Simple Secrets

Simple Secrets
Nancy Mehl

BARBOUR
PUBLISHING

© 2010 by Nancy Mehl

ISBN 978-1-60260-512-1

Scripture taken from the HOLY BIBLE, NEW INTERNATIONAL VERSION®. NIV®. Copyright © 1973, 1978, 1984 by International Bible Society. Used by permission of Zondervan. All rights reserved.

This book is a work of fiction. Names, characters, places, and incidents are either products of the author's imagination or used fictitiously. Any similarity to actual people, organizations, and/or events is purely coincidental.

For more information about Nancy Mehl, please access the author's Web site at the following Internet address: www.nancymehl.com

Cover image: © Chris Reeve/Trevillion Images

Published by Barbour Publishing, Inc., P.O. Box 719, Uhrichsville, OH 44683.

Our mission is to publish and distribute inspirational products offering exceptional value and biblical encouragement to the masses.

ecpa Member of the
Evangelical Christian
Publishers Association

Printed in the United States of America.

DEDICATION

A parent always hopes that in some way, they will be their child's hero. But I am blessed because I have a son who is my hero. I love you, Danny, and I will always be thankful to God that He has allowed me to be your mother.

ACKNOWLEDGMENTS

No writer writes alone. There are always others who help to make a story ring true. I want to thank the wonderful people who helped me to create Harmony, Kansas and its citizens—past and present.

First of all, my thanks to Judith Unruh, Alexanderwohl Church Historian in Goessel, Kansas. I don't know what I would have done without you.

A big thank you to the woman I now call my "fruity friend," Sarah Beck, owner of Beck's Farm in Wichita. You are a joy to work with!

Thank you to Marjorie Shoemaker from the Mennonite Heritage Museum in Goessel who took the time to answer all my questions and give me a "guided tour."

Thanks to Penny and Gus Dorado for helping me with my Mennonite research. You guys are real blessings in my life.

To my wonderful and unique friend Elly "Singer" Kraai: thanks for the Sunrise!

I also want to acknowledge my wonderful agent and friend, Janet Benrey and my first editor, Susan Downs, both of whom have opened doors of blessing for me.

My deep and abiding appreciation to Becky Germany and all the incredible folks at Barbour for giving me a chance.

To my wonderful husband, Norman: I love you so much. This "writing thing" would be impossible without you.

To my critique partners Faye Speiker, Kim Woodhouse and Alene Ward: thanks for your invaluable help.

To my readers who have been so encouraging and supportive: you'll probably never know in this life how much you mean to me. YOU are the reason God gave me this opportunity. I will never take you for granted.

To the Mennonite people who have given our country such a rich heritage of faith and taught us to respect the things in life that are really important: I hope I've represented you well. I've certainly grown to love and admire the principles you stand for.

Lastly, and most importantly: to my Very Best Friend. You are the air I breathe. . .

Chapter One

"She wants a talking pizza on the cover."

Grant slid my proposal across the desk until it rested in front of me. His dark eyes narrowed, warning me not to argue. We both knew it was useless, but I couldn't stop myself. I'd worked hard on a menu cover for Pizzazz Pizza. The lines were clean and bold, the graphics eye-catching.

"You know pizzas don't actually speak, right?" An attempt to keep a note of sarcasm out of my voice failed miserably.

He sighed and ran his hand through his short salt-and-pepper hair. Managing an advertising agency isn't easy, and Grant works with more problem clients than most. Grantham Design is a mid-range firm. Not the worst but not the best. Grant's dream is to make it to the top like Sawyer, Higgins, and Smith, the number one advertising firm in Wichita. I'm pretty sure I knew what those guys would tell Olivia Pennington to do with her chatty Italian pie if this was their account. But unfortunately for Grant and me, we couldn't afford to lose her as a client.

I sighed and picked up my beautiful proposal. Maybe I could make it work for someone else—a client who was savvy enough to leave designing to the designers.

"A talking pizza," he said once again. "And don't get too creative, Gracie."

"Exactly what every designer strives for, a complete lack of imagination."

"Just make it work." With that, he turned and strolled out of my office, leaving me with a rejected design and a verbal food product in my future. I stared out the window at the deli across the street. Feeling hunger pangs, I glanced at my watch. Maybe I could consider the new menu design over lunch. Uptown Bistro serves the best hummus in town. Just thinking about it made my mouth water. My jaw dropped when I saw the time. Nine thirty? How could it only be nine thirty?

I flashed back to the excitement I'd experienced two years earlier when I graduated from college with a degree in graphic design. I was determined to set the design world on fire. But since then I'd discovered that the real world is a lot different than what I'd imagined. Most clients aren't interested in seeing *my* ideas. Instead, they boldly declare that they "know exactly what they want." Unfortunately, their brilliant suggestions are simply remakes of overused, hackneyed concepts, completely inappropriate for their needs. Like a talking pizza. I rubbed my forehead, trying to rid myself of the beginnings of a tension headache. Sometimes I felt like a kid who'd been handed a box of crayons and admonished to "color in the lines" without any chance for creativity or fresh ideas.

I put the Pizzazz Pizza packet in my drawer and stared at my computer screen. Well, if she wanted chatty food, I'd give her chatty food. At that moment, several ideas popped into my head that would make for interesting dialogue. Of course, none of them were appropriate for a family night out at the local pizza parlor. Then I began to wonder just what a pepperoni-covered pastry would say if it could talk. I was pretty sure it would scream "Help!" as loudly as possible since it was about to be sliced into pieces and devoured. However, I doubted seriously that Olivia Pennington would appreciate the humor behind such an idea. A few other entertaining concepts were drifting through my mind when the phone rang.

"Hello, Snicklefritz!"

I sighed into the phone. "Dad, I thought you were going to stop calling me that."

"Grace Marie, I've been calling you Snicklefritz ever since you were a little girl. You used to like it."

I leaned back in my chair and stared at the framed photograph of my parents that sat on the edge of my desk. "But I'm not five anymore. What if you accidentally use it in public again—like you did at graduation?"

My dad laughed. "Your friend Stacy said I was 'darling.'"

"Stacy was not and never will be my friend, Dad. She told everyone about that silly nickname. There are still people from school who call me Snicklefritz."

My dad's hearty laughter made me grab a strand of hair and twirl it around my finger—a nervous habit I couldn't seem to shake.

"So what's up?" My stomach tightened a notch. He usually never contacts me at work unless something's wrong. Like two weeks ago when he told me he'd broken his leg and would be out of commission for a while. And the call last year after Mom was diagnosed with cancer. Thank God, she's fine now.

"Honey, we got word today that your uncle Benjamin passed away."

My stomach relaxed, and I let go of my hair. I'd never even met my father's only brother. He lived in a little Mennonite town somewhere in northeast Kansas.

"What happened, Dad?"

There was a prolonged silence. When he spoke, my father's voice trembled slightly. "It was his heart, Gracie."

"Are you okay?"

"I'm fine, honey. I just wish. . ."

"You tried everything you could to mend your fences with him, Dad. You have nothing to feel guilty about."

A shaky sigh came through the receiver. "I know that, but it doesn't make it any easier right now."

"Do you need me to come home? When's the funeral?"

"The community has already held the service."

"You mean no one told you about your own brother's funeral?" I didn't even try to keep the indignation out of my voice. "What kind of people are these? Is it because you're banned or something?"

"Now don't jump to conclusions. Turns out Benjamin left strict instructions that this was the way he wanted it. The pastor who called me felt badly but didn't know what else to do except to honor my brother's wishes. He—he also wanted me to know about Benjamin's will."

"So what did he leave you?" It couldn't be much due to Benjamin's lifestyle.

"He didn't leave me anything, honey. My brother left his house in Harmony, along with all of his belongings to you, Gracie."

Goofy talking pizzas had obviously warped my brain. My father's words made no sense.

"What? He left what to who?"

"Left what to *whom*, Gracie."

"Dad, this is *not* the time to correct my English. Why in the world would Uncle Benjamin leave me his estate? He didn't even know me."

"I don't know, honey. The congregation we belonged to when I was young believed in The Ban. Benjamin embraced the practice the rest of his life, even though the church as a whole doesn't do it anymore. You were born after your mom and I left Harmony. Since you were never part of the church, I guess in Benjamin's mind you're the only relative left who isn't off-limits." He sighed.

"You know, my brother wasn't always so judgmental. Originally, Benjamin fully supported my decision to leave Harmony. But after your mom and I settled in Fairbury, something happened. He changed—and not for the better." My father paused. "I wish I'd taken him with me when I left. Maybe things would have turned out differently."

"I'm sorry, Dad. I really am. But this still doesn't make any sense." It would take some time before I could grasp the idea that I was now a property owner in a little Mennonite town.

"I wish I could help you more, Gracie. But with this leg, I can't travel. And Mom needs to stay here to take care of me. I'm overnighting the papers so you can look at them yourself. You'll have to decide what to do from there."

"Seems to me that Uncle Benjamin took a big chance leaving everything to someone he didn't know. I might decide to sell the land and plant a Motel 6 in the middle of Harmony."

My dad chuckled. "Well, that would definitely shake things up a bit." He hesitated for a moment. "Your mother and I left Harmony because the bishop of our church opposed our marriage even though our parents supported us. He ruled that town, Gracie. His judgmental attitudes made life unbearable. But your mother reminds me that he's been gone a long time. Pastor Mueller, the man who called today, seemed nice. Very understanding. Not at all like Bishop Angstadt. I'm not crazy about the idea of your going to Harmony alone, but your mother tells me I'm overreacting. Pastor Mueller said he would do everything he could to help you. He sounded very sincere."

"Send me the papers, Dad. I honestly don't know what I'm going to do about this."

"I don't want to make your mind up for you, Snickle. . .er, Gracie. But maybe you could go for at least a week or two. See if you can find someone to buy the place. The money would certainly create a nice nest egg for your future. And while you're there, you could rescue some of the possessions that belonged to Mama and Papa so they can stay in the family. When my folks left Harmony, they deeded the house to Benjamin and left almost all their belongings behind. My guess is that Benjamin kept most of our family heirlooms. It would mean a lot to me if we could get them back." He paused and took a deep breath. "But once you get them, if you feel uncomfortable in Harmony, I want you to turn around and come home. Forget the stuff. You're more important than any heirlooms. Promise me, Gracie."

"Okay, I promise." My dad tends to be overdramatic when it comes to me. His emotional response to their old hometown didn't alarm me. I suddenly thought of my grandfather. "Dad, are you going to tell Papa that Benjamin died?

"No. Mom and I have talked about it. I don't know if he even remembers Benjamin anymore. It would just confuse him, I'm afraid."

Papa Joe lived in a nursing home and was in the last stages of Alzheimer's. Mama Essie had passed away almost five years ago. They'd never been able to understand why Benjamin had turned his back on the family and stayed in Harmony. Now it was too late for them to reconcile. At least in this world.

Harmony. Strange name for a place that had brought so much destruction to the Temple family. Would this gift from my uncle help to heal the past, or would it bring even more pain? It was impossible to know the answer to that question by just sitting in my office.

I smiled down at the sketches of Pizzazz Pizza's new logo. Let Grant figure out what conversational cuisine says.

I was going to Harmony.

Chapter Two

With a promise from my best friend, Allison, to look after my cat and a warning from Grant that I had to be back in two weeks for an important client meeting, I took off Friday morning for Harmony, Kansas. After leaving Wichita, the only towns I saw along the way were small, rural places where life looked much slower and more relaxed than it did in the city. I was reminded of life in tiny Fairbury, Nebraska, where I'd been raised. As a teenager, I felt as if I lived behind a big picture window, destined to watch the world go by without actually being a part of it. Getting a job and moving to the big city had been a dream come true. Surprisingly, as I watched the countryside rush by, I felt a twinge of nostalgia for the way things used to be. My reaction surprised me. I had everything I wanted in Wichita—a job with an ad agency, an apartment downtown, and more friends than my entire high school class in Fairbury. I dismissed my errant feelings as a case of homesickness. It had been almost two months since I'd seen my mother and father. After I returned from Harmony, I'd schedule a weekend trip to Nebraska.

I stopped for lunch in a place called Walalusa. As with many small towns, the local diner had two distinct qualities you could count on—curious stares from the regulars and a burger loaded with grease, fried onions, and dripping cheese. Thirty minutes later I left with a full tummy, a bag of homemade peanut butter cookies, a pat on the back from a waitress named Floreen, and a vow to stop by again on the way home.

After about an hour and several wrong turns, I finally found an old, crooked, weathered sign that pointed the way to Harmony. I kept the notes I'd written from my father's verbal directions on the seat next to me and drove slowly, watching street signs so I wouldn't get lost. Homes with modern farm machinery were interspersed with older farmsteads that had horses, ancient tractors, and plows.

I rolled my car window down and breathed in the aroma of wet earth and burgeoning fields planted with wheat, alfalfa, and corn. I'd almost forgotten what the country smelled like.

Eventually I found a signpost that announced my entrance into Harmony. Instead of heading straight to Benjamin's, I decided to drive around a little. I turned onto what seemed to be the main road, a wide dirt street dotted with buildings. On the corner sat a large white building with a bell tower and a sign that read BETHEL MENNONITE CHURCH. A group of people stood in the front of the church, laughing and talking together. Most of them wore the kind of clothing I'd expected to see. The men had on dark pants, solid-colored shirts, and black or dark blue jackets along with the large brimmed hats that made them recognizable as Mennonites. The women wore dresses that reached almost to their ankles. A couple of them had added another covering—almost like a jumper or apron. A few sported the traditional head covering. But to my surprise, there were also women and men in more contemporary outfits. Jeans, sweatshirts, flannel shirts—even one young woman who wore shorts and a T-shirt.

Several of them looked my way. At first I wondered if it was because of my car, a bright yellow Volkswagen Beetle. But a quick look around revealed I was mistaken. Along with the black buggies and horses I'd expected, quite a few cars were parked on the streets. Some plain and dark with painted bumpers and others quite modern—even new.

On the other side of the huge church was a park with a massive stone water fountain, a small lake, various types of colorful flowers that reached up from well-tended garden plots, freshly painted shelters, and wooden picnic tables large enough to hold an entire family. The landscaping and careful maintenance showed extreme care and concern. I promised myself a visit some afternoon during my trip, accompanied by one of the novels I'd packed away in my suitcase.

As I drove farther down what was obviously the main drag, I couldn't help but notice the street signs. Although I was currently on the obligatory Main Street, the other interconnecting roads had interesting names like Bethel, Resurrection, and Charity Lane. I wondered if Hope Road was ahead somewhere since Uncle Benjamin had lived north of Main Street and Faith Road.

Harmony certainly had a small town atmosphere, but unlike so many of the abandoned and dying rural communities throughout Kansas, this place was vibrant and alive. I checked out some of the various businesses. Among the rows of neat, colorful buildings with hand-painted signs, I discovered a meat market, a bakery, a candle shop, a clothing store, and a secondhand emporium. Ruth's Crafts and Creations caught my eye, and Mary's Kitchen looked to be doing a brisk business, even though it was three in the afternoon. Lights sparkled from inside several buildings, and a bearded man in dark clothes and a wide-brimmed straw hat was using a phone attached to the wall outside. Old-fashioned streetlamps lined both sides of Main Street, and benches sat along the boardwalk, each one filled with men deep in conversation or women doing needlework while they talked and laughed together.

Harmony bustled with activity, and the residents certainly

weren't the dour, grim people I thought I'd encounter. This wasn't the town my father had described at all, but a charming place full of happy people. Spring flowers blossomed in window boxes. Honeysuckle bloomed over handrails and climbed up the sides of buildings. Children ran up and down the covered, wooden sidewalks, giggling and playing just like children anywhere else. I had the strangest feeling I'd stepped back in time and landed inside a Norman Rockwell painting. The real world seemed far away from this place—as if Harmony had found a way to banish it outside its borders.

I drove all the way through town, continuing to draw stares from people I passed. Just like every other small town, everyone knows when a stranger is among them. Feeling a little uneasy with the attention, I headed for Uncle Benjamin's. At the place where the businesses ended and houses began, I found the hand-painted street sign that read FAITH ROAD. At the corner of Faith Road and Main Street stood another church, this one much more modern. The square redbrick building sported a sloping roof and a large metal cross attached to its front face. A sign sat a few feet from the road that read HARMONY CHURCH. Two churches in a town this size just added to my list of surprises. Dad had only mentioned Bethel—the Mennonite church my family had once attended.

Following my father's instructions, I turned north and drove for about a mile, leaving the town behind. This area was much more rural with only a few simple houses nestled in the middle of fields planted with newly budding crops. Before reaching my final destination, I came upon a huge, red Victorian-style house with white trim. It sat back from the road and was surrounded by a large orchard. I slowed my car and stared. It had a wraparound porch with a creamy white railing. Two gleaming ivory rockers sat on the porch, and baskets of flowering green plants hung from the roof. The effect was striking—almost breathtaking. I noticed a very modern tractor parked next to a large red barn and an old beat-up truck in the driveway. I'd anticipated stark houses without beauty or style. Either my preconceived notions were wrong, or the people who owned this house weren't Mennonite.

I continued down the dirt road until I found Uncle Benjamin's. His house had the plain white paint I'd expected, but the two-story structure was actually quite charming. A nice-sized porch was attached to the front of the home. Large yellow tulips bloomed next to the steps, and beautiful purple irises, surrounded by a circle of stones, graced the middle of the yard. Purple irises. Mama Essie's favorite flowers. Had she originally planted the garden? Since it was late April, the flowers were anointed with the joie de vivre of spring, and as I stepped out of the car, their aroma greeted me. An old oak tree sheltered the porch, and a lone, cream-colored rocking chair sat waiting for an owner who would never return. I'd seen quite a few wooden rockers on Main Street. It was a safe bet they'd been crafted in Harmony.

As I approached the steps, I noticed two sparrows sitting on the railing. I thought they'd take flight when they saw me, but instead they stared at me with interest until I put my foot on the first wooden stair. As I watched them fly away and land on a branch in the oak tree, I discovered the reason for their lack of fear. Dangling from the branches was a brightly painted bird feeder. There were also several birdhouses hanging nearby, along with a large, multiholed house attached to the trunk of the tree. I'd never seen birdhouses like these. Each was solidly built out of wood and adorned with pictures of birds and flowers. Beautiful and colorful cardinals, blue jays, and sparrows decorated each structure. Tiny heads poked out of the houses while the birds from the porch sat on branches near the large feeder. They were obviously used to being cared for.

I fumbled around, trying to find the key that had been sent with Benjamin's papers. I'd just grasped it when the sound of a loud, gravelly voice split the silence. I almost dropped my key.

"Hey, just whatcha think you're doin' there, lady?"

I turned around to find a woman staring at me suspiciously. A round orb of a human being, she wore faded denim overalls over a dingy, torn T-shirt. Her feet were encased in old ratty sneakers caked with dirt. A lack of makeup and graying hair pulled into a messy bun made it hard to determine her age, but I guessed her to be somewhere near sixty.

She took a few steps closer. "I asked you just what you was doin' at that door, lady," she said, her face screwed up like a prune. "I knowed the man who lived there, and you ain't him. You ain't even his ghost."

After my initial shock, I recovered my voice. "I–I'm Benjamin Temple's niece. He—he left this house to me." I cleared my throat and forced myself to calm down. "I'm Gracie Temple," I said more forcefully. "And you are?"

Unfortunately, she took this as some kind of invitation and clomped her way up to the porch. She squinted as she looked me up and down. I met her gaze without flinching.

"Well, I guess you might actually be lil' Gracie," she said finally, her face cracking a smile that showed some gaps in her teeth. "You sure look a lot like old Benny. He was a nice-lookin' man, your uncle. Even more important, he was a good man. We was close friends. I been watchin' for you ever since he passed away. Promised Benny I'd keep an eye on this place."

"My uncle told you I was coming?"

The old woman leaned over the porch railing and spat on the ground. "Yeah, he did. It sure was important to him. In fact, it was all he talked about toward the end."

"Well, thank you for watching the house." I flashed her a smile and put my hand on the doorknob, hoping she would take it as a dismissal. I wanted to get inside, unpack, and settle in.

Instead of taking my hint, she extended her grimy hand. "I'm

Myrtle Goodrich, but folks call me Sweetie. Pleased to know ya. I live just down the road a piece. I'm sure we'll be good friends."

I couldn't help but stare at the hand she held out. She noticed and pulled it back, wiping it on her overalls. "Sorry. Been workin' in my orchard." After transferring most of the dirt on her hand to her clothes, she reached out again. This time I took it, forcing myself not to check it for cleanliness. Her grip was firm and her hands rough and calloused.

"Nice to meet you, Myrtle." I looked my new neighbor over carefully. Besides the fact that I didn't like cutesy names, if I was ever knocked senseless and a name like Sweetie fell out of my mouth due to severe brain damage, I still wouldn't apply it to this odd woman. I couldn't even call my cat "sweetie." Of course, with a name like Snicklefritz, he'd already suffered as much indignity as any one cat should have to. He'd acquired his name as a defensive maneuver on my part. Hopefully, the next time my father called me by that loathsome nickname, I could claim he had dementia and had confused me with my feline friend.

She flashed me another strange grin. It reminded me of a baby with gas. "Yep, when I was born, my mama took a gander at me and said, 'Will you look at that little sweetie?' And that was my name from then on."

"Well, that's interesting." I tightened my grip on the doorknob. "It was nice to meet you. But I really need to get unpacked. Maybe we'll see each other again before I go." Feeling as though I'd handled my escape the best way possible, I began to fiddle with the key, attempting to fit it into the keyhole. Instead of taking the hint, Myrtle advanced again.

"It's a good thing you finally got here," she said, looking around as if someone was hiding around the corner, listening. Of course her loud, rather rough voice pretty much made any attempt at secrecy useless. "Your uncle had a troubled mind, Gracie girl. I 'spect I never seen a man so full of worry. He sure was countin' on you comin' here. Toward the end it was all he talked about."

I took my hand off the doorknob, disturbed that my uncle was afraid and focused on me before he died. "I thought Uncle Benjamin died of a heart attack. Are you saying he knew he was going to die?"

Myrtle shrugged her rounded shoulders. "His heart was bad for years. He got worse and worse this last year. Then a couple of months ago, he started gettin' real weak and sickly. Couldn't stay on his feet for long. He figgered his time was finally up. Guess he was right."

"I—I didn't realize he had a heart condition. He didn't keep in contact with his family."

She nodded vigorously. "It's a cryin' shame, too." She swiped at her eyes with her muddy hand, leaving a trail of grime on her face. "He was a good man, Gracie girl. A good man."

"Thank you." I put my hand back on the doorknob. "Now if you'll excuse me. . ."

"Sure, sure." She frowned and took a step back. "Well, if you need anything, alls you gotta do is set this pot of petunias on the porch rail." She bent down to pick up a large pot of flowers sitting near the steps and handed it to me.

"Wouldn't it be easier if I called you?"

She exploded with coarse laughter, and her face turned beet red. "You're gonna have to get used to livin' like the old Mennies," she sputtered after regaining her voice. "There ain't no phone here."

No phone? I hadn't counted on that. "I have a cell phone. . ."

"I wouldn't count on it workin' out here," she said, interrupting me. "But you can go down to one of them shops in town. There's phones there. Not all these Mennies live by the old rules like your uncle. Only a handful of those kind left now." She grinned at me like a deranged Cheshire cat. "You got lucky and inherited one of the few houses around without no electricity or a working phone. For a city girl like you, it'll be quite an adventure, I reckon."

20

I stared at the woman as I set the flowers on the porch. Even though I found her irritating, it occurred to me that she might be one of the only people who really knew my uncle. Although I abhorred the choices he'd made, seeing the house where my father had grown up sparked a desire to learn what I could about Benjamin. "You know, I am rather curious about my uncle. Maybe while I'm here you could answer some questions I have about him."

"Well," she said, staring up at the sky, "it's gettin' pretty late. I got a roast in the oven that'll be burnt to a crisp if I don't get a-goin'." Myrtle waved once and jumped off the porch. Then she headed down the road like her overalls were on fire.

I shook my head as I watched her scurry away. Had I scared her off? Maybe it was best not to question my good fortune. I had to consider that maybe old Sweetie was a few bricks shy of a full load. Besides, I was determined to stay focused on my goals. I fully intended to sell the house, grab a few things for my mom and dad, and leave well within my two-week deadline. Trying to learn more about my uncle would probably only sidetrack me.

Before opening the front door, I glanced up and down the road. Besides the big, red home in the distance, I spotted a couple of other houses on Faith Road. They sat like silent sentries in the middle of crop fields. It didn't make any sense, but I suddenly had the strange feeling they were watching me—wondering what I was going to do next. A curious sense of uneasiness filled me, and I couldn't stop my fingers from trembling as I slid Benjamin's key into the lock.

Chapter Three

I had to jiggle the ancient key several times before the front door creaked open. Anticipating the worst from a lifelong bachelor, I was pleased to find a clean, orderly, and rather attractive living room. A bright rag rug lay on the polished hardwood floor, adding a splash of color to the surroundings. To the right of the entryway, a carved wood staircase led to the upstairs. The massive cherry secretary next to the window was beautifully carved and intricate, with a drop-down lid that doubled as a desk. The makeshift desktop held paper, pens, and a large leather Bible. Another wall was lined with bookcases. A rocking chair, a close cousin to the one on the porch, sat in the corner, and against the farthest wall, I was surprised to find a lovely couch upholstered in a rich gold brocade fabric. The material had been well cared for but appeared somewhat faded by time. Someone had carefully folded a colorful handcrafted quilt and laid it across its back. In another corner of the room, next to a cast-iron stove, was a brown leather upholstered chair, and next to it stood a tall grandfather's clock made from some kind of dark wood. Perhaps mahogany. The pendulum sat unmoving. I fumbled around on top of the clock and found the key that unlocked the front piece. Same place we kept our key at home. After checking my watch, I set the time, pulled up the weights, and started the pendulum moving. The slow ticking filled the silent room, making it feel as if life were coming back into the abandoned house.

The furniture surprised me. Rather than being plain and without character or design, I found well-crafted pieces that had obviously been created with excellence.

I checked out the old potbellied stove that was probably used to supply heat to the main room during the winter. Good thing it was spring. I didn't relish the idea of having to gather wood and start a fire on a frigid Kansas morning.

Two paintings hung in the living room. One was of horses standing near a fence. The other, a landscape depicting a field of golden wheat under gathered storm clouds. Both displayed a high level of talent, and I wondered about the artist. Against the far wall a large cross-stitch sampler declared "Fear not for I am with thee." The scripture touched my heart, as if God were speaking directly to me, reassuring me that even in this rather strange situation, I wasn't alone.

As I began my search through the rest of the house, I felt happy beyond words to find a fairly modern bathroom. The large claw-foot tub was different than what I was used to. I found the lack of a shower rather annoying, but I could make do. I'd been expecting an outhouse. I still remembered the summers my family went camping and fishing at a lake not far from our home. The only available facilities left much to be desired. Not much more than holes in the ground, I visited them only when absolutely necessary. My cousin, Jonathon, used to tell me stories about big, hairy spiders that lived at the bottom of the toilets. Needless to say, any outing to the bathroom was made in great haste and with severe trepidation. Thankfully, I wouldn't be having nightmares about spiders while I was here.

I liked the kitchen with its lemon yellow paint and handmade oak cabinets. A small oak table with two chairs sat near a window that looked out on the property behind the house. The table was covered with a green-and-white-checked tablecloth, and matching valances hung over the windows. A large tublike sink with a water pump sat directly under one of the windows. Two colorful rag rugs lay on the floor. A white hobnail hurricane lamp hung from one of the wooden beams that stretched across the ceiling. The stove and refrigerator bordered on antique, but at least they appeared to be clean. A stainless-steel teapot waited on the stove. As Myrtle warned, I couldn't find any electrical outlets. I peeked out the window and discovered that a propane tank had been set up next to the house. That explained how the appliances worked.

A sudden knock on the front door startled me, and I sighed with frustration. So far, my visit to what I'd pictured as a peaceful Mennonite community had turned out to be something quite different. Hoping Sweetie hadn't made an unwelcome return, I cautiously opened the front door. A nice-looking man stood on the porch, dressed in jeans and a blue-checkered shirt. I guessed him to be not much older than me. He flashed me a crooked grin.

"Sorry to bother you," he said, "but I wonder if you're Benjamin's niece, Grace?"

For crying out loud, did everyone in this town know me? "Yes, I'm Gracie Temple. And you are?"

He brushed a lock of sun-bleached hair out of his face. "I'm Sam. Sam Goodrich."

"Goodrich? Any relation to. . .?"

"Yeah," he answered a little too quickly, his face flushing. "I'm her nephew. Don't tell me she's been here already."

"Yes. In fact, she introduced herself before I even got inside the house."

He shook his head. "Sorry about that. My aunt was pretty close to your uncle. She took his death hard. I think she's still trying to look out for him."

I couldn't leave this man standing on the front porch much longer. It was becoming evident he wasn't going anywhere. Reluctantly, I pushed the screen door open. "Would you like to come in?"

"Thank you, I would. But first let me get something from my truck. I brought you a housewarming gift."

I watched as he bounded off the porch and hurried over to a battered, weather-beaten truck that must have been blue at one time before rust took over. With a start, I realized it was the truck I'd seen parked in front of the beautiful red house down the road. Did this guy live there? I found him handsome in a roughshod, country kind of way. Not anything like the guys back home. Most of my dates came through hooking up with other people in advertising. I was used to the slicked-down, suited-up type who sported black-framed glasses and had their hair carefully styled to look messy. Never could quite understand the popularity of that look. I achieved it every morning when I rolled out of bed, and it didn't cost me a cent.

Frankly, Sam reminded me more of the boys in Fairbury—the ones I'd wanted to get away from. Funny how they'd never made my heart beat faster—the way it did now. Sam grabbed a large wicker basket from the back of his truck and trudged back to where I stood waiting.

"I thought you might like some fresh fruit," he said, smiling. "I have a farm about half a mile down the road. I brought you some fresh blackberries and strawberries. I also grow peaches and apples, but they're not ready to harvest yet. I stuck in some jars of peaches from last season, along with some apple preserves and a jar of apple butter." He carried the basket straight to the kitchen. He'd obviously been here before.

"Thanks. I appreciate it. It will be nice to have something to eat. I haven't had time to look around to see if there's anything else in the house."

He set the basket on the table in the corner of the kitchen. "You don't need to worry about that." He stepped over to the refrigerator and swung the door open. To my amazement it was stocked with food. "After your father called Pastor Mueller to say you were coming, we made sure you'd have what you needed." He stepped over to a door next to the kitchen cabinets. "There's also quite a bit of food in the pantry."

Inside a small room lined with shelves, I found almost every kind of canned food imaginable. Lots of collard greens, spinach, hominy, and bags of white beans sat waiting for someone who might appreciate them. That sure wasn't me. I was relieved to see a jar of peanut butter, a loaf of bread, and on the floor, a few bottles of pop.

"There are two wooden boxes on the floor near the door," Sam said. "They contain bird food and squirrel food for Ben's friends."

"I saw the bird feeder, but where did he feed the squirrels?" I closed the pantry door and almost ran into Sam. He colored slightly and took a step back. "There's a feeder on the south side of the roof. Ben has a ladder leaning up against the house. Just carry the food up there and dump it in. You'll have all kinds of squirrelly visitors. I mean besides my aunt and me." He grinned when I laughed. "Why don't you let me feed them the first time? It will only take a few minutes."

"Thanks. That would be great. I. . .I can't thank you enough for everything. If you'll tell me how much you spent on supplies, I'd be happy to write you a check."

His friendly smile ratcheted down a notch. "You don't owe us anything. That's just the way things are done around here. Besides, Ben was our friend."

Although my first reaction was to insist once again that he allow me to compensate him, I could tell it was best to back off. I didn't want to offend him. "Why don't I get us something to drink while you feed my uncle's pets? Then maybe we could visit for a while?"

His answering smile indicated that our rather awkward moment had passed. Sam showed me where the glasses were kept. Then he shoveled some bird and squirrel food into two metal pitchers and carried them outside. I checked out the fridge and found a pitcher of fresh lemonade. As I poured some into our glasses, I heard the ladder hit the side of the house. I carried the ice-cold lemonade into the living room and waited for him to finish. As promised, it took him less than five minutes. He came in, put the pitchers back in the pantry, and joined me in the living room. I sat on the couch while he took the rocking chair.

"I have to admit that the furniture in this house surprises me," I said after he'd made himself comfortable.

He smiled. "You thought it would be plain? A lot of straight lines and lack of decoration?"

I nodded.

"You're thinking of Shaker furniture. For the most part, even Old Order Mennonites were allowed to have nice furniture." He pointed at the secretary. "I believe that's been in your family for many years. If I remember right, Ben told me it was built by your great-great-grandfather."

"Really? My dad sent me down here to rescue our family heirlooms. I'm certain he'll want it." I shook my head. "There's more furniture here than I anticipated. We'll have to rent a pretty big trailer to get all this stuff to Nebraska."

Sam nodded and took a drink from his glass. After a few seconds of awkward silence, he smiled. "One of the reasons I came by was to show you how to use the propane tank and explain how the plumbing works.

"We do have plumbing in the big city."

He laughed. "I know that, but in this house, water is collected in a cistern that flows into a tank in the basement. If you want to take a bath or wash clothes, you have to turn on a small gas-powered generator that runs water through your pipes."

"Well, how does the. . .um. . .the. . ."

Sam grinned and put me out of my misery. "I won't explain all the intricacies to you, but an air compressor allows everything else in the bathroom to work the way you're used to. And let me put one other rumor to rest. Old Order Mennonites do use toilet paper. You'll find it in the bathroom cabinet."

The relief I felt must have shown in my face, because he chuckled again. I liked the way he laughed. It was deep and real. His irises were an unusual shade of bluish gray. I'd never seen eyes that color before. His blond hair almost reached his shoulders, and he kept pushing it off his sunburned face. It gave him the kind of romantic look many movie stars would probably sell their souls to possess.

"One other thing," he said. "There's an old wringer washer downstairs. Not very modern, but you'd be surprised how clean it will get your clothes."

"Thankfully, my grandmother used a wringer washer when I was young. She taught me how to operate it. When it broke down, she finally got a modern washer, but she always swore that her old machine got her clothes cleaner."

"My aunt used to say the same thing. However, she was willing to trade cleanliness for convenience. She'd never go back to the old way."

Feeling that we'd exhausted the clothes washer topic, I tried another tack. "Sam, do you mind if I ask you a few questions?"

He shook his head. "Of course not. That's why I'm here."

"It's about my uncle. You see, I never got the chance to know him. I must say I'm shocked he left his property to me. I have to wonder about it. You and your aunt were close to him. Do you have any idea why he'd pass along his inheritance to a niece he'd never met?"

Sam cleared his throat and frowned. "I'm sorry, I don't. He made it very clear that his personal life was off-limits. I guess he was friendlier with me than most, but there was always a side of Ben that he kept to himself. As you know, he was raised in the Old Order. Never really left it. Most of the other folks in town have adopted more modern ways, although they hold true to the Mennonite principles, plain living, and everything. But not Ben. He and a few others clung to the old ways. Funny thing was, he didn't hang around them much either. It was like he was protecting himself against something and he couldn't allow people to get too close." He stared down at the floor, looking uncomfortable. "Toward the end, he said some things I didn't quite understand. I got the feeling he hadn't meant to let them slip out." He lifted his head and looked at me. "Honestly, I'm not sure I'm comfortable telling you something said in private. If I really thought it was important, I would be willing to chance it. But at this point, I don't see how it would help anything."

A good-looking man with principles. Quite a rare find. Without realizing it, my eyes drifted to his left hand. No ring. For a few seconds, I felt a sense of relief. Then I realized I was having some rather serious thoughts about a hick farmer in a town so small it wasn't on most maps. This wasn't what I was looking for. I'm definitely a big city girl. I forced my mind back to the situation at hand.

"You said my uncle didn't spend much time with people who believed the way he did? Didn't he go to church?"

Sam shrugged his broad shoulders. "Well, the Old Order folks don't have a formal meeting house anymore. They hold services in each other's homes. Ben went to all the meetings and did everything he was supposed to do, but he rarely just sat down and carried on a conversation with anyone, even those who believed the same way he did. There were a few people he trusted, including my aunt and me. But I can't say he was ever completely forthcoming with us." He gulped down some lemonade then set down the glass. "I believe there was something going on with your uncle—something he never talked directly about. As far as I know, he died without ever sharing it."

"But he did tell you about me."

Sam frowned and leaned forward. "Ben asked me to come by and talk to him about something 'private' a couple of months ago. I thought he was finally ready to share whatever it was that bothered him so deeply. But he only talked a little about your family—who you were and how he hadn't seen you for so long. Didn't really explain why except to say there were some differences that separated you. Then he told me that I should watch for you to come. He even told me that he'd had all his property put in your name." He sighed and leaned back in his chair. "That was as personal as he got. I only wish he would have trusted me more. I think he went to his reward with a heavy burden. That shouldn't have happened. Benjamin Temple deserved better."

"Maybe he would have told you if he'd had more time," I offered.

Sam stared at his empty glass. "Possibly, but I don't think so. Ben knew he didn't have long. His heart was giving out. In the last year, he got worse and worse."

I felt a rush of indignation. "Why in the world wouldn't he call my father to let him know how ill he was? Except for my grandfather who is in a nursing home, my dad was his only close relative."

"He had his own way, Grace. It might not make sense to you, but over the years I came to respect your uncle for many of his beliefs. He didn't choose an easy life."

"But turning your back on people who don't believe the same way you do isn't right."

Sam shrugged. "I don't agree with it either, but I think in Ben's mind it was the only choice open to him. I guess he thought somehow your dad and your grandparents would repent and come back into the fold."

"That's ridiculous. My parents and grandparents are the best people I've ever known. They have nothing to 'repent' from."

Sam pushed back his chair and stood up. "Well, Pastor Mueller agrees with you. He talked to Ben several times and encouraged him to contact your family. Your uncle wouldn't budge. I tried to reason with him, too, but he shut me down. I finally let it go because I didn't want to lose his friendship."

I smiled at Sam, but I was thinking that although his words sounded right, I wished someone had been more forceful with my uncle. He'd left a lot of hurt behind him, and that certainly didn't seem very Christlike to me.

"I've got to get going," Sam said, "but first I want to make certain you know how to fire up all your appliances."

I obediently followed him around while he demonstrated each piece of equipment. I wanted to grumble that in Wichita, all I had to do was turn a knob, but I kept my mouth shut. I appreciated his help. After our informative tour, I walked him to the front door.

He put his hand on the doorknob to leave but suddenly hesitated. "Why don't I stop by tomorrow and take you to breakfast in town? You'll get a chance to visit a few of our shops and meet some of Harmony's residents. There are still a few folks who remember your family. I'm sure they'd love to meet you."

I started to turn him down. I wanted a few days to myself before taking on the town of Harmony. But as I looked into his incredible smoky gray eyes, I forgot what I'd wanted to say. Instead, I found myself nodding and asking him what time he'd be by. After agreeing to nine o'clock, I said good-bye and closed the door after him. As it clicked shut, I breathed a sigh of relief. Finally, some time alone. Hopefully, there wouldn't be any more interruptions from friendly neighbors.

It was still early, so I decided to carry my bags in from the car, poke around some, and then have a little supper. I'd already noticed several oil lamps scattered throughout the house. I searched until I found some matches in my uncle's desk. At least I would have some light after the sun went down.

As I closed the drawer, my eyes were drawn to the black leather Bible that lay on the desktop. I'd picked it up, intending to see if Benjamin had written family information in the front, when something slipped out from between the pages and fell to the floor. It was an envelope. I gasped involuntarily when I bent down to look at it.

My name was scrawled in large block letters on the front.

Chapter Four

I left the letter sitting on Benjamin's desk while I carried in my bags and had supper. I assumed my uncle had written it, but I couldn't decide if his message from beyond the grave was something I really wanted to read. Was this some last-ditch attempt to seek forgiveness? I didn't have to scratch very deep to uncover the resentment I felt toward him. The hurt he'd caused my family made it difficult for me to forgive him no matter what he had to say. Of course, my uncle may have left a very different kind of letter—a scathing missive full of judgment and retribution. Except that Sam and Myrtle had painted him in different colors. Unfortunately, most people have two faces—the one they show in public and the one they keep hidden behind a carefully constructed mask. Not knowing my uncle made it impossible for me to guess his motives.

A look through the refrigerator presented me with several options for supper. I finally settled on a bowl of beef stew that smelled absolutely wonderful. I found myself searching for the microwave before I remembered where I was. I discovered a small metal pan that I filled with stew and set on the stove. After locating a box of matches, I turned the knob under the pan, struck the match, and watched as the flame whooshed beneath the raised burner. A few minutes later, the aroma of homemade stew filled the homey kitchen. I added a slice of bread and butter, and before long my meal was ready. I sat down at the kitchen table and gazed out the window. A row of trees lined the back of the property. I wondered what was on the other side and decided to scout it out when I had time.

I finished my supper, put the dishes in the sink, and lit the oil lamp on the table. My mother had kept a couple of oil lamps in Fairbury even though we had electricity. A holdover from her childhood, I guess. The smell of burning oil took me back to leisurely nights on our old porch swing, listening to the cacophony of cicadas while my mother's old lamp burned in the window. I'd been in such a hurry to leave Nebraska I guess I'd forgotten a few of the things I'd actually enjoyed.

I grabbed my largest suitcase and headed for the stairs. Since the main floor consisted of the large living room, a bathroom, the kitchen, and the pantry, the bedrooms had to be on the second floor. The stairs were much steeper than I was used to, and each step creaked as I climbed. They twisted at the top and ended at a dark hallway. It occurred to me that perhaps it would have been better if I'd checked out this part of the house before the sun had gone down. The light from my lamp cast a rather ominous glow that made my surroundings look a little spooky. I left my heavy suitcase on the landing and proceeded down the hall.

There were three rooms upstairs. The first bedroom had probably been Benjamin's. The bed was covered with a rather plain blue bedspread. There was a mahogany dresser with a mirror. The top of the dresser held a comb, some kind of hair tonic, a small bowl of change, and two bottles of prescription medicine. An old wooden chair sat next to the wall, and a small battered trunk rested at the foot of the bed. Across the room I found a closet door. I slowly opened the door, which protested loudly in the silence.

An array of men's slacks and shirts hung on wooden hangers. All the pants were either black, dark brown, or dark blue. The shirts varied from light to dark. It was almost impossible to distinguish exact shades in the yellowish glow of the lamp. A wide-brimmed black hat hung on a hook on the side of the closet, and another hat just like it, but made out of straw, sat on a shelf.

I closed the door and stood in the middle of the room. "Hello, Uncle Benjamin," I said softly into the still, quiet space. "You wanted me here, and I'm here. Too bad you didn't make a move to see me while you were alive."

Feeling a little silly for talking to myself, I left that room and stepped out into the hallway. I held the lamp out in front of me and followed its flickering light to the next door. I turned the knob and swung it open. This room was larger than Benjamin's. A beautifully carved bed was pushed up against the back wall, next to the windows. A colorful patchwork quilt covered it. I walked over to the bed and ran my fingers across the hand stitching. I recognized the design. Mama Essie. She'd made one just like it for me. I'd tucked it away in my closet at home, afraid to use it because it was so precious I didn't want to damage it.

Of course, Mama hadn't seen her creations as something to be protected. "Why, honey," she'd said when I confessed to storing the precious gift away, "I made that quilt to be used. When you wrap yourself in it, I want you to imagine you're getting a big hug from your grandma."

I swung the lamp around and found a dresser like Benjamin's—but bigger and more ornate. A large homemade rag rug lay on the floor, and a cast-iron stove in the corner waited for the next chilly night. This had obviously been Papa Joe and Mama Essie's room. This was where I'd sleep. I could almost feel my grandparents, and the sensation gave me a sense of peace. I wondered how long it had been since the room had been thoroughly cleaned. I ran my fingers across the dresser and found it relatively free of dust. The quilt and the bedsheets looked freshly laundered. Had Benjamin tidied up in anticipation of my visit? The thought made me feel a little funny—as if he'd reached out to touch me from the great beyond. A shiver ran up my spine. Of course, as sick as he'd been, it was more likely Myrtle or Sam who had spruced the house up. I doubt my uncle thought much about housework during the last days of his life.

I lit the lamp that sat on the dresser but kept the one I had with me so I could use it to navigate my way back up the narrow stairs in the dark when I was ready for bed. I swung it around and had turned toward the door when I noticed an old photograph on the wall. I held the light close to it. It was a family portrait. A young Mama Essie and Papa Joe looked stoically at the camera. Mama was lovely, her dark hair pulled back into a bun with a few loose curls caressing her cheeks. Her dark eyes were framed by thick eyelashes that didn't need any help from mascara, and although the picture was in black and white, her cheeks were shaded with what might have been a rosy hue had the photograph been taken in color. Papa Joe stared at the camera with a rather humorless expression. But the hint of amusement in his eyes was unmistakable. I knew that look. He'd had it every time he'd told me one of his awful jokes. I didn't figure out how bad they were until I was an adult. To a child who worshipped her grandfather, Papa Joe put the professional comedians on TV to shame.

"Did you ever wonder why bread is square and lunchmeat is round?" he'd ask. Or "If you're eating cured ham, Gracie girl, don't you ever wonder just what was wrong with it before it got well?"

I also recalled the times he'd swing me around in circles with his strong arms, singing "I've Been Working on the Railroad." After leaving Harmony, he'd worked for the railroad until he retired. I guess that's why he loved the song so much. But even more than that silly song, Papa Joe had loved me—and I loved him and Mama. Seeing them so young made me realize how much I missed them. Even though Papa was still alive, he seemed only a shadow of the robust man he had once been. I'd give almost anything just to hear another one of his terrible jokes. I moved the lamp a little closer. I'd never seen any pictures of my father as a child—but there he was, probably all of ten years old. And next to him a smaller boy with deep, piercing eyes. Eyes that spoke of intelligence and reason. Uncle Benjamin. Although hair color is difficult to define in a black and white photo, it was easy to see that while the rest of the family had dark hair, Uncle Benjamin's was lighter. I would have bet all the money in my checking account, which wasn't much, that he'd had red hair like me. And that the spots across his nose were freckles just like mine. Although my mother told me my dimples came from an angel's kiss, I found that, in fact, they'd come from my uncle. I wondered if his eyes were green, too. They looked lighter than my dad's, which were brown.

It took a little while for me to recover from the shock I felt. Why hadn't anyone told me I looked so much like Benjamin? Had it been too painful for my parents and grandparents to talk about? When my father looked at me, did he see his brother?

I turned on my heels and left the room, slightly disturbed. Looking at that picture, I'd experienced a feeling of connection with an uncle I'd never met and never would on this side of life. Benjamin's actions toward my family had left me a solid sense of disdain for him. Finding out that I looked like him left me feeling confused.

One room remained at the end of the hall. I tried to turn the door handle, but it was either locked or jammed. I pushed against it a couple of times but couldn't get the door to budge. For tonight this last room would have to remain a mystery. At one time, it must have been my father's bedroom, but he'd been gone for thirty years. Probably relegated for storage, lack of use had caused the door to stick.

I put my suitcase in Mama and Papa's room, unpacked some of my clothes, and put them in the dresser drawers. When I opened the closet door, I discovered several women's dresses. According to my folks, Benjamin had never married. They must have belonged to Mama Essie. I'd look more closely tomorrow, when I had enough light to see them better.

I pushed my empty suitcase under the bed, picked up the lamp, and walked across the squeaky floor to the stairs, being careful to grasp the wooden railing with one hand while I held the lamp out in front of me with the other. Once downstairs, I realized I was going to have to get better at figuring out this lighting thing. If I'd lit a couple of lamps down here before I'd gone upstairs, the house wouldn't be so dark. I quickly fired up a lamp in the living room and put the one in my hand back in the kitchen. It sure wasn't like having electricity, but at least I could see well enough to get around.

I moved the bag with my makeup and toiletries into the bathroom, and grabbed the remaining overnight bag, carrying it into the living room to unpack. Although with my mother's prompting I'd purchased a windup alarm clock, I quickly realized that my cell phone charger was useless. Maybe I could buy an adapter for my car. That way I could at least charge my phone once in a while. Since I hadn't seen any kind of auto parts store in Harmony, I would probably have to drive to Council Grove.

The silence around me seemed almost deafening. In Wichita, I'd grown used to the sounds of cars honking, people talking as they walked past my windows, and long train whistles that woke me up in the middle of the night. It had been a long time since I'd been in the country—and so far Harmony was turning out to be even quieter than Fairbury, where the neighbors lived much closer. At least in Fairbury, you could hear dogs barking at night.

Suddenly remembering something else I couldn't get in Wichita, I went out on the front porch and down the steps. After walking a few feet away from the house, I stopped and looked up. Across the dark expanse of the night sky, the vista of stars sparkling like scattered jewels almost took my breath away. This was a sight only visible in the country. The lights of Wichita muted the stunning portrait of God's heavens, but in Harmony, they glittered with fire, anointing the night with His majestic, creative touch. It was beyond beautiful. I stood there, staring up until my neck began to ache. Reluctantly, I made my way back into the house, reminding myself that I had two weeks here—several more chances to behold this awesome sight.

Once inside, I checked my watch. A little after eight. I crossed my arms and gazed around the room. This was the time of night I'd usually pop popcorn, turn on the TV, and veg out until I got tired enough to go to bed.

"Not much to do here, Uncle Benjamin. What did you do for entertainment?" My voice sounded strange in the quiet. Like it didn't belong. Maybe it didn't. Maybe I didn't. I glanced over at the bookshelf and considered checking out the books lined up there, but I knew I was only trying to put off the inevitable.

My eyes rested on the letter lying on Benjamin's desk. Might as well get it over with. Funny how I dreaded reading it even more now that I knew about the similarities I shared with my uncle. Would my opinion of him be altered? And if so, which way would it go? I scolded myself for trying to anticipate something I couldn't possibly know anything about unless I actually got enough gumption to open the envelope. I moved the lamp to a small table next to the rocking chair, picked up the letter, and sat down. With trembling fingers, I pulled out the sheets of paper, unfolded them, and began to read:

Dearest Niece Grace,
It is difficult to write this letter for many reasons. First of all, I am unsure that you have even honored my bequest.

I am aware that this letter might fall into different hands than yours. I placed it within our family Bible, believing that only a family member would discover it. I pray my assumption proves correct. However, since I cannot be sure of the outcome, it is with great trepidation that I pen these words.

First of all, I must tell you that although my family believes I have rejected them, I assure you I have not. I love them deeply and miss them. It is true that they have chosen to leave the old ways, but I cannot judge them right or wrong for this. God's love transcends our habits and choices. The reason for my separation from them is for motives they have never been made aware of. However, as I am dying and will not be able to protect them much longer from a terrible secret that has held me captive all these years, I have no choice but to pass it to someone else. And unfortunately, that person, my dear niece, must be you.

I cannot see into the future, and I don't know you, so I have no idea if you will be able to discover and navigate a path never found by me. However, my conscience will not allow me to die with this secret buried beneath years of deceit and lies. I have asked God's forgiveness for keeping it to myself—and for my part in it. But even with that forgiveness, justice has still not been served. Perhaps it never will. Unfortunately, you will now have to decide the matter. I pray your choices will be better than mine have been.

Reading by the light of the old lamp proved difficult, and my uncle's cramped script wasn't easy to read. His words filled me with a sense of dread. Either I was about to find out something I was pretty certain I didn't want to know—or I would discover that my poor deranged uncle had fallen way off his wooden rocker. With a sense of misgiving I turned the letter over and once again held it near the flickering lamplight.

Many years ago, an evil man lived in Harmony. Maybe you think I am being dramatic by using the word evil, *but I assure you that this man epitomizes the term. On the night my brother, Daniel, your father, planned to leave town with Beverly Fischer, the young woman who would become your mother, Jacob Glick was killed. No one in Harmony knows this. They believe he left town because he was so disliked. All these years I have been the only person who knew the truth. Now I must pass it on to you. Sadly, it is yours to bear alone.*

You see, I found Jacob's body that night. He'd been struck on the head with a large rock that still lay near his feet. The force of the blow took his life. I buried his body, the bloody rock, and a suitcase filled with his belongings amid the grove of trees on our property. His body lies there still.

I had to read the last paragraph several times to be certain I understood its meaning. My uncle had buried a body—here? A feeling of cold fear moved through me. I tried to tell myself that he was sick and that this letter was the result of his illness. But the thoughts seemed so well constructed and clear of confusion. With dismay, I continued to read.

You are probably asking yourself why I would do something like this. Why would I bury the body of a man who obviously lost his life by the hand of another and spend the rest of my days separated from my family, afraid to leave this property because the truth might be revealed? The answer will shock you, my dear niece, but I cannot keep the matter hidden any longer. It is because the man who killed Jacob Glick was my brother—your father, Daniel.

I put the letter in my lap. "This isn't true," I whispered into the dark corners of the room. "My father would never do something like that."

Of course, there was no response. What kind of a man would leave a poisonous letter like this behind him? What was he trying to accomplish? I knew my father. He was a man of peace—of forgiveness. The idea that he would take a human life was ludicrous. I had no desire to read another word of the hateful letter, but something compelled me to pick it up again. My hands shook, causing the paper to quiver beneath the amber-tinted glow of the lamp. I pulled the second page to the front and continued to read.

Please understand that I love my brother. I know this sin of murder was not planned. Jacob must have done something to provoke Daniel. Jacob was reprimanded many times for conducting himself inappropriately with several of the town's young women. Perhaps his conduct toward your mother was the impetus for my brother's reaction. I will never know the answer to this question in my lifetime. And please understand this: I am confident my brother did not know of Jacob's death. I came upon them when they were having words, arguing about something. I have no idea as to the nature of their disagreement. I left them to their contentious confrontation and went home. I found Jacob a couple of hours later. I am certain Daniel had no idea his blow had taken the man's miserable life. If my brother had been aware of the result of his anger, he would have stayed and paid for his crime. But I, in my desire to protect him and the girl he loved, took matters into my own young hands. I wanted Daniel and Beverly to get away from Harmony and have the life I knew could be theirs. So I took care of the problem and spent the rest of my days protecting our secret.

There are days when I regret my actions, even though

I still love my brother. There are days when I hate him for what his careless actions have cost me. But there are many more days when I love him as much or more than I did when we were children.

With apprehension I turned the second page over and read further.

Now, dear niece, I am forced to turn my secret over to you. You must decide what to do with it. Should you call the police, my brother will probably be arrested for murder. Should you keep this horrible secret, you may suffer the same fate I have—life in Harmony, protecting the land that holds the proof of my brother's dreadful deed.
Forgive me for passing this terrible legacy along to you. I realize it is unfair, but I did not know what else to do. I could not die with this unconfessed sin on my conscience. Perhaps I forfeited my life on earth to protect my family, but I am too weak to forfeit eternity.
Please know that I have prayed earnestly for you.
Your loving uncle, Benjamin Temple

My fingers trembled so much as I attempted to refold the horrible letter, I dropped it on the floor. All I could do was stare at it. It couldn't be true. It had to be the rantings of a man sick not only in his body but also in his soul.

I tried to figure out what to do next. Should I call my father and read the letter to him? But what if Benjamin was telling the truth? I knew my dad. If he thought he'd really caused the death of another human being, he would contact the authorities. And then what? Would he go to prison? And what about my mom? The cancer that had tried to take her life was in remission. Would the stress cause it to return? And what if I decided to keep this

43

secret to myself? Burn the letter and leave town without revealing Benjamin's secret? Someday, someone would probably find Jacob Glick's body. Would they tie it to us? Even though confusion jumbled my thoughts, I attempted to think the situation through. This property had been in my father's family for several generations. Glick's death would certainly be blamed on a Temple. Would it be Benjamin? For a moment, the idea of pointing the finger at him seemed to be a way out. But if the body was identified, my father would realize the truth and take responsibility for it. Of that I was certain.

My legs felt like lead. I couldn't move. Suddenly, an odd noise from outside caught my attention. What was it? Again, a scratching sound near the window drew my eyes there. I got up slowly, actually stepping on the letter, and crossed the room. I moved the curtain aside and looked out. I couldn't see anything, but another sound—a bumping noise—came from the other side of the house. I quickly realized how incredibly vulnerable I was.

I ran to my purse and pulled out my cell phone. Although it was almost out of power, there was still a little juice left in it. I quickly punched in 911, not knowing if emergency services even existed out here. All I got was a series of beeps telling me I didn't have enough power to make this call—or any call. I could run out to my car and drive to Sam's, but I had no intention of exposing myself to the darkness—and whatever waited outside.

It was entirely possible that the noises I heard belonged to an animal—but what kind of animal? I knew that in Kansas I wouldn't have to contend with a bear or a lion, but there were other things to consider. Like packs of wild dogs that banded together after their owners dumped them in the country. And rabid smaller animals that would attack humans if they felt threatened.

And of course, there was the possibility that whatever waited outside was altogether too human. Someone who knew there was a woman alone in this house without any way to get help.

Simple Secrets

I checked the front and back doors, making certain they were locked. Then I sat down on the couch and wrapped myself up in the quilt that lay over the back. Probably another one of Mama Essie's. "I need a hug, Mama," I whispered. As I sat there shaking, I put my trust in the only One who could really help me now. I repeated the comforting verses in Psalm 91 until the noises outside ceased, and I fell asleep.

Chapter Five

A loud knock on the door roused me. Was I late for work? Would Grant be mad? I opened my eyes and looked around. Where was I? This wasn't my apartment. I was in Harmony, and there was a body buried on my property.

The knock came again. I got up and shuffled to the front door. When my hand touched the knob, I remembered that someone or some*thing* had been outside last night. Daylight streamed in through the windows, so I felt safer, but still. . .I yearned for my door in Wichita. There was a peephole where I could see who stood outside, waiting to come in. I'd just stepped over to the front window, hoping I could get a look at my visitor, when a face popped up right in front of me. I shrieked involuntarily before I realized it was Sam, looking as surprised as I felt. Trying to pat my hair into place, I cracked open the door.

"Do you scream at everyone who stops by?" His eyes were still wide with alarm.

"No, just you." I swung the door open so he could come in.

"Is that what you're wearing to breakfast?" He stared at my rumpled clothes.

"Oh. Breakfast. I forgot." I pointed toward the living room.

"I'm sorry. Come in. It will only take me a few minutes to get ready."

Sam entered the living room and walked straight to Benjamin's letter, still lying on the floor. "Did you drop something?"

I reached over and grabbed it out of his hand before he had a chance to look at it. "Yes, sorry. Please have a seat. I don't have any coffee. I—I just. . ."

"Woke up?" He offered me an uneven smile. "I couldn't tell."

"Funny."

He glanced at the letter in my hand and then looked at me strangely. I'd planned to put it back inside the Bible, but that was out now. I'd have to take it upstairs with me.

"I had a rough night. Something outside. Guess I'm not used to living this way—so far from other people."

He chuckled and plopped down in the rocking chair. "I understand. It definitely takes some adjustment."

"Actually, it was rather frightening. And I had no way to contact anyone."

"I'm sorry," he said, the smile slipping from his face. "It's important to have a way to get help if you need it. We'll work out something." He pointed toward the roof. "Most of the time, squirrels only feed during the day, but Ben mentioned that he heard something at night sometimes. Could even be raccoons or possums. That's probably the noise that frightened you."

I frowned at him. Great. Nocturnal squirrels or something even bigger. His explanation might explain the scratching noises, but it certainly didn't cover the odd thumping. Unless these were the biggest critters in the world.

"Excuse me while I get ready."

"Sure. Is it okay if I wait inside? It's a little nippy out there this morning."

I nodded, clutched the letter to my chest, and hurried away, somewhat charmed by the idea that he'd actually asked if he could

47

stay inside the house while I changed my clothes.

First I stopped by the bathroom to brush my hair and fix my makeup. Then I ran up the stairs to Mama and Papa's room where I'd stored my clothes. I changed out of my wrinkled jeans and T-shirt and pulled on a clean pair of jeans and a dark green sweater that complimented my coloring.

I stuck the letter from Benjamin in the top drawer of the dresser, underneath my socks. It would stay there until I could figure out a safer place for it. I had no idea what I was going to do with the information my uncle had passed on to me, but for now, I didn't want it falling into the wrong hands.

In the soft sunlight of a new day, the letter seemed like a bad dream. I wanted to read it again, just to make sure I'd understood it, but first I needed to seek God's council. Before I went downstairs, I prayed, "Father, I'm asking You to show me the way. Give me wisdom. I don't know what to do. Thank You for Your guidance."

Remembering Sam's comment about a chill in the air, I grabbed a light jacket from the closet and put it on. When I went downstairs, he was still sitting in Benjamin's rocking chair. He stood up as I entered the room.

"Wow, you really do clean up quick." An odd look flitted across his face. "Please don't take this wrong, but you sure look like. . ."

I sighed. "I know. My uncle Benjamin. I saw a picture of him last night."

"It's just the coloring. I don't want you to think you look like a middle-aged Mennonite man."

"Oh, thanks. Because that's certainly not the look I was going for."

He laughed and walked to the door, holding it open for me. "Then you've succeeded. Ready for breakfast?"

I searched for my purse and found it next to the couch. "I don't usually eat much in the morning. Sometimes I grab an energy bar on the way to the office or some coffee cake from Starbucks."

His expression registered confusion.

"Oh, Starbucks is. . ."

His hearty laugh stopped me in my tracks.

"Grace, I know what Starbucks is. I may have lived in Harmony most of my life, but I do get to the city quite a bit. Besides, we actually do have television out here." He shook his head. "You're still in America, you know. This isn't a foreign country. I was just wondering how anyone can get their day started without breakfast. It's the most important meal of the day."

Now it was my turn to laugh. "Yes, I know. My mother tells me that all the time. And sorry about the Starbucks comment. It's just so different here. Sometimes it feels like I'm living a long way from civilization."

He pointed toward the door, his gray eyes twinkling. "Just the reason I want to introduce you to Harmony. I think you'll be pleasantly surprised."

I stepped outside to a chilly morning. I tugged my Windbreaker closed and locked the door.

Sam trotted down the steps in front of me. "There is a lake behind us," he said. "On the other side of the tree line. You'll find that it's cooler living near the water. We'll warm up fine in a couple of hours." He pointed up the road toward his house. "My place is even closer to the shore. Believe it or not, it's a little colder in my backyard than it is in yours."

I pushed back a desire to ask him if I could see the inside of his fabulous house, but I was afraid he'd misunderstand my intentions. Besides, running into "Sweetie" wasn't something I looked forward to.

On the way to the restaurant, Sam told me some of the history of Harmony. Founded in the late 1800s by a group of German immigrants, it was once called Bethel. In the early 1900s it was changed to Harmony because of another Kansas town that adopted the original name.

"Although at one time, most of the residents lived under Old Order rules, now the population is largely Conservative. There are a few, like Ben, who still live under the old traditions, but along with the conservative Mennonites are those who are much more liberal."

"I noticed two churches here," I said. "We just passed Harmony Church, and on the other side of town is Bethel Mennonite Church."

Sam nodded. "Bethel serves the conservative Mennonites. Harmony members are either more liberal Mennonites—or not Mennonite at all. Harmony Church is nondenominational." He turned to smile at me. "That's where I attend. I'm not Mennonite and never have been. But the pastor there, Marcus Jensen, was raised Mennonite."

I stared out the window of Sam's truck. Main Street bustled with activity. The shops were open and people meandered down the sidewalks, stopping to visit before proceeding on to their destination. Most wore clothing I would associate with Mennonite culture, but quite a few were dressed just like Sam and me.

"How do the two churches get along?"

"Surprisingly well," he said. "For the most part, Harmony's name fits the town. Of course, that wasn't always the case. Although this was before my time, back when your family lived here, the church's bishop was a man named Amil Angstadt."

"My dad mentioned him. I guess he's the reason my parents left Harmony."

Sam nodded. "From what I've heard, he ran this town with an iron fist. He died about ten years after your father left. That was about a year after your grandparents moved away. Some people thought they'd come back, but they never did." He smiled at me again. "I understand they didn't want to leave behind a granddaughter they'd grown to love."

"They stayed away for me?"

He shrugged. "That's what Ben told me. I believe he exchanged a few letters with his parents."

"I—I didn't know that. He certainly never wrote to my father."

"Ben wouldn't talk about his brother much. That was a closed subject."

The mention of my uncle's name brought back the memory of that awful letter. "Sam, have you ever heard of a man named Jacob Glick?"

Sam frowned. "Jacob Glick? Sounds familiar. I think Sweetie mentioned him once. Some really unpleasant man who used to live here. If I remember right, he moved away a long time ago, but I'm not sure. I could ask my aunt if you'd like."

"No. That's okay. Just forget it." I didn't want Myrtle Goodrich involved any deeper in my life than she already was.

I turned away to look out the window again. I could feel Sam's eyes on me, probably wondering why I'd asked about Glick. I really didn't want to think about him now. I was in Harmony, and I wanted to experience it without the specter of Glick or my dead uncle hanging over me. I tried to concentrate on the shops and people we passed, putting the letter out of my mind. But its presence hung on me like a heavy coat—not so easily shed.

Sam pulled up in front of Mary's Kitchen. The old two-story redbrick building looked as if it had existed almost as long as the town. Wooden beams held up the sloping porch roof. The second story windows were thin and topped by stone carvings that resembled intricate valances. Four white rockers sat on the front porch, two each in front of the wide glass windows that framed a bright red wooden door. Signs in the windows read OPEN and NO SHOES, NO SHIRT, NO SERVICE. A menu was posted in one window and flyers from both of Harmony's churches in the other.

"There aren't any wimpy city breakfasts here," Sam said with a chuckle. "I hope you're hungry."

51

Surprisingly, I was starving. There was something about the country air and the wonderful aromas drifting from the restaurant that stirred up memories of Mama Essie's big Saturday breakfasts. We'd drive to Mama and Papa's house every weekend and gorge on homemade pancakes with lots of butter and maple syrup. And spicy link sausages with crusty edges. Without warning, my mouth started to water. "I don't think you need to worry about me. This morning I feel like I could eat my breakfast *and* yours."

Sam laughed and jumped out of the truck. I started to put my hand on the door latch, but before I had a chance to flip the handle, my door swung open. He stood waiting for me to get out of the truck. Add being a gentleman to his other great qualities. I flashed back briefly to my last several dates in town. Not one of my escorts had opened the car door for me. In fact, now that I thought about it, none of them had opened any doors for me. After I exited the truck, he hurried up the steps to the diner and held that door open, too. I could certainly get used to this kind of treatment.

"Hey, Sam!" several patrons called out when we stepped inside. Burnished wood floors and wooden booths reminded me of an old diner in Fairbury that had never left behind its '70s motif. A few tables sat against the front window. Stainless-steel legs with yellow laminate tops and matching chairs held the obligatory salt, pepper, sugar, and orange plastic container with nonsugar sweeteners. Cerulean blue walls were covered with photographs. Many of them looked pretty old. Without closer inspection, I assumed they were pictures of the town down through the years and of the people who had called Harmony home. Some of the portraits looked to be from the 1800s or early 1900s. Scattered among lots of smiling faces, several dour looking families frowned upon the easygoing patrons enjoying their food.

Sam pointed to a table for two next to a wall near the window. "How's this?"

I nodded and sat down on one side of the table while he took the other chair.

"Mary! You got customers!" An older man in overalls who sat in a nearby booth hollered toward the back of the restaurant.

A long wooden counter that matched the booths held large glass containers filled with slices of pie and cake. An old cash register sat underneath one of the café's hanging lights, which consisted of large, white, round globes positioned around the interior of the room. Most of them were glowing even though the intense daylight that streamed through the front windows made their attempt to provide proper illumination completely futile. Steam rose from two coffeepots sitting on a warmer behind the counter, and overhead someone had mounted a couple of dead fish on the wall. Next to the stuffed fish, two large chalkboards contained the day's specials. A hallway next to the backward L-shaped counter led to restrooms and a door that had to be the entryway into the kitchen. An old metal step stool pushed against the door held it open. A couple of minutes later, a rather harried-looking young woman came out carrying plates of hot, steaming food.

"If you yell a little louder, Harold, they can hear you in Council Grove."

The chastised Harold greeted her good-natured ribbing with a raucous laugh.

"Just tryin' to keep you on your toes, Mary," he said with a grin. "Didn't want nobody starvin' to death due to your pokiness."

The woman plopped a large plate in front of him. "I don't think you have anything to worry about." She jabbed at the man's large belly. "You could live on what you've got stored up for quite some time."

The other two men sitting with Harold exploded with laughter. I noticed that one of the Mennonite families sitting nearby joined in the merriment. The overall feeling inside the restaurant was one of cozy familiarity.

53

After serving the rest of the plates in her hands, Mary headed our way. Her quick smile for Sam faded when she saw me. But she fixed it back into place so fast most people wouldn't have noticed.

"Howdy, Sam. Who's this pretty lady? You're not stepping out on me, are you?" She placed her hands on her hips and locked her gaze on me. She had long dark hair pulled back in a ponytail. Long lashes framed deep brown eyes set in a heart-shaped face.

Sam flushed a nice shade of pink. "Now Mary, you be nice." His smile seemed a little tight. "This is Ben Temple's niece, Grace. She's here to take care of his estate."

I saw a flicker of relief in her expression. "Nice to meet you, Grace," she said, extending her hand. "I'm Mary Whittenbauer. I own this joint." Her grip was stronger than I'd expected.

"Most people call me Gracie. Nice to meet you. I hear you fix a mean breakfast."

"Well, Hector Ramirez, my cook, is responsible for most of the meals here. I tell people I taught him everything he knows, but he says it's the other way around."

She looked at Sam. "You havin' the usual?"

He nodded.

Mary pointed to one of the chalkboards on the wall. "That's our menu. What sounds good to you, Gracie?"

I picked the regular breakfast with scrambled eggs, sausage, hash browns, and toast. I said yes to coffee and watched Mary saunter back to the kitchen.

"I take it you two date?"

Sam looked at the tabletop like he saw something interesting there. "We've dated some, yes. It–it's not that serious though."

"Sounds like Mary thinks it is."

His eyes bored into mine. "Let's talk about something else, okay? I'm not comfortable. . ."

"I'm sorry. It's not my business anyway." My eyes strayed to the photographs on the wall next to us. "Tell me about these pictures."

Sounding a little more relaxed, Sam launched into a few stories about the families that had settled in Harmony years ago. Many of the original settlers still had descendants who lived in the small town. He confirmed my suspicion that as a rule, Old Order Mennonites didn't go in for having their pictures taken. They believed capturing your likeness on film was akin to creating a "graven image" and that excessive attention to one's outside appearance could lead to vanity and self-worship. Their lives revolved around aspects they considered to be really important. Faith and family were at the top of the list. However, there were a few scattered pictures of people dressed in clothing that identified them as members of the Old Order community. Sam explained that down through the years, a few pictures had turned up here and there. Some families who really wanted keepsakes had pictures taken in secret, not letting the rest of the community know. I thought back to the photograph I'd found back at Benjamin's. It tickled me to think of Papa Joe as a rebel—even back then. I was certainly grateful he'd had at least one portrait taken. I wondered if there were more somewhere. Maybe a little digging would uncover others.

I was so engrossed in Sam's stories I didn't even notice that Mary had returned with coffee. I looked down to see a cup in front of me. I picked it up and took a sip. Its deep, rich flavor was exactly what I needed.

"You're probably used to that froufrou Starbucks coffee," Sam said. "The only flavors you can add here are cream and sugar."

I laughed. "Who told you I drink 'froufrou' coffee anyway? For your information, Starbucks has regular coffee, too."

He raised his cup. "Point taken. Sorry to make assumptions."

Before I had the chance to admit that I liked many of the flavored lattes and Frappuccinos that probably fit his "froufrou" description, the front door of the restaurant opened and a large man with a dark, bushy beard walked in. He wore the kind of straw hat I'd seen in Benjamin's closet and on some of the other men in Harmony. His black pants and blue shirt reminded me of Benjamin's clothes. However, he also wore a blue Windbreaker not much different than the one I had on.

"Abel!" Sam called to him.

The man raised one of his meaty hands and a wide smile spread across his broad face. "Hello there, Sam."

Sam waved him over, and the man approached our table. His size was intimidating, but he radiated affability.

"Grace Temple," Sam said, "I'd like to introduce you to Abel Mueller. He's the pastor of Bethel Church."

Pastor Mueller's huge fingers enveloped my hand. "Grace Temple? Is this Benjamin's niece?"

I nodded. "One and the same."

He kept my hand nestled in his and covered it with his other hand. "We're glad you're here, Grace. I'm so sorry your family wasn't notified when Benjamin became so ill. I tried and tried to convince him that you would want to know, but he forbade me from contacting anyone."

I had to admit that Pastor Mueller had taken me by surprise. In my mind, I'd lumped him into my preconceived idea of Mennonite leaders—grumpy, judgmental, and humorless. But this man was far from that. "It was Benjamin's choice, I guess. Not much you could do about it."

"Thank you. That makes me feel a little better." He finally let go of my hand.

"Emily and Hannah meeting you for breakfast?" Sam asked.

Pastor Mueller grinned. "Yes, as soon as they're through picking out fabric from Ruth's place. Spring is in the air, so new dresses are on the horizon."

"Why don't you have a cup of coffee with us until they get here?" Sam said.

The pastor looked at me. "If Grace doesn't mind."

"No. Please do."

He grabbed another chair from a nearby table and pulled it up to ours, easing his large frame onto the padded seat. His eyes scanned the room. Mary stood talking to a family seated near the kitchen. The pastor waited until she looked his way and then stuck one of his fingers in the air. The restaurant owner nodded. Seemed as if Mary knew what everyone wanted before they asked for it. In Wichita, I visited the same Starbucks almost every morning, and each time the workers behind the counter acted as if they'd never seen me before.

"So, how long will you be in Harmony, Grace?" Pastor Mueller asked.

"Two weeks. I have to get back to work. And please, call me Gracie." I took a sip from my coffee cup.

"Gracie, it is," he said with a smile. "And what kind of work do you do?"

"I'm a graphic designer. I work for an advertising agency."

The pastor's eyebrows shot up. "An artist, huh? I have a lot of respect for those to whom God has given artistic talent. I'm afraid that's something He neglected to bestow upon me."

"I've always loved to draw. I began when I was pretty young. My mother says I started drawing bugs when I was two years old."

He chuckled. "Bugs, huh? Glad you moved on to other things." He took a sip of coffee and then put his cup down. "What are your plans while you're in Harmony?"

"I need to find a way to let people know my uncle's house is for sale. How should I go about that?"

"Well, if you don't mind, I'd like to spread the word in town first before you put anything in a newspaper outside of Harmony. We have a few young couples that would love a chance at that property." He looked at Sam. "I'm thinking about Kenneth and Alene Ward. They've asked about Ben's place several times."

Sam nodded. "I think they'd buy it gladly."

"I'm not sure why," I said. "The house isn't bad, but there are much nicer places around here."

Pastor Mueller smiled. "Your uncle owns somewhere around thirty acres of the land surrounding that house. When your grandparents lived there, it was farmed for wheat and corn, but Benjamin let it all go after they left. An industrious young couple could bring the land back."

A chill ran through me. Farming meant digging and turning over the soil. A good chance my family's secret would be uncovered. The very thing my uncle had feared.

"You won't have any trouble selling Ben's property," Sam said. "I'll help you get the word out. Maybe we can make some flyers and post them around town."

I nodded dumbly, but my mind was still focused on the body hiding somewhere under a few feet of dirt. Then another thought struck me. "Pastor Mueller, how did my uncle survive? Financially, I mean. Without any crops..."

"First of all, please call me Abel," the gregarious man said. "Pastor Mueller is a little too formal for me."

"Thanks."

"Your uncle's income source is easy to spot as you walk up and down our streets," he continued. "He made all the wonderful rocking chairs scattered all over town. And the birdhouses and feeders. You'll see many of them in Ruth's store when you visit." He shook his head. "Benjamin never lacked for work. He was a skilled craftsman."

"I didn't see any kind of workshop on his property."

"Most of the time, he worked in the basement," Sam said. "Have you been down there?"

"No. I thought about it last night, but without electricity..."

"Too spooky?" Abel laughed. "I can understand that."

At that moment, Mary showed up at our table with plates for

Sam and me. She set his down carefully in front of him. A pile of pancakes topped with butter and a plate of sausage. She shoved my plate toward me without as much care. I looked up to see her giving me a rather frosty stare. Was she warning me? I had no idea why she saw me as a threat to her relationship with Sam. I wasn't going to be around long enough to cause her any problems. But maybe I was misinterpreting her actions.

She refilled our coffee cups. "Anything else here?"

"Thanks, Mary," Abel said heartily. "Emily and Hannah should be along soon. We'll need a round of your wonderful pancakes."

"You got it, Abel." She shot one more pointed look toward me and headed to another table. I glanced at Sam to see if he'd noticed, but he was busy pouring syrup on his plate.

"Abel, would you say grace?" he said after placing the syrup pitcher back on the table.

I bowed my head as the pastor thanked God for our food and the day He'd given us. I silently added a couple of requests of my own, said "Amen," and picked up my fork. The eggs were fluffy and delicious, and the sausage reminded me of Mama Essie's. The coffeemaker behind the counter chortled as it created another round of the fresh, robust brew. I usually try to keep myself down to one cup of coffee a day, but I decided to relax my rule this morning. Mary's breakfast was made to be eaten with the accompaniment of her great coffee.

"So what do you think of Harmony so far?" Abel asked, looking at me.

I quickly swallowed a mouthful of food. "I haven't seen much of it yet. Sam's going to show me around a little." I put my fork down and frowned at him. "This town hasn't had a good effect on my family, you know. I have to say that I came here expecting to find something much different than what I've seen so far."

Abel smiled. "You mean a place full of religious zealots and judgmental people?"

I nodded.

"Gracie," he said with sincerity in his voice, "if you could see Harmony as it was thirty years ago, that might be exactly what you'd have found. Except for a few people, like your father, who stood up against the tyranny in this town, everyone took their orders from a man who certainly didn't follow the real tenets of our faith. Amil Angstadt was a bully who thought his brand of religion was the only way to heaven. You see, Mennonites believe salvation comes through the grace and the sacrifice of Jesus Christ. But Angstadt taught that the price our Savior paid for us wasn't enough. That what you wore, what you did or didn't do, or even who you spoke to paved your way to heaven."

I shook my head at him. "But isn't that the same thing you do? I mean, making these women wear these long dresses and odd caps. Not using electricity. None of these things produce righteousness. That comes from the inside. Not the outside."

I saw Sam's eyebrows shoot up. Maybe I was being too direct, but after seeing the havoc this man's religion had played in my family, I didn't care.

To my surprise, he smiled widely. "First of all, we use electricity. I know your uncle didn't, but he held to some of the old ways that most of us don't. And as far as what produces righteousness, you're exactly right. I agree with you completely."

"I'm confused. Then why. . ."

"Gracie, we don't *make* anyone wear certain clothes or do anything else. You see, we live this way because we want to. There isn't a single person in my church who has ever been compelled to do anything except follow the teachings of Christ: to love Him with all their hearts—and to love their neighbors as themselves." His forehead wrinkled, and then he chuckled. "You know, I haven't had to explain our ways for a very long time. I guess we're rather isolated here." He took a sip of his coffee and then set the cup down in front of him. His eyes sought mine. I saw compassion and kindness in them. Even though I hadn't been prepared to like him, I did. Very much.

"Living a simple life isn't done so we can earn brownie points with God," he said in a soft voice. "It's a lifestyle we adopt because we truly believe it's helpful for us." He held out his open hands. "Take television. Don't even have one. When there's a storm, sometimes I'll come here and Mary will turn the set on so we can get updated weather forecasts. Or if something of national importance happens, I may go to a neighbor's house and watch a news channel for a bit so I can keep abreast of the situation. While waiting for whatever information I need, I've seen snatches of several of today's. . .what are they called. . .sitcoms?" He pulled on his beard. "I think our community is better off without them."

"But there are good things on TV, too," I said. "Shows that spread the gospel."

"I know that. I believe television can be a wonderful way to touch the world with the Good News. But the rest of it. . . Well, we would just rather live without its leaven. Please understand though—it's not a rule of the church or anything like that. It's a suggestion. Just as with many of our other choices. Like what we wear." He leaned back in his chair and folded his arms across his chest. "Let me ask you a question. Some of the schools in Wichita have adopted dress codes. Do you know why?"

I nodded. "Because it stops kids from wearing gang colors. Also, it helps to cut down on the attention to clothes and refocuses it back on schoolwork."

"That's exactly right. In wearing modest, simple clothing, we believe it helps us to focus our lives on God and His service and away from worldly concerns. It's as simple as that." He shrugged. "But please understand—we only ask that our members dress modestly. They choose their outfits. I don't visit everyone's house in the mornings and approve their choices." He chuckled. "Not even for my Emily. She says I have no taste."

I stabbed another sausage with my fork. "Okay, I understand the clothing thing. But why did my uncle turn his back on our family? Sam says you don't actually ban people."

"He's right. If we discovered a church member was involved in some kind of serious error, we would reach out in compassion to him, but we wouldn't turn him away unless there was no other choice. In my entire life I've never seen it happen. I'm not saying I haven't watched people leave the faith, but they always left on their own accord." He hesitated and gazed intently at the table-top for a moment. "I've heard that Amil Angstadt used what at one time was called The Ban, but trust me—when he died, the practice died with him. I visited your uncle many times, trying to convince him that he needed to reach out to his family. He refused to even discuss it with me. I have no idea why."

But I was pretty sure I did. "Abel, I appreciate everything you've said. I had some wrong ideas. I guess it isn't your religion that was the problem in my family. It seems that following the wrong leader caused most of the destruction."

He nodded. "I believe that to be the truth."

I finished the coffee in my cup and glanced toward the front counter. Mary leaned against the back wall and glared at me. I changed my mind about raising my cup to indicate I wanted more coffee. Fortunately for me, Sam noticed I was out and waved to her. She picked up a pot, carried it over, and silently filled everyone's cup. She left the table with a backward glance at me. Let's just say that the small town charm evident in the café didn't carry over to its owner.

"I—I do have another question," I said to Abel while I tried to ignore Mary's obvious distaste for me, "but I'm not sure you can help me. You weren't in Harmony when my parents lived here."

He shook his head. "No, I wasn't. But I have learned a lot about those days from some of the folks who lived through them. Ask away."

"Do you know anything about a man named Jacob Glick?"

A loud gasp from behind me revealed an older woman standing next to a girl who looked to be around fourteen or fifteen. They were dressed almost exactly the same, in long pastel dresses covered by a white pinafore. Both wore caps with ribbons that hung next to their faces.

Sam sat closest to the older woman whose face had gone horribly pale. He reached out and caught her as she staggered.

"Emily!" Abel cried out. "Are you all right?"

She nodded vigorously and pushed away from Sam, steadying herself. But the look of fear in her wide eyes told me a different story.

This woman was terrified of Jacob Glick.

Chapter Six

I hope Emily's feeling better." Sam glanced over to the table where the Muellers sat, waiting for their pancakes.

"Yeah, me, too."

Emily Mueller's hurried explanation of a sharp pain in her side left me with more questions than answers. I didn't want to think she'd lied to me, but her reaction seemed to be more a response to the name of Jacob Glick than to some kind of physical pain.

Eventually she regained her composure, even managing to paste a smile back on her face before Abel ushered his family to their own table. Sam and I accepted an invitation for Sunday dinner tomorrow after church. The request for our presence hadn't come from Emily. I had to wonder if she was as happy as her husband to welcome us to her home.

I watched the Muellers as I finished my breakfast. Although Emily wouldn't look my way, her daughter, Hannah, seemed fascinated by me. I wasn't quite sure why. There were other non-Mennonite people in Harmony. What was so special about me?

The girl's head covering and simple dress couldn't hide her natural beauty. Tendrils of golden blond hair trailed from beneath her cap, and her large sky blue eyes were framed by flawless skin.

A lack of makeup certainly didn't hurt her stunning looks. A teenage boy, eating breakfast with his family at a nearby table, kept sneaking glances at her. I didn't blame him a bit.

As if reading my mind, Sam said, "Hannah Mueller seems quite taken with you. Probably because Abel introduced you as an artist. You'll see some of Hannah's paintings at Ruth's. Harmony has a few artisans, including Joyce Bechtold. She painted your uncle's birdhouses." He lowered his voice. "Although she'd never admit it, I think Joyce hoped someday Ben would become more than just someone she worked with. In all those years, he never gave her any kind of encouragement." He grunted and looked past me, as if viewing something I couldn't see. "I saw him stare at her once when he didn't know I was watching him. I could have sworn I saw something in his face…a tenderness." He shook his head and refocused his attention on me. "Must have been my imagination. If he was interested in her, why wouldn't he have said something? Except for loving God, finding the right person to share your life with is the most important thing in the world."

Was that how he felt about Mary? She kept looking our way, as if checking up on us. Obviously, her relationship with Sam wasn't that secure—in her mind anyway.

I waited while Sam went up to the register to pay our bill. Mary said something to him that seemed to upset him. She tried to grab his arm, but he gently wrestled it away from her. As he turned to walk back to where I sat, the look Mary shot me was one of pure anger. Her expression shook me. I certainly wasn't after her boyfriend. In fact, I had no intention of starting a relationship with anyone in Harmony. Not even a man as nice as Sam Goodrich.

"Let's take that tour," he said when he reached the table. I stood up and was headed for the front door when he put his hand on my shoulder. "Wait a minute," he said. "I just thought of something." He pointed at some pictures against the far wall of the restaurant. "There are some old pictures of Harmony here. I think your Jacob Glick might be in one of them."

I followed him to a grouping of black-and-white photos. Sure enough, they appeared to be photographs of the town down through the years. I began to scan them. Sam pointed to a shot taken of a dry goods store on what must have been opening day. The proprietors stood proudly in front of their business. Off to the side stood a bearded man in dark clothing. He stared straight at the camera. His fierce expression chilled me, and I shivered involuntarily.

"Amil Angstadt," Sam said. "I'm sure he had no idea he would show up in the picture, but there he is. Sweetie showed me this photo years ago, but she won't talk much about him. Pretty scary, huh?"

I nodded my agreement. So this was the man who had caused so much pain in my family.

"Here," Sam said triumphantly, pointing to a picture a few spots away. "Ever since you mentioned this Glick person, I kept thinking I'd seen the name somewhere. This is a picture of the church building in 1980. That's Glick standing in front."

I looked closely. Sure enough, someone had written "Jacob Glick" in the margin of the photograph.

"Glick wasn't actually a part of the church." I jumped at Abel Mueller's voice coming from behind me.

"Then why is he shown in front of the building?"

"He worked around the church," Abel said. "I have some old memoirs written by people who attended Bethel down through the years. They refer to him as a church custodian. Appeared to be a rather solitary fellow. No family. Not well liked. He was asked to leave town—more than once."

"And why is that?"

Abel shrugged. "According to what I've managed to glean though some old letters and diaries, Glick was very interested in finding a wife. Mennonite women are encouraged to marry within the faith. Since he refused to join the church, church leaders rebuffed his efforts. He finally gave up and left town. And that was the end of Jacob Glick."

I wished with all my heart that a bus out of town *had* signaled the end of Glick, but unfortunately, unless my uncle had taken leave of his senses, a rock in the side of the head had been his actual means of departure.

Glick was an unusually unattractive man. I assumed his looks hadn't helped him in his quest for companionship. Dark hair, bushy eyebrows that had grown together, and an unusually long nose worked together to produce a rather frightening visage. His beady, black eyes held an odd hint of wildness to them. This was a man most women would run *from* instead of toward.

"Not what you'd call a good-looking guy is he?" Abel asked.

I shook my head while Sam snorted his agreement.

Abel cleared his throat. "I don't mean to pry, but is there some reason you're interested in Mr. Glick? I mean, he's not part of your family. He wasn't even part of the church."

Wishing I'd come up with a reason for asking about Glick sooner, I blurted out the only thing that came to my mind. "I found his name on something at my uncle's. I was just curious. It's no big deal." Well, at least I hadn't out-and-out lied. I wasn't sure about the "big deal" part, but maybe that would prove true, as well. I decided to change the subject before I was asked more uncomfortable questions. "Sam said Old Order Mennonites didn't believe in having their pictures taken. Is that why there are no pictures of the church members or the families here?"

Abel nodded. "Yes, but there are a few. Ida Turnbauer told me that the cousin of one of the church members was a photographer. It seems a few folks contacted the man privately and had family pictures taken. They weren't normally shown to anyone outside of the family, but I know they were treasured mementos." He pointed to a grouping of family photos showing people dressed in the same kind of clothing depicted in the picture at Benjamin's.

"Why are these here? I would think the families would have kept them."

"Most of them did. These were either left behind when the families moved away or donated by relatives who still live in Harmony." He directed our attention to one of the photographs. A very handsome young man stood next to an older man and woman. "That's Levi Hoffman. He owns our candle shop. Lived here all his life." He motioned toward the other photos. "The rest of these folks moved away. Levi's the only one who still lives in Harmony."

I glanced around at some of the other pictures on the wall. "Kind of sad that there aren't more images of the early Mennonite settlers. Wouldn't they help to keep their memories alive? Help people remember what they accomplished?"

Abel chuckled. "I understand your point, Gracie. But we have no photographs of Christ, and He changed the world. I'm not sure how important pictures really are."

I wanted to tell him how special the portrait of my family hanging in Mama and Papa's room was to me, but I kept my mouth shut.

I looked closer at the face of Amil Angstadt. There was something burning in those eyes—and it didn't reflect the heart of the loving God I'd come to know. A rush of emotions churned inside me. The depth of my feelings surprised me. Being in Harmony, the place where my parents had grown up and fallen in love, was affecting me in ways I hadn't anticipated. It made their experiences so real. I could almost sense their fear and heartache.

While I fought to bring my feelings under control, I studied Jacob Glick again—the man who was buried somewhere on property that now belonged to me. I had a strange urge to blurt out the truth to Abel. I felt strongly that he had the heart of a pastor and would want to help me. But I had to remind myself that I really didn't know him—or anyone in this town. Besides, until I'd prayed more about it, I couldn't risk sharing anything with anyone. I turned around and ran right into Sam. I put my hands on his chest to balance myself.

"Oh, s–sorry," I stammered. Still touching him, I looked up into his eyes. What I saw there made my toes tingle.

"Th–that's okay," he said in a husky voice.

I forced myself to step away from him. Without planning it, my gaze swung toward the back of the restaurant where I'd last seen Mary. She was still there—staring at me. But I saw more than just jealousy in her face. There was hurt.

"We'd better get going," I said more forcefully than I meant to. I was almost to the door when I remembered Abel. I looked back to find him watching me. "It was nice to meet you. I guess we'll see you tomorrow. . .about one?"

He nodded. "See you then, Gracie."

Mary watched as Sam and I walked toward the front door. I thought he'd at least say good-bye, but he seemed to have completely forgotten about her. Although I'd never been in love, I knew the signs. This woman was head over heels for Sam Goodrich, but he didn't reciprocate her feelings. I felt sorry for Mary. I hadn't come to Harmony to cause anyone pain. Maybe two weeks was too long to stay—and then I remembered Uncle Benjamin's secret. I was trapped here until I could find a way to resolve my family mess.

Sam and I stepped out into a bright spring day. "Let's start on this side of the street. Then if there's time, we'll hit the other side." He shrugged. "If not, we'll come back next week. There's no rush."

I nodded and followed him to Ruth's Crafts and Creations. The little store was housed between the restaurant and Menlo's Bakery. At Sam's recommendation, we decided to save the bakery for last. Good idea since I was so stuffed I couldn't even think about food.

A bell tinkled above the door when we walked into the sunny yellow building with cream-colored trim. A gray-haired woman with a wide red face looked up from something she was working on behind her counter.

"Why, Sam Goodrich. It's been a month of Sundays since you've come to see me. What's going on?" She fastened her inquisitive expression on me. "Well, goodness gracious. Who is this?"

Sam put his hand on my elbow and gently guided me toward the counter. "Ruth Wickham, meet Grace Temple, Ben's niece."

The woman's hands flew to her ample chest. "Oh my. Grace, I'm so happy to finally meet you. I'd heard you were coming. I wish Benjamin had let someone contact your family so you could attend his service."

A thought struck me. "Is—is my uncle buried near here?"

Ruth's round face softened into a smile. "Yes dear. In the cemetery outside town." She pointed her chubby finger at Sam. "Sam can show you where it is." She wiped her hands on the calico apron she wore over jeans and a bright red sweatshirt. "I've got some lovely flowers in the garden out back. You come by here whenever you want, and I'll give you a nice bouquet to put on his grave."

"Thank you."

She waved her hand at me. "It's nothing. As persnickety as Benjamin was, we thought a lot of him. Such an honest and ethical man. You should be proud of him, Grace."

"Please call me Gracie," I said. I realized as I said it that Sam kept introducing me as Grace. In fact, I couldn't remember him calling me Gracie once.

"Gracie it is," Ruth said. "Now let me show you around some." She came around the corner and took my arm. "I've got several of your uncle's birdhouses and feeders over here." She sighed heavily. "I can hardly believe there won't be any more."

"Joyce can still paint birdhouses for you, Ruth," Sam said. He reached up and ran his fingers along the smooth side of a beautifully carved house. "I guess no one makes a house quite like Ben, though."

"No. No they don't." Ruth put her hands on her hips and stared at the birdhouses displayed on her shelves. "Benjamin took pride in everything he did. Never rushed the job. Never sacrificed quality for speed, yet he met every order on time." She brushed at her eyes with her hand. "Aren't many men like Benjamin Temple anymore." A quick smile chased the sadness from her face. "Except you, Sam. I swear, if I didn't know better, I'd believe you two were related."

Sam's easygoing expression faltered for a moment, and something dark crossed his features. I wondered what was behind it. Why did he live with his aunt? Where were his parents? He'd mentioned living in Harmony for most of his life. My curiosity was aroused. Sam Goodrich was an interesting man. I found myself wanting to understand him.

Besides my uncle's creations, Ruth's shop was filled to the brink with handmade items: beautiful quilts, dried flower arrangements, pottery, and bolts of cloth. On one wall, I discovered several framed paintings. Most were landscapes; several were of horses. Each one was striking, painted by someone with remarkable natural talent. And every single painting was set into a carved frame that highlighted the scene perfectly. One particular picture really caught my eye. It depicted a man plowing a field, with a storm brewing in the sky behind him. Dark clouds boiled with moisture. The farmer's urgency to beat the impending rain showed in his taut muscles and stalwart expression. I realized the style was familiar.

"These are outstanding," I said. "I believe my uncle has two paintings by this artist hanging in his house. Who. . ." I leaned in and saw the signature. *H. Mueller.* I couldn't hold back a gasp.

"Hannah Mueller painted these?"

"Hannah painted all of them," Ruth said, bustling up next to me, "and the pictures in your house. She's a very talented young lady. Hard to believe she's only fourteen. You know, painting used to be frowned upon by many in the Mennonite community. This kind of art was considered useless."

I shook my head. "That's a shame. I'm glad Hannah's family doesn't believe that."

Ruth smiled. "Well, you can still see influences from those beliefs in Hannah's work. You'll notice that most people are either seen from a distance or their faces are turned away. Landscapes are the prevalent theme, and almost every picture is of local life and community."

"I don't understand."

Ruth shrugged. "I've seen some paintings I wouldn't allow into my house, haven't you? I guess it's just an attempt to keep the subject wholesome and free of vanity. Like it says in Philippians: 'Finally, brothers, whatever is true, whatever is noble, whatever is right, whatever is pure, whatever is lovely, whatever is admirable—if anything is excellent or praiseworthy—think about such things.'"

An image from a lurid art show I'd accidentally stumbled upon during a downtown art crawl in Wichita flashed through my mind. It had left me feeling disgusted. "I—I see what you mean, Ruth. Painting the kinds of things that honor that verse makes sense."

She nodded. "Abel and Emily see Hannah's painting as a gift. They encourage her, but they also make certain she uses it in a way they believe will please God. I think she does that admirably. She's never had any formal training, you know. Unfortunately, the school she attends has no art teacher."

"Her technique is very advanced. I'm surprised." I leaned in closer and inspected the painting a little closer. "Are these for sale? How much for this one?"

"The watercolors are twenty dollars, and the oil paintings are thirty."

"That's not enough. These are worth much more. Goodness, the frames alone. . ."

"These frames don't set Hannah back a penny," Ruth said, chuckling. "They're donated by a very talented man who loves to help other people." She smiled at Sam.

"You?" I said to him. "You carved these frames?"

He shrugged. "No big deal. Something I do while I watch TV."

"Well, it *is* a big deal. They're beautiful. You could sell them." I fumbled in my purse and pulled out my pocketbook. "Here," I said to Ruth. "I won't give Hannah less than fifty dollars for this painting. And it's worth much more."

Ruth put her hand up to her mouth. "Oh, she will be so thrilled. We haven't sold many." She noticed the surprised look on my face. "Not because people don't love them," she said. "It's because Hannah gives them away to everyone. The only people who pay for them are out-of-towners, and we don't get that many. Of course, there is one person in town who's bought quite a few." She crooked her thumb at Sam.

I grinned at him. "So let me get this straight. You give her frames—and you buy the paintings and the frames back?"

He flushed just as he had at the restaurant. "I never had brothers or sisters. Helping Hannah kind of fills the void, I guess."

Ruth chuckled and looked at him fondly. "You're a good man, Sam Goodrich. You know that? I'm proud to know you. I really am."

Sam turned an even deeper red, causing Ruth and me to laugh. He shook his head and walked over to a display of colorful plates, feigning disinterest in our attention.

Still giggling, Ruth grabbed a bag and some newspaper from under her counter. While she wrapped up the painting for me,

I poked around the shop a little more. I found lots of wood carvings and a table full of embroidered towels and pillowcases. I grabbed four of the pillowcases—two for me and two for my mother. A nicely decorated box of homemade fudge called my name, and I added it to my selections.

On the other side of the room sat a table with the most artistically designed stationery, cards, and envelopes I'd ever seen. "These are lovely," I said to Ruth. "Where did you get them?"

She toddled over to see what I meant. "Oh, you mean Sarah's paper." She picked up a sheet of stationery with green and yellow leaves that wrapped around the top and one side. Each leaf was intricately designed. "Sarah Ketterling is one of our few Old Order residents. She and her father live on a farm outside town." She fingered the eye-catching design. "This is called wood-block printing. Do you know anything about it?"

A faint memory from one of my college classes flashed through my mind. "I've heard of it, but this is the first example I've seen. She carves the design into wood, right? And then rolls paint across it. Then the paper is put on top and the design is transferred."

Ruth smiled. "That's the basic idea, but it's a little more complicated than that. I have these patterns in right now, but I sell out pretty quick. People love this stationery. I also have several customers from outside Harmony who order it regularly." She ran her hand over the paper again. "Sarah's about your age. A lovely young woman." She sighed. "But her father keeps her on a pretty tight rein, so I don't get to speak to her often. Her father, Gabriel, was very close to Bishop Angstadt when he ran the church here. He's never cottoned to Abel Mueller—thinks he's too liberal." She touched my arm. "Even though Benjamin was part of that Old Order group, he wasn't too thrilled with Gabriel's brand of parenting. He and Ida Turnbauer tried talking to him more than once. Never did any good. Just made him mad."

"Well, Sarah is very talented. A real artist." I picked up a package of the green leaf stationery, along with some matching envelopes. "I'd love to learn more about this process."

"Gabriel won't let you anywhere near his daughter," Sam said. "In fact, when Ruth sells her work, she has to give the money to him. He won't allow the proceeds to go directly to Sarah."

"He sounds like an awful person. Why doesn't Sarah just leave?"

Sam shook his head. "She's afraid of him, Grace."

"I'm not so sure she isn't more afraid *for* him," Ruth said frowning. "Gabriel used to be a different person before his wife ran off with another man. He always had a good word for everyone. I liked him. But after his wife left, he completely changed. I think Sarah feels responsible for him—as if it's her job to look after him."

Anger churned inside me. "I'm sorry for him, but what about *her* life? She must be extremely unhappy."

"I don't believe he realizes what he's doing to her," Sam said. "He thinks he's protecting her against the world. The same outside world that stole his wife. Of course, Angstadt's early influence in his life has only reinforced his suspicion and fear. One of the bishop's main teachings was that worldly influences cause nothing but spiritual pollution. I guess in his mind, that justifies his treatment of Sarah."

"That preacher left a trail of confusion behind him, that's for sure," Ruth said, shaking her head. "Thank God Abel Mueller came to this town. The difference is night and day."

"If you've spent enough money, we should get going," Sam said. "I didn't think we'd be spending our whole day here."

"Now you let Gracie alone, Sam Goodrich," Ruth said good-naturedly. "She can buy anything she wants."

I took the stationery up to the counter and put it with the painting, the pillowcases, and the fudge. "I'd really better get out of here. I won't have any money left."

"Well, before you leave, I have to show you my pride and joy." Ruth's eyes sparkled as she directed my attention to something silver inside the glass case under the counter.

Sam grinned. "She shows off her pride and joy to everyone who steps foot in this place."

"Now, Sam Goodrich," Ruth shot back, "you just hush."

"Oh my goodness. What is it?"

Ruth smiled. "This is the one thing I won't sell. I let it stay in the store so folks can enjoy it. You see, I live alone. Keeping it in my house just for my tired old eyes doesn't make much sense."

She slid the door behind the case open and lifted out a silver piece that looked like a vase with handles and a top. Under the silver cover decorated with floral finials sat a glass container. The silver itself had been beautifully decorated with rosettes and laurel leaves. Leaves ringed a square-shaped stand, and on the front, a silver flower encircled a crest.

"I've never seen anything like it," I said. "It's beautiful."

"Believe it or not, it's a chestnut vase." Seeing the surprise on my face, she beamed. "That's what it was designed for, but near as I can tell, my ancestors actually kept sugar in it." She touched it lovingly. "It was handcrafted in the 1700s by a rather well-known designer and given to one of my relatives as a gift. It's been handed down for generations. When I'm gone, it will go to my daughter. It's very valuable."

"Does your daughter live here?"

"No, she lives in Kansas City with her husband. But she visits when she can. Next time she comes, I'll introduce you."

"I would like that, but I'm only going to be here a couple of weeks."

Ruth's forehead wrinkled. "That's right. I forgot. For some reason it seems as if you're already a part of us." She carefully put the vase back behind the counter. "Well, it's too bad. Carolyn would have loved you."

She rang up my purchases on a cash register that looked about twenty years old. My total was a lot smaller than it would have been for the same items in Wichita.

"Why don't you leave this stuff here and come back for it later, when you're finished looking around town?" Ruth said. "That way you won't have to lug it around or let your fudge melt inside Sam's truck. It doesn't seem hot outside, but you know how steamy the inside of a vehicle can get when the sun beats down on it."

"Thanks. I will."

Sam stood at the front door, holding it open. "Come on, woman," he said with a grin. "We've only made a little dent in our tour."

"He's getting a little pushy, don't you think?" I said to Ruth, who laughed and waved good-bye.

Back out on the sidewalk, Sam guided me to the next store. Harmony Hardware was exactly what the sign declared. A small hardware store with items you would find in most other shops just like it. However, among the hammers, nails, and other tools, there were handmade wooden spoons and oil lamps. Obviously it was geared to accommodate all of Harmony's citizens. I recognized the outside of the building as the place where Amil Angstadt's had had his picture snapped unawares so many years ago.

Sam introduced me to Joe Loudermilk, a small man with a ready smile and an offer of hot coffee.

"Joe's got the pot going all day," Sam said. "Don't you, Joe?"

"You bet." He lowered his voice and gave me a secretive smile. "Get 'em in for coffee, and they're buyin' stuff they forgot they needed. Works every time."

"Well, I don't want coffee, but I need some things to help Grace live a little better out there at Ben's house." Sam said. "Why don't you give me a good flashlight—and a couple of those battery-powered lamps?" He turned to me. "These will give you a lot more light than those old oil lamps."

"Great idea, but what if I hear another monster clumping around outside?"

"I have a plan that should keep you safe from monsters. We'll have to stop by my place on the way home, though."

I was thrilled to know I was going to get to see the inside of his house, yet disturbed that he called my uncle's house *home*. It certainly wasn't *my* home.

Sam paid for the lamps and flashlight even though I offered. His argument that he could use them after I left took the wind out of my protests, and I finally agreed.

We visited two more stores on that side of the street: a secondhand store that had lots of great items, and a clothing store that carried some of the traditional garb worn by many of Harmony's populace. The proprietors at Cora's Simple Clothing Shoppe were friendly and welcoming, even though my basic questions and ignorance about their practices made it obvious I wasn't Mennonite. They showed me different garments and explained that originally, wearing certain kinds and colors of clothing was an attempt by the Mennonites to show their separation from the rest of the world. But eventually it was determined that although keeping oneself removed from carnality was a positive thing, removing themselves too far from the people Christ called them to love wasn't productive. They showed me dresses in lovely fabrics and styles, along with many skirts and blouses that, although plain, were no different than clothing being sold in regular stores across the country.

"Dressing modestly is our aim," Cora Crandall, the store owner, said. "Quite a few of the women love the traditional prayer coverings while some wear nothing on their heads at all—except in church." Her white cap and peach-colored dress accented her dark skin and large brown eyes. Her husband, Amos Crandall, towered over her and exuded friendliness. I immediately liked this couple.

"Many people believe that the scriptural admonition of a head covering in church isn't relevant for today," Amos said. "Others feel it is. So each person wears what they feel comfortable with. There are no rules set in stone."

I thanked them for their insight. I came incredibly close to buying a lovely apple green dress with small flowers, three-quarter-length sleeves, and a gathered waist. The lace around the collar was light and delicate. Unfortunately, I couldn't think of a single place to wear it. I held it for several minutes before reluctantly putting it back on the rack.

Sam and I spent the rest of the morning visiting the other side of Main Street. I met the owners of the leather and feed store. Paul and Carol Bruner carried everything needed for horses and cattle. Dale Scheidler ran the farm implements store with his brother Dan.

Then we got to Nature's Bounty, a small shop that sold dairy products, fruits, and vegetables.

"I sell a lot of my fruit here," Sam said. "Although most of it is marketed in Council Grove and Topeka."

The store was rather crowded with people buying milk, cheese, and fruit. Sam pulled me aside. "That's Joyce Bechtold," he whispered. "She's the woman who painted the birds on Ben's houses and feeders. We should come back when she's not so busy. I know she wants to meet you."

Joyce was a lovely woman with curly hair the color of molasses, cut to just above her shoulders. She had soft brown eyes and laugh wrinkles. I whispered to Sam, "Is she Mennonite?"

"No, as a matter of fact, she's not. She attends my church."

I wondered if that had anything to do with my uncle's lack of interest in her. Too bad. Even from across the room, her graciousness and kind attitude toward others was obvious. As she finished helping a customer, her eyes swung over to where Sam and I stood. When she saw me, her eyes widened and her complexion grew pale. I saw Sam nod slightly to her.

"Let's get going," he said gently.

When we were outside, I grabbed his arm. "Joyce seemed shocked when she saw me. Why?"

Sam sighed. "She knew you were coming, but none of us knew how much you looked like Ben. It's rather startling."

"You didn't seem surprised when you first met me."

He blushed. "Guess I was just thinking about how pretty you are."

I stared at him, but I couldn't come up with a snappy comeback. All I could think about was that he'd said I was pretty. I tried to change the subject quickly. "I—I get the feeling Joyce really cared for my uncle."

"Yes," he said quietly. "She really did."

Next to Nature's Bounty was Keystone Meats. I started to open the door when Sam caught me by the arm.

"We don't really need to go inside. John Keystone. . ."

"Don't be silly," I said lightheartedly. "We've made the rounds of all the other stores. I want to check out this one, too."

I swung open the old screen door on the whitewashed building with the bright red–painted letters and stepped inside. Unlike Joyce's store, there weren't any customers standing around. In fact, Sam and I were the only ones. My first impression was that there wasn't anyone at all in the store. Then a man came from behind the meat counter. He was tall and slender, probably in his early thirties. His long, aquiline nose and dark eyes enhanced his well-sculpted good looks and tanned skin. Longish black hair only added to his overall attractiveness. I felt my mouth go a little dry.

"Hello, Sam," he said in rich, deep tones. "What do you want here?"

"John," Sam said, acknowledging the man with a nod. "This is Grace Temple, Benjamin Temple's niece."

"Hello," I said slowly. The tension between the two men was palpable. What was this about?

John wiped his hands on the white apron he wore over jeans and a dark blue shirt. He stuck out his right hand, and I took it. He held it a little longer than was necessary, but I didn't pull it away. His eyes locked on mine and for a moment I felt transfixed. A door slammed behind us, breaking the moment.

"Well, here you two are. I was beginning to wonder if you'd left town." Mary sashayed up next to us, a fake smile plastered on her pretty face. Before Sam or I had a chance to respond, she turned her full attention to John.

"I need some ground chuck and twelve rib eyes for tonight, good lookin.' Is that possible?"

He spread his arms apart. "Anything for you, gorgeous." He whirled around and disappeared through a door behind his counters.

"So, Gracie. Have you met everyone in town yet?"

"Of course she hasn't, Mary," Sam said in measured tones. "There are almost five hundred people living in Harmony. We couldn't possibly meet all of them in a couple of hours."

Mary's right eyebrow shot up. "Oh, has it only been two hours? Seems like much longer."

Frankly, I was getting tired of Mary's jealous digs. "Maybe we should go, Sam. I'd like to take a nap sometime today. I didn't sleep well last night."

"Sure. No problem." He walked to the door and pushed it open, waiting for me to exit first. The door slammed loudly behind us.

"Look, Sam," I said when we were a few feet away. "I don't want to be a source of contention between you and Mary. Maybe it would be better if we. . .well, if you and I didn't see each other again."

"No!" His explosive response startled me. He blew a deep breath out between clenched teeth. "I. . .I should explain, I guess." He pointed toward a bench in front of the meat market. "Let's sit down a minute."

81

I lowered myself down on the bench and waited. After a little pacing, he finally sat down next to me.

"Mary and I... I mean... We're kind of engaged."

My mouth dropped open in surprise. "Kind of engaged? How can anyone be *kind of* engaged? Either you're engaged or you're not."

He hung his head and stared at the ground. "I don't know how it happened. To this day, I swear I don't remember asking her to marry me. But somehow she got the idea that I did. Now I don't know how to get out of it. I—I don't want to hurt her."

I let out an exasperated sigh. "You can't marry someone because you don't want to hurt her feelings. That's ridiculous."

"I know, I know. I've been trying to fix this thing for months. But every time I even begin to bring up the subject, she starts crying and I back off."

I put my hand on his arm. "The longer you string her along, the worse it will be. You've got to tell her. Let her get on with her life."

"I know. I know you're right." He put his hand over mine and looked into my eyes. "Thanks."

"You're welcome." I pulled my hand away, my own words ringing in my ears. In two weeks I would be gone. It wasn't fair to either one of us for me to allow feelings to build up between us. Of course, maybe Sam wasn't interested in me at all, but when I looked in his eyes, I could almost swear I saw something stirring there.

I decided to change the subject. "You and John Keystone don't get along very well. Is there a problem?"

He shrugged. "Keystone's only been in Harmony a little over a year. He came here with an attitude. I'm not the only one he doesn't like. No one's been able to forge a friendship with the guy—except Mary."

It seemed odd that someone with no roots in Harmony would move here and start a business, but John Keystone wasn't my problem. I had other fish to fry. I pointed to the last shop on the street. Hoffman Candles. Now there was something I could get into. "I love candles. Let's finish our tour—and then to the bakery."

Sam nodded and stood up. He swept one hand toward the candle shop and bowed slightly. Then he followed me to the white clapboard building with large windows and dark blue shutters. He ushered me into a room that contained a hodgepodge of aromas. Shelves with different kinds and sizes of candles shared space with interesting holders made of wood and metal. Some were freestanding while others were made to mount on the wall. I'd never seen so many different types of candleholders before and mentioned it to Sam.

"Levi Hoffman makes the candles, but the holders are created by Harmony residents," he said. He pointed to a set of burnished metal holders. "These were built by Cora and Amos's son, Drew."

"Wow. They're very good. He's very skilled."

"Yes, he is."

I heard something in his voice that made me look up at him. Sam smiled. "Drew has Down syndrome. Cora and Amos have done an outstanding job with him. They don't treat him as if he has a disability. He's a great kid, and he's achieved so much more than most people expected."

I nodded but didn't say anything. Grant, my boss, had a son with Down syndrome. I'd watched his struggles with Jared and felt great compassion for the Crandalls.

"Who's that out there?" A voice rang out, breaking the silence.

"Levi, it's Sam. I've brought Ben's niece to meet you."

A curtain hanging in the back of the store parted, and a man stepped out. He couldn't have been much older than my father, but his hair was almost completely white. With his bushy beard and chubby body, he looked like a real-life Santa Claus. His eyes twinkled, and he broke out into a big smile when he saw us. Although he had certainly changed since the picture in the café, I could still see traces of the handsome young boy in his face.

"So this is Gracie?" he said in a deep voice. "I've been waiting for her. Abel stopped by a little while ago and told me you were making the rounds." I held out my hand, but instead of taking it, he wrapped me in a robust hug.

"Nice to meet you," I said, my words muffled by his shoulder.

He let me go and then stared at me with interest. "My goodness. She's the spitting image of Ben. I can hardly believe it."

"I know," Sam said. "It's a little disconcerting."

"Well, I think it's wonderful."

I was getting a little tired of being talked about and not addressed directly. "Were you and my uncle close?"

Levi stepped back a few paces. "No one was really close to Ben," he said, a note of sadness in his voice. "But I cared for him." He walked over to a nearby shelf and picked up two tall wooden candleholders. "He made these."

He held them out, and I took them from his hands. They were oak, stained dark. Each one had carved round balls at the top where the candle was supposed to sit. Then they straightened out for about six inches before the bottom spread out into a carved base. I looked closely. The carvings were of birds and flowers.

"They're beautiful, Levi."

"Please, I want you to have them. Let's find some candles to go in them. What would you like? Sandalwood, vanilla, rose, lilac. . ."

"I'd love lilac," I said, "but let me pay for them."

"Pshaw. This is a gift. For the niece of my friend." The candlemaker's eyes flushed with tears. "I'll put them in a bag for you."

"Thank you very much. I'll treasure them."

Levi had just pulled some paper from a stack on a table and was wrapping the candles and the holder when the door swung open behind us. A tall, grim-faced man dressed in dark clothes, a white shirt, and a large black hat stepped inside the store. Behind him trailed a young woman also dressed in black. Her long dress dusted the floor, and even though it was spring she wore full sleeves. Her head was covered with a stiff bonnet, not the light prayer covering I'd seen on other women in town. She kept her eyes downcast as if she were carefully watching her black laced-up shoes. Her attire was almost too morose for a funeral, yet the overall spirit emanating from the pair made that destination a definite possibility.

"Hello, Gabriel," Levi said. "Have you brought me some new candleholders?"

The man stepped in front of Sam and me as if we weren't even in the room. He put a large box on the counter in front of the store owner. "No other reason I'd be here, Levi." His voice was sharp and raspy.

The store owner looked down into the box and carefully lifted out several metal holders. They were actually quite stunning. Intricately formed and freestanding, curved pieces of wrought iron formed the legs that held them up. Other pieces of metal had been twisted into designs that ended up creating a place to hold a candle.

"Why, they're beautiful," I said. "You made these?"

The man swung his gaze around and fastened his angry eyes on me. Even through his black beard I could see his lips locked in a sneer. "I'm sorry. I don't remember addressing you," he spat out.

"Now Gabriel, you mind your manners," Levi said evenly. "This is Gracie Temple. Benjamin's niece."

The man's eyes traveled up and down my body. "Doesn't look like anyone Benjamin Temple would cotton to. He wouldn't have approved of anyone this worldly." His eyes flashed with anger. "Would have been mighty ashamed to call something like this family."

I could feel my blood start to boil. "Now you look here. . ." Sam put his hand on my shoulder, and I caught myself before I said something I would probably regret. I stood there stoically, determined not to start an argument with this man. It was obvious it wouldn't do any good.

Assuming I wasn't going to rise to his bait, Gabriel turned back to Levi and resumed his transaction. I couldn't help but glance over at the girl who stood by the front entrance. So this was Sarah Ketterling. Although she'd kept her head lowered throughout her father's rude behavior, she looked up long enough to find me staring at her. Her lovely dark eyes were full of pain and embarrassment. Her light complexion turned even paler and she turned quickly toward the door.

"I'm going to wait outside, Papa," she said in a soft voice. She slipped quietly out of the store. Gabriel didn't appear to hear her.

"Wait here," I whispered to Sam. I crept to the old screen door and opened it slowly. Then I stepped out onto the wooden sidewalk where Sarah stood with her back toward me, her thin body leaning against a light pole.

"Sarah," I said as gently as I could so as not to scare her. "I wanted to tell you how beautiful I think your stationery is. I bought some of it this morning. You're very talented."

The girl swung around, her eyes wide. She glanced nervously toward the entrance of the candle shop. She reminded me of a frightened fawn with large brown eyes and long dark lashes. The hair under her bonnet was almost black, sharply framing her delicate features.

"Th–thank you," she said in a voice so low I could barely hear her. "It–it's wood-block print. I love to do it."

"It's wonderful," I said with a smile. "I'm an artist, too, although a lot of what I do is on the computer. But I love all kinds of art. I paint and I've done some sculpting. I've never had the chance to learn wood blocking though. I wish you would teach me."

Her eyes swung past me and back to the shop behind us. "I'm afraid Papa wouldn't allow me to give lessons. I—I don't see many people."

I reached out and touched her arm. "Maybe you could ask him? I'd pay you for the lessons, of course. I'm staying at my Uncle Benjamin's house. If you could show me even once. . ."

"Sarah won't be showing you anything." Gabriel's harsh voice broke through the calm morning air. "I'll thank you to leave my daughter alone."

With that, he grabbed Sarah by the arm and pulled her toward him. Then he stomped down the sidewalk, his daughter scurrying behind him like some kind of pet dog. I was so furious with him—with his treatment of Sarah—that tears stung my eyes. How can anyone call himself a father and behave that way?

I swung around, grabbed the door, and pulled it open, once again almost running into Sam. Twice in one day. This had to stop.

"Sorry, Grace," he said. "Gabriel's been like this ever since his wife left. His problems have nothing to do with you. Don't take it personally."

Levi made a clucking sound with his tongue. "He locks Sarah in the house with him. She hardly ever goes out. I think he's afraid of losing her like he did her mother. It's a sad situation."

"Well, Abel convinced me that regular Mennonites aren't like Gabriel," I said sharply as I approached the counter. "But these Old Order people really take the cake. I guess this is what my mom and dad had to deal with."

Levi chuckled as he slid my candles and their holders into a paper bag. "Gabriel's not typical at all, Gracie." He pointed at Sam. "Why don't you introduce her to Ida Turnbauer?" He smiled at me. "Ida lives right down the road from you. She's Old Order. You'll find her to be a wonderful and loving woman."

"Good idea," Sam said. "We'll stop by sometime in the next

couple of days. You'll love Ida. She's a doll." He smiled at me. "You know, people are people, Grace. No matter what group you belong to, some members are gracious and loving, but some are mean, just like Gabriel. That holds true for everyone: Mennonite, Baptist, Pentecostal, Methodist, or any other label you want to use."

I nodded. "I get your point."

"My friends," Levi said, holding out my package. "I'm afraid I must tend to some hot wax that won't wait. I'm sorry to rush you. I'd love to spend some time getting to know you better, Gracie. Maybe we can plan to get together soon?"

"Why don't you and Grace come to my house for supper tonight?" Sam said.

I took the bag from Levi's outstretched hand.

"That would be wonderful," he said, giving Sam a wide smile. "Gracie, would that work for you?"

"Sounds great."

"How about six o'clock?" Sam said.

Levi shook his finger at Sam. "Try and stop me. I hope your aunt serves some of that fantastic applesauce she makes." He rubbed his round stomach. "It's worth the trip, Gracie."

"We'll let you get to your wax," Sam said. Then he turned to me. "I'll go to the hardware store and pick up your lamps and flashlight. Why don't you go to Menlo's and wait for me? After I introduce you to the Menlos, we'll pick up your packages from Ruth's."

I nodded, thanked Levi again for the gift, and set out for Menlo's. By the time Sam got to the bakery, the lovely German couple and I were already friends. Sam and I spent almost an hour listening to them talk about their family and laughing at their funny stories. Finally, Sam made our excuses and we left.

Sam went to the truck to wait for me while I hurried to Ruth's to pick up my earlier purchases. Although she didn't seem to be around anywhere, my sack was on the counter, ready to go. As

I came out of her store, I saw John Keystone standing by his window, watching me. I waved, but he just stared at me. The odd expression on his face made me feel uneasy, and for a fleeting moment I felt strongly that'd I seen him somewhere before. But that was impossible. I would have remembered if I'd met him in Wichita or Fairbury. I rejected the odd feeling and made my way to the truck. As I climbed inside, I noticed Mary standing outside the restaurant with a cup of coffee, glaring daggers at us. I felt confident I'd made some friends today, but Mary Whittenbauer, John Keystone, and Gabriel Ketterling certainly weren't among them.

Sam backed the truck into the street, and we headed down Main toward Faith.

"So, did you have a good time?" he asked.

"I did. Harmony is an interesting place. I just wish I'd come here while my uncle was alive."

"I know. Me, too." He handed me a small sack sitting on the dashboard. "Better put your cherry turnover inside one of your other bags. If you leave it in my truck, I can't ensure its safety."

I laughed and grabbed the bag. "Thank you. I love these. I'll try to save it for breakfast, but I can't promise anything."

"Besides being a nice man, Mr. Menlo is a skilled baker. Cakes, pies, all kinds of pastries. He sells sandwiches, too." Sam smiled. "But these turnovers are my favorite."

We rode in silence the rest of the way. My uncle's letter kept running through my mind. Visiting downtown Harmony had been a welcome distraction, but now I had to face reality again. What were my options? Should I destroy the letter and act as if I'd never read it? Or should I bring it out in the open and let the chips fall where they may? One minute the first choice felt right, and the next minute the second seemed the only alternative. As I considered my options, a new possibility occurred to me. Maybe Benjamin's letter would be enough to prove my father's innocence.

In a way, it was a record of Benjamin's testimony—revealing his belief that Glick's death was an unfortunate accident. Could this be my way out of this awful situation? Even if it worked, it would pull my dad into a whirlwind. Did I really want to do that?

I was so lost in thought I didn't realize that Sam had pulled up in front of Benjamin's house. "Hey, you should wait until you get inside to take your nap," he said gently, pulling me out of my reverie.

"I–I'm sorry. Guess I was somewhere else."

He looked around and smiled. "Nope, still Harmony." He held his hands out for my packages. "Let me carry these in for you."

He grabbed my bags as well as the sacks from the hardware store. Once inside, he put batteries in the lamps and showed me how to use them. Sure enough, they outshone the oil lamps by far. I felt relieved to have them.

"But what about the monster question?" I said, teasingly. "What do I do if Godzilla visits after dark?"

He walked over to the front door. "Sweetie told you about the flowers during the day, right?"

I nodded.

"She and Ben used those flowers as a way for him to let her know if he needed anything. She took care of him for several weeks before he died. Cleaned his house. Fixed meals. Washed his clothes. She'd walk down our driveway several times a day looking for that pot."

"That won't help at night when Godzilla wants to eat me."

"No, it won't. But I have an idea." He smiled, seemingly pleased with himself. "Walkie-talkies. Sweetie and I use them when I'm out working in the orchards. She can call me into supper or tell me when she wants something. I'm going to give you one tonight, and I'll keep the other. That way, if you need me, all you have to do is scream."

"Oh, great. Hopefully, there won't be any actual screaming."

He laughed. "I hope not. It might disrupt my snoring."

"Just don't saw logs too loudly. I'd hate to have to compete."

"Don't worry. I'll keep it to a dull roar. Now you go get that nap you've been planning." He put his hand on the doorknob. "I'll pick you up about a quarter to six. Oh, and bring your cell phone and charger along. We'll charge up your phone, but I don't want to mislead you. Those things are spotty at best out here. Sweetie and I use walkie-talkies because we gave up on cell phones and needed something we could count on."

"Okay," I said, stifling a yawn. My lack of sleep was catching up to me. "I'll see you tonight."

"One last thing. I hope you don't mind that I invited Levi to join us. I did it for two reasons. One was because he's a great guy, but the other is that he's lived in Harmony his whole life. He knew your family. I thought maybe you'd like to talk to him about them." He frowned. "Sweetie was born here, too, but she won't talk much about her life before I came to live with her. I have no idea why." He hesitated a moment. "You know, I don't say this to many people. I love Harmony, but there's something. . .an undercurrent." He shrugged and laughed. "I sound goofy. Maybe I need a nap, too."

Sam was right. There were definitely undercurrents. So deep they threatened to drown my family. I smiled at him. "I'm glad you invited Levi. I'm sure we'll have a wonderful time. And thanks for the tour. I really enjoyed it."

"You're welcome."

I watched as he walked down the steps, got in his truck, and drove away. So Myrtle didn't want to talk about the past. Did she know something? She and my uncle Benjamin were obviously good friends. She was the person who kept his house clean while he was ill. If they were that close, had he told her his secret? I closed the door and leaned against it. The information I'd gotten about Glick interested me and confirmed Benjamin's sentiments.

Glick sounded like the kind of man who might have had enemies. Could his death have been something else besides an accident? Uncle Benjamin believed Glick had died accidentally—by my father's hand. But I knew my dad. He would never walk away from a severely injured man. If he'd hurt him badly, my father would have gone for help.

In the truck, I'd wondered if I should ignore the entire situation or just tell my dad the truth and let him decide how to proceed. But as I stood here, contemplating those choices, I added two more items to my list of possibilities. What if Glick really had been murdered by someone other than my father? Someone Glick had harmed in some way. Should I keep digging? Attempt to find the truth and bring this decades-long mystery to a close?

Of course, the letter could simply be the incoherent ramblings of a dying man, and Jacob Glick might be alive and well—totally oblivious to the mystery his disappearance had caused. If that were true, my decision to walk away from my uncle's strange missive would be the right one.

I might be confused about how to proceed, but one thing I wasn't confused about. I had no intention of spending my life guarding this family secret the way Benjamin had. I needed to choose a course—and quickly.

I ran up the stairs to get the letter and read through it again. Maybe this time I'd see something I hadn't noticed before. Something that would guide me in the right direction. I pulled the dresser drawer open and rifled through my socks.

The letter was gone.

Chapter Seven

I spent the next two hours attempting to convince myself I'd simply misplaced the letter, but I finally faced the fact that it was gone and that someone had broken into the house and stolen it. After making certain no one else was in the house, I checked the front and back doors. The locks were still intact. How had my burglar gained access? A quick check of the front porch revealed a key hidden under the doormat. There was no way to know if someone who knew the key's location had used it to enter—or if the intruder had simply stumbled upon the simple hiding place. I dropped the key into my pocket. At least now, getting into my uncle's house wouldn't be quite so easy.

I sat in the rocking chair on the front porch for over an hour, trying to decide what to do next. I'd lost the only piece of evidence I had that might prove my father's innocence. What did the theft of the letter mean? Had someone else discovered our family secret? Or were they trying to hide the truth for other reasons? And why take the letter now? Benjamin's place had been vacant for almost a month. Why not break in and steal it before I arrived in Harmony? My visit wasn't a secret. Try as I might, I couldn't make sense of it. A tension headache began to nibble at my temples, and I rubbed them, trying to chase away the pain.

My eyes wandered to the flowerpot sitting near the porch railing. Myrtle! Maybe she saw something. Unfortunately, it was a long shot. Sam had mentioned that they'd both been working in their orchards. Myrtle may not have been in a position to notice anyone coming or going from Benjamin's house. I decided to check with her tonight though. Couldn't hurt.

I rocked back and forth awhile longer and stared at my car. I had an almost overwhelming desire to pack up and go home. Confusion combined with a growing sense of fear gathered strength in my mind. Finding the letter was bad enough, but knowing it had found its way into someone else's hands made everything much worse. Who had it and why? Was I in danger? Unfortunately, I had no answers to these questions.

My plan for a quick nap had been chased away by this strange turn of events. As I got up to go inside and change my clothes for supper, I realized that whoever had the letter had obviously been aware of my itinerary. Sadly, that fact didn't narrow the list of suspects much. Almost anyone could have done it. Except Sam. At least I could be certain he wasn't involved since he'd been with me all day.

I went inside and climbed the stairs to Mama and Papa's room. As I picked out a fresh white blouse and a pair of khaki slacks, my fingers brushed against one of the long dresses hanging in the closet—a dark blue and cream calico print. I pulled it out and looked closer. The lace around the collar was slightly yellowed with age and the material was thin beneath my fingers. But even after all these years, there was a feminine quality about it that appealed to me. On a whim I took off my sweater and jeans and pulled the dress over my head. Then I took one of the white caps hanging on a nail inside the closet and placed it over my hair. I closed the closet door and turned to look at the old mirror attached to the dresser. I couldn't help but gasp. The Gracie who looked back at me was a stranger. I even felt a little different. I ran my hands over the material, thinking about Mama Essie. She'd stood in this very spot, looking at herself in these clothes. I wished she were still here. Her sweetness and wisdom had always helped to lead me in the right direction.

As I stared at my reflection, I wondered what she would do in my place, but the answer to that question wasn't hard to discern. Above all, Essie loved her family. There was nothing she wouldn't have done for them. She would have met this challenge head-on, fighting for the truth in an effort to protect her son. She would never have believed that my father had killed another human being. As I removed the dress and put on my own clothes, I knew what I had to do. If I was even a little unsure about my father's innocence before, I was totally convinced of it now. The theft of the letter made it clear there was a secret hidden beneath the seemingly calm surface of Harmony, Kansas—a truth someone wanted to keep hidden. I intended to find out what it was.

I gathered my fresh clothes together and put them in the downstairs bathroom. Then I headed for the basement door. I remembered Sam's instructions about turning on the generator so it would pump water for my bath. I grabbed one of the flashlights purchased in town and walked gingerly down the rickety stairs. Thankfully, there were small windows in the basement walls so the flashlight wasn't necessary.

The basement held several surprises. As Sam had said, Benjamin used this space for his carpentry work. There were eight rocking chairs lined up against the back wall. Six were painted—two were not. About twenty birdhouses in various stages of assembly were stacked up on a large workbench. Another corner of the room held a variety of old trunks and ancient, unused furniture. A quick search through one trunk revealed several beautiful quilts and other handmade items carefully packed away. In another I found a set of china, beautifully decorated with small pink flowers, and silver candlesticks wrapped in cheesecloth. These treasures must have belonged to Mama Essie. They were certainly part of the family heirlooms my father wanted me to rescue.

I finally figured out how to start the generator and hurried back upstairs to take a bath. Although I was used to showers, I had to admit that soaking in the tub felt good. Unfortunately, the knowledge that someone had been inside the house made me uneasy, so I didn't tarry long.

I was ready to go by five thirty. As I sat waiting for Sam, something I'd seen while searching for the letter from Benjamin popped into my head. I got up and went over to the secretary where I'd first found the family Bible. I opened a long drawer underneath the desktop and took out a key attached to a blue ribbon. Maybe this was the key to the third bedroom upstairs.

I still had some time before I had to leave, so I hurried upstairs to check. Sure enough, the key fit and the door clicked open. I pushed it in slowly until the contents of the room were revealed. Unlike the other rooms, everything was covered with dust. Not wanting to get dirty after my bath, I ventured in only as far as the dresser that sat near the door. I carefully opened the cover of an old Bible lying on top of the grime-covered piece of furniture. The name *Daniel Temple* was scrawled on the inside cover. As I'd suspected, this had been my father's room. Why had Benjamin kept the other bedrooms clean and in pristine condition but allowed this one to sit without any attention? There was only one reason I could think of. He'd closed off this room because he wanted to forget his brother. Why? Resentment? Even hate?

Looking around the neglected room, I began to wonder if the letter was actually an attempt to point the finger of blame at the wrong Temple brother. Could Benjamin have killed Jacob Glick? I left the room and climbed down the stairs to wait for Sam.

A new possibility swirled through my mind while I sat staring at the front door. Perhaps the isolation Benjamin had surrounded himself with hadn't come from some noble attempt to protect his family. Maybe it had actually been nothing more than the act of a desperate, guilty man who hated his brother and wanted one last chance to destroy him. But if this were true, how in the world could I ever prove it?

I suddenly felt the need to get out of Benjamin's house. I stepped out onto the front porch while thoughts of the missing letter, the abandoned room, and new suspicions about my uncle created a cacophony of fear inside my brain.

Chapter Eight

I want to make a quick stop before we go to supper," Sam said as he shut the truck door after I slid into the passenger seat.

"A quick stop? I can see your house from here. There are no stops between here and there."

He jogged around the front of the truck and climbed inside. "I'm aware of that," he said with a grin. "We're going the other way."

We drove out of the driveway and turned left—away from the big red house. There were two old homes that sat down the road about a quarter of a mile from Benjamin's. Sam pulled into the dirt driveway of the closest one and turned off the engine. "This is Ida Turnbauer's place. I want to introduce you."

"But she doesn't know we're coming. It's rude to just stop by without calling first."

Sam laughed. "Maybe that's true in the city, but out here you could have company stop by almost anytime. And besides, you can't call Ida anyway. No phone. I want you to meet her. I'm afraid you have some wrong ideas about folks like her."

I started to protest again when an elderly woman stepped out onto the porch and began waving us in. She had on a long, dark blue dress, and her head was covered with a white bonnet.

"Too late now," Sam said innocently. "We're trapped."

I sighed and shook my head.

Sam reached over and put his hand on my arm. "Grace, Ida loves company. She's always ready for a visit. Trust me."

"Okay, I get it. I'm not in Wichita. The rules are different here."

He nodded. "Most of your rules don't even exist in Harmony. Besides, we're only staying long enough to say hello. I promise."

We got out of the truck and walked up to the porch where Ida stood sporting a wide smile. "This must be Grace," she said as we approached. "I wanted so much to walk over and greet you when you first arrived, but I know city folk do not like unannounced company."

Her face held evidence of past beauty. She spoke with an accent, her words slightly guttural. Proof of German descent, just like my grandparents. I instantly felt drawn to her and a little embarrassed to be counted among "city folk."

"I–I'm happy to meet you."

"My goodness," she said as I stepped up next to her. "You are the spitting image of your uncle." She took my face in her hands. I could feel the calluses on her fingers as her faded blue eyes sought mine. "Bless you, child. I know it meant the world to Benjamin—knowing you would come and take care of things after he died. I wish there had been time for him to see you before the end."

I wanted to tell her that my uncle had had all the time in the world to "see me" if he'd wanted to, but I kept quiet.

A tear slid down the old woman's wrinkled face. "Ach, your uncle was a good man," she said softly. "I hope you believe that. No matter what anyone else tells you, you hang on to that, ja?"

She let go of my face and grabbed Sam's arm. "I have some brewed tea and warm cookies inside. You two come and sit a spell with me."

Sam leaned over and kissed her cheek. "Can't do it right now,

Ida. Sweetie's waiting supper, and you know how she gets if I'm late."

Ida smiled. "I know how she gets. But you two will come back, ja?"

Sam looked at me, and I nodded.

"How about Monday afternoon?" he said.

"That would be wonderful. I will look forward to it. I just might make one of those strawberry pies you are so fond of."

"Well, in that case, we'll definitely be here." He turned to look at me. "Ida makes the best strawberry pie in Kansas."

"I'm not so sure about that," I said teasingly. "My grandmother made a mean strawberry pie herself."

The smile slipped from Ida's face. "*Made* pie?" she said. "You do not mean Essie has passed away, do you?"

"Why yes," I answered. "It's been almost five years now."

Ida clasped her hands to her chest. "Ach, no, no." She toddled over to the white rocker that sat a few feet from her front door. Gracious, did everyone in Harmony have white rocking chairs?

"My uncle didn't tell you? I don't understand. . ."

She sat down slowly and covered her face with her hands. "I do not either. Surely he knew."

"I'm sure he did. My father sent him a letter."

Ida lowered her hands. Tears stained her weathered cheeks. "Your uncle was very tenderhearted. Maybe he did not want to cause me pain."

One look at her face made it clear that if that had been his intention, he'd failed miserably. "Were you and my grandmother close?"

Ida nodded. "Ja, we were best friends growing up. I loved her dearly."

"Then why. . ."

"Did I not try to get in touch with her in all these years?"

I nodded.

Ida sighed and stared out at the wheat field across from us. A gentle breeze caused the knee-high, green stalks to sway gently as if caught in some kind of synchronized dance. "It's hard to explain," she said. "I was so hurt when she decided to leave that it was easier to put her out of my mind." She turned her gaze back to me. "I know that does not make much sense. Her leaving had nothing to do with me. I realize that now. But I turned it into something personal, and now it is too late." She shook her head slowly. "She sent me a letter not long after she and Joe moved to Nebraska. I—I never opened it." Ida reached up and wiped a tear away from her eye. "Perhaps it is time I did."

"You kept it all these years?" I said.

She reached over and patted my arm. "Yes. I just could not bring myself to read it."

"So your silence toward my grandmother had nothing to do with some kind of banning?"

Ida's eyes widened. "Of course not." She scowled at Sam. "Ach, what have you been telling this child?"

Sam shrugged. "Didn't come from me."

"Oh. Benjamin. I should have known." Ida shook her head. "Benjamin had his own ways, Grace. In our faith, if someone is caught in sin and they are not repentant, they may be forbidden to participate in some of the ceremonies in the church service, but they are not asked to leave the fold. And we still talk to them. Understand that any action the church takes is not seen as a punishment; it is an attempt to help them get straight with God. But actually excommunicating someone? I saw it a couple of times when I was a girl. One had to do with a man who would not stop beating his wife and child, and the other was a woman who flagrantly carried on an adulterous affair with a man in our community. The elders counseled all of them and only asked them to leave the church after they refused to change their ways. Thankfully, the wife beater left his family behind and the church was able to help restore

101

them." She stared into my eyes. "My guess is that any other church would have done the same thing. You must understand that what happened under Bishop Angstadt was done through his own attempt to control his members. It was not godly nor would the Mennonite Church have approved it—if the area leadership had known about it. Benjamin's attitude toward your family may have originated through Bishop Angstadt, but he held on to it all those years without any help from anyone else. When the bishop died, anyone approving of The Ban died with him." Ida stared down at her feet for a moment. "I want you to know that I tried talking to your uncle many times on the subject, but he wouldn't budge." She looked up at me and frowned. "I often wondered if there was something else behind his stubborn refusal to contact his family. Something he would not tell any of us."

Her sentiments echoed what Abel Mueller had told me. That made at least three people who'd confirmed that after Amil Angstadt died, Benjamin's silence toward my family had been his decision alone—perhaps for the reasons he'd written in his letter—or perhaps for other reasons yet to be uncovered.

"Ida, I'm sorry to break this up," Sam said softly, "but we've really got to be going."

The old woman nodded. She reached for my arm, and I helped her to her feet. "Grace, you leave this big strapping man at home Monday and come by on your own, ja? Maybe we could read your grandmother's letter together?"

"Hey, how come I get cut out of the loop?" Sam said playfully. "What happens to *my* strawberry pie?"

Ida and I both laughed. "I tell you what," I said to Ida. "Why don't I come by around one o'clock and Sam can join us at two? That way everyone gets what they want."

Ida clapped her hands together and a smile lit up her face. "Ach, that would be wonderful. And we promise to save you some pie, Sam."

"In that case, try to stop me." He leaned over and kissed the old woman on the cheek. "Unless you both want Sweetie to come here after us, we've got to get going."

I said good-bye to Ida, and we got back in the truck.

"So do you still think Old Order Mennonites are mean, judgmental people?"

"No, you and Abel were right. I came here with the wrong impression. I'm beginning to understand that as a whole, Mennonites live the way they do because they're trying to protect their community." I glanced at the houses and fields around us. "You know, as much as I love the city. . ."

"You're beginning to appreciate a simpler lifestyle?"

I laughed. "Don't put words in my mouth." But he was right. Outside of the situation with my uncle, Harmony was beginning to grow on me. It must have been very difficult for Papa and Mama to leave here—even with the church problems they faced. The knowledge that being with me meant more to them than their friends and hometown roots touched my heart. I worked to swallow the lump that tried to form in my throat.

"Well, here it is," he said as we pulled into his driveway and he turned off the engine.

Although I'd seen his house from the road, I found it even more striking up close. Deep red with creamy white trim, a large porch, and two turrets it portrayed all the beauty and elegance of the Victorian period. As Sam held out his hand to help me down from the truck, I couldn't tear my eyes from it.

"I think this is the most extraordinary house I've ever seen," I said. "Where did it come from? I mean, it's different from any other home around here."

After I hopped down, Sam shut the truck door behind me. "This house has an interesting history. A man who owned most of the land in this area built it in the late 1800s. When a group of German Mennonites began to buy nearby plots, he fought to drive them out. But in the end, he converted to their ways. Gave away a lot of his land to the settlers. When he died, he left the rest of it, along with his house, to the community."

"How did you and um. . .Sweetie end up with it?"

Sam chuckled at hearing me finally use his aunt's nickname. "Well, these simple people weren't quite sure what to do with a house like this. They couldn't see it as a church building, and no one wanted to move into it. It sat empty for many years. Believe it or not, eventually Amil Angstadt used it as his parsonage."

I snorted. "Now that *is* hard to believe. I thought he was so rigid and uncompromising. Surely he would have seen this house as ostentatious."

He grunted. "I've found that judgmental people generally are more focused on other people than they are on themselves. Goes back to that 'board in your own eye' thing Jesus talked about. Angstadt found a way to accept something for himself that he never would have allowed for folks in his congregation."

I nodded my agreement with his assessment. I'd known a few people whose lives were caught up in trying to decide what was right or wrong for everyone else. On the Internet I'd even stumbled across Web sites totally devoted to judging different ministries. They were disturbing to say the least and always left me feeling as if I needed a shower.

"So how *did* you end up with it?"

"Well, when Angstadt died, the church elders were left to decide what to do with the remaining congregation. Some members left the church altogether, happy to be out from underneath his thumb. Harmony Church was started by ex-members of Angstadt's group who wanted a fresh start." He shrugged. "I think even folks who were close to Angstadt were glad to have the chance to begin again. Those who remained wanted nothing to do with his house. My aunt was a young woman then. She and her father owned one of the few non-Mennonite farms in the area.

My grandmother died when Sweetie and my mother were pretty young. Her father, my grandfather, was severely injured when his tractor flipped in the field one day. Sweetie spent about a year trying to run their farm alone while she cared for him. Eventually he died. Sweetie sold their farm and bought this house and the land. It took almost every penny she had. With the little that was left, she began planting fruit trees and berry patches. Over time, this place became very productive."

"But hard for one person to run."

Sam nodded. "I came to live with her just in time. Together I think we've done a pretty good job." He cocked his head toward the house. "Now, let's get inside before I end up being the main course at supper."

We were almost to the front porch when the screen door flew open and Sweetie stepped out waving a big spoon at us. "Well, it's about time," she screeched. "Didn't I say six o'clock?" She turned around and went back inside, the door slamming behind her. We could hear her mumbling something about learning to tell time.

Sam looked at his watch. "It's four minutes past six." He shook his head. "Sweetie takes being on time very seriously. Unless *she's* late."

"Wow. I'm sorry we upset her. Should we apologize?"

He chuckled. "I guarantee you that by the time we start eating, she will have forgotten all about it. Don't worry about her. She never stays mad for long."

I noticed a black and silver Suburban parked in the driveway. "Is that Levi's car?"

"Yep. Which means we'd better get inside before Sweetie puts the food on the table. Levi can shovel it down faster than almost anyone I know."

I hesitated for a moment. Standing on Sam's porch, I felt safe for the first time since I'd found the letter. An almost overwhelming desire had been building in me all day. I had the urge to grab Sam by the arm and tell him everything—the whole truth. I desperately wanted an ally, someone I could trust. But I still had doubts running through my mind. Benjamin had kept this secret for thirty years, and here I was ready to blurt out the truth after only a day. And I didn't really know Sam that well. What if he decided to take things into his own hands? What if he insisted on calling the authorities? Could I really risk my dad's future with someone who didn't know him or care about him the way I did? That little bit of doubt forced me to shove the whole situation to the back of my mind, where it sat like an uncomfortable ache, waiting to turn into a full-scale migraine. I prayed that by the time supper was over, I'd know what to do.

Sam led me through a wonderful wood-paneled entry hall and into the dining room. The furniture was gorgeous—and certainly not what I'd anticipated from Sweetie. The walls had been painted a lovely shade of deep red with white wainscoting almost halfway up. Crown molding accented the ceilings. Long windows let in plenty of light, overpowering the soft glow from the brass chandelier that hung over the table. The furniture in the room perfectly fit the Victorian styling. A massive Victorian sideboard sat against one wall. It matched the mahogany dining-room table and chairs.

I was so stunned I froze in my tracks.

"Not quite what you expected from a couple of hick farmers, huh?" he whispered in my ear.

"I don't think you're a hick farmer," I hissed back. "But where. . . ?"

"Some of the furniture came with the house, but the lion's share of the decorating was done by my aunt. She's spent years trying to bring back the original style of the house."

A gentle push sent me toward the table where Levi sat waiting. I could hear Sweetie rummaging around in the kitchen. I sat down in the chair Sam pointed to and smiled at Levi.

"Quite a place isn't it?" he said. "I've watched it change little by little over the years, but I'm still impressed every time I come here."

I made a mental note to remind myself about not judging a book by its cover. I'd certainly done that with Sweetie—or Myrtle—or whoever she was. One thing I knew: There was a lot more to this woman than a loud voice, coarse mannerisms, and a nosy attitude.

Sam said something about helping his aunt bring in the food and disappeared. Levi and I made small talk about the weather for a few minutes before they came back carrying a large platter of fried chicken and bowls of mashed potatoes and creamed corn. Another trip to the kitchen resulted in big, fluffy rolls straight from the oven, along with strawberry preserves and a bowl of homemade applesauce. Levi's face lit up when he saw it.

I sipped my delicious brewed iced tea until everyone sat down. Sam said grace and then began to pass plates of food around the table. I quickly discovered that Sweetie was more than a crack decorator; she could hold her own in the kitchen as well. Her flaky fried chicken had a buttery taste along with just a hint of spice. I had to admit that she may have even surpassed Mama Essie's skill in chicken frying. In fact, she could give the Colonel a big run for his money. And the applesauce had so much flavor I had no desire to sample the canned variety ever again. Levi filled his bowl with the flavorful sauce.

"So, Gracie, what do you think of Harmony so far?" Levi asked. "I hope your little run-in with Gabriel Ketterling hasn't soured you on the whole town."

I swallowed a scrumptious mouthful of mashed potatoes and gravy. "No, not at all. I like almost everyone I've met. Sam introduced me to Ida Turnbauer right before we arrived here. She's a lovely woman. Nothing like Gabriel."

"So that's why you're late for supper," Sweetie said, glaring at

Sam. "I swear, boy, you can't get from A to B without a few Cs and Ds thrown in, can you?" She shook her head, but I caught the hint of the smile she tried to cover up by holding a chicken leg up to her mouth. Her love for her nephew was obvious.

Sam held up his hands in mock surrender. "Sorry, Sweetie." He looked at Levi and me with a big goofy grin on his face. "I take after my aunt. I just can't keep my nose out of other people's business."

Sweetie's face turned pink. "I got no idea what you're talkin' about. I don't go stickin' my nose where it don't belong. Goodness gracious."

Levi chuckled. "Now Myrtle. You and I may not be churchgoing folks, but I know a whopper when I hear it. You need to repent to these two young people right now."

Sam and I laughed, and after a few feeble attempts to defend herself, Sweetie gave up and joined in.

"Okay, okay," she sputtered as the laughter wound down, "I guess I am a little interested in what goes on 'round here." She wiped her eyes. "My mama said I was a curious child, and I seem to have grown up into a powerful curious adult."

"*Curious* being a nicer word than *nosy*?" Sam asked with a wink.

She shook her head. "You'd better watch it, boy. I got apple pie in my kitchen, and it ain't gonna shake hands with your gullet if you don't knock it off."

"My abject apologies for casting aspersions on your veracity," Sam said mockingly.

Sweetie looked at me, her face screwed up into a frown. "I got no idea what he's talkin' about sometimes, but I know I heard somethin' like an apology in that mess, didn't you?"

I nodded my agreement. "It didn't make sense to me either, but I think it's safe to assume he's sorry."

"Well, in that case, I guess you can have pie—after you finish your supper," she said to Sam.

"That won't be a problem." He loaded up his fork with potatoes. "As usual, you've outdone yourself, dear aunt."

"Yes, this is absolutely delicious," I said. "You're a terrific cook."

Sweetie blushed again and mumbled something about people bein' silly, but I could tell she was pleased.

Levi had just started to tell me some of Harmony's history when there was a loud, insistent knock on the front door.

"Now, who in the world would come botherin' folks at suppertime?" Sweetie sputtered as she got up from her chair.

I guess the idea of visiting neighbors whenever you felt like it actually did have some rules attached: Never drop by during supper.

We could hear Sweetie open the front door and say something to whoever was outside. Then the door closed and footsteps neared the dining room. Sweetie came into the room followed by Ruth Wickham. Her normally red face was a couple of shades darker than usual.

"Ruth's got somethin' important to say to us," Sweetie said. Her expression made it plain she still wasn't happy about her meal being interrupted.

Ruth stepped up next to the table, wringing her hands.

"Why, Ruth," Levi said. "What's the matter? Is something wrong?"

She nodded. "I–I'm not in the habit of accusing anyone of stealing," she said haltingly. "But as hard as it is, I have no choice."

"Stealing?" Sam said. "What in the world are you talking about, Ruth? What's been stolen?"

A tear slipped down her cheek. "My—my chestnut vase is gone. I'm—I'm sorry, Sam. But as far as I know, there was only one person who could have possibly taken it."

To my horror, she fastened her gaze on me. "Gracie Temple, you give me back my vase. Right now."

Chapter Nine

"I'm really sorry about this," Sam said again.

We were seated in the living room. It was as beautifully decorated as the dining room with the same crimson walls and white wainscoting that matched the fireplace mantel. But I couldn't focus on the decor. I was far too upset.

Sam sat across from me on a plush brocade love seat that matched the couch where I waited to be exonerated. I'd told Ruth she could search Benjamin's house and my car if it made her feel better and had given her my keys. Levi had gone with her.

"It's not your fault," I said. We were beginning to repeat ourselves. Sam had apologized, and I'd assured him he wasn't to blame at least four different times.

"When they don't find anything, Ruth will acknowledge her mistake and everything will be back to normal." His eyes kept darting from me to the hallway that led to the front door.

I didn't respond. It would never be "back to normal," whatever that was. My previous feelings of being charmed by Harmony and its residents had vanished like smoke in the wind. I was sorry about Ruth's chestnut vase, but I had the distinct impression that I was her prime suspect because I didn't live here. I'd only been accused of stealing one other time in my life. That was when a girl in high school told several people I took her favorite CD. When she found it in her boyfriend's locker, she didn't even bother to tell me she was sorry she'd accused me. But I made sure everyone who knew me found out the truth. I only learned when I got older that it would have been better to keep silent about it, letting God be my defense.

I realized that I needed to do that now, so I quietly put the situation in His hands. There was nothing I could do about it anyway. The truth is, people believe whatever they want no matter how much we try to defend ourselves. I looked over at Sam. His dark brown shirt made his sun-bleached hair look almost white. He flashed me a quick smile that I'm sure was supposed to comfort me, but I related more to the nervous tapping of his left boot on the hardwood floor. The sound stopped suddenly, and I looked up to see his eyes fastened on mine. Something that felt like electricity traveled up my spine.

"I didn't take it, you know," popped out of my mouth before I could stop it.

His eyes widened. "There was never any question in my mind, Grace."

"But you didn't see what was in my sack when I left Ruth's."

"It wouldn't have made any difference. I know you're not a thief. But you might be interested to know that I actually did look inside your bag. It's just like the one from the hardware store. I mixed them up when I went looking for the lamps after we got back to your place. Believe me, if the chestnut vase had been there, I would have seen it."

I felt a quick stab of relief. At least one person knew I was innocent. I felt certain Ruth had already tried, convicted, and sentenced me. I didn't think she was intentionally trying to frame me, but I had to admit that having Levi go with her made me feel more comfortable.

I looked at my watch. "They've been gone a long time."

"It's only been about thirty minutes. It's taking longer because they can't find anything."

The clatter of dishes from the kitchen highlighted another problem. Sweetie was fit to be tied. Her supper had been ruined. Was she angry with Ruth—or with me? With Sweetie it was hard to tell.

The sound of a car door slamming told us that Ruth and Levi had returned. I waited for them to come inside and tell me they'd found nothing—followed by an effusive apology from Ruth. But no one entered the house. A moment later we heard a second car door slam, followed by the sound of someone starting up a vehicle and driving away.

"What's going on?" I asked Sam.

"I don't know, but I'm going to find out." He'd just stood to his feet when the front door creaked open and we heard the sound of footsteps in the hall. Levi walked into the room, and the expression on his face made my heart sink so low it felt like it hit my shoes.

"What's going on, Levi?" I hated the squeaky sound my voice made, but I couldn't seem to control it.

He came over and sat down next to me, taking my hands in his. "Gracie, we—we found the vase in your basement. It was in a trunk, hidden under some old quilts."

I tried to say something but didn't seem able to form anything coherent. All that came out of my mouth was "But…but…but…" I looked over at Sam, whose mouth hung open—the color drained from his face.

Levi squeezed my hands. "Ruth isn't going to press charges. Folks in Harmony don't call the authorities very often. We like to handle these things ourselves. But she did ask that you stay out of her store from now on."

After another squeeze, he got up and walked toward the entryway. At the doorway he stopped and looked back at me.

"Gracie, Ruth isn't angry with you. You'll find that most people in Harmony are very forgiving. We work hard to deserve our name." He shook his head. "I must admit that I find it hard to understand how this happened. You certainly don't seem like the kind of person who would take something that doesn't belong to you. Whatever's going on, I want you to know that I'm here for you. If I can do anything to help you—anything at all—you come see me. Anytime, night or day." With that, he turned and left the room. A few seconds later we heard the front door close.

I tried to hold back my tears, but I couldn't. I covered my face with my hands and sobbed. Until that moment, I had no idea how much I'd begun to like this town and these people. But now I was marked as a thief—for something I hadn't done.

I felt Sam sit down next to me and put his arm around my shoulders. I leaned into him and cried until I couldn't cry any more. He handed me a handkerchief from his pocket. I took it and wiped my face.

"Sam, I swear. . ."

He reached over and touched my lips with his fingers. "Don't even go there." He reached under my chin and pulled my face up to his. "I think it's about time you told me what's going on, don't you?"

"What. . .what do you mean?"

His eyebrows knit together in a frown. "Oh, come on, Grace. Your uncle had some kind of secret. He leaves his property to a niece he's never met. You're asking questions about Jacob Glick, a man who left Harmony years ago. And you've had something weighing on your mind ever since this morning. I know you didn't take that vase. That can only mean one thing. Someone is trying to frame you. My guess is they're hoping this accusation will make you leave town." His eyes sought mine, and I couldn't look away. "So tell me what this is all about. You can trust me. You know that, don't you?"

As I stared into his face, I was aware of two things. One: that I really could trust him. And two: that he was going to kiss me. Both of those realizations forced my heart from my throat and back into my chest where it belonged. His kiss was tender and sweet. And when he pulled back, I could still feel the pressure of his lips on mine. I kept my eyes closed for a few seconds afterward just savoring the moment. When I opened them, he was smiling at me.

"Look," I said, keeping my voice low so Sweetie wouldn't overhear us. "I'll tell you what I know, but you have to promise that you won't take matters into your own hands. This situation is very serious, and it has to do with my family. I have to decide what to do about it without pressure from anyone else. Can you live with that?"

"Of course. All I want to do is help. I'm not planning to cowboy up and 'take care of the little lady.' I know you can handle yourself just fine."

"We need to go somewhere else. Someplace where we can talk without being overheard."

Sam stood up and took my hand. Then he led me toward the front door. First he stopped by the kitchen where Sweetie was still banging pots and pans around.

"We're going out to the barn for a while," he said in a voice loud enough to be heard over the racket. "Sorry about supper. It was great." He rubbed his stomach with the hand that wasn't holding mine. "I'm still hungry. I don't suppose we could have some leftovers when we get back?"

Sweetie's expression didn't offer us much hope of anything— let alone remnants of her abandoned meal. But she finally nodded. "You go do whatever you need to do, boy. I'll heat you up somethin' when you're done."

She wiped her hands on her apron and shot me a look that took me by surprise. It wasn't so much anger as it was fear. Was she afraid her nephew might be getting involved with someone she didn't trust? We stared at each other for a moment longer until Sam pulled me away.

The barn sat about one hundred yards from the house and was painted the same color. As we approached, a small tricolored dog ran around from behind the structure. He looked like a cross between a Jack Russell terrier and a rat terrier. His big ears stuck straight up, and his short legs moved so quickly he almost appeared to be flying.

"Hey, Buddy!" Sam called. He knelt down as the little dog jumped up into his arms and licked his face. "Grace Temple, meet Buddy Goodrich. The third member of our little family."

After Sam set the small, wiggly dog back on the ground, I dropped to my knees and got an almost identical welcome. Buddy had big brown eyes that stared deeply into mine. It was as if he were trying his best to read my thoughts.

"Hi there, Buddy," I said after he'd finished handing out wet doggy kisses. His stump of a tail wagged so hard his whole backside quivered. I looked up at Sam. "I figured you'd have some kind of big farm dog."

"Buddy's a stray. We kind of picked each other. I'm probably not the kind of owner he had in mind either—but our relationship works just fine." He pointed toward the barn, and I followed him inside with Buddy hot on our trail.

Sam sat down on a hay bale, and Buddy jumped up next to him, laying his head on Sam's lap. I plopped down on a bale across from him. A quick glance around the barn revealed stored farm equipment, bags of seed and fertilizer, and a couple of horses. One was dark and shiny, while the other, a pinto, matched Buddy's colors. Although I'd never owned a horse, a friend back in Nebraska had kept several. She'd had a pinto pony almost exactly like this one. I breathed in the barn's sweet, earthy mixture of hay and horses. The setting sun sent its rays through the open windows and bathed our surroundings in a golden glow.

"Now, what in the world is going on, Grace?"

Even though I'd decided to tell him the truth, for just a moment, fear nipped at my heels. Benjamin had spent his life guarding this secret, even from Sam who had been his friend for many years. Could I really trust this man who sat waiting to share my family's strange secret? One day in this town and my life was in chaos. Up was down and down was up. I sighed and stared into Sam's eyes, silently asking God to show me if I should spill my guts.

"Look," he said quietly, noticing my obvious reluctance to take the dirty Temple laundry out of the bag, "if it helps any, I'm going to tell you what Ben told me. Once when he meant to talk to me—and one time when he didn't. Maybe it will help."

I nodded. "Go on."

Sam sighed and stared at something above my head. "About two weeks before he died, I stopped by his house. Sweetie had made up some food for him although he wasn't eating much. I was trying to talk him into a bowl of her chicken and rice soup when he suddenly stopped me. 'Sam,' he said, 'I need you to make me a promise. I want you to help my niece when she comes to Harmony. It won't be easy for her.' I tried to get him to tell me more, but he wouldn't say another word."

"Did you promise him?"

"Yes I did. I figured it was the least I could do for a dying man. Someone I considered my friend." Sam smiled. "I have to say that I was certainly pleased when you opened the door yesterday. I had this image of Ben in a dress that I couldn't get out of my mind. The truth was much better than my imagination."

"Thank you." I rubbed my hands over my upper arms. The gentle spring air was beginning to chill. "Now tell me the thing you overheard that you weren't supposed to."

Sam stared down at the hay-covered floor. "This happened a

few days before Ben died. He was getting weaker but refused to go to the hospital. I'd come by to see if he needed anything and to try once again to convince him we should contact your father." Sam took a deep breath and let it out slowly. "But he was adamant that we not call him. Abel and I debated the situation more than once. It was a difficult decision."

I waved my hand at him. "Look, I have no idea what I would have done in your situation. Hindsight is twenty-twenty. I'm not angry with anyone in Harmony for abiding by my uncle's last wishes. It wasn't your fault."

"Well, thanks for that. Now that I know you, I wish we'd gone a different direction. But what's done is done, I guess."

"Getting back to your story. . ."

"Oh yeah. Sorry." He fixed his gaze over my head again. "Anyway, I'd actually walked out the front door and gone to my truck when I realized I'd forgotten to give Ben the flowers Sweetie had sent over for him. I grabbed them and went back into the house. Ben was still sitting at the kitchen table where I'd left him. As I approached the door, I heard him praying. He was asking God to protect you and to forgive him, and he was crying." Sam acted as if he were brushing the hair out of his eyes, but I could tell he was moved emotionally remembering Benjamin's distress.

"Is that it?"

He shook his head. "No. Suddenly he rose to his feet and walked over to the kitchen window. Then I heard him say something like, 'You will not have the last word, Jacob. You hear me? We will be rid of you. Somehow. Someday. You may have imprisoned me, but another one will take my place. Maybe I couldn't defeat you, but I'm praying *she* can.' And with that, he staggered back to his chair and collapsed." Sam lowered his gaze, and his stormy eyes fastened on mine. "I backed out of the room and left the flowers on the table in the hall. I never told Ben that I'd overheard him. When you first asked about Jacob Glick, it didn't mean anything to me.

But when you brought him up again at the diner, I remembered Ben's words and realized they may not have been the crazy ravings of a dying man. He could have been referring to Glick. I just didn't know why—or what it had to do with you."

Could this be the sign I'd asked for? I felt a peace settle over me. I had my answer, and now it was time to share the burden I'd carried alone over the last twenty-four hours. I took a deep breath and just let the story tumble out. I told Sam about the letter, what it said, and how it had been stolen. I also explained that I was becoming convinced someone else was concerned about keeping Glick's death covered up, because there were secrets even my uncle didn't know.

"My father would never kill anyone," I said finally. "Nor would he leave someone fatally injured and just walk away. I believe he fought with Glick—but I also believe someone else killed him. To be honest, I suspected my uncle for a while. I wondered if he was trying to blame my father for his own misdeed. But after thinking about it, I realize it doesn't make sense. No real Christian who knew he was going to die would leave behind such an awful accusation. He'd care more about the hereafter than the here and now. Benjamin even wrote about being afraid of carrying a lie into the next life. And he sure didn't take that letter from my dresser, nor did he try to frame me by stealing Ruth's chestnut vase. Someone is extremely interested in keeping the truth about Jacob Glick buried. Literally and figuratively."

Sam, who hadn't moved a muscle since I'd begun my discourse, just stared at me with his mouth open.

"S—say something," I said finally. "You're scaring me."

He shook his head as if trying to clear his brain. "I—I had a few ideas about what you were going to tell me, but I must admit they didn't come close to the reality. The only thing I got right was that Ben was talking about Jacob Glick." He looked down at his scuffed leather boots. "Wow. I don't know what to say." He swung his gaze back to me. "So you're saying there's an actual body buried on your property? Someone who's been there for thirty years?"

"That's about the size of it."

He stood up, waking Buddy who looked at him accusingly before he put his head back down and dozed off again. Sam paced back and forth a couple of times. Then he stopped. "We've got to call the sheriff, Grace. We can't fool around with this."

I jumped up, too. "You promised you'd let me make the decisions about what to do, remember?"

"Yes, but I'm pretty sure having a buried body on your property is illegal," he said sarcastically. "Especially if the person was murdered."

"Listen, Sam. That body's been there for thirty years. Another two weeks isn't going to make a difference. I want some time to try to figure out what really happened to Glick."

"And if you can't?"

"Then we'll decide what should be done. I agree that we'll probably have to call the sheriff. I have no intention of living here for the rest of my life, guarding the body of some guy I don't even know."

It felt good to say "we." Bringing someone else into the mess my uncle left behind lifted a weight. But that still didn't bring me the answers I needed.

Sam sauntered back over to his bale of hay and sat down. He reached over and scratched Buddy behind the ears. "Wait a minute. This might be easier than you think. If you never mention the letter, no one will know who killed Glick. They won't be able to prove Ben knew anything about it even though they might suspect him. He can't be hurt by this anymore. Maybe we could just accidentally uncover the body, call the police, and act dumb."

I sighed. "You're forgetting my dad. Trust me. He'll try to take responsibility for Glick's death."

"But why would he connect the remains to Glick? Your father thinks he moved away years ago. It might never occur to him that the dead man is someone he knew."

"Benjamin packed a suitcase to make it look like Glick left town and buried it with him. It won't be hard for the authorities to figure out who the body belongs to. Look, Sam. In the time I have left here, let's see what we can find out about Jacob Glick. There are still people in Harmony who knew him. I think we might be able to figure out what really happened if we talk to the right person. And in the process, we'll probably find out who took Ruth's vase and planted it at my place. Until then, everyone's going to think I'm guilty."

Sam stared at the floor for several seconds. Finally, he raised his hands in surrender. "I might be making the biggest mistake of my life, but okay." He pointed his index finger at me. "But if we can't solve this thing. . ."

"Like I said, we'll probably have to call the sheriff."

"Probably?"

I reached for a strand of hair and twirled it around my finger. "Just what kind of man is he?"

Sam's eyes widened, and then he laughed. "He's a jerk. I know it's not nice to say things like that, but folks in Harmony try their best to keep him out of their business. He doesn't like religious people, and he sees our little town as a hotbed of crazy zealots."

I snorted. "Oh great. That's encouraging."

"Sorry. Just being honest."

"Well, let's keep that prospect in the background for now." I looked at my watch. "It's getting late. Let's see if we can talk your aunt into having pity on us. I'm starving. Then I need to get back to my uncle's and get a good night's sleep. We have a lot of work to do. . ."

Sam held his hand up like a cop stopping traffic. "Whoa right there, little lady. I might have promised not to interfere in how you handle your family secret, but that doesn't mean I'm going to stay quiet about everything you do."

I frowned at him. "What are you talking about?"

He stood up again. Somehow, Buddy knew this time Sam intended to leave. The small dog jumped down and waited at his master's feet. "You heard noises outside Ben's place last night. Today someone's been inside your house twice. There's no way on God's green earth I'm letting you stay there another night. I'll drive you over so you can get whatever clothes and supplies you need, but then you're coming back here. And you're staying with us until we know beyond a shadow of a doubt that you're safe." He folded his arms across his chest and glared at me.

My own stubbornness raised its ugly head and met his expression with one of my own. I desperately wanted to inform him that he wasn't about to tell me what to do. But to be honest, the idea of staying at Benjamin's alone gave me the heebie-jeebies. "Don't get used to pushing me around," I growled at him. "However, in this case, I think you're right." I nodded toward the house. "What will Sweetie say?"

"Sweetie won't say a word. She trusts me. If I say you need to stay with us, she'll go along with it."

Great. Just what I needed. A hostess forced into extending hospitality. I sighed. "Let's see if she'll feed us, and then you can give her the news. I'm sure she'll be overjoyed."

He chuckled and pointed toward the large barn door. Buddy and I headed out, but when I turned around, Sam wasn't behind us. He stood in front of one of the horses, petting its head and speaking softly to it. I waited while he said good night to both of the beautiful animals, admiring his tenderness with them. Sam Goodrich was different than any man I'd ever known—except my father. Was that why I was drawn to him? I made an inner vow to keep a little distance between us—physically and emotionally. It would be hard. His long blond hair glowed in the dusky light, and the muscles in his arms moved as he stroked the horses. The remaining sunlight caught the light golden hairs on his arms. His lean body moved with an unusual grace. I suspected it came from working on the farm. I couldn't call him cover-model handsome, but his looks were appealing, even though I got the feeling he wasn't aware of it. More importantly, Sam Goodrich was an honorable man. To me, there was nothing more attractive than a man with a virtuous heart. And there weren't enough of them around. I ran through a short mental list of the men I'd dated in the past year—every one a polished professional. Yet none of them held a candle to this Kansas farm boy.

Sam checked the padlocks on each stall and faced me with a smile. "Sweetie and I rescued Ranger and Tonto from a man in Council Grove who abused them. When we brought them here, they were sick, skinny, and afraid of people. They've come a long way."

"Ranger and Tonto? Like on *The Lone Ranger*?"

"You're too young to remember that show," he said with an amused grin.

"So are you."

He ambled over to where Buddy and I stood waiting. "When I was a kid I watched reruns. I used to pretend the Lone Ranger was my father—and Tonto was a wise uncle I could go to when I needed advice."

I stepped outside so Sam could close the barn door. Dusk was giving way to darkness. The light above the barn door created a safe, golden circle for Sam, Buddy, and me. I'd told Sam my secrets. Was it time to ask him to reveal his? I took a deep breath and dove in. "I hope you don't think I'm being nosy, but where are your parents? Why do you live here with your aunt?"

"You're not being nosy. It's a natural question." He leaned against the barn door and crossed his arms. "My mother died when I was young. I never knew my father. Sweetie is my mother's only sister. She applied to be my guardian, and here I am."

122

"I'm sorry."

He shook his head. "Don't be. Sweetie's been a wonderful substitute parent. I had a great childhood, and there's no other place I'd rather live than on this farm. I love Harmony and the people who live here." He smiled at me, but it didn't quite reach his eyes. "Really, don't feel sorry for me, Grace. I don't." He leaned down and petted Buddy on the head. "Now, let's see what kind of mood Sweetie's in. I swear, my belt buckle feels like it's hitting my spine."

I nodded and followed him and Buddy back to the house. I was glad I'd asked about his parents, but I'd noticed that he hadn't told me how his mother had died or why he'd never known his father. Maybe I was splitting hairs. I guess he'd tell me when he was ready. Right now, Sweetie's fried chicken and mashed potatoes called my name.

By the time we reached the porch, we could tell by the aroma that she had decided to have mercy on us. Sure enough, when we walked in the door, she yelled at us from the kitchen to "sit down at the table before I change my mind and throw this food in the trash." A few minutes later, we were eating.

At first Sweetie didn't say anything to me directly. She made sure I had some of everything on the table. After my second helping of mashed potatoes, she finally addressed me.

"So how do you imagine that silly vase of Ruth's found its way to your place?" Her tone was sharp and confrontational, but there was no condemnation in her expression. I got the feeling she was testing me.

After swallowing the bite of biscuit and strawberry preserves in my mouth, I met her fixed gaze, refusing to look away. "I have no idea. Someone put it there, and I intend to find out why."

After a brief staring contest, she lowered her eyes and nodded slowly. "Good for you. You might find it a little uncomfortable in town for a while, but sometimes you just gotta stand up straight and do whatcha gotta do. Backin' down from a fight ain't never the right way to go. You gotta face your adversaries with your head held high."

"Sweetie, I want Grace to stay here with us," Sam said. "Someone broke into Ben's place and left that vase there to implicate her. It's not safe."

His tone didn't invite discussion, and to my utter amazement, Sweetie didn't offer any. The disagreeable look on her face was either due to my extended visit—or because she had indigestion. I couldn't be sure, but to her credit she nodded.

"I'll put clean sheets on the bed in the south bedroom."

"Sw–Sweetie," I said with a gulp, "did you see anyone at Benjamin's house today while Sam and I were in town?" I patted myself mentally for finally spitting out the silly name.

She frowned so hard her two eyebrows became one. "What kind of a fool do you take me for?" she snapped. "If I'd seen someone snoopin' around your house, don't you think I woulda told you already? For cryin' out loud. . ."

"Now, Sweetie," Sam said in a soothing voice, "I intended to ask you the same question. Grace just got it out before I did. We're not saying you'd forget to tell us if you saw someone. But sometimes we don't realize until later how important some little detail might be in a situation like this."

"Well, I didn't see nothin'. I was workin' today. Not gallivantin' around town."

"Thanks," Sam said. "That's all we needed to know. And thanks for this great supper. No one cooks the way you do. Not even Hector down at the café."

Sweetie's face relaxed, the storm seemingly abated for now. Sam certainly knew how to control his aunt. She stood up. "You two ready for some of my apple pie?"

I was so full my stomach wanted to scream "No!" but I found myself nodding along with Sam. It was as if my head had no actual connection to my brain. Within a few minutes we were eating the best apple pie I'd ever tasted, covered with cream. I'd had apple pie and ice cream before, but never warm pie with pure cream ladled over it. It wouldn't be the last time.

Finally, when there was no way to put another bite of food into my body, Sam and I left to pick up my things from Benjamin's. As we approached the house, a clap of thunder exploded overhead, and I jumped.

"Hope you're not afraid of storms," Sam said. "In the spring, we get them all the time. Sometimes one right after the other. The farmers look forward to the rain—as long as it's not too much."

"No, I love rain. I just didn't realize we had a storm coming in."

As if on cue, thick sheets of rain began falling on us. Sam parked as close to the door as he could, but we still got soaked before we hit the front porch. It didn't take me long to gather what I needed. Before we left, I carried a lantern to the basement. I wanted to look inside the trunk where the vase had supposedly been found. It was still open, and except for a quilt that had been moved to one side, it looked just as it had when I'd gone through it the first time.

"The trunk was unlocked?" Sam had followed me down the stairs.

"Yes."

"And where was the letter?"

"That was upstairs, in Mama and Papa's room." It made me nervous to think that someone had not only been in this basement, but also in the main room and the upstairs. The entire house felt tainted somehow.

Sam closed the chest. "I don't like leaving the house un-protected." He shook his head. "In Harmony, we don't usually worry about locking our doors. I don't think I've ever thought about someone breaking in and stealing something as long as I've lived here. But now I'm uneasy. This house is way too accessible."

I reached over and put my hand on his arm. "Look. Whoever broke in was here for a specific reason. To get that letter and to plant the vase. I don't think anything else is missing, and I doubt they'll be back—especially since they know we'd be watching for them."

He stared at the closed trunk. "Maybe you're right," he said thoughtfully, "but some new locks and dead bolts wouldn't hurt." His face creased in a deep frown. "Grace, how could anyone know about that letter? I mean, I doubt seriously that Ben told anyone else about it. If he had, they could have gotten it before you came to town."

"I've wondered about that myself. I don't know the answer."

He turned toward me. "I might. I think the noises you heard last night were more than squirrels. I think someone was watching you and saw you read the letter." He reached over and put his hand on my cheek. "You need to consider the idea that whoever is behind this may not take kindly to your probing and prodding around for information. I'm beginning to wonder if you might actually be in some danger."

Although I already shivered from the chilled rain outside, his words made me feel even colder on the inside. Seeing my distress, he opened his arms, and I leaned into him. In the circle of his embrace, I felt safe. But I couldn't shake the feeling that right at that moment, someone else in Harmony had very different intentions—and my safety was the least of that person's concerns.

Chapter Ten

After a hot shower and clean clothes, I felt more like myself. I crawled into bed and gazed around the room Sweetie had prepared for me. Although only a guest room, it matched the rest of the house in charm and decor. Deep purple violets adorned the wallpaper. The thick oak furniture was delicately carved. A gorgeous lavender and gold Victorian rug lay in the middle of the gleaming wood floor. Flowers and vines decorated its edges. A fireplace with a thick oak mantel held a large basket of silk lilacs. I tried to imagine lying in this tall bed and snuggling down into the soft, stuffed mattress while snow fell outside and a fire crackled in the fireplace. Even though it wasn't winter, it made me feel warm and comfortable. Over the bed hung a beautiful painting of children playing in a meadow full of flowers. I pulled myself up so I could see the signature. *H. Mueller.* Still another painting by Hannah. After hearing that Sam regularly bought her work, I felt confident I'd find more of the young girl's paintings throughout the house.

I lay back down in the bed, pulled the thick, handmade quilt up to my chin, and stared up at the decorated ceiling tiles. The glow from a bedside lamp made the room seem so cozy and safe that the tension from the day's earlier events began to lessen. I listened to the rain pelting the roof overhead and prayed for guidance. One of my favorite times to talk to God was after climbing into bed at night. Everything is dark and still, and His presence seems so real. Although no voice boomed out of heaven with the answers to my problems, a solid sense of peace washed over me, reminding me that I am never alone and that my Father is never surprised by any turn of events. Nor is there anything He can't handle.

After praying, my mind wandered back to the intruder at Benjamin's. The rain had successfully washed away any clues, such as footprints or tire tracks—not that they would have helped us anyway. If my visitor had left something behind that could identify him, it would likely be inside the house, and I hadn't noticed anything that didn't belong.

My silent musings drifted back to Sam's embrace in the basement. Since then, he hadn't tried to kiss me again, and I wondered why. Did he regret that first kiss the way I did? We had no future. It was pointless to stir up yearnings that could never be fulfilled. Keeping ourselves in check was the only sensible thing to do. I let out a deep sigh that seemed extremely loud in the silent room. Then why couldn't I get that kiss out of my mind? And why did I get butterflies in my stomach every time I looked at him? Obviously, I knew the answers to my own questions— and they weren't acceptable. "Stop it, Gracie," I whispered. "Get control of yourself." I had no intention of creating any additional problems in my life. I already had more than I could handle. In two weeks, come hell or high water, I intended to head back to Wichita, leaving Sam Goodrich and Harmony far behind me.

I forced myself to stop thinking about Sam. My priority right now lay in another direction, and I couldn't allow errant feelings for some good-looking fruit farmer to interfere.

I turned out the light and listened to the rain for a while. Sam had asked me to go to church with him in the morning. At first I'd said no because I knew Ruth would be there. Finally, he'd convinced me that if I didn't go, I would look guilty. Reluctantly, I'd agreed, but I was having second thoughts now. How would people treat me? Was the story all over town? Even as a part of me dreaded confronting the accusing looks and whispers, my stronger, more independent side rose up in indignation. I hadn't done anything wrong, and I had nothing to feel embarrassed about. My parents had drilled several strong beliefs into me down through the years. One of them had to do with only playing to an audience of One—and that His opinion was the only one that mattered. I knew He wanted me to be kind and forgiving, yet He didn't expect me to accept condemnation.

I thought about Mama Essie and Papa Joe and how much courage it took for them to walk away from the town and the people they loved because they knew Amil Angstadt was leading his congregation away from the Bible as well as the tenets of their faith. I figured if they could stand up for what was right in such a big way, I could certainly attend church knowing my conscience was clear and the charges against me were false.

I flipped over on my side and had just started to drift off when I heard the door to my room open slowly. I turned over to see who it was. The light in the hallway illuminated the empty doorway. I kept staring but no one appeared. Great. What now? Ghosts? Suddenly, something hurtled toward me, and a scream escaped my lips. A hairy face sought mine, and a wet tongue licked my forehead. Buddy!

"You scared the snot out of me," I hissed accusingly.

Seemingly unfazed by my brief bout of hysteria, Buddy settled down next to me. I'd just put my arm around him and snuggled closer when the ceiling light suddenly clicked on. I turned my head toward the door. Sam stood there in a dark blue T-shirt that read ROCK CHALK JAYHAWK and matching sweatpants that had JAYHAWK printed down the side.

"KU fan?" I teased.

His tousled hair and "deer in the headlights" expression made it clear he'd been sound asleep. "I thought I heard you scream."

Even though I wore a T-shirt and sweatpants myself, my usual sleeping attire, I pulled the covers up closer to my chin. "You did. I was just attacked by a vicious beast."

As if on cue, Buddy lifted his head and stared sheepishly at his perturbed owner.

"Buddy," Sam grumbled. "What are you doing here?"

I quickly ran my hands through my hair, trying to rid myself of bedhead. "He's attempting to sleep—just like me." I smiled at him. "Thanks for running in to save me, but I'm fine. I can handle monsters this cute and cuddly." I stroked the little dog. "Please don't make him leave. Having him here makes me feel better."

Finally, the stricken look on Sam's face softened, and he shrugged. "Fine, he can stay, but only if you promise there will be no more screaming unless you're being mauled by something a little more dangerous than Buddy."

"You got it. Now if you don't mind?"

Buddy's mouth opened in something close to a doggy grin. Then he put his head down again.

"Boy, loyalty means nothing in this house," Sam said accusingly. "Good night."

"Good night." I watched as he closed the door. It felt great to know he was looking out for me. And having Buddy in the room only added to my feeling of security. "Thanks," I whispered into the darkness, "for two angels named Sam and Buddy. I know You're watching over me. Please help me to uncover the truth. I'm counting on You." Once again, I cuddled up next to Buddy and promptly fell asleep.

It seemed like only minutes passed before I awoke to Sam's voice saying, "Time to rise and shine, sleepyhead!"

I sat up in bed and looked at the clock. It was a little after eight. Buddy stood up, yawned, and then jumped down off the bed and ran toward his master.

"Sure, *now* you pay attention to me. When you want food and you need to go outside." He grinned at me. "Sweetie's making breakfast."

"Be down as soon as I get dressed."

He nodded and closed the door. I could hear Buddy's nails clicking on the wooden floor in the hall. I rolled over on my back and gazed up. The specter of accusing stares and angry murmurs from the citizens of Harmony floated like fuzzy visions across the ceiling. But the words of Jesus whispered louder. *"Peace I leave with you; my peace I give you. . . . Do not let your hearts be troubled and do not be afraid."*

I spent a few minutes thanking God for the day before me. Then I put myself into His capable hands. I rolled out of bed, grabbed my clothes, and made my way to the bathroom, as my slippers made a *slap, slap, slap* sound on the floor.

It took me about twenty minutes to scrub my teeth, change my clothes, apply some makeup, and run a brush through my hair. I'd brought one of my few dresses along. I usually wore slacks to church, but I hadn't been certain what to expect in Harmony. Although my simple light aqua frock was modest and thankfully hung below my knees, the apple-green dress that I'd seen in Harmony popped into my mind. I really wanted it but was worried that the Mennonite shop owners might think it was inappropriate for someone not of their faith to purchase it. How could a simple dress make me feel so insecure? I stared at my reflection in the mirror. "You can buy any dress you want, Gracie. Get the dress. You don't have to wear it here. Wear it in Wichita."

Having a quick talk with myself made me feel better. I would buy the dress. But I'd probably wait until right before I left town.

I picked up my T-shirt, sweatpants, and slippers and went back to the bedroom where I put them away. Then I made my bed and went downstairs. Sweetie and Sam were already sitting at the table. The smell of fresh-brewed coffee tickled my nose as I entered the kitchen. Sweetie got up when she saw me.

"My waffles are gettin' cold, girl," she said, her tone accusatory.

I glanced over at Sam who rolled his eyes and shook his head. I was beginning to learn that Sweetie's nickname smacked more of irony than reality. This woman was about the sourest person I'd ever met.

"Sorry," I said softly. "I got ready as quickly as I could. I'd never purposely be late for one of your delicious meals."

My statement seemed to take the wind out of her sails. She paused with a plate of waffles in her hand. "Th–that's okay," she said finally. "I'll have them to you lickety-split."

Sam gave me a thumbs-up when his aunt wasn't looking. I remembered the scripture that promised a gentle answer would turn away wrath. Wow. Obviously it worked.

Before long, I was full of waffles, bacon, and coffee. When Sam announced it was time to go, I got up and followed him to the front door. Sweetie stayed behind.

"Doesn't your aunt ever go to church?" I asked when Sam closed the front door behind us.

He shook his head. "She used to when she was younger, but I guess something happened that changed her. She encourages me to go, and she reads her Bible and prays. She just won't step foot inside a church building." He shrugged. "I used to try to get her to tell me why, but I finally gave up. Whatever her reasons, she's determined to keep them to herself."

I thought about Sweetie as Sam's truck jiggled down the dirt road toward Harmony Church. I'd met quite a few ex-church members like her—people who used to be part of congregations but had left for various reasons. Sometimes they'd pulled out because the church didn't seem to be meeting their needs. And sometimes it was because they'd been hurt. I couldn't help but wonder what would happen if more churches took care of the people already inside its borders instead of concentrating so much on bringing in new bodies. Numbers are great. I have no problem with large churches as long as they care for their members. But I'd seen firsthand what happens when people are neglected. I thought about a friend of mine who belonged to a small singles' group at his church. Because of work, he missed several meetings in a row. "Wow, Gracie," he'd told me. "Not one person ever called to ask me if I was okay—or to tell me they missed me." I could still see the look on his face. He quit going to that church. A simple phone call—a little concern—would have made a huge difference in his life. Jesus' admonition to Peter, "Feed my sheep," slipped into my mind. Unfortunately, some of His sheep seemed to be starving.

Sam turned into the parking lot at Harmony Church, forcing me to put my thoughts on hold. "Here we are," he said as he pulled into a space. "Are you nervous?"

I looked out the window at the people headed for the large brick building. Not one of them stared at the truck or seemed interested in who was inside. "A little bit." The scripture about God's peace came back to me. "I'll be fine. Let's go inside."

I waited for Sam to open my door, and then I climbed down carefully, keeping my skirt in place. He was incredibly handsome in his black slacks and gray striped shirt.

"You look really nice this morning," I said as I stepped out of the truck.

"And you look absolutely beautiful," he said in a low voice.

I felt the blood rush into my face and had to turn away so he wouldn't notice. He took my arm and escorted me toward the front entrance. Several people stepped up to introduce themselves as we entered. Sam told them who I was, yet no one acted as if they'd heard about my supposed thievery. I'd started to relax until we almost ran smack-dab into Ruth and her companion—Mary Whittenbauer. Their expressions made it obvious they'd been talking about me. Mary already had it in for me. Combining forces with Ruth made for a poisonous mix.

Sam's grip on my arm tightened, and he steered me right toward the two women, even though I pulled away from him and tried to go the other way.

"Hello, Ruth. Hello, Mary," he said, his voice a little too loud for my liking.

Ruth's mouth dropped open. Mary just glared at him.

"G—good morning, Sam," Ruth said after she regained her composure. "Gracie."

"Good morning," I mumbled. I fought a quick rush of embarrassment and had to remind myself that I had nothing to be humiliated about. "Good morning, Mary," I said a little more forcefully.

"Good morning, Gracie." She fired her words back at me like small, potent bullets.

I felt Sam tug on my arm, but I wasn't quite finished. A small fire of indignation burned in my gut. "I'm looking forward to today's sermon," I said with a smile. I directed my gaze toward Ruth. "Maybe the pastor will preach about the ninth commandment, Ruth. Do you know it by any chance?"

"Let's go," Sam said gruffly. This time he didn't try to gently lead me away from the women. Instead, he yanked me so hard I almost toppled over.

"Let go of me," I hissed once we were out of earshot.

He stopped in his tracks and faced me. His eyes flashed with anger. "Do you feel better now that you put Ruth in her place?" He shook his head. "Don't you know that you don't fight wrong with more wrong? It never works."

"She had it coming. Bearing false witness is a sin."

"So is not turning the other cheek," he said in a tight, controlled voice. "God is all about love and forgiveness, Grace. With your name, you'd think you'd have figured that out by now."

As we made our way to our seats, an internal struggle was going on inside me. Self-righteousness screamed that I'd been wronged, while humility whispered that no one was more wronged than Jesus—yet He had forgiven the world. Of course, humility won, quickly followed by conviction and its close friend, repentance.

Sam sat silently beside me. As the music ministers began taking their places on the platform, I turned to him. "You're right," I whispered. "I'm sorry. Hope I didn't embarrass you."

He let out a big sigh. "I'm not embarrassed. I overreacted, too. You only said what I was thinking. But we can't pay back evil for evil. It always blows up in our faces."

"I know. I'll apologize after the service."

"You pray about that. If you feel the need, I'll go with you." He put his hand on mine. "You're a wonderful person, Grace. You don't deserve to be in the spot you're in. I hope I'll be able to help you."

"Me, too." My eyes drifted past Sam. Two rows up, Mary turned around and glowered at us. I quickly looked away. "Mary may be more of a problem than Ruth," I said softly.

Sam grinned down at me. "You could be right. We usually sit together in church."

I turned toward him in surprise. I wanted to tell him that ignoring Mary to sit with me wasn't wise, but before I could get the words out, the praise and worship music began. I took one more quick look at Mary, but she'd turned her head toward the platform. As much as I resented her talking to Ruth about me, I felt uncomfortable knowing my presence caused her pain. By the time the music came to an end, I'd made a firm decision. Sam and I would have to talk about the reality of our relationship. That there wasn't one—and never would be. He and Mary would have to sort out their own problems. I couldn't be in the middle anymore.

As the singers and musicians left the platform, a man came up and stood behind the pulpit. I figured him to be somewhere in his middle forties, although with his receding hairline, he could have been younger. He towered over the retreating musicians by quite a bit. His thin frame and rather large nose put me in mind of drawings I'd seen of the fictional character Ichabod Crane. When he opened his mouth to speak, a rich voice rolled out. I sighed deeply as he introduced his sermon topic—"Walking in Love." In other words, God had my number. I could almost feel the target on the top of my head. By the time Pastor Jensen finished, I'd been properly spanked. I'd learned long ago that God disciplines his children through His Word. When a sermon reaches into your heart and shines a light on your wrong attitudes, it is the Holy Spirit bringing His loving conviction.

I was convicted all right. I glanced over at Mary. My visit to Harmony had disrupted her life. Perhaps it wasn't my fault, but my reaction to her situation *was* my responsibility. When the sermon came to a close and we were dismissed, I asked Sam to wait for me in the truck. I knew he'd offered to go with me if I decided to talk to Mary, but I felt strongly that this was something I had to do alone. He gave me an odd look but headed for the exit. I caught up to Mary just as she scooted out of the pew where she'd been seated.

"Mary, may I speak to you privately for a moment?" I put my hand on her arm and held on.

"I—I don't know. . ." Her expression reminded me of a fox I'd found caught in a trap once when we lived in Nebraska. It had taken quite awhile for him to trust me enough to let me open the trap and free him. I kept the light pressure on her arm.

"Please."

She sighed, and resignation registered on her face. "I suppose it would be okay." She pointed toward a small alcove to my left. I released her arm and followed her there. As she walked in heels higher than I'd be comfortable with, her dark, silky hair bounced in rhythm to her full but rather short skirt. I tried not to think about the appropriateness of her outfit for a church service. It wasn't my job to judge her. Especially now. When we reached our destination, she turned and folded her arms across her chest, her red mouth pursed in a pout. "What do you want, Gracie?"

I prayed silently for the right words, clearing my throat to give me a second to hear from God. "We seem to have gotten off on the wrong foot, Mary," I said finally. "I'm not sure why, but I'd like to clear it up if at all possible." I gazed into her deep brown eyes and saw the hurt and insecurity there. A wave of sympathy washed through me. "I'm not interested in Sam romantically," I said gently. "He's a wonderful man and has been a good friend since I arrived in town—but that's all. Whatever's going on between you two has nothing to do with me. Please understand that I'm not your problem—or your enemy. In fact, I'd like to be your friend if you'll let me. Like Pastor Jensen said, we're a family. We should act like one."

Instead of the warm reaction I'd hoped for, her mouth tightened and she stepped away from me. "I honestly don't know what kind of game you're playing, but I know Sam Goodrich. He has feelings for you. It's obvious. Maybe you don't return them, but that doesn't change a thing. We're engaged—at least we were until you showed up."

Well, I guess the soft-answer-turning-away-wrath thing doesn't work all the time. This certainly wasn't the reaction I'd prayed for. "Look, Mary," I said slowly, "surely you realize that if your relationship with Sam is secure, my presence won't interfere with it in any way. If you two are meant to be together, no one will be able to come between you—on purpose or accidentally."

"How dare you!" she huffed. Her face flushed an angry red. "I couldn't care less about your opinion on any subject. I understand stealing fiancés isn't the only kind of theft you're interested in."

My good intentions flew out the window. Anger coursed through me in a torrent. "Look here, you little. . ."

"That's enough, Grace."

Sam's stern tone caught me off guard. I turned around to find him standing behind us, Ruth at his side.

"But she said. . . ," I sputtered.

"This is all my fault," Ruth said, interrupting what promised to be a scathing report of the injustice leveled against me.

Her words stopped me cold. "Wh–what?" I managed to get out between clenched teeth.

Ruth reached over and took my hands in hers. "I said, I guess this is all my fault." She glanced up at Sam and shook her head. "Sam told me that you couldn't possibly have taken the vase. I've known him ever since he came to live here, and if there's one thing I can count on in this life, it's the truthfulness of Sam Goodrich." She squeezed my hands. "I can't say I understand how my vase got into your trunk, Gracie. To be honest, it will take a leap of faith for me to believe you had nothing to do with stealing it. But I trust Sam. And I didn't actually see who took it. Those two facts have to outweigh my suspicions. I have no choice but to give you the benefit of the doubt." She smiled at me. "Could you possibly find it in your heart to give me another chance?"

"Of course, I can. I'm not a thief, Ruth. Really. I would never take something that doesn't belong to me." I swung my gaze toward Mary. "Not on purpose anyway."

Ruth hugged me. "Let's just put the whole situation behind us, okay? You're welcome in my shop anytime. Maybe we need to have a cup of coffee together this week and get to know each other a little better."

"I–I'd like that."

A quick glance at Mary made it clear her anger was now not only directed at me but at her friend, as well. She mumbled something I didn't understand and stomped away, stopping to speak to a couple exiting a pew several rows away from us.

"Don't worry about Mary," Ruth said. "I can handle her. She gets pretty angry sometimes, but she usually finds a way to move past it." She put her arm around my shoulder. "I'm going to walk you back to Sam's truck." She frowned at him. "I just said some nice things about your willingness to be honest, Sam Goodrich. You need to do that now." She glanced toward Mary and then back at Sam. "You understand me, boy?"

He nodded, his face pink. "Yes ma'am," he mumbled.

Ruth guided me away from Sam and Mary. When we were out of listening range, she let me go. "Sorry to rush you off like that, but Sam owes Mary a frank talk. It should have happened a long time ago." She sighed and shook her head. "Mary pushed and prodded him into this so-called *engagement*. At first, Sam was too nice to tell her he wasn't certain about it. Finally, I think he just gave in. Sometimes when you live in a town this small, you can start thinking that your choices in life are limited to what's here. I think in the back of Sam's mind, he figured he might as well hook up with Mary because there would never be anyone else." She smiled at me. "Since you've come to town, he's started rethinking that attitude."

I started to protest, but Ruth pointed toward the doors of the church. "Let's talk outside. Esther Crenshaw is on her way over here, and she's the biggest gossip in town."

Over my shoulder I saw a woman with curly brown hair wearing a bright red dress and a large flowered hat making a beeline toward us. Ruth quickly pulled me out the door, and we hurried to Sam's truck where we stood on the side not facing the church. Esther followed us outside but stopped to talk to someone else, seeming to forget us completely.

"Listen, Ruth," I said when we'd safely escaped Esther's attention, "I have no romantic interest in Sam. He's a nice man, and I think we're building a friendship—but that's all it is. For goodness' sake, I've only known him for two days. That's not enough time to fall in love."

Ruth's round face crinkled as she laughed. "Oh, Gracie. My husband and I fell in love on our first date. I knew he was the man for me, and he knew I was the woman he wanted to spend his life with. We were married almost forty years before he died. And every single year was happy." She reached over and patted me on the shoulder. "Love isn't something you buy at the store when you're ready," she said gently. "It's a gift that can arrive all of a sudden—without warning. It can come at the most inconvenient time—and it almost never looks the way you expect it to." She reached up and touched my face lightly. "The worst thing you can do is not take the gift when it comes. It may never come your way again. Believe me, I know."

I stared at the older woman, unable to find the words to respond to her. Sam couldn't possibly be the man for me. Everything about him was wrong. Wrong kind of man. Wrong profession. Wrong town.

"I understand what you're saying," I said, trying to sound convincing, "but honestly, Sam and I are not a couple. Nor will we ever be. We're not a good match."

She smiled. "Maybe not. Sorry. Guess I shouldn't stick my nose into other people's business."

"It–it's fine." I cleared my throat and tried to offer her my most sincere expression. "Look, I want you to understand something. For reasons I can't explain right now, I'm convinced someone took your vase and placed it inside my uncle's house just so they could cast a bad light on me personally. I know that doesn't make sense to you now, but I hope to prove it before I leave Harmony."

Ruth's forehead puckered. "You don't have to prove anything to me, honey. But if someone was actually trying to set you up. . ." She shook her head. "You know, Benjamin Temple was the loneliest man I ever met. Now don't get me wrong—I adored him. His

140

honesty, his compassion. But there was something bubbling below the surface of that man. Now you come to town and things start heating up." She studied me for a moment. "You be careful stirring that pot, Gracie. If it boils over, people can get burned."

Was she warning me or threatening me? Truth was, I had no idea who was my friend—and who was my enemy. Could Ruth have planted the vase at Benjamin's house? Maybe she put it there herself. And what about Mary? She had a good reason for wanting me out of town.

I looked around at the people heading toward their cars. Nice people. Friendly people. But someone in this town hid a dark secret, and I had no intention of leaving until I uncovered it. "Here he comes," Ruth said suddenly.

I looked past her and saw Sam coming our way. His face was set in stone without a hint of a smile. No sign of Mary.

"Let's get going," he said brusquely as he approached the car. "We don't want to be late for dinner at Abel's."

He opened the truck door for me, and I climbed inside. He slammed it shut and rounded the front of the truck toward the driver's side. A determined-looking Ruth blocked his way. The window on his side was rolled down, which made it easy for me to hear their conversation.

"Did you talk to her?" she asked in a firm voice.

"Yes I did." By the look on his face and the tone of his voice, it was obvious Mary hadn't taken it well.

"Good. Now you both can move on."

Sam grunted. "Not necessarily. She's pretty angry. I think I'll have to make myself scarce for a while."

"Nonsense. She'll come around. I'll speak to her. Trust me."

Sam leaned down and gave Ruth a kiss on the cheek. "Well, if there's anyone who can settle her down, it's you. But I'm not sure even your powers of persuasion will work this time."

Ruth's light, musical laugh drifted through the air. "Oh ye of little faith." She stepped out of Sam's way, and he slid into his truck. Then she leaned on the open window and frowned at me. "You be careful, Gracie. And remember what I said." With that she turned and walked away.

"What did she say?" Sam asked as he turned the key in the ignition.

"She told me I might be getting ready to bite off more than I can chew." I sighed. "I'm beginning to wonder if she's right."

"Phooey." Sam backed the truck up, being careful to avoid distracted churchgoers involved in animated conversations in the parking lot. "You can't give up now. You must be on the right track. You certainly caught someone's attention."

I had to agree with him on that point, but as we drove to Abel Mueller's, Ruth's admonition kept ringing through my mind. *You be careful stirring that pot, Gracie. If it boils over, people can get burned.*

Chapter Eleven

This chicken is delicious, Emily," I said, taking another bite. "And this stuffing. I've never had anything like it."

"It's called *bubbat*," she said with a smile. "The raisins add a nice flavor, I think."

"It's wonderful. And these rolls." I picked up a round roll with another round knob on top of it. It looked like a little snowman without arms and legs.

"Zwieback," Hannah said. "Mama makes it all the time. She's a great cook."

"She certainly is." I smiled at Emily. "I'm amazed. How did you put together a meal like this so quickly? Doesn't your church let out about the same time as Sam's?"

"I cook Sunday's dinner on Saturday," Emily said with a small laugh. "We don't like to work on the Sabbath. So you see, all I had to do was heat everything up."

"Well, you're the best heater-upper I've ever met."

Hannah giggled, and Abel laughed warmly.

Thankfully, dinner was relaxed and enjoyable. Whatever had caused Emily to react so violently to me in the diner wasn't evident today. I'd been a little nervous on the way over, wondering if Abel and his family had heard about my supposed criminal activity. Sam had assured me that even if Ruth had wanted to tell Abel, there wouldn't have been any opportunity. Two different churches, two different schedules, not enough time. Hopefully, now that Ruth had removed me from the top of her suspect list, the rumor wouldn't go any further.

I glanced over to find Hannah's brilliant blue eyes fastened on me. She seemed intrigued by the new guest in the Mueller house. I was very interested in her, too. A girl with so much natural talent needed encouragement and training. Her chances of receiving it in Harmony were slim to none.

Abel's house felt cozy and welcoming. Not much different than my folks except for the lack of a TV or DVD cabinet. The Muellers had electricity, and a quick peek into Emily's kitchen revealed modern appliances. What Abel told me at the diner appeared to be true. His day-to-day existence wasn't much different than mine except for an effort to keep life simpler and free of outside distractions.

The dining room where we gathered to eat was spacious and homey. The large oak table with twelve chairs spoke of big dinners and lots of guests. Our small group assembled at one end. A large painting of Bethel Church hung over the carved oak buffet pushed up against the wall. On the other side of the room, I spotted another painting. A girl with a white prayer cap sat under a tree and gazed out at a lake graced by a family of swans. The figure was in the distance with her face turned away. I remembered Ruth's comment about Mennonite paintings not showing features or figures close up. Even so, there was something achingly sad about the image. The young girl had wrapped her arms around her knees, almost in a fetal position. I started to ask about the origins of the work when Abel spoke up and redirected my attention.

"Hope you saved some room for dessert," he said energetically. "My wife makes the best peach cobbler in Harmony."

"Oh, I didn't realize cobbler was a Mennonite dish."

Abel's eyes widened and he let out a belly laugh, his beard bouncing up and down. "Oh, Gracie. Emily made you some special dishes passed down from her mother and grandmother because she thought you might enjoy them. But we eat the same things you do. Emily makes a mean pizza, and I'm partial to Chinese food. We even drive to Topeka once in a while to eat at the Chinese buffet." He wiped his face with his napkin, still grinning. "And I doubt very seriously that the Mennonites can take credit for cobbler."

Hannah seemed particularly amused by my gaffe. I smiled at her. "I'm sorry. I guess I have a lot to learn about the Mennonite way of life."

"There's not much to learn," Emily said softly. "We're really pretty normal."

"I keep confusing the way things are with the way they used to be when Bishop Angstadt ran the church."

The smile quickly left Emily's face, and the tense look I'd seen when I first met her returned. Amil Angstadt seemed to be a sore subject to almost everyone who lived here.

"As I explained to you in the café, Harmony *is* a much different place now," Abel said. "During Bishop Angstadt's day, I doubt that our little town would have deserved its name. There was a lot of unhappiness in Harmony back then."

"My folks don't talk about it much," I said. "They believe in forgiveness, so I guess that makes them unwilling to dredge up the past. But there's still some anger and mistrust even if they don't acknowledge it."

Abel nodded. "I understand. In Philippians, Paul talks about forgetting what lies behind. But over the years, in counseling folks in the church, I've discovered another truth: that sometimes we try to bury things that aren't dead."

"What do you mean?" Sam asked.

"Well, in Paul's mind, his past had been dealt with. It was dead. He could look forward and knew that looking back would simply stop him from achieving everything God had called him to do. But sometimes people try to bury things they *haven't* dealt with. And when that happens, the past won't stay silent. It manifests in other ways—interfering with your life and not allowing you to move forward."

Abel's wise admonition appeared to be pointed in a specific direction. I noticed that he looked at Emily several times while he spoke.

"You've just described Benjamin Temple," Hannah said in her light, girlish voice. "I think something awful happened to him. He always seemed so sad."

Hannah had been so quiet throughout dinner that hearing her speak startled me. I smiled at her. "You're very perceptive."

"Benjamin isn't the only one," she said matter-of-factly. "It doesn't take much perception to know that Harmony is a town full of secrets. You haven't been here very long. Just wait."

"Hannah!" Emily's sharp tone startled me. She turned my way, her face flushed. "I must apologize for my daughter. She is at an age where a little drama goes a long way."

"Well, what about John Keystone?" Hannah shot back. She gave me a conspiratorial wink. "That man's hiding something all right."

"Hannah, that's enough. This family does not gossip." The seriousness in Abel's deep voice caught his daughter up short. It was obvious that when Abel stepped in, Hannah knew she had overstepped her boundaries.

"There certainly *is* something wrong with that man," Emily murmured under her breath.

Abel frowned at his wife. "I'm sorry, Gracie. For some reason, Emily has taken a dislike to our town's butcher. I have no idea why."

Emily didn't respond, but the look on her face displayed

something fiercer than dislike. What was that about?

I glanced over at Hannah. Just what secrets could she be privy to? Perhaps talking to her privately might reveal something that would help me find out what happened to Jacob Glick. It was a long shot since she wasn't even alive when Glick lived in Harmony, but I knew from past experience that many times children overhear things they aren't supposed to. Most parents would be mortified if they were aware of everything their children repeated outside their homes.

Hannah didn't respond when her father rebuked her. Instead, she pouted. Typical teenage reaction. I tried not to smile.

I had every intention of bringing up Glick's name again. After Emily's reaction at the diner, I was certain she knew something. But it felt wrong to do it now. The Muellers had graciously welcomed us to their home. Using them for information at the dinner table seemed somewhat impolite. I suddenly realized that I'd been plotting the best ways to use my hostess and her fourteen-year-old daughter for information. My stomach lurched at the prospect. Finding the truth was important, but at what cost? What lines would I cross to protect my father?

I tried to deal with my guilty conscience as Emily and Hannah cleared the dishes. When they'd finished, Emily brought out cobbler and ice cream.

"Why don't we eat our dessert on the porch?" Abel said. "Hannah, get everyone fresh coffee, will you?"

Sam and I picked up our bowls, napkins, and forks and followed him and Emily out of the dining room toward the back of the house. At the end of the hall, Abel opened a door and we stepped out into a large screened-in porch lined with pots of colorful flowers and plants. Lovely white wicker furniture with dark blue cushions and small white flowers sat against powder blue walls. A white ceiling fan turned lazily, moving fresh spring air through the room.

"Oh, this is charming," I said. "If I lived in this house, I think I'd spend every minute I could right here."

For the first time since I'd met her, Emily's expression completely lost its haunted look. She smiled widely and her eyes twinkled with life. "That's exactly what I do." She set a pot of coffee on a small, nearby table and opened the lid to a large cream-colored trunk that sat in front of a set of matching love seats. "All my sewing supplies are kept in here. I sit in this room almost every day and sew for hours." She sighed happily. "It makes me happy. When it's nice, I love to listen to the birds singing. But I especially enjoy rainy days. I feel so safe and cozy in this special place." She put her hand over her mouth and giggled. "I sound silly, don't I?"

When she laughed, I got a quick glance of the beauty she had once been—before some kind of sadness chased away much of her vivacity. Her dark eyes sparkled and her cheeks took on a rosy hue.

"I sound a little unhinged, I know. But this room is very important to me." She smiled at her husband. "Abel built this porch. He said I needed a room of my own."

Emily clearly loved the big, burly man who stood next to her. Although he blushed from the attention his wife gave him, it was obvious her joy pleased him. These two were still crazy about each other even after many years of marriage and a teenage daughter. I wondered if I would be as blessed someday as they were now.

I glanced over at Sam who'd settled down in one of the padded chairs. His expression as he gazed at me made me feel warm inside. I quickly glanced away and had started to sit down when I noticed something in Emily's chest. I put my bowl of cobbler on the floor next to my chair. "That material," I said, picking up a large, folded piece of apple green–colored cloth with small, white and yellow flowers. "I saw it in the dress shop."

Emily took it from me and smiled. "Why, yes. I made a dress out of this."

"You made it?" I knew dresses didn't just grow on trees and fall on the ground for people to pick up, but I'd never really known anyone who made clothing. My grandmother used to, when she lived in Harmony, but she only did it because it was seen as her duty. When my grandparents moved to Nebraska, she'd informed my grandfather that unless he wanted to run around naked, he'd better learn to buy his clothes from a store. Thankfully, he did just that. Mama Essie had also detested baking bread. Although she was a wonderful cook and baked all the time, she never made another loaf of bread after leaving Harmony. "For goodness' sake," she'd quip. "Why spend all that time on something when it's right there on the shelf?"

Of course, there were lots of things on grocery shelves she could have substituted for homemade—but bread was the only thing she ever skimped on. Papa Joe explained it to me once, after he made me promise not to tell Mama. Seems that when she was a girl, her mother had been especially hard on her when it came to bread making. In fact, she'd informed her daughter that if she couldn't bake a good loaf of bread, no man would ever marry her. And no matter how hard she tried, Essie's bread-making skills stayed woefully inadequate.

Then she met the handsome Joe Temple who didn't seem to know that rule. If she couldn't even find the oven, he didn't care. He told me he fell in love with the beautiful Mennonite girl with the reddish gold hair and flashing green eyes the first minute he laid eyes on her. Thankfully, my great-grandparents approved the union. Although marriages weren't actually arranged in their community, they had to be agreed upon by the parents. Joe and Essie weren't allowed to date, but they were allowed to attend church functions together and to sit next to each other at supper when the two families would meet for fellowship. Essie, on the other hand, wasn't completely sure about Joe. She'd laugh when telling the story about how one day she watched him pick up a baby bird that had fallen out of its nest. He climbed the tree with one hand while holding the bird in the other, and carefully put it back where it belonged. Joe had no idea that he'd been seen by anyone—and he never mentioned it. Yet he would stop by that tree frequently to check on the little bird's progress. Essie figured that if he could care that much about a baby bird, he would care even more for her. She was right.

Emily's voice startled me out of the past and brought me back to the present.

"This shade is perfect for your coloring. Perhaps you'd allow me to make a dress just for you?"

"Oh, my," I said quickly. "I—I can't allow you to go to all that trouble. I'll just buy the one in the store."

Emily's eyes ran up and down my body. "Nonsense. That dress is for someone larger than you. It won't fit right." She gave me a sincere smile. "It isn't any trouble, really. Sewing makes me happy. Please allow me to do it."

I swallowed the lump that tried to form in my throat. Here I'd been planning to use this woman for information, and all she wanted to do was to bless me.

"I would absolutely love it, Emily. I don't know how to thank you."

"No thanks are necessary. If you have time before you leave, I'll take some measurements and we'll talk about how the dress should look. I know our styles aren't very hip."

Abel burst out laughing. "Did you just use the word *hip?* And where did you learn that word, my dear?"

"Well, goodness gracious, Abel," Emily sniffed as she closed the trunk and rose to her feet, "we don't live in a barn. I *do* know a little bit about the world."

Abel's hearty chuckle filled the room. I looked over at Hannah who grinned at her parents' antics.

"I'm sure you do," Abel said with a broad smile. "I'm just

trying to imagine the conversation you had where this word was used." He stroked his beard and gazed at the ceiling. "I know. Perhaps it came from the widow Jacobs. She probably showed you her new support stockings. Or was it eighty-year-old Fred Olsen commenting on his newest pair of 'hip' overalls?" He sighed dramatically. "It's so hard to figure out. There are so many hip people in Harmony."

Emily lifted her flushed face toward her husband as the rest of us laughed. "You're very, very funny—you know that? Actually, it was one of the children in my Sunday school class. They told me I was a 'hip' teacher. Now what do you think of that?"

Abel leaned down and kissed the top of his wife's head. "I think they're absolutely right," he said gently. "You're the hippest person I know."

Emily turned on her heel while mumbling something about taking the material she held into the bedroom, but I could see the smile on her face as she left the room.

Still chuckling, Abel encouraged us to eat our cobbler while it was warm. The crunchy topping was perfect for the warm peaches dusted with cinnamon. The ice cream tasted homemade. It had a rich, creamy goodness that store-bought ice cream couldn't begin to match. Sam and I finished our desserts, and Hannah took our bowls and refilled the coffee cups. A sense of peace settled all around me, and I realized I was really enjoying my time in the Mueller's house. However, a glance at the clock on the wall reminded me that I really needed to call my parents. I'd originally planned to call them from Sam's, but it was later than I'd suspected. I was afraid they might be worried. I asked Abel if I could use his phone, and he led me to a small alcove at the end of the hallway where a built-in shelf held their telephone. I got my calling card out of my purse and dialed the necessary numbers to have the charges billed to my home phone. After a couple of rings, my father's deep voice boomed through the receiver.

"Hello?"

"Hey, Dad! It's me."

"Snicklefritz! It's about time. We've been concerned about you."

"I know. Sorry, Dad. Benjamin's place doesn't have a phone. I knew you'd be wondering about me—even if it's only been two days."

His warm laugh drifted through the phone. "I know it doesn't seem long to you, honey. But to parents, two days feels like an eternity. Now tell me what's happened so far. How do you like Harmony? Who have you met? Are people being nice to you?"

"Whoa. Too many questions. Why don't I just start from the beginning?" I told him about my arrival in his old hometown, but of course I left out the most important things: the letter, the theft, and the fact that I wasn't staying in Benjamin's house. My father seemed most interested in the people in Harmony. If I mentioned someone he knew, he'd stop me and ask about them. He knew Emily and wondered how she was. When I told him she was married to the pastor who'd called him about Benjamin's death and that they had a daughter, he seemed very pleased. He was interested to hear that I'd met Levi Hoffman but even more excited that I planned to spend some time with Ida Turnbauer.

"Ida and your grandmother were such close friends," he said. "I always liked her. An honest woman and a wonderful Christian. She encouraged your mother and me when we told her we were leaving Harmony. One of the few people who did. Please tell her we said hello."

"I will," I promised. "She certainly was shocked to find out that Grandma had passed away. Uncle Benjamin didn't tell her."

"I wanted to contact Ida when Mama died, but Papa said no. He still had some resentment toward a few folks in Harmony. I guess Mama tried to explain their leaving to Ida, but she wouldn't listen. That church. . ."

"Actually, it wasn't the church, Dad." I proceeded to explain the situation to him.

"Goodness," he said after taking a deep breath I could hear clearly through the receiver. "I guess I blamed everything on the church. Perhaps that wasn't completely fair."

"I'm finding out that most of the bad things that went on here came from Amil Angstadt. A lot of people disagreed with him, just like you and Mom."

"Well, more of them should have stood up to him. That man caused a lot of grief and confusion." I recognized the sharp tone in his voice. It meant *this discussion is off-limits. Move on to something else.* Life in Harmony had certainly left my father with some unresolved feelings.

I changed the subject and started telling him about Benjamin's house and the things I'd found there. I debated telling him about his old room, but when he asked about it, I knew I couldn't lie.

"He left it like it was when I moved away?" He repeated his sentence twice as if he couldn't believe what he was hearing. "I—I don't understand."

"I don't either, Dad. Maybe it's best not to try to figure it out. I—I mean, at least he kept all your things. M—maybe that means something."

With everything that had happened, I was certain Uncle Benjamin had truly loved my father, even if his decisions made it look otherwise. But my main proof was contained in the missing letter, and I couldn't tell my father anything about that yet. I could only pray that someday, when the truth came out, Dad would know that his brother cared deeply for him. After sharing with him that there seemed to be interest in the house and land, I informed him that we'd need a moving truck to cart all the family heirlooms to Nebraska.

"That's not a problem. I'll rent some storage, and we can put everything there until we decide what to do with it. When do you want me schedule the truck?"

I named the last Saturday before the Monday I was supposed to be back to work.

"Can't you put the sale of the house in someone else's hands and leave sooner? Maybe you could come here for a few days before heading back to Wichita. Mom and I miss you."

"I miss you, too, Dad. I'll visit you guys the first free weekend I have after I go home. I promise. But I really think I need to spend the next two weeks here. There's a lot to do, and besides, I really like Harmony. Since I'll probably never be back, I'd like to hang around as long as I can."

The silence on the other end of the phone told me that my father was having a hard time accepting my sentiments about a place he still held in a negative light.

"It's really different now," I continued. "The people are very nice, and the pastor isn't anything like Angstadt. He's more like Pastor Buchannan at your church."

"Well, I must admit that even though we only spoke briefly, Pastor Mueller seemed like a very nice man. I–I'm glad things are going well for you there. I'll have to take your word about the positive changes in Harmony. If you say things are different. . ."

"I do."

I promised my father I'd call him again in a couple of days. Now that I was at Sam's, it would be much easier to contact him. However, not telling him the truth about where I was really staying made me feel a little guilty. It suddenly hit me that I'd only been in Harmony a couple of days and I was already collecting secrets of my own.

I started to say good-bye when I decided to take the plunge and ask him the question I really wanted to. I prayed it wouldn't make him suspicious.

"By the way, Dad," I said as casually as I could, "do you remember a man named Jacob Glick?"

154

The deep intake of breath from my father was matched in stereo from behind me. I whirled around to see Emily Mueller standing a few feet down the hall, the same look of terror on her face that I'd seen at the diner. I told my dad I had to hang up, and I'd call him back. I didn't hear any response, but I knew I had to speak to Emily right away. I quickly put the phone down. I'd have to square things with my father later.

"Emily," I said in a low voice, "I need to know about this Glick person. I can't tell you why, but it's very important. Please, please, tell me the truth. Why does he frighten you so much?"

She lifted a trembling hand to her face and pushed back a stray strand of hair that had escaped from her bun. We studied each other for several moments before she spoke in a sharp whisper. "I don't understand why you feel the need to dredge up Jacob Glick. Why can't you just leave the past buried? It won't do anyone any good to talk about him."

My mouth almost dropped open at the use of the word "buried." "Listen Emily, as I said, I can't tell you why I need to know about him. But it's very important. People's lives could be adversely affected if I don't find out the truth." I frowned at her and took a step closer. "If you know anything. . .please, please, help me. I promise it will stay between us. You have my word." Even as I gave her my promise, I wondered if I'd be able to keep it. Eventually the truth about Glick was going to come out. Keeping Emily insulated from the fallout might be impossible.

I could actually see her internal struggle play out on her face. Finally, she grabbed my arm and started pulling me toward a door in the hallway.

"I'm taking some measurements for Gracie's dress," she called out loudly enough for her husband to hear. "Stay out of the bedroom."

"All right, dear," Abel yelled back. "I'm going to take Sam outside to see the garden. Hannah's with us."

Emily waited until we heard the door to the porch slam shut. Then she opened the bedroom door and guided me inside. It was a lovely room with lace curtains and dark mahogany furniture. A homemade spread covered the bed. Emily sat down on top of it, still clutching the material for my dress. She pointed to a spot next to her. I took a seat, curious yet almost apprehensive about what she was getting ready to share.

"Growing up in a Mennonite home was wonderful," she said slowly, measuring her words carefully. "We had no distractions like television or video games. We just had each other. I played with my brothers and sisters all the time—and we knew each other. I mean, really knew each other. And I read. A lot. I especially loved the classics. Dickens was a favorite. And *Little Women*. But then Amil Angstadt came to Harmony." Her eyes shone with tears. "Everything changed. I lost all my books. We were only allowed to read the Bible and certain religious books approved by the church. Children were supposed to work—to be productive. Playing was discouraged. It was worse on the girls. Bishop Angstadt made us feel that unless we were being prepared for marriage, we were useless. And he insisted that all engagements come through him for approval. I cared deeply for one young man, but the bishop forbade me to see him. It broke my heart to tell this man we couldn't marry." She sighed and wiped away a tear that slid down her cheek.

"Why didn't someone stand up against Angstadt?"

She shook her head. "Mennonites are taught to be respectful and submissive to authority. Many of the adults were confused. They were torn between their responsibility to the church and their concerns about what was happening. Some people did leave. Like your parents. Others met secretly, trying to find a way to change things, but they were faced with resistance by certain members who felt they were trying to personally attack Bishop Angstadt." She sighed so deeply her body trembled. "It was a

156

terrible time for everyone."

"I–I'm sorry you had to go through that," I said gently. "But what does this have to do with Jacob Glick?"

"I swore I would never mention that man's name again." Her voice shook with emotion.

I held my breath and waited for her to continue. I could see my questions were causing her distress. After reading my uncle's letter and remembering something Abel had said at dinner, I had a pretty good idea what she was getting ready to tell me. On the one hand, I wanted to hear it. On the other hand, I dreaded the words I feared were coming, but I couldn't do anything to stop her. I had to know the truth. This was too important to me—and to my father. Finally, she took a deep shuddering breath and looked into my eyes. The raw pain I saw in her face shook me.

"Jacob was hired to do maintenance work around the church. Although he wasn't actually a member, he was almost like the bishop's second in command. Anyone wanting to see Bishop Angstadt had to get through Jacob first. He was always at the church. He even lived in the basement." She cleared her throat and stared at the material in her hands for a few moments. When she looked up, her face was pale—almost ghostly white. "No one else knows what I am about to tell you. I vowed I would never say anything, but I'm afraid you're going to keep digging until it comes up in a way I—I can't control."

I put my hand over hers. "Emily, please understand that unless it was absolutely necessary, I wouldn't put you through this. Glick may be involved in something that could seriously hurt my family unless I find out everything there is to know about him. I realize it seems unfair to ask you to tell me your secrets when I can't tell you mine, but if you could only trust me a little."

She smiled slightly and nodded her head. "I hope I can, Gracie. Because what I'm about to tell you could damage my family, as well."

Once again, something rose up inside me that wanted to stop her. To stop this entire thing. To go home and forget that Harmony, Kansas, existed. But somehow I knew that the secrets buried in Harmony were meant to come out. That the truth would set people free. Something Abel had said at dinner floated through my mind. *But sometimes people try to bury things they haven't dealt with. And when that happens, the past won't stay silent. It manifests in other ways—interfering with your life and not allowing you to move forward.* I suspected this was true for Emily. Maybe today would be the day she would take a step forward from her past. I prayed it was true.

I squeezed her hand. "I understand. Please..."

She grabbed my hand back with such force I almost yelped in pain.

"I—I was only seventeen. My—my mother sent me to the church to pick up some hymnals that were torn and needed mending." Her voice trembled and tears fell down her cheeks. "J—Jacob was there. He—he told me the hymnals were in the basement. I—I followed him down there."

She took a breath and held it. Without realizing it at first, I held mine, too. Even before she spoke, I knew what was coming. Then in a rush of words she said "When I got down there, he led me to a room—his room. And then he..."

I put my fingers on her lips to stop her. Neither one of us needed to hear the rest. I opened my arms, and she leaned against me and sobbed as if her heart would break. After several minutes, she gently pushed me away.

"After it happened," she said haltingly, "I ran to a special spot near the lake. I liked to go there sometimes to think...you know, to be alone."

I could only nod, afraid to trust my voice at that moment.

"I sat there for a long time, looking at the water, wondering what to do. Finally, I got up and went home. I made the decision to never tell anyone." She sighed. "You see, I was afraid. Afraid of what people would think about me. Afraid that my parents wouldn't love me anymore. Afraid Jacob would tell lies about what happened." She shook her head. "I couldn't stand that." She patted her prayer covering with trembling fingers. "I never went back to my favorite spot again. It always reminded me of. . . of. . ." Emily straightened her back and stared at me with a frank expression. "I'm certain I'm not the only one Jacob molested— or tried to molest. There were complaints, but Bishop Angstadt always protected him."

"The picture in the dining room. That's you, isn't it?"

She nodded slowly. "I loved to paint when I was a girl, but it was frowned upon in our community. I painted that picture at school after the. . .incident. When the year was out, I snuck it home and hid it in our attic. I should have thrown it away, but for some reason I didn't. I brought it with me when Abel and I married. Even though I hid it, he found it and insisted we hang it in the dining room. He said he was proud of my talent. I couldn't tell—tell him. . ." She wiped her wet face. "I don't know why I kept it in the first place. Maybe because it was the last thing I ever painted. I don't know. It was a stupid thing to do."

"So Abel has no idea what it represents?" I couldn't keep the incredulity out of my voice. "You've kept it to yourself all these years?"

Emily grasped my arm with her small fingers. "Yes. I hate that painting. Every day it mocks me. Reminds me of what Jacob took from me." Her fingers tightened on my skin. "I've wanted to say something—to tell Abel the truth, but I couldn't. Not in all these years. If only I'd told someone what happened after Jacob. . .um, left, but I was still too ashamed. And afraid. Of course, the longer I waited, the harder it became to confess. Now, I just want the whole thing to go away."

"But like your husband said, these kinds of situations don't just fade away by themselves." I tried to keep my voice soft and nonthreatening, but there was a sense of fury building inside me. Against Glick and men like him. And against toxic secrets that people hide inside themselves, ruining their lives. Was the church to blame for some of this? Are we too afraid to be honest with each other?

As if reading my mind, Emily said, "Please don't blame anyone in the church—except Bishop Angstadt. There were many people who cared about me. I alone made the decision to keep this secret. No one forced me to." Another deep sigh escaped through her lips and shook her thin body. "I realize now that I could have told my parents. They would have believed me. And they would have done something. Maybe the truth would have even stopped Jacob from hurting another young woman. I live every day with the guilt of my decision and wonder how much damage my cowardice caused."

"This secret has been kept too long, Emily," I said matter-of-factly.

She smoothed her hand over the apple-green cloth in her lap. "It's too late now, Gracie. I will not allow Abel and Hannah to be hurt by something that happened so long ago."

"But don't you realize that Abel already suspects there is something you haven't told him? Didn't you understand that his admonition about buried secrets was directed at you?"

Her head shot up and she stared at me with wide eyes. "No. He's never said anything. . ."

"Look, I'm not married, but I've watched my mom and dad through the years. They know instinctively when something is bothering the other one. It's a kind of radar."

"You know," she said in a dreamy voice, "after what happened, I made up my mind that I would never marry. The young man I told you about earlier begged me to marry him after Bishop Angstadt died, but I turned him away. I was convinced no man

160

would ever want me—and I would never want another man. But then Abel came to Harmony. There was something about him. He brought out feelings in me I'd never had before. It—it was as if we were meant to be together. Although I rebuffed him at first, I finally realized I couldn't live without him."

"Oh Emily," I said with a smile. "I've only known your husband a short time, but if I've ever met anyone you could talk to about something like this, it would be Abel. Don't you know that about him?"

She was silent for a few moments. Then she nodded. "Yes. Yes, he probably is. But I just can't ruin his image of me." She turned her head and stared at me, her eyes wide and shiny. "I lost myself a long time ago, Gracie. The only time I feel real is when I see myself through Abel's eyes. If you take that away from me, I'm afraid I won't exist anymore."

"But don't you know that when God sees you, He only sees His dear and precious daughter? Isn't the reflection we see in His eyes the true image of who we really are?"

She smiled sadly and patted my hand. "I know in my heart that what you say is true. But my mind is still full of shame and sorrow. I will not allow Jacob Glick to spread his hateful venom to Abel and Hannah. I will not."

She spoke the last three words carefully and with absolute conviction. I had no response. She obviously blamed herself somehow for the awful thing Glick had done. She needed help—some kind of intervention. But I wasn't the one to provide it. She needed her husband's support and counsel. Suddenly, something else she'd said popped into my head.

"You said you were still afraid—even after Glick left town. That doesn't make sense. If he was gone, why would you still be afraid of him? He couldn't hurt you anymore."

Emily pushed her hair back again, tucking it under her cap. She straightened her back and closed her eyes. In a voice so soft

I could barely hear her, she said, "That's easy to answer. There was a new evil in Harmony. Something we'd never experienced before. I could feel a dark cloud hanging over the town. Our first murder. Our first murderer. I had no way of knowing if Jacob Glick would be the only victim."

Chapter Twelve

I sat silently on the bed while Emily got up and looked out the window. "Abel is showing off his roses," she said in a monotone. "He's so proud of them."

I finally overcame my shock enough to speak. "Emily. . .you know that Jacob Glick is dead?"

She came over and stood in front of me, her hands folded tightly together as if she didn't know what to do with them. "I didn't see him die, nor have I ever heard anyone else admit it."

"Th–then how. . ."

She sighed, picked up the material for my dress, and sat down next to me. "I really do need to take some measurements. You look to be about Hannah's size. Of course, you're much more womanly than she is."

I grabbed her arm. "Emily, how do you know Jacob Glick is dead?"

She smiled sadly. "A few days before he. . .disappeared, I overheard him talking to Bishop Angstadt. They were in the hardware store, looking for new door latches. I was in the next aisle. Mama needed a pot to replace the one I'd accidentally scorched, and I'd found some on the bottom shelf. I was crouched

163

down, looking them over. That's why they didn't see me."

"What does this have to do with Glick's death?"

She reached over and patted my hand. "Don't worry, Gracie. I'm getting there." She smoothed the dress material with her hand. "Jacob knew something about the bishop—something he wanted to keep quiet. I'm certain it's the reason Jacob was free to do almost anything he wanted without fear of retribution. It's also why I was afraid Bishop Angstadt wouldn't help me if I went to him about what Jacob did to me." She shook her head. "I have no idea what it was. Neither one of them mentioned details. They simply referred to it as the bishop's 'secret.' Bishop Angstadt was clearly frightened. When Jacob demanded that he find him a wife, the bishop mentioned three women he might be able to deliver as marriage candidates, because he believed he had some kind of influence over them or their families."

"Who were they?"

"Kendra McBroom, the daughter of one of the church's elders. Her parents thought the sun rose and set on Bishop Angstadt."

"Who else?

An odd look crossed her face. "Are you sure you want to know?"

"Yes. Tell me, please. It's important."

"Beverly Fischer."

She said the name so matter-of-factly, for a moment it didn't register. "My—my mother?"

She nodded.

I felt my throat go dry. This wasn't welcome news. It gave my father a motive for murder. If he'd found out that Angstadt planned to auction off the woman he loved to a lowlife like Glick, he would have gone ballistic. At least now I knew what their fight was about. Then something occurred to me. "My grandparents would never have allowed it."

She shrugged. "Bishop Angstadt acted as if he could convince them. Of course, he might have simply been trying to placate Jacob. I don't know."

I almost laughed. At one time, Marvin Fischer may have allowed the bishop too much influence into his life. But if he'd tried to touch his daughter, Angstadt would have seen another side to my grandfather. When his family was threatened, Grandpa Fischer was like a pit bull with a bad attitude. "You said there were three women?"

"Yes. The last was a young woman who was trying to run her family's farm single-handedly. Her mother was dead and her father an invalid. Even though several people in the community had tried to help her, no one believed she could possibly succeed. Bishop Angstadt thought she would marry Jacob if she were offered enough cash to help run the farm and pay for an operation that might restore her father's health. Jacob seemed pretty happy about that idea. I think he was interested in this young woman above the others. He insisted that the bishop approach her. Of course, this meant the bishop would be out a great deal of money. I'm sure the prospect didn't appeal to him."

"But where would Angstadt get that much money? I can't imagine a Mennonite minister being paid enough to handle something like that."

Emily shrugged. "There were a lot of things about the bishop that didn't make sense. I overheard my father telling my mother that some property had been signed over to the church when someone in the community died. The proceeds were supposed to go to restoring the church building. But as far as I know, it never turned up. It's possible Bishop Angstadt intended to use that money for Jacob's bride. It's also possible that's what Jacob had on him. But that's only conjecture. Gossip wasn't acceptable in our community—especially when it was about our leadership." She took a deep breath and let it out slowly. "I don't believe in gossip either, but if there had been more honesty in the church, a lot of bad things might have been averted."

I nodded my agreement, but my mind was still working on Angstadt's agreement with Glick. Actually, blackmail gave the old Mennonite bishop a pretty good reason for wanting Glick dead. Although I had my doubts that Angstadt would go that far beyond his faith, I began to understand that my father was only part of a long list of people who'd wanted Jacob Glick removed from their lives. A thought struck me that made me go cold inside. "Emily, who was the third woman?" Even though I knew the answer before she said it, I was still shocked when she spoke the name out loud.

"Myrtle Goodrich. Sam's aunt."

I stared at her while I tried to sort this information out in my mind. Sweetie? Had Angstadt actually approached her? Was Sweetie involved in his death? I had to shelve these thoughts for now. I couldn't deal with them and concentrate on my final questions for Emily.

"Let's get back to how you know Glick is dead," I said.

She shrugged, her face expressionless. "I wasn't absolutely certain until today. But I suspected it because Jacob had Bishop Angstadt in his pocket and the bishop was preparing to give him the one thing he wanted more than anything in the world. There's no way he'd leave Harmony right before his dreams of companionship came true." She sighed and shook her head. "So many people hated Jacob. It didn't take much to figure out he'd finally been dealt with. After a few months, I began to believe that whoever killed him had no intention of hurting anyone else. They'd killed Jacob for a reason, and now that he was gone, they had no need to hurt anyone else. I was very young, and the idea of one human being murdering another was very frightening. I guess my fear came from the suspicion that a murderer lived in Harmony." She shivered involuntarily. "It still bothers me. It's like finding a spot on your favorite dress that won't come out.

Eventually you learn to live with it, but you don't like it. Harmony is...well, it's not a place where murder...belongs." She frowned at me. "Does that make sense?"

I nodded. "Actually, I think I understand exactly what you mean."

The sound of voices drifted down the hall. Emily paled. "Stand up and let me measure you."

I stood to my feet while she took a tape measure out of her pocket. She held it up to my neck and measured to the end of my shoulder. Then she wrote the figure down on a small pad of paper on the dresser. Next she wrapped the tape around my chest.

"Emily, did you ever tell anyone about your suspicions?"

Her eyes flew toward the bedroom door. "Shhh. No, never. After Jacob disappeared I felt nothing but intense relief. Not just for me, but for any other girl he might have hurt. I decided to leave well enough alone."

After writing down my chest measurements, she measured from my shoulder to my bustline and then from my shoulder to my waist. While she worked, I thought about the information she'd given me. I wasn't sure how much it helped, but at least it had opened up some new possibilities. Emily tugged on the tape measure she'd wrapped around my waist.

"Thank you for being honest with me," I said. "Hopefully, it will lead me to the truth."

She pulled the measuring tape to just below my knee, and then she stood up and stared at me, her features tight with emotion. "What I told you today is in confidence, Gracie. If at all possible, you must keep it to yourself."

"Sam is aware of the situation, and I trust him, Emily. What you overheard between Glick and Angstadt is very important and could help us immensely. I need to tell him about that, but I won't reveal anything personal about your...situation. Can you accept that?"

She studied my face for a moment. "I—I suppose so." She grabbed my arm. "But if at some point you feel you must bring me into whatever you're doing, will you come to me first? My husband deserves to know the truth before anyone else in Harmony."

I reached out and took her hands in mine. "Okay, but I sure wish he'd heard this from you before I did. Please—please, consider telling him everything you shared with me. I suspect keeping these secrets has cost you dearly. Isn't it time Jacob Glick stopped interfering in your life?"

A small groan rose from somewhere deep inside her. "I understand what you're saying, Gracie. I really do. But I'm so afraid. I love my life. What if the truth ruins it?"

"Jesus said that the truth would set you free, didn't He?"

"Yes. Maybe you're right, I don't know. But it must be my decision." She carefully put the tape measure back in her pocket and picked up the pad of paper, which she placed on top of the material. "I'll begin working on your dress tomorrow. It will be so pretty with your lovely auburn hair."

"Thank you." I turned to open the bedroom door. "Everyone will be wondering what happened to us."

"Wait a minute," she said. I stopped with my hand on the doorknob. "I've told you what you wanted to know. Are you going to tell me why it's so important to you? And how you've discovered that Jacob Glick is dead?"

I hesitated. "Not yet. But as soon as I can. . ."

"It's okay," she said, wrapping her arms around herself in a hug. "Believe me, I know what it's like to be forced to keep secrets."

The sorrow on her face touched me. "Why don't we pray that God will bring us both to a place of freedom, Emily? A place where we won't have to keep secrets anymore."

She hugged herself a little tighter. "I've lived with this so long. . ."

"Too long, I think." I took a deep breath and pushed the door open. "Ready?"

She nodded. "Thank you, Gracie. Telling you helped a little bit, I think. Even though I didn't want to."

I fixed a smile on my face and followed her down the hall to the sun porch. Abel, Hannah, and Sam were laughing at something Abel had said. Obviously their conversation was more lighthearted than the one Emily and I had just shared.

"Well, there you are!" Abel bellowed. "I was just telling Sam about the time Mabel Samuelson brought her sweet plum pudding to the church dinner but accidentally used salt in her recipe instead of sugar." He wiped a tear of laughter from his eye. "No one said a word because they didn't want to hurt her feelings. Until Teresa Harker's boy, Jonathon, spit his out on the table and said the pudding 'sucked big-time.' " Abel chuckled. "You remember that, Emily? Mabel was so embarrassed, but everyone at the table started laughing and it turned out to be one of the best church dinners we ever had."

Emily smiled at her husband. "Yes, I do remember. I also remember that Mabel's older son, Michael, had to do extra chores for teaching Jonathon that phrase."

Sam grinned at me. "What took you two so long? Abel and I were beginning to think you'd come out of there with your dress already made."

"Oh, you know. Girl talk." I looked at the clock on the wall. It was already after three. "Are you about ready to go?"

Sam stood up. "Well, if we don't get out of here soon, I'll probably fall asleep."

Abel snorted. "Are we really that boring?"

"That's not the problem," he said. "My stomach is so busy digesting Emily's fantastic food, the rest of my body is almost useless."

"I'm glad you enjoyed it," Emily said. "You and Gracie will

have to come back soon. We love having you here."

I turned around and gave her a hug. "We will. Thank you so much for your hospitality." Emily clung to me for several seconds. When we broke apart, there were tears in her eyes. I felt a deep connection to her and a desire to help her rid herself of the demons from her past. My dislike for Jacob Glick had grown to a smoldering fire. No one had the right to take his life, but something inside me couldn't mourn for him.

Abel and Emily escorted us to the front door with Hannah bringing up the rear. After saying our last good-byes, as Sam and I walked to his truck, the front door of the small yellow house swung open, and Hannah came running out, calling my name. I stopped to wait for her.

"I—I just wondered if sometime we could paint together or do something. . ." The words tumbled out so quickly I really had to concentrate to understand her. Her china blue eyes were wide and her cheeks flushed a delicate pink. Such a beautiful child. For a moment, I saw Emily in her. Was this how she looked when Glick violated her? My heart ached at the thought.

"Of course," I said, trying to keep my voice steady. "I'd love it. Maybe one afternoon this week? After school?"

Hannah nodded enthusiastically, and a smile erupted on her face that only added to her loveliness. "That would be wonderful. Will you call me?"

I barely got out the word "Absolutely" before she wrapped her arms around me.

"Oh, thank you, Gracie. I can hardly wait." With that she turned and ran back to the house, her pale blue skirt flapping around her long legs. She turned once to wave at us before closing the front door behind her.

"Hannah hasn't had anyone in her life who could help her with her art," Sam said. "Ida told me Emily was a pretty good artist as a young girl, but she gave it up. Lost interest in it, I guess. Seems strange to me—with a daughter like that." He shrugged. "But what do I know? I'm just a man. I don't pretend to understand women."

I swallowed the lump that rose in my throat and tossed him a sideways smile. "We're not that hard to figure out. We're just like you—only smart."

He swung the truck door open for me. "Funny. If you all are so smart, why do you hang around us?"

I climbed into the seat, holding my skirt. "Because God took one look at Adam and said, 'Wow. This guy's going to need all the help he can get.' And here we are."

He raised one eyebrow and cocked his head sideways. "I don't remember those words from the Bible."

"I'm paraphrasing, but that's exactly what He meant."

Sam laughed and closed the truck door. Then he got in and started the motor. "Did you talk to your dad?"

I slapped my forehead. "Oh man. I hung up on him. I need to call him back."

"It will only take a few minutes to get to my place. You can call him from there."

I nodded and stared out the car window. As Sam backed up, I noticed a car parked in front of a detached garage near the back of the property. "Is that Abel's car?"

"Yes. You're wondering why all the chrome is painted black?"

I nodded. "I noticed a few cars like that when I came into town. My father mentioned something once about Mennonites who still affiliated themselves with the old ways but felt cars were a necessity in today's world. They paint their bumpers dark so their cars won't look too 'flashy.' He called them 'black bumper' Mennonites. I just assumed Abel was more progressive than that."

"Harmony is a town full of all kinds of people, Grace. You've seen that. Old Order, modern Mennonites, conservative

Mennonites, non-Mennonites—even some folks who don't go to any church at all. Yet for the most part, everyone gets along. They care about their neighbors." He backed out of the driveway and pointed the truck toward Main Street. Then he stopped and turned toward me. "This is a special place, you know? It's not perfect, but there's something. . .unusual here. As cliché as it sounds, I feel like I found myself in Harmony." He grinned. "I know. I sound like a throwback from the sixties."

"Well, kind of."

He laughed. "Get ready to think I've really gone over the edge, but here goes. Ida Turnbauer told me that after Angstadt died, a bunch of the women got together and prayed that God would protect Harmony from the kind of divisive spirit that ruled this town during his reign. That God would bless this town with peace and make it a special place where people truly feel at home and treat each other like family. She believes He answered that prayer."

"Maybe you need to talk to Mary and John Keystone. I don't think they've heard this story."

"I didn't say people can't get angry and upset. I just said it won't rule. We've had our share of spats and problems, but I've been here since I was a kid, and I've never seen them go unresolved. Eventually peace comes." He put the truck in gear and started down the dirt road.

"Well, that's very interesting, but what does that have to do with Abel's painted bumpers?"

"Oh yeah. Almost forgot. Well, Abel painted his bumpers black as a way to bridge the gap between the modern Mennonites and the few Old Order folks who live here. He saw it as a compromise. Abel cares more about not offending someone than he does about how good his car looks. I think it's a great example of humility, and it goes a long way toward keeping the spirit of peace alive in Harmony."

I smiled broadly at him. "Oh, now I understand your truck. You're trying to be the humblest, most peaceful person in Harmony."

He burst out laughing. "Oh man. You're brutal." His hands caressed the old, cracked steering wheel. "Actually, I just like this truck. We're comfortable together. I realize it's an eyesore, but I don't care. I'll trade her in one of these days." He reached out the window and adjusted the side mirror. "You know, I used to own Levi's Suburban. His old station wagon broke down, and he needed transportation. He asked about this truck, thinking I might be willing to sell it since I had two vehicles. But I just couldn't let it go so I sold him the Suburban instead."

"You chose this truck over that nice Suburban?"

"Yep. I sure did." He winked at me. "Now don't tell me you're ashamed to be seen in this fine vintage vehicle."

"Heavens no. I drive a Volkswagen. That proves I have no ego whatsoever."

We both laughed. As Sam's truck shook and jiggled down the uneven road, I gazed out the window at the passing houses. Families were out in their yards playing together. Happy dogs ran around with toys in their mouths while being chased by children who screamed with delight. Old people sat in rocking chairs on their front porches, watching their antics while mothers and fathers cleaned their yards and prepared barbeque grills for dinner. Sam was right. There *was* something about Harmony. Something I'd never felt before—even in Fairbury. Sometimes I had the strangest sense that I'd been here before—that I knew this place. It was a passing feeling—one that came and went so quickly it was almost like a quick flash of lightning. I suppose it was seeing Mama and Papa's house—talking to people who knew my family. Whatever it was, the sensation left me feeling slightly unsettled.

My mind drifted back to Emily and my discussion with her. What was I going to do about her revelations? What should I tell

Sam? I'd promised Emily I'd do my best to keep her secret, yet I didn't want to lie to Sam. I settled on a compromise.

"Sam, do you trust me?" I asked more sharply than I meant to.

He frowned at me. "Yes. Why?"

"Emily told me some things I think will help us find the truth about what happened to Glick, but I can't tell you all of it. Some of it is very private—to Emily. Will you respect that and not push me for information I can't share?"

"I suppose so. If that's what you need me to do."

"Thank you." I began to recount the conversation Emily overheard as a child, leaving out her past involvement with Glick. I hesitated before actually naming names.

"I guess we need to find out just what Glick had on the good old bishop," Sam said. "We also need to uncover the names of the three women being dangled as bait."

"I—I know who they were."

Sam glanced over at me. "So tell me."

"A woman named Kendra McBroom."

He nodded as he turned onto Main Street. "Kendra married a man over in Clay County. I don't remember his name, but she has a sister who still lives here."

"Sam, my mother was one of the women."

He didn't reply, but he slowed down and pulled over to the side of the road. We were parked right in front of Levi's candle shop. All the shops on Main were closed except for the café.

"Your mother?" His voice quivered with surprise. He stared through the windshield at the almost empty street. "That could explain the fight your father had with Glick. If he'd found out about it. . ."

"But how?"

A look of confusion crossed his face. "What if Angstadt went to your grandparents and told them he wanted their daughter for Glick?"

"I don't think so. First of all, my grandparents would never have agreed to it. They fully supported my parents' relationship. Besides, I'm pretty sure Glick had someone else at the front of the line. I'd think if Angstadt had approached anyone, it would have been her."

"You mean Kendra?"

I shook my head slowly and stared at the dashboard. "No. From what Emily told me, Glick favored one woman over the rest."

Sam waited silently. Even before I could get my next words out, his eyes grew wide. "It's not. . .not. . ."

I put my hand on his. "It's Sweetie, Sam."

His face hardened. "I don't believe it."

"Look, it's hard for me to accept, too." I didn't tell him that I couldn't see Sweetie as a romantic figure. She must have changed a great deal over the years.

"Tell me everything Emily said about my aunt," he said, his voice hot with anger.

"Emily said Sweetie was trying to run the family farm by herself and that her father was disabled. Angstadt mentioned some operation that might help him—but that Sweetie couldn't afford it. He believed that if he offered her enough money to save the farm and pay for her father's surgery, she might agree to marry Glick."

Sam focused an icy stare out the window. "That's true about the operation. My grandfather's broken bones weren't set correctly. He developed a pressure ulcer that restricted his blood flow, and he died. If he'd had surgery to put those bones where they belonged, his life might have been spared."

"That's awful Sam. I can't imagine what your aunt went through. I'm so sorry. I hate the thought of dragging her into this situation and making her relive what must be the most painful time of her life."

His hands gripped the steering wheel so tightly his knuckles turned white. Finally, he released his hold. "There's nothing for you to be sorry about. You didn't cause this situation. Besides, now we really are in this together. You don't have to fight this battle alone."

I smiled at him. "I was never alone. God has been with me from the beginning. But even before the moment I told you about the letter, I believed He sent you to help me. After I told you the truth, I *knew* He had."

Sam turned in his seat and pulled my face to his. His kiss was gentle but determined. Before I realized it, my arms were wrapped around his neck and we were locked in a tight embrace. When his lips left mine, I looked into his eyes and almost gasped at the raw emotion I saw there. I pulled back and straightened up in my seat.

He scooted back behind the steering wheel. "I—I keep apologizing to you. I don't know what came over me. I shouldn't have...I mean..."

"It's okay." I felt something bold rise up inside of me. "I wanted you to kiss me, Sam. It's not just you."

He ran a trembling hand through his hair. "Look, I know we've only known each other a few days..."

"Two days," I interjected. "Two short days."

"Well, they don't feel short to me. I feel like I've known you all my life."

The sincerity in his voice made my breath quicken. I gazed into his eyes. I had to fight to slow my breathing and catch my breath. What was happening to me? I'd never felt anything like this before. "I–I'm not sure if I can concentrate on this situation with my uncle if I'm thinking about you all the time. Can we agree to put our feelings on hold until we find a way out of this dilemma? My dad's future hangs in the balance."

Sam's eyes ran over my face as if he were trying to memorize it. "Yes. Of course." His voice was low and husky. He ran his finger down the side of my face. "But once we figure this thing out. . ."

I smiled. "We'll talk."

Sam started the truck. As we pulled out in the street, I noticed someone near the entrance of the café staring at us.

Mary Whittenbauer stood with her arms folded, her expression full of naked anger. If looks could kill, I'd be breathing my last.

Sam's attention was focused on a passing horse pulling a buggy. In his attempt not to startle the horse, he missed seeing Mary. As we drove by, she and I locked eyes. And what I saw there gave me chills that even a warm day like today couldn't drive away.

Chapter Thirteen

What's wrong?"

"It's that obvious?" I couldn't remember anyone ever hating me with the kind of passion I'd witnessed on Mary's face. The experience shook me to my core. "Mary was standing outside the café. She saw you kiss me."

"Oh great," he mumbled.

"Maybe the next time you decide to get romantic, you shouldn't do it right in front of your girlfriend."

He gave me a withering look. "First of all, Mary isn't my girlfriend. To be honest, right now, she's not even my friend. Secondly, I'd like to draw attention to your use of the words 'next time.' I assume that means there will be a 'next time'?"

Before speaking I carefully measured my words. "It would be dishonest of me to say that I don't want you to kiss me again. But besides trying to stay focused on the business at hand, we've got to remember that I'll only be here two weeks. Do you really see any kind of a future for us?"

"You make it sound impossible—as if we're both immovable."

"But aren't we? You have a farm. You can't leave it—or Sweetie.

And I'm a graphic designer." I waved my hand toward the small businesses lined up along Main Street. "Do you see any advertising firms in Harmony? I have a great job in Wichita that I can't walk away from. Besides, I'm just not a small town girl. I need the excitement of the city."

His expression grew pensive, and his lips tightened into a thin line.

I waited for him to say something, but he stayed silent. I stared out the window and watched downtown Harmony pass by me while I tried to drive the picture of Mary's face out of my head. I'd tried to make peace with her. Of course, I'd also assured her I wasn't interested in Sam. At the time, I'd meant it. But what she saw today made me look like a liar. I wasn't sure what to do. Should I leave it alone or try once again to soothe her hurt feelings? My last attempt had been a disaster.

I forced myself to think of something else. There wasn't anything I could do about Mary right now. I tried to focus on the uniqueness of Harmony as we drove down Main Street. I'd never seen a town with so much personality. Every building was painted a different color—and each one had its own design. Whether expressed through brightly colored or plain exteriors, or store names painted with individual flare and imagination, the individual buildings somehow added up to a complete picture. A desire to paint Harmony welled up inside of me. I hadn't painted anything in a long time—ever since I'd started working for Grant. Perhaps Hannah and I could come down here together. It would be a great way to teach her the mechanics of painting. Not that she hadn't picked up most of it through pure talent and instinct. The problem was finding the time.

"What did you tell your father?" Sam said, interrupting my thoughts.

"What?"

"Your father. What have you told him?"

I sighed. "I'd just asked him about Glick when Emily interrupted us. I'm sure he's wondering what's going on."

We reached Faith Road, and Sam turned the truck toward his house. "You know, it would be helpful if you could get his side of the story."

"Without spilling the beans?"

He nodded.

"I guess I'll do what I'd originally planned. Just tell him I've heard stories about Glick and was wondering if he knew him."

"You don't think he'll find that the least bit suspicious?"

I shrugged. "Why would he? I've already brought up other people I've met."

"Yeah, but you haven't met Jacob Glick."

I slowly blew air out between pursed lips. "Well, in a way I have. It's like he's haunting me."

"Don't be silly. People aren't really haunted by ghosts."

"Well, he won't go away, and he follows me wherever I go. What do you call that?"

"Point taken." Sam pulled into his driveway and parked next to the house. "Listen, I know I need to question Sweetie about Glick, but I can't just go in there and ask her if he tried to buy her for his wife. Obviously, if he approached her, she didn't accept his offer."

"Maybe. Or maybe her father died before she had the chance to act on it."

Sam vigorously shook his blond head. "I can't accept that. She would never consider it. I know her. She's not that kind of person."

I reached out and took his hand, wrapping my small fingers around his large, strong ones. "Sam, if Sweetie could save *your* life, what would she be willing to do?"

His face took on a stricken look as he considered my question.

"I rest my case," I said gently. "None of us know what we'd do to protect someone we love. Besides, this happened years ago, and people change."

"I don't want her to think I don't trust her."

"Why would she think that? We'll just ask her if she knew Glick. Give her a chance to tell us on her own what we need to know."

Sam shook his head. "We can't keep asking everyone about Jacob Glick. It looks weird. We need a cover story."

The curtains in the front window moved slightly. Sweetie was probably wondering why we hadn't come inside.

"What if we say we found something of Glick's and it got us to wondering about him."

Sam frowned at me. "But that's a lie."

"Well, you come up with something better," I said with exasperation.

His forehead wrinkled in thought. "What about the truth?" he asked after a long pause.

"The truth? What truth? We can't tell what we actually do know—and we have no idea what we don't know..."

"Could you repeat that?"

I slapped him lightly on the arm with my free hand. "Seriously, what are you suggesting?"

"That we simply tell people we've heard some interesting things about Glick and we're curious about him."

"And if someone asks what we've heard?"

He smiled angelically. "We say we can't tell them. That's the truth."

I let go of his hand and pushed myself back against the truck door. "You know, that may actually be a rather brilliant idea. People who have nothing to hide will probably accept it as simple curiosity. But someone who had something to do with his death will see us as a...as a..."

"I think the word you're searching for is 'threat.'" Sam rubbed his hand over his face. "Suddenly my brilliant idea doesn't seem so brilliant."

"Nonsense. We don't have a lot of time, and we need to flush out the truth. This could do it." I grinned at him. "Besides, no one is going to try to hurt us as long as we're together. You're a rather intimidating fellow, you know."

He snorted. "Sure. I can lug around baskets of fruit with the best of them. If it comes down to that. . ."

"Listen. I think it's evident that whoever killed Glick did it out of anger. We're not hunting a serial killer. Sure, someone is trying to keep me quiet, but so far, all they've done is steal a letter and plant a stolen vase in Benjamin's house. If they'd really wanted to harm me, wouldn't they have done it by now?"

Sam stared at me glumly. "It's not like I work for CSI or something. And yes, before you ask, I've seen *CSI*. Truth is, I'm a simple farmer. I have no idea what the person we're looking for is capable of. I have every hope that whoever hit Glick on the head with that rock didn't mean to kill him. But that doesn't mean he isn't determined to keep his involvement quiet—and that he's not willing to do whatever it takes to accomplish that goal."

"I understand, but after finding out more about Glick, I'm convinced his death was a crime of passion—totally unplanned. I mean, who cooks up a scheme to murder someone out in the open where there could be witnesses? And no one *chooses* a rock as a weapon. It was used because it was handy."

The curtains in the front window moved again. Sweetie was getting antsy.

"Well, I'm glad you've got this all figured out," Sam said caustically. "But just in case your skills as a profiler are lacking in any way, I think I'll keep an extra close watch on you."

I stuck my hand out. "Agreed."

He shook my hand but didn't let it go right away. Finally, I pulled it back. "Sweetie's been watching us ever since we got here. If we don't get inside, she'll probably come out and drag us in by our hair."

As if she'd heard us, the front door flew open, and Sweetie stepped out on the porch. Buddy ran out from behind her. When he saw Sam's truck, he raced toward us, barking happily.

"I think this is Sweetie's way of telling us our time is up," Sam said. "Let's go. I want to show you something."

We got out of the truck and headed for the porch where Sweetie stood glaring at us with her hands on her hips. Today's overalls were cut off at the knee, and she wore a red T-shirt without stains or tears. I fought the urge to ask her if this was her special Sunday outfit.

" 'Bout time," she shouted. "I thought maybe you two was plannin' to move in there permanently."

"Well, we would," Sam said, "but you'd have to bring our food out to the truck, and I wouldn't want to inconvenience you."

"Wouldn't inconvenience me none, 'cause I'd let you both starve to death."

Sam quickly climbed the stairs and pulled his aunt into a big bear hug. "Now, Sweetie. You know you love me too much to let me waste away."

She pushed him away laughing. "Boy, you are a mess. A really big mess."

Sam leaned over to pet Buddy, whose joy at welcoming us home caused him to wag his stumpy tail so hard he could barely stay on his feet. "At least someone is glad to see us." Sam was quickly rewarded with a sloppy kiss.

He clumped back down the stairs. "Grace and I are going down to the lake," he told his aunt. "We'll be back in a while."

She nodded. "Supper at seven. I'm sure you stuffed yourself at Abel Mueller's house. I'm just makin' a fruit salad."

He smiled at her. "Perfect choice, Sweetie. Thank you."

"Shoot, I was gonna make fruit salad anyway," she grumbled as she went inside the house.

"I've been wondering about the lake," I said as I followed him around the side of the house. Buddy trotted after us, stopping once in a while to investigate a weed or a patch of dirt. We walked through the orchards. The apples and peaches were visible but still small.

"We'll start harvesting next month," Sam said. "It's a big job. I hire some of the boys in town to help." He stopped and pointed toward some land to the south of where we stood. "Those are our blackberry and strawberry fields." He smiled widely. "We have some empty fields on the north. We're thinking about planting pumpkins."

"It's wonderful, Sam." I could tell he was proud of what he and his aunt had accomplished. The orchards were beautiful. The trees looked strong and healthy and the fields lush and green. I breathed in the scent of wet earth and growing things. It was intoxicating. The city had its smells, too. Unfortunately, they weren't anything like this.

"The lake is this way." He pointed toward a row of cottonwood trees that stood about fifty or sixty yards away from the last row of fruit trees.

"Man, if your house is closer to the lake than Benjamin's, it must be quite a hike from his back door."

"It is. Ben's property is bigger than you think."

We trudged on until we reached the cottonwoods. A worn dirt path wound between them. The tall trees reached toward the sky, their thick gray trunks furrowed with age and nature. Puffs of cottony seeds sailed gently on the air like small dancers in an impromptu spring ballet. The white fibrous masses reminded me of large feathery snowflakes. I stopped in my tracks to watch the magical performance. Sam paused beside me as if he understood my captivation. However, Buddy ran ahead, oblivious to my sudden enchantment. When we finally exited the trees, Sam grabbed my hand and pulled me up next to him. A large azure blue lake lay before us, lined with cottonwoods and wildflowers. The flowers grew unchecked and added splashes of color against the green grasses, creating a soft patchwork blanket that surrounded the clear blue lake. A long dock stretched out before us, the wood aged and ripened by years of sun, rain, and snow. Sam guided me toward it.

"It's absolutely beautiful here," I said, awestruck. "I–I've never seen anything like it."

Buddy ran to the end of the dock and sat down, gazing out at the water as if he also found it captivating.

"I love it out here," Sam said softly. "It's so peaceful. I come here a lot just to think."

"If I was going to be in Harmony longer, I'd paint it."

"Let's sit here." He pointed toward the edge of the dock where Buddy waited for us. "I like to take my boots off and dangle my feet in the water."

I settled down next to Buddy who leaned up against me. We were becoming fast friends. I reached down to untie my shoe, and he quickly kissed me on the cheek. I found the gesture endearing and kissed the top of his head. "Thanks, Buddy. I love you, too," I whispered.

Sam put his boots and socks behind him, rolled up his jeans, and let his feet dip into the still water of the lake. "Brrr. It's a little chilly this early in the spring."

I swished my toe around, creating a small ripple. "You promise fish aren't going to nibble at my toes?"

His laugh was deep and warm. "I'm not promising anything. But if you catch one, make sure he hangs on until we can pull him out. Sweetie fries a mean catfish."

"Oh great. I didn't get a pedicure just to become fish food."

Sam frowned at me. "A pedicure, huh? You really are a city girl."

I giggled. "Oh, sorry. How do you country folks do it? File your nails down with a rock?"

He snorted. "Ha, ha. No, we use clippers. Believe it or not, they work just fine." He held his feet up to show me. "See? My toes don't look like they should belong to the Wolfman or anything, do they?"

Actually, he had fine feet. Large, well-formed, with light golden hair that snaked up toward his ankles. I noticed an odd spot on the side of his right foot. "You've got a nice scar there. What happened? Did you step on a rake?"

He shook his head. "No. Unfortunately, once in a while we get hunters who like to set traps around the lake. Hunting isn't allowed in this area, but it doesn't keep everyone out. I check the shoreline as often as I can for traps." He wiggled his foot. "I found one the hard way."

"You and I have more in common than I thought." I told him about living in Fairbury and the fox I'd released from a trap.

"Wow, Grace." His forehead furrowed with concern. "You took a real chance there. Most wild animals don't understand that you're trying to help them. They can be very dangerous, especially when they're in pain."

I reached over and ran my hand down Buddy's back. "I couldn't leave him there, Sam. I just couldn't. I took the risk knowing what could happen. Fortunately, it turned out okay."

"Well, I won't be taking you with me to check for traps, that's for sure."

A family of Canada geese swam past us, the little goslings struggling to keep up. Their soft gray feathers ruffled in the gentle breeze that moved across the deep blue water. A group of ducks squawked loudly from the other side of the lake. From their frantic bobbing, I could tell they'd found a school of small fish. As my eyes drifted a little to their right, I couldn't help but gasp. "Oh my goodness. I don't believe it!"

Sam turned his head my way. "What is it you don't believe?"

"That—that looks like a whooping crane!"

"It *is* a whooping crane. We've got all kinds of wildlife out here. Several kinds of owls, eagles, hawks, raccoons, skunks, possums, foxes, deer—almost anything you can think of."

"Wow. It's just incredible. I could sit out here forever."

"I understand, but unfortunately you need to call your father and we both need to talk to Sweetie."

"Maybe you should do that by yourself. She might feel uncomfortable with me there."

He sighed and swirled his right foot in a circle. The water rippled around it. "I don't know. It might seem strange if I approach her alone. Why don't we start a conversation tonight about the town and its history? We'll slide Glick's name in and see what happens. Hopefully, she'll open up and tell us something helpful." He stopped moving his toes and fixed his gaze on the duck family that had eaten its fill and was now gliding across the lake. "Maybe we should just tell her the truth. I mean, about your uncle and all. She might be a great help to us."

I hesitated a moment before answering him. I didn't want to offend him or make him think I didn't trust his aunt, but ever since our first meeting, I'd had the odd feeling she was hiding something. "Look, Sam. I don't think that's a good idea. I—I know you're not going to like this, but. . ."

"You think she's a suspect?"

I put my hand over my eyes to shield them from the sun and turned to look at him. "I don't know. I just think we need to keep our. . ."

"Investigation?"

"It sounds silly when you actually say it, but yes. We are searching for the truth, so I guess it is kind of an investigation. Anyway, I think we need to keep it quiet for now."

"I trust Sweetie with my life," he said in a somber voice.

Nancy Mehl

"And I trust my father with *my* life," I responded gently. "But here I am, asking questions that could end up implicating him in a possible murder."

Sam cleared his throat and stared at his bare feet. "Okay, okay," he said finally. "But it would be nice if we could bring someone else into this who knew Glick. We're shooting in the dark here."

"Who would you suggest? Emily's already told us what she knows. She can't help us any further even though she suspects Glick is dead. . ."

"You didn't tell me that," he said sharply. "Why does she think that?"

"Well, think about it. If Glick was finally about to get himself a wife, why would he leave town? Emily told me she's suspected he's been dead all these years."

"But then why. . ."

"That's all I can say about that for now, Sam. Please don't ask me any more about Emily." I patted his arm. "I'll tell you everything when I can. Just trust me when I tell you that Emily has helped us as much as she can."

"Okay." He stared at the water for a few moments before suddenly snapping his fingers. Buddy took it as an invitation and moved next to him.

"Fickle dog," I said teasingly while I scratched him behind the ear.

"I know exactly where we can go," Sam said. "Levi."

"Will he keep what we tell him secret?"

"Absolutely. Levi was here when Glick lived in Harmony, and he knew Angstadt very well. He used to be one of his elders but got so disgusted with the way things were being handled he left the church. He was also really good friends with your uncle. In fact, I think Levi was one of the people Ben trusted the most."

"Well, if you think it's a good idea, it's okay with me. He doesn't appear to have any real connection to Glick. If we're going to bring anyone else into this situation, it should be someone who has no motive to want Glick dead."

He nodded. "Okay. I'll set up a meeting." That settled, he pointed at a spot to my right. "Look. You can see your dock from here."

"I have a dock?"

"Just like this one, only not quite as long."

I followed his finger. Sure enough, off in the distance, I could see another dock stretching out into the lake. It was almost hidden by the natural grasses that grew out of the water. I stared at it for several seconds, feeling unsettled for some reason. "I have the strangest feeling I've seen this lake before," I said. "It started when we first came through the trees, and it's even stronger now."

"But didn't you say you've never visited Harmony?"

"Yes. I've never been here. I have no idea why it seems so familiar."

He smiled. "Déjà vu. You've been somewhere else that reminds you of this place. Have you spent much time at any other lake?"

"Yes. Near Fairbury where we used to live. My dad took us camping and fishing there."

"That's probably it."

"Does this lake have a name?"

Sam laughed. "Well, the early Indians who settled here called it Trouble Lake."

"What an odd name. Not very fitting for this beautiful, peaceful spot."

"Actually, it is. The Indians believed that when they came here and bathed in the water, their troubles were washed away."

I gazed out on the tranquil scene. "Wow. That's inspiring. Maybe if I floated for a few hours..."

Sam grinned. "I'm afraid you'd only get waterlogged."

"That's probably true." I glanced at my watch. "I've really got to call my dad. It wasn't fair to drop Glick's name and then hang up on him." I reluctantly took my feet out of the water and began pulling on my socks. "When we talk to Levi, let's start off asking him what he knows about Glick. If we don't get what we want from that, then we'll drop the bombshell. But only after he promises to keep what we tell him to himself."

Sam slid his socks on. "Okay, but I really think we can trust him with the whole story, Grace. I just hope he can point us in the right direction. I sure think it's worth a try." He finished pulling on his boots and stood up, holding out his hand to help me to my feet. Buddy ran halfway up the dock and turned around to look at us as if he was wondering why we were so slow.

"The idea of actually telling someone else is a little scary," I said. "But we only have two weeks. I guess we have no choice."

Sam nodded. "Let's get you to a phone. And don't forget our strategy at supper."

I followed him and Buddy back to the house. Were we making a mistake telling Levi about Benjamin's letter? I couldn't see any other option. At the end of two weeks, I would have to do something. If I couldn't discover some information that would help my father, the situation could head in a terrible direction. One that I didn't want to face.

Sam led me to the back of the house and opened a door into a screened-in porch. It reminded me a lot of Emily's. He laughed at the expression on my face.

"Look familiar? This is where Emily got the idea for her porch. She fell in love with this one and told Abel. He came out and looked at it and built a similar one for her."

"Does Emily spend a lot of time here?" I couldn't see Emily and Sweetie as close friends.

"Oh, she probably drops by a couple times a month at least." Sam checked a large potted plant near the corner windows. Then he picked up a nearby watering can and added some moisture to the huge green fern. I almost laughed. I had a fern in my apartment that looked like some kind of sickly cousin to this one. And I'd thought mine was pretty healthy. Obviously I'd been deluded. "Sweetie and I hire some of the teenagers from the church to help during harvest—and for a few other chores around here. Abel and Emily drop by to make sure they're working hard." He flashed me a big grin. "Sweetie and Emily actually like each other very much. Emily loves this house, and Sweetie loves to show it off. I guess when people find something they have in common, anyone can forge a friendship."

"I guess so." Spending time in Harmony had begun to change the way I looked at people. I was beginning to see that I didn't have everything and everyone all figured out after all. I watched Sam examine some of the other plants and couldn't help but once again compare him to the men I knew in Wichita. Sam was intelligent, compassionate, courteous—and he really listened when I talked. My last date had spent the entire evening talking about himself. The only chance I'd had to speak came when he occasionally took a breath, and even then I'd felt he was just waiting for me to finish so he could launch into another boring story about his supposed success as a copywriter at another advertising agency in town.

"You'd better call your dad," Sam said after inspecting several of the pots scattered around the room.

I nodded. "My dad and your aunt in one day. It's a lot to face."

"Well, at least it should be interesting," he said as he opened the door into the main house.

I walked past, brushing against him as I stepped up into the kitchen. He smelled of aftershave and the outdoors. My mind went back to our kiss in the truck, and I felt my cheeks grow hot. I hurried ahead of him so he wouldn't see how much he affected me.

"Why don't you use the phone in the study?" he said. "It's down the hall and to your left."

Without turning around or acknowledging him, I followed

his instructions. The first door on the left opened into a beautiful room lined with tall oak bookshelves. Against the back wall, long windows looked out on the orchards. Two leather, high-backed chairs sat near a wood-burning fireplace in the corner of the room. An intricately carved wood mantel above the fireplace held several framed pictures. I moved closer so I could see them. In the first, a young boy held the hand of a handsome woman who smiled at the camera. I realized with a start that the boy was Sam and the woman was Sweetie. Sam's long blond hair almost covered one eye. Although he smiled for the camera, his eyes held a deep sadness. The picture must have been taken not long after he came to live with his aunt. I stared at Sweetie's picture. I guessed her to be in her late thirties. Curly amber-colored hair cascaded down to her shoulders. Her large dark eyes held the guarded look I'd come to know. The next picture was a head shot of an achingly beautiful woman with sandy hair and bright blue eyes. Sam's features were unmistakable. His mother. I stared at her for several seconds. A quick look through several of the other framed photographs showed no shots of her with a man. Where was Sam's father?

The rest of the pictures were of people I didn't recognize, although I suspected that a portrait of an elderly couple was of Sam's grandparents. The very last picture caught my attention. A young woman with blond hair piled up on her head smiled at the camera. Although I almost couldn't believe it, I realized it was an earlier photo of Sweetie. She had to have been in her late teens or early twenties. She was breathtaking. In her large, luminous eyes I detected no hint of the hardness that would change her. I saw only happiness. This picture must have been taken before her father's accident. Had that loss changed her into the gruff, suspicious woman she had become? Or could it have been something else? Had Jacob Glick's touch of evil driven the hope from her life?

I found the phone on top of a large mahogany desk. I slid into the leather chair behind the desk and dialed my dad's number. He answered on the first ring.

"I'm sorry I had to hang up so fast, Dad," I said quickly. "We were having lunch at the pastor's house and. . ."

"Why in the world did you ask me about Jacob Glick? Where did you hear that name?"

My dad's sharp tone startled me. I thought back quickly to my conversation with Sam. I needed to sound nonchalant without actually lying to my father. "I've been hearing lots of names, Dad. His was just one of them. It seems he wasn't a very nice man."

I waited quietly for my father to respond but was greeted with total silence. "Dad?" I said finally. "Are you there?"

"Is that man back in Harmony? Has he approached you, Grace Marie?"

My dad had called me by both my given names—a sign that at that moment he was as serious as he could possibly get. And he'd asked if Glick had come back to Harmony. He had no idea the man was dead. My knees felt weak. If I hadn't already been sitting down, I think I would have collapsed. I trusted my father, but a little corner of my brain had held on to a small pocket of fear—fear that my father had been someone else once. Someone I didn't know. I knew now, beyond a shadow of a doubt, that he was completely innocent of Glick's death.

"N—no, Dad. He's not here. I guess he left not long after you did."

"Well, thank God for that. He was a terrible man. He's the only person I ever hit, Gracie. I'm not proud of it. I don't believe in violence. Never have. But that man. . ."

"What did he do?"

"It doesn't matter. I don't want to talk about it."

"I'm twenty-three years old, you know. Not a baby."

"I know that."

My dad's stern voice didn't welcome any further challenge.

But with what was at stake, I took a chance and pressed on. "Someone told me he was a little too friendly with the girls in Harmony. For you to hit him, he must have made a move on Mom."

My dad's exasperated sigh echoed loudly through the receiver. "Why in the world is this important to you? If Jacob is gone, who cares what he did or didn't do?"

If I could tell my father what Glick had done to Emily Mueller, he'd probably tell me whatever I wanted to know. But I couldn't do that. "Look, I'm just interested, that's all. Sam's been showing me around town, and I'm learning all kinds of things about Harmony—past and present. Jacob Glick is just one of the people whose name came up. Why are you so defensive?"

He sighed again. "I don't know. Jacob is a part of the past I'd like to forget. I suppose if it's important to you, I can try to remember whatever I can. I haven't thought about the man in over thirty years."

"Well, it's not *important* really. I'm just curious."

"Okay, okay. He was the maintenance man for our church, but he spent most of his time skulking around town, following young girls, and being a general nuisance. He bothered your mother on more than one occasion, even though he knew we were seeing each other." He paused for a moment as if gathering his thoughts. "There were rumors that he'd been extremely inappropriate. You know, actually grabbing some of the ladies in town. I have no idea if that's true. My parents didn't discuss unpleasant things in front of my brother and me, so what I know is only through rumors."

"But why did you get in a fight with him?"

"The night before your mother and I left Harmony, we were supposed to meet in a small clearing in the trees behind my house. Even though our parents and a few other people knew we were going away to get married, we didn't want too many people involved. If Bishop Angstadt found out, he would have exerted great pressure on our families to stop us. When I arrived at the spot where I was to meet your mother, I found Jacob hiding behind a tree, watching her. He'd been bothering her for months. She'd had to rebuff him more than once. I'd warned him to stay away from her. When I confronted him, he told us he knew what we were planning and he intended to tell Angstadt. I guess everything just boiled up inside me. I hauled off and slugged him so hard I bruised my knuckles."

"Your—your knuckles? You hit him with your fist?"

He snorted. "Of course I did. What did you think I'd hit him with?"

"Not a rock," I mumbled to myself, not realizing my father could hear me. He hadn't hit him with a rock at all. That meant...

"A rock?" Dad said. "Of course not. I only wanted to stop him from bothering Beverly. I wasn't trying to kill him, Gracie. Goodness gracious. You sure get some funny ideas. Must be all that television..."

"Okay, Dad. I get it." I didn't have time for another lecture on the evils of television. Boy, he and Abel were like twins when it came to that subject.

"All right," he said. "I told you about Jacob Glick. Now, who's Sam?"

I launched into a narrative about Sam and Sweetie, leaving out that I was staying with them.

"You say this Sweetie person has been in Harmony for a while?" He sounded puzzled. "I don't remember anyone with that name. It's certainly not a name I'd likely forget."

"Her real name is Myrtle, Dad. Myrtle Goodrich."

"Oh my goodness gracious. Myrtle Goodrich. Wow. She's still there? I figured she'd left after her father passed away."

I told him about the farm and the house she'd renovated. I also explained that she'd taken Sam in when he was a boy.

"Well, that's very interesting," he said softly. "I always felt so sorry for Myrtle. I didn't really know her very well, but the whole town was aware of her plight. I'm really happy to hear she's made something of herself and overcome her past." I heard him move the phone away from his mouth and say something I couldn't make out. Then he laughed into the receiver. "Honey, your mother is pestering me to give her the phone. I'm going to hand you over. You call us back again in a couple of days, okay?"

"Okay, Dad. I love you."

"I love you, too, Snicklefritz."

I talked to my mom for another ten minutes before we finally hung up. I put the receiver down and stared at the phone for quite some time, trying to turn over the information I'd gotten from my dad. He'd hit Glick with his fist. My father hadn't killed Glick at all—on purpose or accidentally. I felt as if a major weight had been lifted off me. I started to get up to find Sam, when the door to the study swung open and he came inside.

"Are you finished?" he asked.

I nodded and motioned to him to close the door. He latched it and came over, sitting down in a chair near the desk. I told him everything I'd learned from my father.

"So you see," I said when I'd finished, "my father not only doesn't know Glick is dead, but he couldn't possibly have killed him. Dad didn't hit him with a rock, Sam. Someone else did that. Someone else killed Jacob Glick."

Sam studied me for a moment. "And you believe your father told you the truth?"

I nodded. "I know him better than I know myself. I'm convinced of it."

He shrugged. "That's good enough for me." He sat forward in the chair and put his head in his hands. "Glick never made it from the spot where your father hit him. So if we can figure out who met Glick in the clearing after your father and mother left and before Ben found him, we've got our murderer." He straightened

Simple Secrets

up and frowned at me, his face creased with concern. "Since we know your father didn't accidentally kill Glick, I think the person who hit him with that rock probably intended to kill him, Grace. They probably saw your dad hit him—and then when your parents left, they picked up a rock and finished him off. I suspect Glick was a little woozy after being punched in the face. Most likely, that made it much easier to approach him."

"That makes sense," I said, thinking it over. "The problem is that no one we've talked to actually saw who hit him. I'm beginning to think our only chance at finding the truth is to discover the identity of the person who took my letter and planted Ruth's vase at Benjamin's. That person must be the real killer."

Without warning, a side door to the library opened and Sweetie stepped in, holding something in her hand. "I can't help you with Ruth's vase, and I can't help you figger out who killed that stinkin' varmit Jacob Glick. But I can tell you exactly who stole your letter." She walked over and slammed the papers she held in her hand onto the desktop right in front of me. "It was me. I took your blasted letter."

Chapter Fourteen

I had no intention of ever talkin' 'bout this. I'd hoped it was dead and buried. . .just like that miserable old letch Jacob Glick."

Sam and I sat quietly at the kitchen table. Sweetie had refused to explain her surprising admission until she was ready. She'd ordered us into the kitchen where we sat waiting while she scooped out three bowls of fruit salad and shoved them in front of us. The salad looked and smelled delicious, but my appetite had vanished. From the somber expression on Sam's face, it was evident he felt the same way.

After her comment, Sweetie stared at me as if I might want to respond, but for the life of me, I couldn't think of a single thing to say. Her shocking revelation seemed to have affected my ability to voice anything coherent, so I simply nodded. She took it as a sign to continue.

"I barely knew Jacob. I only seen him when I went to town. Didn't go to that church where he worked or nothin', so there weren't much call for me to run into him." She sighed and shook her head. "Whenever I did cross his path, that man always gave me the willies. He had a look in his eyes that was. . .well, *lustful* is the best word I can come up with. I tried to keep my distance from him. My daddy told me not to ever give him a reason to approach me." Her features softened, and for just a moment I saw a quick flash of the young woman I'd seen in the pictures on the mantel. But instantly her expression hardened, and Sweetie was back.

"But...but what does this have to do with why you took Grace's letter?" Sam's harsh tone caused his aunt to glower at him.

"I'll get to that, boy. You need to hush up and let me tell the story my way. It's the only way you're gonna get it. You understand?"

"Whatever." Sam shrugged, then jabbed a forkful of salad and shoved it into his mouth.

"Anyways," she continued, "I kept to my daddy's advice, but every time I seen Jacob in town, he'd watch me with those sharp, beady eyes of his. After a while I got kinda used to it. And then my daddy had his accident. I didn't make it to town much 'cause I was takin' care of him after he came back home." She stared at the tablecloth as if she could see the past woven into its design. "Several of the nearby farmers helped me, tryin' to take care of our fields. Some folks from town came with food and medical supplies." Her voice caught. "Your grandma and grandpa were there for me almost every day, Gracie. Along with Levi and the Turnbauers. Good people. But then that Angstadt fellow started comin' around. Not too often, but even a little of that man was too much for me. I always felt like he was checkin' me out, you know? Pretending he wanted to help—but like he had another motive hidin' behind his fake smile."

She paused for a moment before she rose from her chair and grabbed the iced-tea pitcher from the counter. She refilled her glass and Sam's. I hadn't even touched mine. When she finished, she sat back down with a grunt.

"Well, Daddy just got worse and worse. The doc from Council Grove came out to check on him. He's the one who told me Daddy's bones hadn't set quite right. Unless he had an operation to fix them proper, he could die. Had to do with the way the blood flowed through his body. I didn't have no money, and I couldn't figger out a way to get it quick enough. I thought about sellin' the farm, but that would take time—time Daddy didn't have."

"We know about the deal Angstadt offered you," I said gently. "He'd give you the money for the operation if you'd marry Jacob Glick."

Sweetie's eyes grew wide. "Now how in tarnation did you hear about that?"

I started at the beginning, from reading the letter, to deciding to tell Sam the truth. I finished with the conversation Emily had overheard between Glick and Angstadt when she was young. The only thing I left out was Glick's awful attack on Emily.

"My, my. You two have been busy little beavers, ain't ya?" The touch of amusement in her tone seemed in stark contrast to the seriousness of the situation. She leaned back in her chair, folded her arms, and stared at us. "So you want to prove that Daniel Temple didn't kill Jacob." She snorted. "Shoot, I coulda told you that. Daniel was one of the nicest boys I ever met. He wouldn't harm a hair on no one's head. Not even that low-life Jacob's." She shook her head slowly. "No, Daniel didn't kill Jacob."

"Do you know who did?" Sam asked solemnly.

To our amazement, Sweetie laughed. "Now boy, set your mind to rest. I didn't kill Jacob. If'n I had, wouldn't nobody ever find his body, and all this trouble wouldn't be happenin' now." She reached over and touched Sam's hand. "No, I didn't kill that varmint, boy, and I don't know who did. Wish I'd seen it though. I'd like to help Daniel out. That boy was always nice to me. Always respectful. After Daddy got sick, he'd come with his parents and work on my farm until he was about ready to drop. Never asked for nothin'. Willin' to do anything he could to help. Him and his brother, Benny. They was both special."

I was beginning to get exasperated. Sweetie was taking her

own sweet time and still hadn't explained why she took my letter. I tried to think of a way to hurry her along.

"Guess I better get to what happened that night and why I snuck in and took that letter," she said as if she'd recognized my growing frustration.

I settled back in my chair and waited. Hopefully, we were rounding third base and heading toward home. My stomach growled lightly, and I picked up my fork. The first taste of Sweetie's fresh fruit salad convinced me I could actually eat and listen at the same time.

"Angstadt came to our house two nights after the doctor told me Daddy needed that operation. He told me he would pay for it if I'd marry that snake in the grass Jacob. I was appalled and told him to get outta my house. I didn't tell Daddy nothin' about it. But in the next few days he started gettin' worse and worse." She sat forward in her chair and clasped her rough, work-worn hands together as if she were getting ready to pray. Her knuckles turned white, and the end of her fingers grew red with exertion. She stared at them instead of us. "I—I know what I'm about to say sounds awful, but I just couldn't let my daddy suffer that way. I decided to take Angstadt up on his offer." She looked up at us, her face a mask of pain. "There wasn't nothin' else I could think of to do. The idea of lettin' that man. . .well, let's just say that I loved my daddy more than I loved my own life. It's as simple as that. If either one of you ever loves someone that much, maybe you'll understand." Her expression hardened, and she set her jaw. "After Jacob died and then my daddy passed away, all I wanted was for the whole situation to fade away. I tried to put it out of my mind." She looked at Sam, and the tightness in her face softened. "Then Sam came into my life. I vowed he would never find out that I'd almost sold myself to someone like Jacob Glick. I woulda done anything to keep my decision secret." She sighed. "I didn't want Sam to be ashamed of me."

"So that's why you took my letter?" I asked. "Because uncovering Glick's death would bring all of this to light?"

"That's a big part of it, Gracie girl. But there's more."

Again, I nodded at her to continue. Sam stared at his aunt as if he didn't know her. I understood his shock at finding out Sweetie had kept secrets from him and had my letter all this time, but I was pretty sure some assurance from him would mean a lot to her right now. Her eyes kept flicking toward him, but the look on his face offered little encouragement.

"You see, after I told Angstadt I'd accept his offer, he arranged a meetin' between Jacob and me. We was to get together by the lake. When I came up to the spot where he was supposed to be, I seen he weren't alone." She looked at me. "Daniel and your mama was there, and your daddy was yellin' at Jacob. Seems I wasn't the only girl he had his eye on." She stared at her hands again. "I was standin' behind the trees watchin' when Daniel hauled off and hit Jacob. That nasty man fell down on the ground, but he sure weren't dead. And your daddy didn't hit him with no rock the way the letter says. I couldn't believe it when I read that. What in the blue blazes was Benny thinkin'?"

"What did my father do after he hit Glick?" I asked.

"He and Beverly left. Jacob got up on his feet and stood there cussin' up a blue streak." Sweetie pointed her fork at me. "He was fine, Gracie. Your daddy left him alive. Believe me."

"What did you do then?" Sam asked.

Sweetie ran a hand over her face. "I ran. I chickened out. I hated Jacob, and for some reason, seein' Daniel stand up to him made me want to do it, too." She blew out a long breath between clenched teeth. "But when I got home and was faced with Daddy's pain, I went back, hopin' Jacob was still there."

"And was he?" I asked.

"Oh, he was there all right. Deader than a doornail, his head all busted in." She rubbed her palms together. "All I could do was look at him and think about the money for Daddy's operation. I wasn't sad Jacob was dead. I was just feared my daddy's chances were all gone."

"So you really don't know who killed him," I said with a sigh.

"Nope. But as I told you, it sure weren't Daniel Temple. And I know one other person who didn't do it."

"And who's that?" Sam asked. Thankfully, the tension in his face had eased somewhat. At first I'd thought he was angry with his aunt, but I realized now that he'd just been worried. Afraid she'd killed Glick. Afraid he'd lose the only parent figure he had left.

"Benny Temple. You see, I watched him find Jacob's body. And I watched him bury him. I figgered it was because he thought Daniel had killed him. Weren't no other reason for him to be hidin' Jacob's body."

My mouth dropped open. "You knew Benjamin buried Glick and never said anything?"

"You got that right, missy," she retorted. "I was glad that piece of human scum was dead and gone. And I was determined to keep Benny's secret."

"That's why you took my letter? To protect my uncle?"

She nodded slowly. "That was part of it, surely. But that's not the only reason. You see, I thought Benny saw me that night. After he started buryin' Jacob, I tried to get outta there, but I stepped on a big dry twig, and it cracked real loud. I ran away as fast as I could, tryin' to stay amid the trees so Benny wouldn't see me, but I could hear someone followin' behind me most of the way. It musta been him. And I could swear he looked at me kinda funny after that night. I was feared he thought I killed that nasty old man instead of his brother. I was worried he'd tell folks I did it."

"You never asked him about it?" Sam said incredulously. "In all these years?"

"Nope. Never did. And Benny never brought it up neither. It

were our secret. Anyway, until she came to town." Sweetie crooked her thumb my way.

"But how did you know about the letter?" I asked.

"Because Benny said somethin' about it. Toward the end, he'd sleep a lot. I'd come up to check on him and find him thrashin' around on the couch, mumblin' stuff. One day I found him havin' one of them nightmares. When I tried to wake him up, he grabbed my arm with all the strength he had left and started shoutin' your name, Gracie. He kept yellin', 'The truth's in the letter! The truth's in the letter!'" Sweetie's eyes locked on me, her face puckered in a fierce scowl. "I was sure he was talkin' about Jacob. I couldn't let him bring all that back. I didn't know if he named me as Jacob's killer. Or maybe your daddy. I had no idea what kinda 'truth' was in that letter." She sighed. "Too many lives could be ruined by diggin' up things that are better left dead. I respected your uncle, but in this case, I thought he was all wrong."

"But don't you realize that this letter could clear my father?"

Sweetie leaned back in her chair. "You ain't thought this out, Gracie girl. That letter says your daddy *did* kill Jacob. Even if he didn't mean to."

"You could testify," Sam said. "You can clear Mr. Temple."

Sweetie looked at him as if he'd lost his mind. "And how am I supposed to do that? I can't come forward now, thirty years later, and tell someone I kept quiet about it all this time. Ain't no one gonna believe me. Especially since I probably have more motive than anyone else for killin' him." She shook her head. "Nope. That won't work. I won't do it."

"Then what do we do now? What do we do with the letter?" I could hear the hint of hysteria in my voice, but I was tired and confused. It seemed now that the letter actually made things more complicated. Benjamin had been wrong all these years. He'd assumed his brother was guilty of murder—even if it was accidental. But now we knew that my dad wasn't guilty of anything except maybe giving Glick a well-deserved punch in the face. And the only person who could back that up wasn't willing to do so.

"I wish I'd found that letter before you did and destroyed it," Sweetie said harshly. "It's nothin' but trouble. It should disappear just like Jacob. If it goes away, our problems go away. We can get back to normal."

"Aren't you forgetting the body buried on Grace's property?" Sam asked.

Sweetie shook her head vigorously. "I got a solution to that problem, too. I buy your land, Gracie. I been wantin' to expand anyway. Nobody will think nothin' about it. Jacob stays right where he belongs, and we all go on with our lives."

For just a moment, I saw a ray of hope, but it quickly became clear that Sweetie's plan was flawed. "But Jacob Glick *was* murdered by someone," I said. "We can't just ignore that."

"Anyone living in Harmony coulda bashed in that old coot's head," she said with contempt. "You can't investigate the whole town in a few days, girlie. Besides, maybe the person who killed him already moved away—or died themselves. You could be wastin' your time."

I wrapped a strand of hair around my finger while I thought about Sweetie's theory. "But what about Ruth's vase? Someone took it and planted it in Benjamin's house. Why would anyone do that unless they were afraid I was getting too close to the truth?"

"Was probably Mary," Sweetie said triumphantly. "I heard tell she hates your guts. She did it so you'd get upset and leave town."

"No," Sam said. "It wasn't Mary. I already thought of that. I asked Hector where she was Saturday. She never left the café."

I frowned at him. "You didn't tell me you'd checked up on Mary's whereabouts."

He shrugged. "I just wanted to be sure it wasn't her. I didn't say anything since I was pretty sure she wasn't involved. No point rring up any more bad feelings between the two of you."

Sweetie's jubilation over her hypothesis had taken a swift nosedive. She scrunched up her face while she considered this revelation. Finally, she clapped her hands together. "Maybe Ruth took it herself. She and Mary are tighter than two thieves. They probably planned it."

"I don't believe that," I said. "I haven't known Ruth long, but she seems like an honest woman who would never accuse an innocent person of a crime."

Sweetie started to make a snide comment, but Sam jumped in before she got it out. "You're absolutely right, Grace. She wouldn't." He flashed his aunt a warning look, and she shut her mouth.

I leaned forward and caught Sweetie's attention. "Even if we really believed no one would ever find Glick, *we* know he was murdered. And it's not right."

"Even though we might never find out who killed him?" Sam asked.

"Yes. I realize he was a bad person, but he was also someone's son. Maybe someone's brother." I directed my next comment to Sweetie. "Maybe someone's nephew. How can we just leave him in the ground?"

"I understand what you're sayin'," Sweetie said, raising her eyebrows, "but if you can't figger out who knocked him off, this thing could blow up in your face and hurt a lotta people. I say you two do your investigatin', but if you don't find nothin', I buy the land and we leave well enough alone."

"I don't know. You might be right," I said.

"You sound hesitant," Sam said. "Is that really what you want to do?"

I exhaled slowly. "I don't know. It's confusing. I don't want to cause my family trouble, but if we just walk away, it's like Glick will haunt us the rest of our lives. He'll never be put to rest."

Sweetie's rough laughter told me she didn't understand. But

06

Sam's worried expression mirrored my own. He knew I was right. I was beginning to understand how my uncle felt. Sometimes, doing the right thing is more complicated than it should be.

Sweetie stood up. "Well, since we're bein' all honest and everything, I have somethin' you should see."

Sam and I followed her out of the kitchen toward the study. I had my uncle's letter clasped tightly in my hand, and I had no intention of losing it again. Sweetie swung the study door open and motioned us inside. Then she crossed over to a painting on the far wall. Probably another one of Hannah's. She grabbed the left side of the picture and pulled. To my amazement, it swung out, revealing the door to a safe in the wall.

"I had no idea this was here," Sam said to his aunt. "Why didn't you tell me?" He sounded slightly offended.

"I don't gotta tell you everything, boy." She reached over and patted him on the shoulder. "Wasn't 'cause I don't trust you. Just felt it was better if you didn't know nothin' about it." She quickly turned the dial. I could hear the tumblers fall into place. "I found this after I moved in. Don't know who first put it here, but Amil Angstadt was usin' it—that's for sure. It's also for certain his flock knew nothin' about it." She swung the heavy door open to reveal a deep interior full of papers and a large metal box. She pulled the box out and carried it over to the desk. Sam and I shot each other questioning looks and trailed behind her. Sweetie was turning out to be full of surprises.

"So what is it?" Sam asked.

"When Angstadt came to see me, he asked me how much my daddy's operation was gonna cost. I told him it was five thousand dollars. He offered me ten thousand. It was enough for the operation and to get our fields in shape. I figgered I could save the farm and get Daddy healthy again so when he was ready, he could take up where he left off."

"Ten thousand dollars was a lot of money back then," I said.

"Where in the world would Angstadt get that much?"

Sweetie's eyes were burning coals of hate. "I don't know, but I'm certain he coulda helped my daddy without askin' me to sell myself to Jacob Glick." The timbre of her voice rose. "He was supposed to be a Christian man—no matter what group he belonged to. And he let my daddy die. When Jacob disappeared, he refused to help me. Said he was no longer bound to the bargain 'cause Jacob wasn't in the picture. Yet he had all of this." She flung the top of the box open to reveal stacks and stacks of bills.

"You—you said you found this here?"

She nodded. "After I bought the house, I found the safe. I was gonna crack it open but realized the number was written on the back of an old tapestry that hung here. Evil thing it were. Hell and all its demons torturin' souls. Just like somethin' Angstadt would have. I threw it out and put up an old print that belonged to my daddy until Sam brought home one of Hannah's paintings while I was workin' on this room."

Sam ran his hands over the money. "How much is in here?"

"A little over twenty thousand dollars." Her expression grew tight. "And I ain't never spent one stinkin' dollar of it. I kept it here all these years just 'cause I could. I hope that rotten scoundrel knows I got his money." Her voice trembled with emotion.

"Sweetie," I said softly, "he probably doesn't know. And even if he did, I don't think it matters to him anymore."

"Well, it matters to me. It matters a great deal to me." Tears coursed down her face. "That so-and-so minister watched my daddy waste away when he coulda saved him. After Angstadt dropped dead, I sold daddy's farm and bought this house just to spite him." She looked around the room. "'Course once I realized it weren't the house's fault, I started to love it here. I fixed it up my way. Ain't no part of that man here no more." She gazed down at the box. "'Cept his cursed money. The thing he loved most in the world."

Sam and I just looked at each other. Sweetie had imprisoned

herself with hate for a man who'd died years ago. A wave of compassion swept through me. Sweetie's gruff exterior housed a broken soul.

"Why don't you put it back now, Sweetie?" Sam said gently. "We'll talk about it later."

She slammed the lid shut and picked up the box. "I'll put it back, but there ain't no reason to talk about nothin'. I ain't gonna spend it. And I ain't gonna never get rid of it. It will sit in that safe until it rots away. Just like that no-good preacher." She pointed at the letter still in my hand. "You might as well put that letter in the safe, too. No one can get to it there. I ain't gonna bother with it anymore. You have my promise."

I wordlessly handed her the letter, which she carried along with the box to the open safe door. Once they were safely ensconced inside, she shut the door and twirled the knob. Then she swung the painting back against the wall.

"I know it's early, but I'm plumb tuckered out," she said yawning. "If you two don't mind, I'm gonna take a bath and watch a little TV in my room till I nod off." She pointed her index finger at Sam. "You gotta help me in the orchard tomorrow, boy. We gotta repair the irrigation lines. Them rabbits been chewin' on 'em again."

"Yes ma'am," he said. "I'll be up at the crack of dawn." He leaned over and gave his aunt a kiss on the cheek. She reached up and put her arms around his neck, giving him a quick hug. "You're my blessin', you know," she whispered. "The good Lord mighta been sleepin' when my daddy died, but when He woke up He felt bad and sent you to me." With that she turned on her heel and headed for the door.

"Sweetie," Sam said before she had a chance to make her escape, "you shouldn't have worried that I'd be ashamed of you, you know. That would never happen. Never."

The elderly woman didn't respond. Nor did she turn around.

She hesitated for a moment and then walked out of the room.

"Wow," I said when the study door closed.

"Yeah, wow," Sam echoed.

"I know where the money came from."

Sam gaped at me. "How could you know?"

I told him about the church member who died and left some land to the church when Angstadt was still running things. "Emily wondered what had happened to the money. It never showed up. Now we know."

He nodded. "And we also know what Glick had on Angstadt."

We stood for a moment staring at the door as if Sweetie was going to burst in at any moment with some new revelation. Finally, Sam shook his head and suggested we sit out on the back porch. After stopping by the kitchen for some iced tea, we made our way to the porch. Sam sat beside me in a wicker love seat that looked almost exactly like Emily's. We watched the sunset for a while without speaking. I wasn't certain what he was thinking, but I kept trying to process Sweetie's surprising disclosure with all the other information we'd managed to gather.

Finally, Sam broke the silence. "So now what?"

I shook my head. "I wish I knew. Frankly, I don't think anything's changed. Just because Glick's killer didn't take the letter, we're still dealing with someone who doesn't want me to uncover the truth."

"Has it occurred to you that stealing that vase from Ruth's in broad daylight was really risky?" Sam asked with a deep frown. "He could have easily been caught."

"Yes, I thought about that. It smacks of desperation."

He nodded slowly. "It certainly does. It also means that whoever did it was watching us in town yesterday. He knew you'd been to Ruth's."

"And he knew I'd be back to pick up my purchases. How could anyone possibly know that?"

"I have no idea." Sam let out a deep sigh. "I'm still processing the fact that Sweetie had your letter and has been keeping twenty thousand dollars in a hidden safe."

I placed my hand on his arm. "She's still the same person she was before she told you about the letter and the money." I stared out the window at the remnants of the sun as it slipped behind the reddish-bronze horizon. "I can't stop thinking about the pain she's been through. If I had to watch my father die. . ."

"You know, you and Sweetie both know what it's like to have to fight for your father. You two have a lot in common."

His words jarred me. Sweetie seemed so odd—so different than me. Yet when it came down to our hearts, we *were* a lot alike. I tried to put myself in her place. Would I have made the same decision she had? I wasn't certain and prayed I'd never have to find out.

"At least we know who *didn't* kill Glick," I said slowly. "Now we just have to figure out who did. Sounds like the entire town of Harmony is suspect."

Sam chuckled. "This is starting to remind me of a mystery novel I read once. A man was killed by an entire group of people on a train. Each one struck a blow that could have been the fatal one so no one would know who the actual murderer was."

"*Murder on the Orient Express* by Agatha Christie," I said. "Great book. Great writer."

"Yes, she was," he agreed. "Do you remember how Hercule Poirot figured it out?"

"Not a clue."

"Me either."

We both laughed, and Sam scooted closer to me. A chill ran up my spine along with a message of caution. The light in the room grew dim and with it, my resistance.

"You do realize that Sweetie knows exactly where Glick is buried, don't you?" Sam said.

"Yes, but until we find out how he got there, I don't want to know where he is. It's too creepy."

Sam didn't answer. Somehow talking about the location of Glick's grave made everything seem way too real.

"I sure hope we find out something useful from Levi," Sam said after a long pause.

"Me, too. If he can't help us. . ."

"We might be out of options. At least he doesn't have a dog in this hunt."

"A dog in this hunt?" I said with a smirk. "Is that some kind of colloquial farm boy saying?"

He laughed. "Sorry. I forget you city girls don't understand our country phrases."

"I'm starting to learn some of them, and I have to admit it worries me."

Sam chuckled again. "Well, don't get too concerned. I'm pretty sure it takes a lot to drive the city out of someone like you."

"Not as much as you might think," I said softly.

Sam was silent for a moment. Before I realized what was happening, he leaned over and kissed me. Just like the time in the truck, I didn't have the power to fight back. My mind told me to stop, but my heart urged me on. After a long, sweet kiss, he leaned back.

"Sometimes I'm almost grateful to Jacob Glick," he whispered.

"Grateful? To that awful man? Wh–what are you saying?" The soft light of sunset highlighted Sam's strong profile. I had the strangest urge to touch his face—to run my fingers across the stubble on his firm chin.

"I'm not grateful for the evil he did, but I'm grateful he's kept you here so I could get to know you."

"It—it would have been better if I'd come here for another reason, b–but I know what you mean. I—I wouldn't trade the time we've had together for anything." My voice had an odd squeak to it that I couldn't seem to control.

He started to lean toward me again, but I held my hand up to his chest to stop him. "I—I think we need to get back to planning our next step. It would be easy to get sidetracked, and we can't afford that right now."

He let out a ragged breath. "You're always the voice of reason, aren't you? Just so you know, it's really beginning to get on my nerves."

I couldn't hold back a giggle. "Sorry, but someone's got to keep us grounded. You certainly don't seem capable of it."

"You got that right." He leaned across me, his hair brushing against my face. The musky smell of his shampoo made me almost forget my former admonition. I started to protest his attempt to kiss me again, but a small click and a flash of light confirmed that his target had been the lamp next to me. It provided just enough light to chase away the darkness but kept the warm ambience created by the soft glow of dusk. As he moved back to his side of the seat, I fought the urge to grab him and throw caution to the wind. The depth of my feelings toward this man didn't make sense. What was happening to me?

"I'm supposed to be at Ida's tomorrow at one o'clock," I managed to croak out.

"I'll meet you there at two. After I fix the irrigation system."

"From the attack of the vicious bunnies?"

He laughed. "Yeah, and the vicious mice. There are quite a few wild animals that like to nibble on our irrigation lines. Fixing them is a constant chore."

"Do you think Ida might have any information that could help us?" I asked, guiding the subject away from crazed crunching critters.

Sam stretched his legs out in front of him and yawned. "Maybe. You don't plan to tell her about Glick do you?"

"No. Levi's it unless we're pointed specifically to someone

who might know the whole truth."

"Except the person who knows the whole truth might just be the killer. I doubt seriously that whoever it was ran around sharing that information with anyone else in town."

"You've got a point. Should we talk to Levi after we leave Ida's tomorrow?"

"I'll call him. See if he can meet with us around five." He grunted. "I'd suggest we all go to the café for dinner, but I may never be able to set foot in there again."

"That's not practical, Sam. Maybe you should give Mary a chance to react normally to you. You two can't avoid each other forever. Harmony's too small for that. Besides, you have just as much right to eat in the café as anyone else."

He sighed. "You might be right, but I want to give her some time to settle down. She's way too upset right now."

The look Mary had given me this afternoon made me wonder if he wasn't making a wise choice after all. "Why don't we get some sandwiches and dessert from Mr. Menlo? We could meet Levi in the park. I'd love to spend some time there. It's so beautiful."

"Yes it is," he agreed. "The churches keep it up."

"Together?"

He grinned. "Yes, together. I told you Harmony is a special place. The churches get along great. In fact, Abel and Marcus are good friends."

"It *is* a special place," I said quietly. "In more ways than one."

Sam started to say something but then hesitated.

I looked at him questioningly. "What?"

"Well, you may think this sounds crazy."

I shook my head. "Listen, Sam. With what I've been through the past few days, nothing sounds crazy."

"Okay, here goes." He took a deep breath and slowly let it out. "Harmony is almost like a person, you know? With its own personality. But it's been hiding something. A secret. When you came to town, it's like the town. . .like the town decided to use you to uncover those secrets. You know, so it could heal. I feel like you were meant to come here. Meant to find that letter. Meant to finally bring the truth to light." He turned toward me. "Does that sound nuts?"

Although he tried to keep his tone light, I knew he was dead serious. And the funny thing was that the same odd thought had been flying around in my mind lately, trying to find a place to roost.

We said good night and went off to bed, but I couldn't sleep. I lay in bed and stared at the ceiling for quite a while, wondering if God really had led me here. If what was happening was more than coincidence. If my life and the small Kansas town of Harmony were tied together in some kind of divine destiny. Finally, with Buddy curled up next to me, I drifted off to sleep.

Chapter Fifteen

I awoke to a cloudy, overcast morning. A quick glance at the clock told me I'd slept later than I'd planned. I roused Buddy, found my slippers, and headed downstairs to a silent kitchen. A note on the table told me that Sam and Sweetie were already out in the orchards and that Sweetie had left breakfast for me in the fridge. Sure enough, I found a plate with scrambled eggs, ham, and a couple of biscuits covered with plastic wrap. I popped it into the microwave and checked the coffee. It was still hot. I poured a cup while I waited for my breakfast to heat up. The trick is to heat food up slowly in a microwave. That way it doesn't taste like it's been nuked. Years of living alone had forced me to learn the intricacies of microwave cooking. Not really something to be proud of.

I took my coffee cup, stepped out into the enclosed porch, and looked out the windows for Sam and his aunt. Buddy ran to the door and whined to go out, so I opened it. I finally spotted Sam kneeling on the ground near the edge of the orchard and remembered Sweetie's directive about repairing the irrigation lines. After Buddy finished his business, I watched as he ran over to Sam and enthusiastically jumped up on him. Sam put down his tools and hugged the little dog while Buddy licked his face.

I didn't see Sweetie anywhere and figured she was somewhere deep within the orchard. When I heard the microwave ding, I went back inside and took my plate out. Sweetie's culinary skills translated very well to any meal, and this was no exception.

After breakfast I took a shower, dressed, and bundled up my dirty clothes. I scouted around downstairs until I found the laundry room and tossed my dirty things in to wash. I'd just stepped out into the hall when I heard Sam call my name.

"Back here," I yelled. He came around the corner wearing a black T-shirt that highlighted his flaxen hair. When I looked into his eyes, I was reminded of prairie storm clouds. I felt my heart skip a beat or two.

"Man, it's about time. How late do you city girls sleep?"

"Look you, I'm usually out of bed by six in the morning every weekday and in the office by eight. I suppose you get up earlier."

He leaned against the wall. "I get up by five, and I'm out in the orchards by seven. I imagine you're still drinking coffee and putting on your makeup."

"Okay. You got me beat. So what are you doing now?"

He pushed off the wall and turned toward the kitchen. "Came in to get another cup of coffee. Hope you didn't drink it all."

"Nope. I'll join you if it's okay." I followed him to the kitchen. "I'm washing some clothes. I hope Sweetie doesn't mind if I use her washing machine."

Sam pointed at the kitchen table, so I sat down while he poured us both a cup of coffee. "She won't mind. As long as you don't break anything."

"I actually have washed clothes before. I think her appliances are safe."

"Then you should be okay." He pushed my cup in front of me and sat down on the other side of the table. "So, yesterday was quite a day, huh?"

"Yeah, that's an understatement." I stared through the window, making sure Sweetie wasn't on her way back. "What do you really think about that money?" I kept my voice low just in case she was in the vicinity. "I mean, it belongs to the church, doesn't it?"

He shrugged. "You're guessing about its origin. Truth is, we don't really know where it came from. It's in Angstadt's house, so for now, it's Angstadt's. Of course, his being dead makes it a little difficult to return."

"Even though we can't prove this money is the missing money Emily told me about, this house originally belonged to the church. Doesn't that fact make it clear it should go to them?"

Sam leaned forward, wrapped his hands around his cup, and stared into it. "I honestly don't know," he said after a brief hesitation. "I don't think Sweetie would give it to them. I told you before that she doesn't go to any church." He sighed. "At least now I understand why."

"But Sam, she's judging everyone by Amil Angstadt, and that's not fair. I came to Harmony with a negative opinion of the Mennonite church here—but I was wrong. Dead wrong. Just because Angstadt was a bad apple, that doesn't mean the whole barrel is rotten."

Sam cracked a smile. "Are you trying to put this into fruit terms so I'll understand it?"

I chuckled. "Not on purpose. Maybe you're rubbing off on me."

"You're becoming fruitier?"

"Sadly, that seems to be the case. But back to the money. . ."

"Look, Grace," he said, the smile leaving his face, "I'm not going to pressure my aunt about that money. I had no idea everything she'd been through. Now that I know, I'm going to let her decide what to do. I'm not Holy Spirit Jr. She and God are going to have to work it out between them. My job is to love her—and support her no matter what she does."

I didn't argue with him; this wasn't the time for it. Sam loved his aunt deeply, and finding out how Angstadt and Glick had tried to manipulate her had caused him pain.

"Okay. Let's just leave that alone for now." I glanced at my watch. "Wow, I can't believe it's almost noon. I have to be at Ida's by one."

"I'll make us some sandwiches."

"Oh my, no. I just finished breakfast. And Ida plans to stuff me with strawberry pie."

"You're right," Sam said, frowning. "Maybe I'll just eat half a sandwich. . ."

I laughed. "You'd better be careful. I would hate for you to drop over from starvation."

"Very funny." He winked at me. "I'll have you know I'm a growing boy."

"I'm surprised you don't weigh five hundred pounds the way Sweetie cooks."

He shook his head. "Working out in the orchards keeps me fit. God help me when I get too old to do it anymore. My only hope is to marry a gal who can't find her way around a kitchen."

He gazed at me with a serious, fixed stare, and any humorous retort I might have tried to sling back died in my throat. I quickly dropped my gaze to my coffee cup and took a sip.

"Do you want me to drive you to Ida's?" he asked, his voice a few notches lower than normal.

"N—no. It's just down the road. I'd like to walk." I stood up and pointed toward the porch. "Think I'll go down to the lake for a while before I head over to her house. There are some beautiful flowers growing along the shore. Thought I might pick some to take to her."

Sam smiled. "She'd love that, Grace. How nice of you to think of it. I'll eat a little something and get back to work. See you at two."

"Okay." I headed out the kitchen door onto the porch and

then out the back door. The overcast sky added a chill to the air. My sweatshirt wasn't enough to protect me from the cold that nipped at me. As I broke through the trees, the beauty of the lake struck me again. Trouble Lake. If only I could jump in the water and leave all my troubles behind just as the Indians had done so many years ago. It was hard to believe that I'd only been in Harmony four days. It felt as if I'd been here forever. Wichita seemed far away—almost like someplace I'd only dreamed about.

I gathered some of the lovely wildflowers that lined the water's edge, winding my way around until I reached the dock behind Benjamin's house. Even though it was smaller than Sam's, it looked sturdy and inviting. I walked out to the edge and looked back toward the big red house. It was barely visible above the tree line, but I could see Sam's dock clearly. I turned to walk away when I noticed someone standing at its edge. It was Sam. He stood there, staring into the water. He remained motionless for several minutes. Finally, he took something from his pocket and stared at it. Then he suddenly threw it into the water and walked back toward the house. What in the world had he tossed into the lake?

I turned and headed toward Benjamin's house, wondering if Sam was keeping a secret from me. And if so, what? I was so wrapped up in my thoughts I didn't pay much attention to my surroundings until I entered the grove of trees between the lake and the house. I'd no sooner stepped into the clearing when I stopped dead in my tracks. Was this where Jacob Glick was buried? Was I standing on his grave? Talking about a dead body on your property is one thing. Being faced with the reality of it is quite another. Sweat broke out on my forehead and my knees felt like rubber. I looked back, trying to get my bearings. Although not obvious from the road, Benjamin's house actually sat on a small hill.

As I stared at the lake, that odd feeling of déjà vu came rushing back. Even though it made no sense, I knew I'd definitely been here before. I'd looked at Trouble Lake from this very spot. No, wait a minute. Something wasn't quite right. I walked through the clearing to a grassy knoll right above the tree line. Now I knew where I'd seen this view of the lake. In Emily's heartbreaking self-portrait. This was where she'd sat all those years ago, after Glick's heinous crime, frightened and wondering what to do. I looked around, saddened to think of a young Emily sitting where I stood now, terrified and alone, afraid to tell anyone what had happened to her. And now, years later, Glick's body lay hidden beneath layers of earth. Was this some kind of divine justice or just a bizarre coincidence? I thought about Paul's admonition to the Galatians, that a man will reap what he sows. Jacob Glick had sown evil, and his end had been violent and deadly. A deep sadness washed through me for Emily and, oddly, for Glick himself. If only he'd chosen a different path and given God a chance to make something good of his life. Of course, it was too late for him, but it wasn't for Emily.

Without warning, a sudden gust of wind moved quickly through the trees. The rustle of their leaves seemed to whisper to me, "Beauty instead of ashes. The oil of gladness instead of mourning." I knelt down in the soft grass and prayed for Emily— that she would find a way to exchange the ashes of her past for the beauty God had waiting for her. Too much evil had occurred here. It was time to vanquish it. I knelt before the Lord for several minutes, praying until I felt a release. Trying to shake off the odd sensations that surrounded me, I got to my feet and almost ran out of the grove and into the sunlight. I hurried past Benjamin's silent house and made my way to the road. As I approached Ida's house, I noticed the old woman waiting for me on her front porch. She rocked slowly back and forth in her rocking chair but stood to her feet as I approached.

"I'm so happy to see you, my dear," she said with a delighted smile.

Her friendly expression helped to banish the disturbing remnants of the past that tried to cling to me. "I picked these for you." I held out my armful of flowers, grateful to be out of the clearing and in the presence of this sweet woman who radiated friendliness.

She clapped her hands together and then took them from me. "Ach, wildflowers. I love them so. My husband used to pick them for me. After he died, I would go once in a while to gather them, but as I got older, it became harder and harder to make it down to the lake." She pulled open her screen door. "Come inside and sit while I find a vase."

The inside of her house reminded me of Benjamin's. Homey but simple. I sat down in a lovely chair with quilted upholstery. The open windows picked up the spring breeze and moved it through the house, fluttering Ida's sheer curtains in a slow spring dance.

She left the room for a few minutes but tottered back with the colorful flowers arranged in a cut-glass vase. She put them on a dark wooden table next to the couch and sat down beside them. The floral scent wafted through the room, carried by the gentle air currents. Even though it was still early afternoon, I suddenly felt sleepy. The peaceful quiet of Ida's home made me compare it to my own. Seemed like the television was always on—or music CDs. But now I could hear the wind moving through the trees, the birds singing in different tones and voices, and Ida's clock ticking away the seconds of a lazy April afternoon.

"I thought we would read your grandmother's letter first, dear," Ida chirped in a voice that quivered with the sound of age and contentment. "I baked a strawberry pie this morning. And the coffee is on. It should be ready soon."

"That sounds lovely," I said. "Please, read the letter."

She reached into the pocket of her long, dark blue dress and pulled out an old envelope, faded and yellowed with age. Carefully opening the brittle seal, she reached in and pulled out the folded pages inside.

"I was foolish to leave this unopened all these years," she said, her words heavy with the accent of her heritage. "Herman, my husband, passed away about three months before your grandmother and grandfather decided to leave Harmony. Essie and I were so close. I felt she had deserted me." She shook her head slowly. "It was selfish of me. I should have understood. They had finally freed themselves from their commitment to the church and wanted to spend time with you. Benjamin was old enough to fend for himself and encouraged them to go." She wiped a tear from her wrinkled cheek. "Poor Benjamin. Essie was confident he would follow them someday. But as soon as they left, he shut himself in that house and refused to have anything to do with anybody. I asked him about his parents frequently, and all he would say was that they were fine. About two years after they left, I finally questioned him about why he had not left Harmony to be with them. I will never forget what he said. Or the look in his eyes. They were so dark and cold. 'They have made their bed, Ida,' he said. 'I have made mine. And that is the end of it. I have no need of anyone but my God.'" She made a clucking sound with her tongue. "Never could figure out why he cut them off." She looked at me with sadness in her face. "Did Essie and Joe ever try to contact him?"

"I honestly don't know a lot about it. No one talked to me much about Uncle Benjamin. But I did hear Mama Essie say something once about trying to talk to him. He told them he wanted nothing to do with them—or my father. Papa Joe made plans to come here and try to reason with Benjamin, but then Mama died and Papa Joe started having problems with Alzheimer's. He never did make that trip."

"But now you are here," she said. She smoothed her skirt and smiled at me. "You came here for them. In their place, ja?"

"I—I never thought about it that way. Of course, I was too late for Uncle Benjamin."

"I am not so sure about that, child. God has a whole different sense of time than we do. What looks too late for us is sometimes right on time for God." She held the letter to her chest. "Why, just think about your grandmother and me. She left Harmony in 1990. You were jus a toddler." She shook her head. "Bishop Angstadt pitched a fit, he did. Your grandparents were leaders in the church, you know. When they started to doubt his leadership, things began to fall apart for him. Others in the church began to leave. He died a couple of years after your grandparents moved away. Even if Benjamin could not leave because of his loyalty to the bishop, his death should have made his way clear. I guess the bishop's beliefs about The Ban overcame Benjamin's loyalty to his family. It's a shame."

"One thing I don't understand, Ida. Wasn't there anyone keeping an eye on Angstadt? Someone from your denomination or something?"

"Bishop Angstadt himself was an overseer, but there were no other congregations except ours in this area. And those whose job it was to watch over him were far removed from Harmony. They assumed everything was fine. None of us complained. Perhaps we should have." She lifted her hands in surrender. "It is hard to explain now, child. But at the time we thought we were doing the right thing. Criticizing our bishop was looked upon as an awful sin."

"Seems to me that following your 'old ways' led to a lot of heartache. Yet you still cling to these same principles. I don't understand. . ."

"Now let me stop you there, child," the old woman said with a smile. "I *do* embrace many of the old ways, but it is only because I want to. I love my life—the way it is. Of course, not all my choices are made out of the desire for simplicity. For example, I certainly have nothing against electricity. If it didn't cost so much, I might

224

put it in." She sighed. "But you know something? I love the glow of a lamp at night. And I love sitting in front of a fireplace in the winter and snuggling under the quilts my mother made." She shrugged. "I must admit that I am not a fan of really hot days, but I can harness my old horse, Zebediah, and ride my buggy into town. I sit in the cool café and visit with my neighbors." She put her hand to her mouth and giggled like a schoolgirl. "Now this must stay between you and me, ja? Sometimes, I strip down to my underwear and soak my feet in a tub of cool water. Good thing I can see anyone who turns into my driveway. That way I am able to get decent before they see me in my altogether." She pointed her finger at me. "And is there anything as wonderful as a cold glass of lemonade on a blistering day?" She clapped her hands together. "How can we enjoy the good things in life if we don't understand what it is like without them?"

Ida's simple delight in her lifestyle made sense to me. "I think I understand. If someone had tried to tell me a month ago I'd be envious of people like you, I'd have thought they were crazy. But now. . ."

"You're beginning to like us, ja?" she said laughing. "I'm so glad. If nothing else, you have made some friends here. Maybe someday your mother and father will come back for a visit. I am afraid they have some bad feelings toward Harmony. But this town is special—and very resilient. Even someone like Bishop Angstadt could not break its spirit."

"Sam told me that a long time ago you and some of the other women in Harmony prayed that this would be a peaceful place."

She nodded slowly. "Ja, we certainly did. And our Lord has honored that prayer all these years. I would like your father and mother to see the work He has done here."

"Maybe they will. I intend to tell them about Harmony and what it's become. I think it would heal them to come back for a visit."

"I agree, child. You are very wise." Ida's eyes twinkled with an inner joy that drew me to her.

"You know, you remind me a lot of Abel Mueller. Do you mind if I ask why you don't attend his church? I mean, it's Mennonite and all. Is it because you think he's doing something wrong?"

Ida's eyebrows shot up. "Ach no, child. That is not it at all. Pastor Mueller and I have talked about the reason I am still with our small group, and it has nothing to do with him." She sighed and looked out the window. "Truth be told, I would love to go to Bethel." She swung her gaze back to me. "I will tell you the real reason, but it must stay between us. Is that something you can abide by?"

"Of course."

"It is because of Sarah Ketterling. We have developed a fine friendship, and I just can't desert her, Gracie. The poor child is so isolated. At least Gabriel lets me talk to her. And he even allows her to visit me from time to time. I am afraid if I start attending Bethel, he will forbid our relationship."

I told Ida about running into Sarah in town and my desire to learn wood-block printing from her.

Ida nodded slowly. "I wonder if Gabriel would allow her to teach you if you met here in my home."

"I—I kind of doubt it," I said. "He wasn't very nice to me. Told me my uncle would be ashamed of me."

Ida's face flushed crimson. "That man had no business speaking to you that way. He is so filled up with hate, he can't love anyone." She shook her head. "Your uncle would be so proud of you, Gracie. You are such a lovely young woman. Good and kind—and full of love. Do not listen to Gabriel. I knew Benjamin better than most folks. He was a troubled man—but he was a good man."

She turned her attention to the old letter and unfolded its yellowed pages slowly. "Now, let us read this letter before that handsome, young Sam Goodrich breaks in, looking for a piece of my pie."

I nodded and settled back in my chair. Listening to a letter from my grandmother written twenty years ago gave me a lump in my throat. How I wish I could talk to her one more time. Feel her hug my neck or call me her "little gift of grace."

" '*My dearest friend, Ida,*' " the old woman read in her age-crackled voice. " '*I know our leaving has caused you pain. I am so sorry. When we drove away from Harmony for the last time, all I could think of was you. I know you have felt alone since Herman's passing. In the past few years, our friendship has grown even stronger. Surely you realize how much I treasure it—and you. But I cannot allow Grace to grow up without her Mama Essie and Papa Joe. When we visited Daniel and Beverly, my heart broke when we had to leave. Gracie cried for us as we walked away. I cannot bear it, Ida. Can you understand that, my friend? If I could have both of you, I would. Joe and I talked about asking you to come with us. But I know you do not want to leave your home, and I respect that. Can you respect the yearning in my heart for my beautiful grandchild? I wish you could see her, Ida. She has the most beautiful green eyes and bright red hair. She looks so much like Benjamin. Joe and I are hopeful that he will join us soon. My little gift of grace will love her handsome uncle—I am sure of it. And oh, Ida, if you could only see Daniel and Beverly. What a lovely home they have made for themselves. They are so much in love, even today. It is such a blessing to be near them.*

" '*I know Bishop Angstadt was angry about our decision, but I have come to realize that the love of God I read about in the Bible is not the kind of love I see in him. I will not speak ill of anyone, Ida, but I will ask you to remember that Mennonites are dedicated to following God's love and living in peace with everyone. It is because of my love for Him and*

*His ways first, and the love of my family second, that I have
embraced the decision my husband made to move to Nebraska.
This does not mean that my heart is not broken because I had
to leave Benjamin and you behind. Maybe someday soon I
will be able to come to you—to greet you once again with a
holy kiss. I pray for this.*

  *"'Please take care of yourself, my dearest friend. And if
you can find it in your heart, please forgive me for any pain
I have caused you. I want you to know that I will love you
every day I live. And if I never hear from you again in this
life, I will wait for that kiss in the fields of heaven where we
will take off our socks and shoes and dip our toes into God's
holy waters. I love you today and forever.*

  "'Your loving sister in Christ, Essie Temple.'"

Ida lowered the letter with trembling fingers. Tears coursed
down her face, and I realized with a start that my face was wet,
too. As we looked at each other, I was filled with a desire that
seemed to speak straight from my heart. I rose to my feet and
walked up to Ida. Then I leaned over and kissed her lightly on the
cheek. "This is from Essie," I said, trying to keep my voice from
breaking.

The old woman's breath caught, and she reached up and put
her arms around my neck. I hugged her back while we both cried.
When I straightened up, my shoulder was damp with her tears.

"Oh, my dear Gracie," she whispered. "My dear, dear Gracie."

I sat back down and tried to compose myself. I couldn't help but
compare this letter to the one my uncle had left for me. The first
letter brought fear and confusion. This one had delivered healing
and love. Ida reached into her pocket and took out a hankie, which
she used to dry her face. Not having a tissue handy, I wiped my
tears with my sleeve. Finally, I started to giggle. "My goodness, if
Sam finds us like this, he'll think we've lost our minds."

A grin erupted on Ida's face, and we soon found ourselves wiping away tears of laughter instead of sorrow.

"My goodness," she said once she managed to stop. "What joy you've brought to my home today. I am so grateful and happy I read Essie's letter with you. It made it even more special."

"She always loved you, Ida." I followed that statement with a rather loud, high-pitched hiccup.

Ida chuckled. "I think it is time for something to drink, ja? Coffee or lemonade?"

"Lemonade, please." I tried to stop the next hiccup before it got past my lips. My attempt only made it worse, culminating in a sound that was a cross between a hiccup and a squealing pig.

Ida hurried off to the kitchen, probably afraid I might actually implode before her eyes. She was back almost immediately with a tall, cold glass of homemade lemonade. I swallowed half the glassful in only a few seconds. When I pulled the rim away from my mouth, we both waited in anticipation. Thankfully, my embarrassing bout was gone. Peace reigned once again in my body.

"I–I'm sorry," I said. "I guess laughing and crying at the same time makes me hiccup. I have no idea why I can't hiccup like a normal human being. It's humiliating."

Ida's eyes filled with tears once again even though she smiled. "Your grandmother sounded exactly like that. I used to tease her about it unmercifully."

"You're right. I'd forgotten." Sometimes at family gatherings, my father and grandfather would purposely pester my grandmother until she got the hiccups. She would scold them for it, but somehow it just made the situation funnier. Mama Essie had a way of wrinkling her nose when she was amused that reminded me of a young girl. I fought against the emotions the memory brought. There had been enough crying for one afternoon.

"You know," Ida said in a dreamy voice, staring out the nearby window. "Growing up Mennonite wasn't bad at all. Oh, there were challenges as a young girl, but the positive things always outweighed the negative."

"Tell me about it, please. My father never talked much about his childhood."

"Well, school was the hardest. I grew up in Pennsylvania. We moved to Harmony when I was ten. In Pennsylvania we had our own community school. But when we moved here, I had to go to regular school in Sunrise, a town about ten miles from here. That was hard. We looked different than the other children. And we weren't allowed to participate when they stood for the Pledge of Allegiance."

"I don't understand," I said, frowning. "What's wrong with the Pledge?"

"We were taught that our allegiance was only to God and His kingdom. Not to any government."

"Oh. Did the other kids tease you?"

She nodded. "And not just about that. The way we dressed, the way we wore our hair, and the buggies we rode to school in. There was always something, it seemed. As a child, your heart cry is to fit in. Yet we never did."

"Do those memories make you sad?"

Ida smiled. "No, child. When I was young, it seemed as if my life was very hard. But now, I'm grateful. I would not want it any other way. Being raised the way I was taught me what is really important in this life. Goodness, God has blessed me so much. I could never repay His kindnesses to me. Why, look at the blessing He has given me through you. I know we are going to be very great friends."

I started to remind her that I wouldn't be here long, but I couldn't get the words out. Of course, driving to Harmony for weekend visits wasn't impossible. This town had grabbed a piece of my heart, and I knew I'd have to return whenever I could.

We sipped our lemonade in satisfied silence. I could look out

Ida's front window and see Benjamin's house. The sight of the silent, deserted structure reminded me of a question I wanted to ask her.

"Ida, did you happen to notice any cars at Benjamin's house on Saturday?"

"Let's see." Her forehead wrinkled in thought. "I did see one automobile there. I can't quite remember what time it was."

"Do you know who it belonged to?"

"Why, certainly. It was Sam's."

Disappointment must have shown in my face, because Ida frowned and reached for my hand. "I'm sorry, my dear. That doesn't seem to be the answer you were looking for. Were you hoping I had seen someone else?"

"It doesn't matter. It's not important." I had no intention of telling her about the vase. I felt certain she would believe in my innocence, but I didn't want her to worry about me.

I heard the rumble of Sam's truck on the dirt path that led to Ida's house. The old woman rose to her feet.

"Sounds like I need to cut some pieces of pie," she said happily. "It is so nice to have company. I—I certainly wish you lived here, Gracie. It would be wonderful to have you close." With that, she headed toward the kitchen.

"Let me help you," I called after her.

She turned around and smiled. "Not necessary, child. You stay there and let Sam in, ja? I'll be back lickety-split."

I got up and opened the front door. Sam came bounding up the steps. "Hey, there," he said when he saw me. He looked like he'd just stepped out of the shower. His hair was still damp and he'd changed into a clean shirt.

"Hey, yourself. I hate to tell you this, but Ida and I ate all the pie."

He stopped cold and gaped at me. "I hope you're kidding. . ."

I tried to keep a straight face but found it impossible. His shocked expression made me laugh.

"You are in so much trouble." He flashed me a crooked grin. "I will get you. Somehow. Someway. Somewhere."

"Wow, watch out. I'm shaking." I opened the screen door for him, and he stepped inside. Before I knew it, he had his arms around me in a big hug. He smelled of bath soap and cologne. Startled, I pushed him away. He stepped back quickly and tried to smile, but I could see the hurt in his eyes.

"Sorry. I'm just glad to see you."

"No, I'm sorry," I said. "I shouldn't have done that. You—you just surprised me."

"Forget it," he said brusquely. "I understand."

He walked away from me before I could say anything else. Regret coursed through me. He'd obviously showered and dressed for me. And in his mind, I'd just rejected him. I chided myself for shoving him away. Why had I reacted that way? For some reason, an uncomfortable tension grew inside me that had nothing to do with Jacob Glick or the stolen vase. There was a war waging in my soul. A war I couldn't afford to acknowledge.

I sat down in Ida's chair and listened to Sam and Ida teasing each other in the kitchen. They had a wonderful friendship based on mutual trust and admiration. I wasn't sure I had that in my life. I had friends, sure, but after spending a few days in Harmony, they were beginning to look more like acquaintances. Maybe it had to do with living in a small town. Whatever it was, I couldn't seem to put my finger on the difference.

"Here we are," Ida called out. Sam followed behind her, carrying a tray with three plates of pie and three cups of coffee. Ida wrinkled her nose and laughed. "I told this man I could carry that tray by myself, but he would not let me do it. Thinks I am an old lady, I guess."

"That's not it," Sam said, winking at me. "I just need the exercise so I can keep up with you."

I smiled at him. Thankfully, the friction between us seemed to have disappeared. Ida moved the flowers off the table next to the couch and pulled it over so it sat between us. Sam put the tray on top of it while Ida carried the vase over to a long table against the wall.

"Did you see the flowers Gracie brought me?" she asked Sam.

"They're beautiful," he said, smiling.

She fingered them for a moment and then leaned over to smell them. When she turned around, her eyes were moist. "They remind me so much of Herman. Thank you again, Gracie."

"I'll bring you flowers after Grace leaves," Sam said. "Wish I'd thought of it myself."

Ida tottered back over to the couch. "Pshaw. Men don't understand flowers. Women do though. And my Herman." She reached over and tousled Sam's hair. "You show your concern every time you drop by to see if I need anything. And when you fix things that are broken." She looked at me. "This man completely replaced my roof when it got weak and water began to leak in. He also built new back steps and fixed Zebediah's barn when it started to rot. I could not ask for a better neighbor."

"Oh hush," Sam said good-naturedly. "You know I only do those things so you'll feed me."

Ida chuckled as she took the pie plates and coffee off the tray. She handed me the tray, and I set it down next to my chair.

"This table is not very big, but it will hold our pie," she said. "Now before we eat, will you say grace, Sam?"

We bowed our heads while Sam prayed over the food and asked God's blessings on his friend. We all said, "Amen," and dug into our yummy-looking dessert. It was topped with a rich whipped cream, and the strawberries were encased in a flavorful gelatin. All this was supported by a flaky piecrust that practically melted in my mouth.

"This is delicious," I said after taking my first bite. "My goodness, you definitely would give my grandmother a run for her money."

"I almost forgot," Sam said after swallowing a big bite of pie. "Did you read the letter?"

"Yes, we did," I said. "It was wonderful. We both cried, and I got the hiccups."

Sam laughed. "Oh, great. Don't show it to me. I don't want to cry, and people laugh when I hiccup. I make this strange squeaky sound. Can't control it."

"Thanks for the warning," I said. "I'll try to keep you happy."

Sam gave me a strange look and shoved another piece of pie in his mouth.

"You two young people talk like you have known each other all your lives," Ida chirped. "Gracie, didn't you just arrive here on Friday?"

I nodded. "Yes, I did. But for some reason, it seems like a lifetime ago."

Ida raised her eyebrows. "My goodness, are we so boring?"

"No, not at all." I sneaked a quick look at Sam who returned my gaze with an overly innocent look. "I—I guess it's just that I've been learning so much about the town and its people. And about my family. Things I never knew."

"I understand that." Ida sat her plate down and picked up her cup. "There is a lot of history in Harmony. Many people have come and gone. In fact, few people are left from Bishop Angstadt's days. Most of the old folks have passed—and the young ones have moved away. Only a handful of us left. But the town has changed. People stay now. Things are better. More peaceful."

I was certain she believed what she said, but I knew Harmony still had ghosts. Ghosts that needed to be exorcised. "Abel told me he has diaries and memoirs left behind by past residents. He seems to be an expert on Harmony history."

An odd look crossed Ida's face. "Well, he does have some information, but. . ."

"But there's nothing like actually being there?" Sam finished for her.

Ida sat her cup down and folded her hands. "People only write down what they want people to know in their memoirs. They tend to leave out the unpleasantness—especially their own failures and disappointments." She smiled at us. "Now mind you, I am not saying Abel is misrepresenting anything, but he just has written words. He cannot see the hearts behind the words."

"You're probably the best source of information in town," Sam said. "People should come to you when they want to research Harmony's past."

"Well, I do not know about that, but folks have come around from time to time to ask about past incidents and residents."

I caught Sam's eye, and he gave me a little nod.

"Ida," I said, trying to keep my tone light, "do you remember a man named Jacob Glick?"

She frowned at me. "Jacob Glick? Now why would you ask me about him?"

"I—I ran across his name somewhere. Seems like an interesting man."

The old woman grunted. "Interesting? About as interesting as a snake in the grass." She screwed up her face in a grimace. "The bishop's sidekick, that's what he was. But there was no pretense of godliness in that man. Evil intentions. Evil thoughts." She shook her head. "Herman and I kept our eyes on him. We were determined to keep him away from the young women in our town. Herman confronted him more than once, but Jacob slithered back to the bishop who always protected him."

"That must have been frustrating," Sam said. "Why did you and Herman stay here? Why didn't you leave?"

"Because she felt she had to protect people," I said softly. "Just like she's trying to protect Sarah now."

Ida's head bobbed up and down. "Ja, ja, that's one reason. But we also felt Harmony needed us." She stared past us. "You know," she said dreamily, "too many people are looking for a place where they feel comfortable. But life is not just about comfort. It is about being in a place where you are needed. Comfortable or not, we all have a special place where God wants to use us. A place where someone is waiting just for us. I belong to Harmony. I belong to the people He sends to me. I may not know why—but I know it's important to His plan." She refocused her attention to us. "And I intend to be in the center of His will. That is my calling, you see. Even if He only has me here for one person—it is His plan, not mine that counts."

Sam nodded as though he understood. I just shook my head. I also believed God had a plan for everyone's life, but I had no idea what mine was. Sometimes I worried that I'd completely missed it. Maybe I was so far off track I'd never find my way to that place Ida talked about.

"I—I suppose other people felt the same way about Glick that you did," I said, trying to shift the conversation back to the dead man buried on Benjamin's property. "I mean, he had enemies, right?"

"Oh my, yes. Most of the parents who had young girls. And to be honest, even though Bishop Angstadt protected Jacob, I got the feeling he did not like him any better than the rest of us. He certainly seemed relieved when he left town."

"What made Glick leave?" Sam asked.

"It was strange timing," Ida said slowly. "The last time I laid eyes on the man, he looked like the proverbial cat that had swallowed the canary. Happy as a lark. Never could figure out why."

"I'll bet a lot of people were happy to see him go," I said. Sam and I had hoped Ida would point to someone who specifically wanted Glick gone. But it seemed that everyone in Harmony wanted him out of town. This wasn't getting us anywhere.

Ida rose to her feet. "More coffee?"

"Sounds great," Sam said.

"Let me help you with that." I started to get up when she waved her hand at me.

"You two sit still." She picked up the tray and headed to the kitchen. "I'm not so old I cannot fetch three cups of coffee."

As she toddled away, she mumbled something that I couldn't completely understand. But before she got much farther, a couple of the words brought me to full alert.

"Ida," I said, a little louder than I meant to. "What did you just say?"

Sam shot me a concerned look, but I held my finger to my lips, signaling to him to be quiet.

Ida stopped and turned around. "I am sorry, dear. It is nothing. I—I just said that it is odd so many people are interested in that terrible Jacob Glick."

Sam got to his feet and crossed over to where the elderly woman stood, still holding the tray. He gently took it from her. "What do you mean? What people?"

Ida looked back and forth between Sam and me, a look of confusion on her face. "I guess I should not have said *people*. Just one person who asked me all kinds of questions about Jacob. I had almost forgotten about it. It was awhile ago."

"And who was that?" I asked.

"Why, it was John Keystone, the butcher. He visited me not long after he moved to Harmony. Wanted to know about the early days of our little town, but our conversation kept angling back to Jacob Glick. I found it odd at the time. He said he was doing some kind of family research." She shrugged and headed toward the kitchen, leaving Sam and I to stare at each other with our mouths hanging open.

Chapter Sixteen

Sure didn't expect that," Sam said after we climbed into his truck and waved good-bye to Ida.

"Me either. Why would John Keystone ask about Glick? Could he possibly know something about his death?"

Sam shook his head as he turned onto the main road. "How could he? He was a baby when Glick died. Besides, he only moved here a year ago, and he barely knew Ben. It doesn't make sense."

"He said it had something to do with family business. What could that mean?"

"I don't know, but he must have been referring to *his* family. I remember Abel saying Glick had no relatives."

"So John was talking about his own family," I repeated. "Glick was a predator. We can't assume all his victims lived here. John's interests may have nothing to do with anyone in Harmony."

"You could be right. But what if he lied? Maybe he was just trying to keep Ida from getting suspicious about his questions."

"But why? Who is Glick to John Keystone?"

Sam just shrugged.

My brain kept trying to wrap itself around this new twist. What information was John fishing for? I thought back to Saturday.

John's meat market was right across the street from Ruth's shop. He easily could have slipped in and stolen the vase after Ruth left. But why would he want to cause trouble for me? I was no threat to him.

"Could Mary have overheard me asking about Glick and told John?"

"They're pretty good friends," he said slowly. "I think she'd tell him whatever he wanted to know." He frowned. "But was Mary even in the room when you mentioned Glick?"

"She was there all right. Every time I looked her way, she was shooting me dirty looks."

He sighed. "Well, Abel's pretty loud. Even if Mary didn't hear you, she easily could have heard him. And he mentioned Glick very clearly."

"I—I don't know what to make of this." I stared at him. "Can you ask Mary if she talked to John about me? And if Glick's name came up? I have to know if John had any reason to take Ruth's vase."

"Oh man. You don't know what you're asking. Mary would like to take off my head and serve it as the main course for supper. Besides, even if she did mention our conversation, it doesn't mean John had any reason to frame you for theft."

I patted his arm. "I know that. I'm just trying to follow the trail to see where it leads—even if it's a dead end. Talking to Mary might be difficult, but you've got to mend fences with her anyway. Surely you're not planning to avoid the café for the rest of your life."

"Well, actually that was the plan," he said with a smirk. "It may be the safest alternative."

The silly look on his face made me laugh. "I think you can come up with something better than that."

His only answer was a grunt.

We passed Ben's house and reached Main Street. I looked at

my watch. Four fifteen. We were supposed to meet Levi at four thirty. A little early for supper, but he had something else planned around six. We had just enough time to pick up sandwiches. "You know, even if we find out that John knows of my interest in Glick, we still have no idea what that means."

"I agree. That's why we have to confront him."

"Confront him!" I tried to keep a note of hysteria out of my voice, but I failed miserably. "Since coming to Harmony, I've taken a long-held secret and blabbed it to so many people I'm surprised my family skeletons haven't danced their way onto the front page of the local paper!"

Sam cast a disapproving look my way. "First of all, we don't actually have a local paper. Secondly, if we did, I hope we could come up with something better than your exploits. Besides, just who have you blabbed to? Me? Sweetie found out on her own. You didn't tell Emily the truth."

"But I more or less confirmed her suspicion that Glick was dead. And as far as Sweetie goes, she found my uncle's letter because of me. Because of my carelessness."

"Now hold on there," Sam said sharply. "You weren't careless. Sweetie was overly nosy. There was no way for you to know her part in all this or that she was actually spying on you. That's not your fault."

"I guess you're right, but it sure feels like this situation is spiraling out of control."

"This situation has been out of control for thirty years. We're the ones who need to bring it back under control. You've convinced me that discovering the truth is our only hope."

Of course, he was right. Every moment I'd spent in Harmony had only proved that secrets buried in emotional graves eventually turn deadly. The truth had to come out. I was also well aware of the fact that at the end of my two weeks, if I still didn't have the answers I needed, I would have to tell my father everything. Now that I knew he hadn't actually caused Glick's death, I certainly felt better about that possibility. However, just because I knew my father wasn't involved didn't mean the authorities would believe it. As of now, he was the only person we knew about who'd fought Glick the night he died. And then he'd left town. No matter how you sliced it, Dad looked guilty. The only outcome that would absolutely protect my father was handing over the real killer. I prayed God would help Sam and me find him before it was too late.

We were nearing the bakery. "So what are we going to tell Levi?" I said.

"I don't know. I guess we'll tell him the truth."

"Will he keep our conversation secret?"

"If we tell him to, yes." He pulled up in front of the bakery.

"I hate passing this burden on to someone else."

"I do, too." He turned off the engine. "But we've got to have more information, and he's the only person I can think of who might be able to give it to us." He smiled at me. "Don't worry. I've known him all my life. If there's anyone in Harmony we can trust, it's Levi Hoffman. He's been like a father to me."

I nodded. "Okay, okay. Guess I'm just getting a little antsy. Seems like we take off down one rabbit trail and another pops up. I just hope this journey we're on has a satisfying conclusion. We're dragging a lot of lives behind us."

Sam reached over and turned my face toward his. "You've got to have some faith, Grace. God brought you here for a purpose. He won't desert us now. The results of this journey, as you called it, aren't on your beautiful shoulders. They're on God's strong ones."

I gazed into his eyes and saw the sincerity there. "Exactly what I've been telling myself. But you might need to remind me several times a day. Think you can live up to the challenge?"

He laughed softly. "I'll try." He learned over and kissed me on the forehead. "Now, let's go pick out some sandwiches."

We exited Menlos' a few minutes later, loaded down with sandwiches, pop, and cookies warm from the oven. Mrs. Menlo gave us paper plates, napkins, and plastic utensils—something I hadn't thought about. She also stuck three pieces of baklava into our sack.

We got back in the truck, and Sam drove while I balanced our meal on my lap. I'd passed the city park on my way into town, but this was my first chance to actually scout it out. We turned onto a dirt road that wound around the small lake. A group of geese glided smoothly across the shimmering crystal water. Several small ducks quacked noisily as a woman and her daughter threw pieces of bread to them.

We passed a lovely stone water fountain surrounded by whitewashed wooden benches. Water gently danced down the four-tiered stone fountain. "It's beautiful," I said to Sam. "Looks expensive. Where did it come from?"

He slowed the truck down, backed up, and pulled over to the side of the road. "We've still got a few minutes. Get out and I'll show you something."

I followed him down a stone path leading to the fountain. It was even more beautiful close up. I peered over the edge of the bottom tier. The floor of the fountain was layered with coins dropped in by people with wishes in their hearts.

"I left my purse back in the truck," I said. "I want a penny to throw in."

I turned to go back to the truck when I felt Sam's hand on my shoulder. "Here." He reached into his jean pocket with his other hand. "I've got change from the bakery." He pulled out several coins.

I took a penny, thought a minute, then threw it into the sparkling water.

"You really think that will help?" he asked with a smile.

"I don't actually wish when I throw coins in a fountain. I pray. I just prayed that God's will would be done in Harmony—and in my life."

"Pretty dangerous prayer," Sam said in a quiet voice, the sound of water splashing lightly in the background.

"How so?"

"What if God's will isn't your will?"

"I'm not sure I understand what you mean."

He cocked his head to one side and raised both eyebrows. "A real prayer of consecration—saying not my will but Yours. It means your life may take a turn you hadn't planned on. Are you ready to accept that?"

I stared into the water. Had I really meant what I prayed? Or was I trying to fit God into *my* plan? Doubt flooded my mind. "I—I don't know. I guess I'll have to think about that."

Sam laughed easily, his blond hair blowing gently in the afternoon breeze. "You'd better decide pretty fast. You may have to face that question sooner than you imagine."

I squinted up at him, not quite sure what he meant. The look in his eyes caused a strange tickling sensation to run down my spine. I swallowed hard. "We—we better get going. Levi will be here soon."

"I told you I wanted to show you something." He grabbed my hand and led me around to the other side of the fountain. He pointed to a plaque attached to the front of the structure. It read:

HARMONY, KANSAS
WHERE LOVE REIGNS
1 CORINTHIANS 13:8—LOVE NEVER FAILS
DONATED BY THE MENNONITE WOMEN OF HARMONY

"Oh my," I said. "How wonderful."

"The women I told you about—the ones who got together

after Angstadt died? One of them, Kendra McBroom, had a brother who was a stonemason. The women worked hard to save enough money for his materials, and he donated his labor. They gave this fountain to Harmony as a symbol of their prayers, asking God for His blessing on the town. Your grandmother was one of them, you know."

"I—I didn't know that. No one ever told me."

He nodded. "Your grandparents were well loved in this community. I've heard stories about them ever since I came to live here. Wish I could have met them."

"They were very special people," I agreed. "But I didn't realize just how special until I came here. Funny how sometimes we see those we love through fresh eyes when we see them through the eyes of others."

Sam nodded. "I wish people would see my aunt through my eyes. She's an amazing woman. Just because she comes wrapped in a rough exterior, people sometimes miss how beautiful she really is."

His voice cracked with emotion, and I reached over and slid my arm through his. We stood for a few moments, watching the water dance from tier to tier.

"Levi just pulled up to the shelter," Sam said finally. "We'd better get going."

Sure enough, Levi's Suburban was parked next to a picnic table at the farthest point of the lake. We got into the truck and drove to where he waited. He waved as we approached. Sam carefully carried the sack from Menlo's to the table, and within a few minutes I was chomping away on the best chicken salad sandwich I'd ever tasted.

Sam laughed at my sounds of satisfaction. "I take it you approve of your simple supper?"

"Harmony could have restaurants on every street the way people cook here. I've never had so many delicious meals."

Levi nodded and patted his rounded stomach. "I used to be skinny," he said with a sigh. "But eventually I gave in. Life is too short to miss out on all this great food."

Sam raised his eyebrows and tried to look serious. "Life might actually last a little longer if you said no once in a while."

Levi sighed deeply. "But it wouldn't be as enjoyable."

I laughed. "We haven't even told you about the baklava Mrs. Menlo gave us."

"Oh mercy," he said. "She makes the best baklava in town."

"Well, I'll just add that to my growing list. The best strawberry pie, the best peach cobbler, the best baklava. I see a trend here." I put my sandwich down and wiped my mouth with my napkin. "When do I get something healthy?"

"Now wait a minute," Sam said. "We did have fruit salad the other night. That was very healthy."

"One healthy meal. Great. It's a wonder I can still fit into my clothes. Beginning immediately, I'm cutting down."

Levi chuckled. "My goodness, you're barely there as it is. If you lose any more weight, we won't be able to see you."

I reached over and patted him on the arm. "I knew I liked you the first minute I saw you. Now I know why."

Sam and Levi laughed. The conversation turned to weather forecasts, crops, and harvest. As they exchanged information, I glanced around me. Several families ate together in the lush park. A small playground on the other side of the lake entertained a handful of happy children who shrieked with laughter as they begged their parents to push them higher on the swings or run faster as they clung to the merry-go-round. A man wearing jeans and a T-shirt pushed a little girl, who wore a long dress and a prayer covering on her head, on the swings. And a man with a beard and a large straw hat played ball with a father and his son who both wore jeans and T-shirts. My eyes wandered over to the fountain erected by the praying women of Harmony, and

I got a lump in my throat. God had so clearly answered their prayer. Could what Sam said be true? Would my foray into the past actually bring healing to this community? Or would it tear a fabric in the peace that hung over this place like a comforting quilt? I silently cried out to God, asking Him to bind me to the prayers of my grandmother and the other women who had lifted up this town to Him. *Show me the truth, Lord. Use this situation to help Harmony.*

"Did you hear me, Grace?" Sam's voice cut through my thoughts.

"I–I'm sorry. What did you say?"

He frowned at me. "You okay?"

"Yes. Sorry. I just drifted away for a minute. This really is a beautiful park. I guess it's owned by the city?"

"Actually, the church owns it," Levi said. "They donated the land for the city's use. Both churches worked together to put in the facilities and the playground equipment. And they maintain it together."

"That's amazing," I said. "Unfortunately, there aren't a lot of churches that cooperate like that."

Levi shrugged. "I guess Harmony is unusual."

"You said something to Sweetie about not being a churchgoer," I said. "Yet I understand you used to be an elder at Bethel. I don't mean to be nosy but. . ."

"But what happened?" Levi sat his sandwich down and wiped his mouth. "Let's just say that I've had all the religion I can stand."

"Jesus felt the same way," I said gently. "He told us to strive for. . ."

"I know. Relationship not religion. Abel has told me that more than once." He rubbed his hands together and smiled at me. "Maybe one of these days I'll give in and go back to church. I have to admit that Abel and Marcus Jensen aren't anything like Amil Angstadt." He shook his head. "I'm sorry. Amil Angstadt was the old bishop at Bethel."

246

"I—I know who he was, Levi. He's one of the reasons Sam and I asked to talk to you this evening."

His eyebrows shot up as he looked at Sam. "I figured you two had some specific reason to meet with me. Why in heaven's name would you want to talk about Bishop Angstadt? That man's dead and buried. Best to leave him where he is."

"Levi," Sam said slowly, glancing around to make sure no one was near enough to hear us, "something odd has happened. Grace and I need your help. We want to ask you some questions about your old bishop. And about a man who worked for him. Jacob Glick."

Levi's eyes widened. "Jacob Glick? My goodness. I haven't heard that name in many, many years. Why would you want to know about him? He left Harmony a long time ago. And good riddance, by the way."

Sam reached over and knitted his fingers through mine. "We have something to tell you, Levi. But first we need you to promise you'll keep it between us."

"You can tell me anything—you know that, Sam." Levi stared at us quizzically.

Sam shook his head. "You need to consider our request more carefully than that. What we're going to share involves a very serious crime."

Levi's mouth dropped open. "You and Gracie. . ."

"No, not us," Sam said quickly. "Someone else. A long time ago."

Levi wrapped up the remainder of his sandwich and pushed it to the side. "Listen, you two," he said evenly, "whatever you say to me will stay right here. You have my word. Although I can't imagine. . ."

"Jacob Glick didn't leave town," I blurted out. "He's dead. And buried on my uncle's property."

Levi looked as if I'd just slapped him in the face. "Wha–what? What are you talking about?"

In slow, measured tones, Sam told Levi the whole story—everything that had happened since I'd arrived in Harmony. He carefully left out Sweetie and Emily's involvement. Levi finally lost his shocked expression, but the gravity of our situation wasn't lost on him.

"Goodness gracious," he said finally. "All this time. . ." He shook his head. "Ben kept this secret all these years?"

I nodded. "Yes, but he was wrong about what happened. Someone besides my father killed Glick. We need to know who it was. You seem to be the only person left in Harmony who worked closely with him and Angstadt. And Sam said we could trust you to keep this quiet until we find the truth."

"And if you don't uncover the murderer?"

Sam and I looked at each other. "Then we call the authorities," I said. "We can't keep this buried the way my uncle did. It's got to come out."

Levi stared down at the table for several seconds. "Sorry. I'm trying to digest everything. It isn't easy."

"I know it's a lot to take in," Sam said. "Can we ask you some questions about Glick?"

Levi nodded.

"What did you think of him?" I asked.

"He was a terrible man," Levi said. "He and Bishop Angstadt were almost always together. I never could understand it. As an elder, I took my concerns about Jacob to the bishop on several occasions." He took a deep breath and let it out slowly. "There were accusations about his behavior toward several young women. Yet every time I mentioned it to the bishop, he dismissed me, saying I had wrong information. Or he'd accuse me of spreading gossip. It was very frustrating."

"You were aware of his inappropriateness with some of the women?" I asked. "Do you remember who he approached?"

Levi grunted. "Almost every female in town was bothered by

that lecherous man. Didn't matter how old they were, but he liked the young ladies best. Many of them too young, if you know what I mean. That man was shopping for a young wife." He picked up his pop can and took a drink. Then he wiped his mouth. "I remember specifically his interest in your aunt, Sam. And Kendra McBroom. She left Harmony a long time ago."

"What about Emily Mueller?" Sam asked.

Levi's face went blank. "I—I don't remember anything about that." He frowned. "Emily was only a child when Jacob lived here. I would hope he never approached her."

"What about the parents of these women?" Sam asked. "Did any of them know about Glick's proclivities? Was there anyone you can think of who might have had a reason to kill him?"

Levi hesitated for a moment. "I'm really trying to remember, but it's so long ago. . ."

"I know," Sam said. "Take your time."

Levi stroked his white beard and stared off into the distance. Finally, he shook his head. "I just don't remember anything that will help you. The thing you must understand is that the bishop worked hard to protect Jacob—to keep him from suspicion."

"Well, he didn't succeed," I said. "Someone killed him."

"Give me some time to ponder on this. Maybe I'll remember something helpful." He folded his arms and looked at me. "You said he was killed on your property?"

I nodded. "Yes. Somewhere just inside the tree line."

"Seems like a stupid thing for a man like Jacob to do," Levi said. "Isolating himself. Standing out in the open with all those trees surrounding him. Anyone could have been hiding there, watching him. Waiting for a chance to get rid of him. You know, there was no love lost between that man and at least half of the folks in Harmony. When he disappeared all those years ago, I assumed his leaving was a result of his lechery. Guess I was right, but I just envisioned the wrong kind of departure."

"Angstadt couldn't protect him from everything," I said. "Although I suspect he was relieved when he realized Glick was gone for good."

Sam opened his mouth to say something but stopped when a commotion from Main Street caught our attention. A fire truck with a large tank in its bed bounced down the street while several men ran behind it. A couple of them grabbed the back of the truck and held on while the rest scrambled for their cars.

"What in the world. . . ," I said.

Levi jumped to his feet. "There's a fire."

Sam stood up, too. "Stay here, Grace," he said.

As he and Levi sprinted toward their vehicles, I quickly gathered up the remnants of our abandoned supper and stuffed everything except the opened pop cans back in the sack.

"Sam, wait for me!" I yelled, running as fast as I could for the truck before he took off. I quickly threw the sticky pop cans in a nearby trash can.

Sam honked his horn impatiently before I reached the passenger door. "I want to help," I said breathlessly as I climbed inside.

He just nodded and threw the truck into gear. We sped down the access road toward Main Street. As we neared Main, Sam slammed the brakes on at the sight of Abel Mueller waving him down.

Sam rolled down his window as Abel hurried up to us. "It's Ben's house," he yelled. "Sweetie called it in."

"My uncle's house?" I said incredulously. A house that had stood for three generations was burning? How could that be?

"Thanks, Abel," Sam said. "We need to get there as fast as we can."

"Emily and I are coming in my car," he said pointing to the church. His black car with its painted bumpers sat near the front door. Emily waited in the passenger seat.

Once again, Sam put the truck in gear and tried to navigate down Harmony's main road. People ran out of their businesses, jumping into cars and buggies. It looked as if the whole town was turning out. I recognized many of them: Mr. Menlo, Amos Crandall from the clothing store, and Paul Bruner from the leather and feed store. Joe Loudermilk locked the door of his hardware store, ran down the street, and got into a car with Dale and Dan Scheidler from the farm implements store. Even John Keystone joined the frantic, disorganized race.

"I don't understand how this could have happened," I yelled to Sam, trying to be heard over the rattling of the truck on the uneven dirt road. "There isn't any electricity in the house. Nothing to catch fire."

Sam shook his head. "I checked everything the last time we were there," he said loudly, trying to be heard while he kept his eyes on the road. So many people were pouring into Main Street we looked like part of a badly organized, last-minute parade. "The propane, the generator downstairs—everything was turned off. I have no idea what could have started it."

"Is that tanker truck the only fire truck in Harmony?"

He nodded. "Sunrise has a volunteer fire department. They'll come if we need them, but they're ten miles from here." He glanced over at me, his face tight with concern. "If the fire is spreading quickly, they won't make it in time. We have fire hydrants in town, but none outside of town. This kind of fire is always a worry."

I found myself praying that the house wouldn't burn down. All I'd wanted to do when I got to Harmony was get rid of my uncle's property. Now, only four days later, the prospect of losing the house where my family had lived all those years deeply saddened me. I tried to stop the tears that slid down my face, but I couldn't. That house meant something to me now, and I didn't want to see it destroyed.

It seemed like it took forever to get to Benjamin's. We hadn't even turned onto Faith Road by the time the large plume of smoke was clearly visible above the tree line. When we finally pulled up, the little house was surrounded with vehicles and people. Several of the men from town were hauling a long yellow hose from the tanker truck.

"The truck only holds about three hundred gallons of water," Sam shouted. "We'll use that along with a bucket brigade from your well."

As Sam parked the truck, I could finally see the fire. Flames danced from the corner of the house where the kitchen was located and licked up toward the roof. If the roof went, the house would most likely be gone.

I jumped down and followed Sam toward the people forming a line from an ancient metal water pump located about fifty yards behind the house. Ruth Crandall and Mary Whittenbauer ran toward the pump, carrying stacks of metal buckets. I was so shocked to see Mary that I froze in my tracks. Sam kept going. He quickly took his place in line, trying to stretch the line from the pump to the fire. I jogged up next to him, but was quickly pulled out of the line by Joyce Bechtold.

"Only men in the line!" she yelled at me. I started to protest, but she grabbed my shoulders. "The buckets are too heavy, Gracie," she yelled. "You won't be able to pass it without spilling it." She pushed me toward a large truck that had a hand-painted sign attached to its side. It read HARMONY HARDWARE. "Here," she said, handing me a stack of buckets from the back of the truck. "Carry these to the pump. That will be a big help."

I took the stack from her hands and ran past the growing group of men that stretched from the pump almost to the house. As I set them down next to the water pump, I noticed a man frantically filling buckets and sending them down the line. I was shocked to see Gabriel Ketterling moving water through that old pump faster than it had probably ever flowed before. He glanced my way but didn't acknowledge me at all. Without thinking, I reached out and put my hand on his arm. Startled, he gazed up at me, his face locked in his usual scowl.

"Thank you."

For a few seconds, his expression softened and he gave me a brief nod. The he went back to his work. I ran back to the hardware truck. By now, several women were carrying buckets. I started to get another stack when Joyce grabbed me again.

"Stand at the end of the line," she shouted. "When four buckets are empty, pick them up and run them back to the pump. Do you understand?"

I nodded yes and took off toward the house. Water from the pumper truck was flowing freely on the fire, and the line from the pump was complete. I was shocked to see all the people who'd left their homes and businesses to help. Some I'd met. Most were strangers. Some wore clothing just like mine. Most wore plain clothing. All of them worked together as if they'd been doing this all their lives. Abel Mueller stood next to Marcus Jensen. Sam and Hector from the restaurant passed a huge bucket of water between them. A young man with Down syndrome moved the bucket down the line and turned to wait for the next one. I could feel the tears streaming down my face, but I didn't care."

"Quick," a deep voice hollered. "Take these to the pump!"

I held out my hands for a stack of empty buckets and looked up into the soot-streaked face of John Keystone. His hair was wet and combed back from his face, and his usual smirk had been replaced with a frown. As I stared at him, a sudden revelation hit me so hard I almost stumbled as I ran back toward the pump. I remembered the odd sensation I'd had when I'd met him on Saturday. Now I knew where I'd seen him before. And the realization shocked me. I dropped off the buckets and ran back to the end of the line, passing Cora Crandall and Emily Mueller. They hurried toward the pump, their arms full of empty buckets, and their long skirts flapping against their legs. If the situation hadn't been so serious, I would have found it humorous.

As I reached the beginning of the line, I realized that the roaring flames were down to a flicker. Our efforts were paying off. My earlier tears of gratitude were turning into tears of relief. Between all the running, crying, and breathing in smoke, I was beginning to feel light-headed. By the time I got back to John, things around me began to spin.

I reached over to pick up the empty buckets stacked next to his feet when I felt myself sway. Strong arms reached out and caught me before I fell. I felt myself lowered to the ground.

"Take a big breath, Gracie," a deep voice said. My eyes, which had closed for a moment to stop the world from turning around me, flew open. John was a few inches from my face. "Are you okay?"

"We need more buckets. . ."

He shook his head and smiled. "No. The fire's under control. The pumper truck can finish the job. I think we need to get you into the shade."

"I feel so foolish."

"Don't be ridiculous," he said brusquely. "You have nothing to feel foolish about." He helped me to my feet, keeping his arm around me, and gently guided me over to a nearby tree where he helped me to sit down."

"Here's some water, Gracie," a soft feminine voice said.

Sarah Ketterling knelt next to me with a cup of water in her hands. Wondering where it had come from, I noticed Mary and Ruth filling Styrofoam cups from the restaurant with water from the pump. They handed them out to the tired and thirsty volunteers.

"Thank you."

Sarah's lovely eyes were full of concern. "Are you feeling any better?" she asked.

I nodded as I finished the water. "Yes. Guess I just got carried away a little. I had no idea I'd react this way about my uncle's house."

Sarah smiled at me. "You mean *your* house, don't you?"

I started to protest, but as I gazed at the old house, I realized she was right. It was my house now. And I didn't want it to burn down. "I—I guess you're right."

"Sometimes we don't realize how much something means to us until we're faced with losing it," John said in a low voice. A look passed between him and Sarah that I didn't know how to interpret.

Sarah's pale face turned pink, and she rose to her feet. "I need to check on Father. I'm glad you're feeling better." With that she turned and walked away. John watched her for several seconds before he turned his attention back to me.

"If you're feeling okay," he said brusquely, "I'd better help the guys clean up the mess."

"Yes, I'm fine. And thank you, John. Thank you so much."

He raised an eyebrow, and his face took on the same expression I'd seen when I first met him. "I don't know what it is about this town," he said with an air of disgust. "It gets in your blood somehow. Even if you don't want it to." He shook his head. "Wish I could figure it out."

With that he walked away, leaving me to ponder his words. I should have found them strange, but somehow I completely understood. I started to get up when a sharp voice startled me, and I sat back down with a *thump*.

"Well, there you are." Sweetie stood in front of me in her ever-present overalls. Usually streaked with dirt from her orchards, this time soot decorated the old, worn denim. Streaks of black across her face told me she'd been pretty close to the fire. "I been lookin' all over for you."

At that moment Sam walked up next to her. His T-shirt clung

to his chest and sweat dripped down his face. "It's really not too bad, Grace," he said. "The kitchen will have to be rebuilt, but the rest of the house is okay. A little smoke damage here and there. It will stink inside for a while, but it could have been far worse. Thank God it was called in before it got too bad."

"Abel said you saw the fire and got help, Sweetie," I said. "Thank you so much."

She grinned widely. "Well, I called it in, girlie. But Ida alerted me to the fire. She saw it from her house and ran down the road to my place to tell me. She fell before she got there, but I spotted her layin' on the road thrashin' about. 'Course, by the time I got to her, I could see the smoke."

"Is she okay?" My voice trembled with concern for my new friend.

"Sure, sure. She's back at her place restin'. I took care of her after I called the fire department in Sunrise and Joe Loudermilk. He contacted the rest of the men in our volunteer fire department. I told him to tell Ruth and Mary about the fire. I knowed those two women would alert the whole town. And they sure as shootin' did."

"But what about Gabriel Ketterling? No one called him."

"Nope. He was just drivin' by in his buggy and saw the flames. Him and Sarah pitched in right away.

I shook my head slowly and struggled to my feet. "I can't believe all these people turned out to help me," I said. "If it hadn't been for everyone here. . ."

"If it hadn't been for Ida," Sam interrupted. "This is a terrible time for your house to catch fire with everyone still in town or out in the fields. If she hadn't seen the smoke, it probably would have burned to the ground before anyone had a chance to call for help."

Abel ambled up to us. "Just wanted to tell you that we're going to clean things up tonight and start fixing the kitchen tomorrow. We'll have things as good as new in no time at all."

"How—how much will it cost, Abel?" I said. "I don't have much money, but I'm sure my dad will be happy to. . ."

"Gracie Temple!" Abel said loudly. "Do you still not understand Mennonites? This is what we do. You don't owe anyone anything—except a promise not to leave an oil lamp burning when you're not around."

"That what started the fire, Abel?" Sweetie asked.

"Yep. Too near the curtains from what we can figure. Just got too hot and started a blaze." Before I could say anything, he patted my shoulder. "Don't worry about it, Gracie. If you're not used to having oil lamps, accidents can happen."

Someone called his name, and he turned and walked away. Sweetie followed him.

"I didn't leave any oil lamp burning," I hissed to Sam.

"I know that," he said in a low voice. "Keep your voice down. Obviously someone started the fire on purpose. I think they wanted to burn down the whole house. They just didn't count on Ida and her determination."

"But why burn down the house? It doesn't make sense."

"I have no idea, but my guess is they want you out of Harmony. Seems to me if someone wanted to physically hurt you, they wouldn't be stealing family heirlooms and setting fires when you're not home."

"You've got a point."

"Look, you've been through a lot today," Sam said. "I'm going to have Sweetie drive you home. I need to stay here." He looked up at the sky. "It doesn't look like rain, but we can't take a chance. We need to make sure the house is protected from any surprise storms."

"Thanks, but I'll drive my car. It's been sitting ever since I got here."

Sam started to protest, but I put my fingers on his lips. "This isn't open for debate. I want to check on Ida. I'll go straight to your place after that."

"All right, but if you start feeling woozy again, you either come and get me or go on to the house, okay?"

I nodded solemnly. "I promise."

With a final look of warning, he joined a group of men talking about what to do next to fix my uncle's house. Correction: *my* house. That concept was going to take some getting used to.

I felt a hand on my shoulder and turned to find Joyce Bechtold standing behind me. "I hope you'll forgive me for ordering you around earlier," she said. "I'm usually not so aggressive." Her face belonged to a beautiful woman who had lived with laughter, but her eyes held shadows of pain. Perhaps some of what I saw was planted there through years of unrequited love for my uncle.

"Please don't apologize. I had no idea what to do. I needed someone to tell me, and I'm grateful for your help."

Her well-used laugh lines fell into place as she smiled. "Thank you, Gracie. I wouldn't want to offend you. Your uncle spoke of you quite often. Especially toward the end of his life. He wanted so much to see you. I—I wish he would have reached out to his family before the end. I never understood his reluctance, and although I asked him about it, he never seemed to be able to explain his reasons."

I nodded but couldn't come up with a response. Not one she would want to hear anyway.

She hesitated for a moment as if she wanted to say something else. Finally, she took a step back. "I guess I'd better go. I left the shop unattended, and I'm fairly sure I left the lights on and the door unlocked. All I could think about was Ben's. . . I'm sorry. I mean your house."

I reached out and touched her arm. "No, that's fine. It's hard for me to call it my house, too. He'll always be a part of it."

She nodded silently. Sadness emanated from her.

"Joyce, I wanted to ask you about the birdhouses."

She raised her eyebrows. "You mean the ones I painted with Ben?"

I smiled at her. "Kind of. Actually, he left quite a few of them unpainted in the basement. I'd really like you to have them."

"Oh dear, Gracie. I—I mean, I could paint them for you, and you could give them to Ruth. . ."

"No no. I don't want to sell them, Joyce. I really want you to take the houses. You can do whatever you want with them. Keep them, sell them. I don't care. I know my uncle would want you to have them. And if there's anything else. . .something you gave him or a memento you'd like to have, please let me know. I realize you were close to him."

A tear slid down her face. "Not as close as I wish we'd been. I'm afraid he kept a wall around himself. I feel blessed to have glimpsed behind it a few times, but in the end, that emotional barrier was too strong for us. I wish. . ."

She didn't need to finish the sentence. I knew what she wished. "As soon as things settle down some, will you come by?"

She smiled through her tears. "Thank you, Gracie. Your uncle would have absolutely adored you. I hope you know that."

As she walked away, Gabriel Ketterling's words rang in my head. *Would have been mighty ashamed to call something like this family.* I wondered which statement was true. Would I ever know the answer?

I jogged over to Sam's truck, found my purse, and grabbed the sack of baklava from Menlo's. Then I hurried to the other side of the house where my car had been parked since I'd arrived in Harmony. As I pulled out onto Faith Road, I passed John Keystone. He was getting something out of his car, but his thoughts seemed to be focused in another direction—on the beautiful Mennonite girl waiting in her father's buggy. Sarah sat with her head bowed and her eyes downcast. She appeared to be oblivious to John's fixed gaze. As I drove past, he saw me and quickly redirected his concentration back to the task at hand. Strange. John Keystone was obviously attracted to Sarah, but there was very little hope for romance there. Gabriel would never allow someone like John anywhere near his daughter. Frankly, I was surprised by his attention. I would have thought someone like Mary would be a more likely match.

As I drove down the dirt road toward Ida's, I turned to my earlier conjecture about John. I felt certain I was right. But now what to do with my suspicion? I needed to confront him, but I really wanted Sam with me. Even though I'd seen a softer side to the butcher, I didn't want to be alone with him when I asked the question I had to ask.

I turned into Ida's and parked near the porch. Zebediah stood near the fenced area behind the house. I took a minute to pet him before going inside. He moved his face next to me and closed his eyes while I stroked his soft face. His gentleness touched me. He was used to being cared for. I couldn't help glancing at my car as I made my way to Ida's front porch. I couldn't pet it or have deep feelings about it. Maybe Ida had a point. If I lived in Harmony, I would definitely have a horse.

I stopped cold at the bottom of the steps. *If I lived in Harmony?* Where had that thought come from? Man, a few days here and I was turning into Fannie the farmer. I shook off the silly thought and bounded up the stairs. The door was open, the screen door closed. Instead of knocking, I called out Ida's name. I heard her holler at me to come in. When I stepped into the living room, I found her curled up on the couch with a pillow, a comforter, and a book in her hand.

"Are you okay?"

She struggled to right herself. "Ach, I am fine. My goodness. An old woman takes a tumble and everyone thinks she is ready to be put out to pasture."

Regardless of her protests, I'd noticed a slight wince when she'd sat up. "I don't think you're ready for the pasture, but I do think you should take it easy for a couple of days. Are you sure nothing's broken?"

She waved her hand at me. "I am absolutely certain. I bruised my hip, but everything is still working just fine. I feel so silly, falling like that." She reached down and stroked her legs. "Getting older is not any fun, you know? God keeps me strong and healthy, but our bodies do start to wear out. And there is not much we can do about it." She smiled at me, her face full of joy. "But with every day that comes, I know I am getting closer to going home. And I can hardly wait. Zebediah and I will ride the beautiful trails of heaven—both of us young and vibrant again."

For just a moment, in the look of bliss on her face, I could see the beautiful young girl she was once, and the woman she believed she would be again. It brought a lump to my throat. I sat down in the chair across from her.

"So you believe Zebediah will go to heaven?" I asked gently.

Ida straightened her comforter and put her book on the table next to her. *The Pilgrim's Progress* by John Bunyan. One of my favorites. "I certainly do. I do not believe God would give us so much love for animals if we would never be with them again. The Bible says they have souls. I know there is more than just body and instinct inside them." She smiled at me. "I realize they do not go to heaven the same way we do. But since nothing is impossible for Him, I am convinced He can bring our beloved pets back to us. There have been a few animals in my life..." The old woman's voice shook with emotion. "Forgive me, dear," she said in a quiet voice. "Herman and I never had children. Some of our pets became like our children. I recently lost a dog I had for quite some time. I have not had the heart to replace him. It still hurts too much. And Zebediah? My goodness. What an old and dear friend he is. I cannot imagine my life without him."

"I understand." Ida's remembrances of beloved pets struck a little too close to home. I'd grown up with dogs, but after we lost Eddie, a darling little Jack Russell, I'd vowed I'd never have another one. When I moved into my apartment and discovered that dogs weren't allowed, I'd felt relieved. My cat, Snicklefritz, was the only companion I needed. Of course, I'd been certain I could never get as close to a cat as I had a dog. My assumption had proved false. Silly cat had found a way into my heart. I was suddenly filled with a longing to see him.

"How is your house, Gracie? I tried to watch the attempt to put out the fire from my window, but unfortunately I could not stand long enough to see much."

"It's going to be fine." I shook my head. "I can hardly believe the way everyone came together to save it."

"That is the way it is in Harmony. We are a family." She adjusted her slightly askew prayer covering over the gray braids piled on top of her head. "Let me see if I can get us some tea."

"I really don't have time," I said gently. "But let me make you something before I go. Have you eaten?"

"No, but I will get to it." She winced again. "I am fine, child. Just a little sore."

"You get comfortable," I said with a smile. "I'll brew some tea, get you some supper, and make sure you have everything you need before I go."

Ida's face flushed. "Oh dear. You really do not need to put yourself out so."

I got up and went over to where she sat. Taking her hands in mine, I said, "Ida, you saved my house. Sweetie saw you even before she noticed the smoke. If you hadn't tried to get help, the house might have burned to the ground. My family and I owe you so much."

"Goodness, anyone would have done the same..."

I shook my head. "No. Not everyone would have done the same thing. Most people wouldn't have risked themselves the way you did."

"Ach, child. I am just happy help arrived in time."

I gave her a quick hug. "Now for that supper." I'd started toward the kitchen when she stopped me.

"Gracie, how did the fire start?"

Not wanting to worry her, I said, "Ummm. . .I guess I left an oil lamp burning."

Ida's face wrinkled in a deep frown. "I do not understand. I leave lamps burning all the time. They have never started a fire."

I shrugged. "I guess the lamp was too close to the kitchen curtains. Anyway, that's what I was told." I took a deep breath and tried to keep my tone light. "I don't suppose you saw anyone at the house late this afternoon did you?

She shook her head. "I must admit that I fell asleep reading and spent the entire afternoon napping on this couch—until I smelled something burning." She raised one eyebrow. "Why? Surely you do not suspect. . ."

"No. No reason. Just wondering."

I left the room quickly before she could ask any more questions. I didn't want to alarm her by telling her I thought someone had purposely started the fire, but I had to know if she'd seen anything.

I put some water on for tea. Inside Ida's small refrigerator, I found cold cuts and cheese. There was bread in the bread box. I made a sandwich and sliced an apple. Then I poured a cup of hot tea and carried everything into the living room. Ida had pulled the small side table in front of her, and I set her supper on it.

"Ach, that looks perfect," she said, smiling. "What a blessing. Thank you so much."

I told her to wait a minute and ran out the front door to my car. I grabbed the sack from Menlo's that I'd transferred from Sam's truck. "I have a special treat for you," I said as I reentered the living room. "I hope you like baklava."

Ida's face lit up. "Oh ja. I absolutely love it."

263

I pulled the gooey desserts out of the sack and put them in front of her. "Three pieces. Is that too many? I can put some in the refrigerator."

She slapped playfully at my hand. "You leave them right where they are," she said, grinning. "I intend to make short work of every one."

I laughed at her enthusiasm. "I have to go, but I'll be back later to clean this up and help you get ready for bed."

Ida's bright smile slipped from her face. "Oh no, Gracie. I am just a little sore. I can get around just fine."

I leaned over and hugged her. "No arguing. I'm going to keep an eye on you for the next few days until I know you're okay. Since I can't call to check on you. . ."

She held her hand up to stop me. "I have learned my lesson this time. If I had a telephone I could have called for help right away instead of having to run down the road to Sam's. I would have been a better help to you and would not have this awful bruise on my hip. I intend to get one installed right away." She shook her head. "Honestly, I have never had anything against telephones. I simply did not think it necessary. I was wrong." She grabbed my hand. "I hope you can forgive me for being so stubborn."

I laughed. "Listen, I've changed my way of thinking in so many ways since I arrived in Harmony. I can't get a signal on my cell phone here. Not having it ring twenty times a day was hard on me at first. But now I find myself enjoying the peace and quiet. I have no intention of being a slave to my phone when I go home. Peace and quiet are much more precious to me now."

She patted my arm. "Thank you for that. Maybe a nice place in the middle of the road will be good for both of us, ja?"

I hugged her again. "Ja," I said softly. "Now, is there anything else you need before I go?"

"There is one thing I would like. Could you go into my bedroom and get my cane? It is in my closet. It will help me get around a little more safely."

"Of course." I followed Ida's finger, which was pointed toward a hallway near the kitchen. I easily found her bedroom. The sparse room held an old iron bed and an antique dresser. The closet door creaked as I opened it. A wooden cane was lying against the wall just inside the closet. I grabbed it and was headed out the door when I took a second look at the bedspread on Ida's old bed. I recognized the familiar pattern. It was one of Mama Essie's, but it was so old and faded, it was only a shadow of the glorious quilt it once had been. I ran my fingers over it. I could see places where the pattern had become worn and the quilt pieces had been patched and mended. I thought back to the trunk with quilts in the basement of Benjamin's house. As soon as I could get back inside, I intended to give Ida a new quilt. I smiled to myself as I pondered the joy it would give her.

I closed the door to the bedroom and delivered the cane to Ida. After assuring her I would be back by nine o'clock, I left. As I drove past Benjamin's house, I saw that there were still quite a few men working. Gabriel was helping Sam nail plywood and plastic sheeting over the exposed areas of the kitchen. The burned areas had been removed. A quick look revealed that Gabriel's buggy was no longer parked on the road, meaning Sarah must have gone home. John's car was gone, too. I glanced at my watch. Almost seven thirty. Although I'd planned on waiting for Sam, my chance to talk to John today was fading fast. After a brief argument with myself, I decided to swing by the market just to see if he was there, although I doubted it. By now he should be home, and I had no idea where that was.

I turned my car toward downtown Harmony. As I neared the market, I began to feel a little apprehensive. When I pulled up in front, I noticed the lights were on. John's car sat in front. I stayed in my own car for a while trying to decide what to do. In my rearview mirror I noticed Ruth leaving her shop. She headed down the sidewalk toward the restaurant. I jumped out of the car and called her name.

"Oh Gracie," she said as I hurried up to her, "I'm so glad the men got the fire out. They were weatherproofing it when I left. Tomorrow we'll start repairs. I want you to know that I have some kitchen things for you if you need them."

"Thank you, Ruth. I can't thank everyone enough for their kindness."

Her face crinkled as she smiled. "We always pull together in Harmony." She closed her eyes and breathed deeply. "Can you smell the honeysuckle blooming? Every spring I wait for its aroma." She sighed and opened her eyes. "I love it here."

I reached out and put my hand on her arm. "Ruth, I need to ask you a favor."

She nodded. "Of course. What is it?"

"Are you going to supper?"

"Yes. Can I get you something?"

"Thank you, but no. I—I. . ."

She put her arm around me. "What is it, child?"

I cleared my throat. "I know this sounds odd, but if my car is still in front of John Keystone's store when you leave the restaurant, will you come looking for me?"

Ruth's gaze swung toward the meat market, and she frowned. "All right," she said slowly. "But why. . ."

"It's probably nothing, Ruth. It's just that John is a little. . . well, different. I need to talk to him about something, and Sam is busy at the house. I will just feel better if someone is watching out for me."

"Maybe I should come with you."

I smiled at her. "No, that's not necessary. Really. If you'd just check on me when you leave—if my car's still there—that's enough."

"Okay. I'll do it. You know," she said quietly, "I think most people have John all wrong. There's something about that man that touches me. I don't think he's as angry as he is sad. He reminds me a lot of Gabe Ketterling." She shook her head. "Maybe it's my imagination. Maybe he's just mean. But I've found that hurting people tend to be difficult because they're afraid to love. What's that phrase?" She thought for a moment. "Oh yes. Hurting people hurt people. It's really true."

"I think you're right, Ruth. Thanks. I'll try to keep that in mind."

The older woman laughed lightly. "Sorry. I've drifted off track here, haven't I?" She grabbed my hand. "You go on. I'm only getting a bowl of chili so I won't be long, but I will wait around until you leave. And if it seems to take too long, I'll come across the street and pretend I desperately need a pound of hamburger."

I hugged her. "Thanks, Ruth. I appreciate it."

I'd turned to leave when I noticed Gabriel Ketterling's Appaloosa horse and buggy tied to a hitching rail a few yards from the entrance to Mary's café. No one was inside.

I hurried across the street to the market. Even though the lights were on, the door was locked. I knocked loudly, praying the whole time I wasn't making a huge mistake. A few seconds later, John stomped out of his back room, a scowl on his face. When he saw me, his eyebrows arched in surprise, and his already annoyed expression deepened.

"I'm closed," he shouted at me through the glass window next to the door.

"I need to talk to you, John. Please!"

With a thoroughly disgusted look, he unlocked the door and held it open. I stepped inside. "I–I'm sorry to bother you," I said quickly, "but I really need to speak with you. I wouldn't come by this late unless it was important."

He pointed to a small table with two chairs that sat against the far wall. "You're right. It *is* late, Grace. I just came back to make sure I'd locked everything up after running out so quickly this afternoon."

As he finished his sentence, I heard a noise that seemed to come from his back room. It sounded like a door closing. "Is someone here? I didn't mean to interrupt. . ."

"No," he said sharply. "There's no one here. Now what do you want? Is it about the house?"

"Well, I did want to thank you for everything you did. But that's not why I stopped by."

His features locked into a frigid stare. "Okay, then why are you here?"

I took a deep breath and met his direct gaze. "I'm here because I want to know why Jacob Glick's son is hiding out incognito in Harmony."

Chapter Seventeen

Although I'd figured John was related to Glick after realizing how much he looked like the picture in the restaurant, I hadn't been certain he was actually his son. He could have been his brother—or even a cousin. It was his age that made me suspect the relationship. John's reaction told me immediately that I'd hit a nerve. Big-time.

"How—how...," he sputtered, his face pale and his eyes wide.

"It's the photo in the café. You have your father's distinct features. Please don't take this the wrong way, but they look good on you. On your father. . .well, let's just say they didn't work as well for him."

John didn't respond at first. Finally, he cracked a small smile. "Well, thank you for that. You can imagine my shock when I first saw that picture."

The tension in the room eased considerably. Out of the corner of my eye, I saw a dark figure hurry across the street. Sarah. She glanced quickly toward the market and then slipped into her buggy. She certainly hadn't come from the café. Was it Sarah I heard leaving through the back door when I arrived? I'd already noticed John's interest in her, but could she actually have feelings for him, too? The bad-tempered John Keystone and the quiet Mennonite girl? Interesting to say the least.

"So why are you here?" I asked. "It seems strange that you would come to Harmony and not tell anyone who you are."

He jumped to his feet and began pacing the floor. "If your father was Jacob Glick would you want people to know?" After crossing back and forth several times, he stopped moving and put his hands over his face. When he brought them down, his features were twisted with distress. "After I arrived and began finding out just who my father really was, I felt disgusted and ashamed. I planned to leave this place and never come back. I wanted to walk away from him and from his embarrassing legacy."

"But you didn't leave."

John shook his head and threw his hands up in mock surrender. "I have no idea why. I just—I just. . ."

"Couldn't go?" I finished for him. "Must be something pretty powerful that holds you here."

A shadow passed the window. Sarah Ketterling's buggy. We both watched her drive away. John turned back to me, and our eyes met.

"Yes," he said softly. "Something holds me here." He came back to the table and slumped into the other chair across from me. "Something about this town. Something about these people." He placed his palms down on the tabletop—his fingers splayed. Instead of looking at me, he stared at his hands. "I—I never really had a home. My mother did her best. Raised me alone. She was always at work. I had no brothers or sisters. She'd told me that my father died when I was young. When she passed away a little over two years ago, I found her diary tucked away in a box. She wrote about my father—Jacob Glick. She'd gotten pregnant, and he'd abandoned her." He finally swung his gaze up and met my eyes. "I wanted to know why. That's all. The diary mentioned Harmony—and that he'd moved away without telling anyone where he was going. I

270

thought Harmony would be the starting point in my search for him. But the opposite happened. Everything ended here. I couldn't find a trace of my father after he left town." He shrugged. "It didn't make any sense. Was he still living somewhere in the area? Had he moved far away? Had he died? Why did the trail go cold? I've looked everywhere for answers, but there are no records to be found. No work records, no social security records, not even a death certificate. I wanted to know why, so I left my practice, contacted a farmer friend in Council Grove, and offered to sell his meat in Harmony. He accepted, and here I am."

"You left your practice? What kind of practice?"

He laughed rather harshly. "I'm a doctor—a family physician. At least, that's what I used to be."

"And what have you discovered about your father?"

He blew air out between clenched teeth. "Well, let's see. I've learned that he was a womanizer, a possible child molester, and an all around terrible person. Seems that his only interest in life was finding an acceptable wife—no matter what the cost."

"But what about your mother? Why didn't he marry her?"

John spit out a curse word. "Sorry. I'm assuming it was because my mother wasn't good enough to marry. You see, she was black."

I'd thought I couldn't dislike Jacob Glick any more than I already did. I was wrong. He was not only a rapist and a child molester. He was a bigot. I thought about the fair-haired, fair-skinned beauties he'd chased in Harmony, and I felt sick to my stomach."

"I–I'm sorry he treated your mother so shamefully. But you can't take it personally. You're not responsible for his behavior."

He shrugged. "I know that somewhere in my mind, but in my heart. . ."

"Your heart knows the truth, too, John. You're not your father."

271

He brushed his dark wavy hair out of his face. "Thank you for that, Gracie."

"So you've never discovered your father's current whereabouts?" I tried to keep my tone light, but guilt ate at my conscience.

He grunted. "Not a clue. Everyone who was around during the time he lived here told me he suddenly left town. Back when I cared where he was, I searched for him. But as I said, I couldn't find him in any public records. It's like he disappeared off the face of the earth."

More like under the earth. "John, I have to ask you something. Please don't be offended. Do you have any reason to want me out of Harmony?"

He stared at me curiously. "You? No, of course not. Why do you ask?"

I shook my head. "Strange things have been happening to me. I get the very distinct feeling that someone in this town would like to see me head back to Wichita. And the sooner the better."

"I can assure you it's not me. But I must admit I've been wondering why you're asking questions around town about my father. Mary told me you were very interested in his picture. I realize your parents knew him, but it seemed odd to me that after all these years anyone would care anything about him."

"I do have a reason, but I can't explain it right now, I'm sorry, but I'm going to have to ask you to trust me. Just for a few more days."

John's eyes narrowed and he frowned at me. "Do you know where he is?"

I didn't answer him. I had no idea what to say.

He sighed and shook his head. "He's dead, isn't he?"

"Again, I'm sorry. You've waited a couple of years to find out the truth about your father. Can you wait just a little longer?"

He shrugged. "I guess so. It's not like I care that much anymore."

I heard his words, but the look in his eyes betrayed him. John cared, all right. He cared very much. My stomach turned at the realization that I would have to confirm his suspicions that his father was gone. It wasn't something I looked forward to.

He cocked his head to the side and frowned at me. "You mentioned some strange occurrences. You mean like Ruth's vase disappearing? And the fire?"

I nodded. "Exactly like that."

"Are you saying the fire was deliberately set?"

"It's possible, but please keep this to yourself. I don't want the person who did it to suspect I know the truth. Everyone except my firebug friend thinks I left an oil lamp burning too close to the kitchen curtains."

A scowl marred John's handsome features. "Maybe you did."

I explained to him about the battery-operated lights Sam had purchased for me.

"Sounds to me like you need to be very, very careful."

I saw something flicker in his eyes. Was that a warning? Could John be the person who had been trying to get me to leave Harmony after all? Something inside me said no. Maybe it was a gut reaction. Or maybe it was the still, small voice of God. I wasn't certain, but I decided to listen to it. "I'm staying at Sam's house. He knows what's going on and is keeping an eye on me."

"Look, Gracie," John said earnestly, "I won't tell anyone about our conversation—if that's what you want."

"Yes it is. For now anyway."

"Fine, but I would also ask you to keep my secret. At some point I may tell people who I really am. I haven't decided, but I'm certainly not ready yet."

"All right, although there aren't a lot of people left who knew Glick. You have nothing to worry about." Even as I said the words, I thought about Emily. How would she feel about it? Although I'd just agreed to keep John's secret, once the truth came out about

Glick's murder, John's identity would most probably be revealed, as well. "I will have to tell Sam, but we'll keep it to ourselves."

He snorted. "I'm sure Sam will find it extremely amusing."

"No he won't. He's not like that at all. Not sure why you two have such animosity for each other."

John shook his head. "Maybe it's my fault. Just seems like he's got it all. People who care about him. Folks who respect him." He sighed. "It's probably my own jealousy."

I noticed the clock on the wall. "I'd better go. It's getting dark. The men working on my house are probably finished for the day."

"*Your* house?" He grinned. "You'd better watch out. Harmony will pull you into its web, too, if you're not careful. A warning from someone who knows."

I smiled back at him. "I have no intention of leaving my life in Wichita behind. I have everything I want there."

John chucked. "Okay. Whatever you say. I'll be at the house that isn't really yours early tomorrow morning. A bunch of us are determined to get you fixed up as quickly as possible."

"I—I don't know what to say. Thank you. I can hardly believe how supportive this community is. I still feel funny about not being able to pay for materials."

"Mennonite community, Gracie. Helping their neighbors is big here. Anyway, the church usually pays for most of the materials. They have a fund set up just for that." He ran his hand through his hair. "The first year I moved here a storm came through and a farmer outside of town lost his barn. The next day he was flooded with volunteers who cleaned up his property and built him a barn twice the size of the first. And they wouldn't let him invest anything except his own time and sweat. It was amazing."

"This place is pretty awesome."

"Yes it is." He crossed his arms and shook his head. "Something else that's pretty awesome: Gabriel Ketterling showed up today to help, and he plans on working with us again tomorrow. This is the first time I've seen him join in anything. I think his love for Ben originally sent him to your house, but his decision to come back. . . Well, it's a surprise. Funny thing is, I think he enjoyed being around people again. I actually saw him smile a couple of times."

"So all it took was catching my house on fire? Maybe I should have done it a long time ago."

"You know what?" he said seriously. "I know you're kidding, but there's truth in what you just said. He responded to being needed. And then he responded to being around other people. Your little accident may have actually been the best thing that's happened to Gabriel in many, many years." He smiled widely at me, erasing almost every reminder of his father, whose photograph had displayed features locked in deep-seated anger and hate. "I think you're good for Harmony, Gracie Temple."

I crooked my thumb toward the restaurant across the street. "Will you tell that to your friend, Mary? I think she would disagree with you."

He waved his hand at me. "Don't worry about Mary. She knows Sam wasn't the man for her. She's known it for a long time. If she could be honest about it, I think she'd tell you the same thing. Right now her pride is hurt. If she could have been the one to break it off, she wouldn't be so mad. It'll pass. Trust me."

"I have a feeling it won't pass until after I'm gone."

He shrugged. "Well, she was there to help during the fire. She didn't have to be."

"I—I guess so. I assumed it was just something she'd do for anyone."

"That might be true—but thanking her might not be a bad idea."

My gaze swung once again toward the clock on the wall. I stood up. "I appreciate the suggestion. I'll try to find a way to tell her how grateful I am for her help. Hopefully, it will go better than the last time I attempted to make things right between us."

John stood to his feet again and stepped over to the locked front door. He turned the lock and held the door open. "I'm glad we got the chance to talk, Gracie. And thanks for keeping my secret."

"You're welcome." I stepped outside onto the boardwalk. The air had cooled considerably and the myriad of stars overhead had begun their nightly spectacular display. I took a deep breath and let it out slowly. The scent of honeysuckle wafted around me like a sweet perfume. As I crossed the street, I replayed parts of my conversation with John in my head. Although I still didn't trust him completely, I doubted he was the person who took Ruth's vase or set Benjamin's house on fire. I also knew now why Emily was so uncomfortable around him. Subconsciously, when she looked at him, she saw his father. Someday when the truth came out, I wondered if her reaction to him would be better or worse. There was no way to tell. I slowly walked up the steps to the café and stood at the door for a few moments, screwing up my courage. Finally, I pushed it open. Ruth sat at a nearby table with her back to me. Just my luck, Mary stood next to her. The two were engaged in a conversation. I had a strong urge to hurry out before the women saw me, but I wanted Ruth to know I'd escaped John's market unscathed.

I walked up quietly and touched Ruth on the back. She cranked her head around and smiled at me. "Oh, Gracie. There you are. I take it everything went okay?"

"Yes, very well. Thanks, Ruth."

I patted her on the back and turned to go.

"I—I guess some of the men will be working at your place tomorrow."

Mary's statement was said as fact, but I responded as if it were a question. "Yes. I mean, that's what I heard. I'm very appreciative."

Although nothing in her expression softened, her next words took me by surprise. "I'll bring lunch by around one fifteen. Have to get through my midday rush first."

"Wh–why, thank you, Mary. I'm sure they'll be happy to hear..."

The rest of my sentence was useless since she turned and ambled off as soon as I opened my mouth. She engaged a couple at the next table in a discussion about the weather. But it was progress. I shrugged at Ruth whose cheery response would have been more appropriate if Mary hadn't walked off and left me standing there with my mouth open.

"Oh wonderful!" she said, rather breathlessly. "I knew she'd come around!"

I nodded without much conviction, thanked Ruth again, and left the café. I headed back toward Benjamin's house, but just as I got to Faith Road, I saw Sam's truck coming my way. I stopped and rolled down my window.

"We're done for the day," he hollered, trying to make himself heard over the noisy truck engine. He pointed in the direction of his house. "Let's go home."

"I've got to check on Ida first," I yelled back. "I'll be there shortly."

He nodded, put the truck in gear, and took off down the road while I turned my car the other way and drove to Ida's. It only took a few minutes for me to find out she was feeling better and didn't need any help. After promising to check on her again the next day, I drove back to Sam's.

When I turned into the driveway of the magnificent red house, I couldn't help but wonder if I'd ever have a home like this. Until I'd seen this place I'd never thought much about what my own home might look like someday. Frankly, I'd always imagined it as much more modern. Most of my designer friends were into clean lines and contemporary styling. They'd laugh at me if they saw this house I'd fallen in love with.

I parked behind Sam and got out of the car. He sat on the front porch steps waiting for me.

"No rain predictions tonight or tomorrow," he said as I reached him. "But just in case, we have everything buttoned up tight. Tomorrow we'll start making actual repairs." He got up and put his hand on my shoulder. "The refrigerator, the stove, and the table are ruined. Sorry. But they can be easily replaced."

"I don't know why I'd do that," I said, more sharply than I meant to. "Whoever buys the property can bring in their own furniture and appliances."

"I guess you're right." Sam's tone was soft, but there was something in his voice that made me realize my attitude was inappropriate.

I grabbed his hand as he took it from my shoulder. "I'm sorry. I have no idea why I snapped at you. I guess I'm just tired. It's been a long day."

He smiled. "Yes, that it has. Let's grab something to drink and sit on the back porch. I have a few things to tell you."

"I have something big to tell you, too."

A few minutes later we were comfortably settled in the beautiful enclosed porch. I almost emptied my entire glass of iced tea in one gulp. I hadn't realized I was so thirsty. Sam got up and refilled our glasses. Then he sat back down next to me in the love seat. The only illumination in the room came from the kitchen behind us. I suddenly became aware of how tired I really was. Sam yawned deeply. Although my weariness was probably more emotional than physical, I realized that he had to be absolutely exhausted.

"I need to tell you what I found out today," I said. "But we can get into it more tomorrow. I'm sure we could both use a good night's sleep."

Sam closed his eyes and leaned his head against the back of the seat. "Sounds good. Go ahead and tell me your big news."

I took a deep breath. "John Keystone is Jacob Glick's son."

His eyes shot open like they were hooked to an electric circuit that had just been switched on. He sat up straight. "He—he's what? What did you say?"

He looked so shocked I laughed. "I said John is Glick's son."

He turned to stare at me with his mouth open. "How. . .I mean. . .how. . ."

I patted him on the leg. "Okay, settle down. How did I find out?"

He nodded dumbly.

"It was the picture of Glick. I know he's not an attractive man, but he has such distinct features. His narrow aquiline nose. His long face and bushy eyebrows. His coloring. John Keystone is a lot better looking than Glick, but the features are the same. When I met him, I kept thinking I'd seen him somewhere before. Today I finally put it together."

"But—but there are other people in Harmony who actually knew Glick. Why didn't they put two and two together?"

"I don't know. Maybe it's my artistic side. I study shapes and contrasts. I remembered the structure of Glick's face and matched it to John's."

"Well, Emily was an artist, and she's known him longer than you. Wonder why she didn't see it?"

I shrugged but didn't say anything. If she had noticed the similarities between father and son, I was certain her mind had blocked it.

He shook his head slowly. "His son. That's incredible." He frowned. "But you're just guessing, right?"

"No. I talked to John. He admitted it."

"Grace Temple!" Sam exploded. "You confronted him? I hope you weren't alone."

I nodded. "Sam, it's all right. He. . ."

He grabbed me by the shoulders. "It's not all right at all. What if he'd attacked you? He could have killed you."

"Ouch," I yelped. "You're hurting me. Let me go!"

Sam released me and jumped to his feet. "I'm sorry, but that was stupid. This means John was the person who took the vase and set the fire."

I sighed deeply. "Yes, Sam, that's it. You've figured it all out. You're Sherlock Holmes in the flesh. You see, as a baby John Keystone crawled to Harmony all by himself. He grabbed a rock and hit his father on the head, killing him. Then he crawled back to Council Grove, where his mother lived, climbed into his crib after washing off all the incriminating evidence, and waited until adulthood to come back to Harmony in case a graphic designer from Wichita showed up to accuse him of murder."

"Okay, that doesn't actually make sense," Sam said sheepishly. "So why does John want you out of town?"

"He doesn't. He's not even aware Glick is dead. Now if you'll just sit down, I'll tell you the whole story."

He came over and plopped down next to me. I filled him in on everything I'd learned. When I finished, he was silent for a while. "Wow. I sure wouldn't want to find out my father was someone like Glick."

"I think it's the reason he's been so defensive."

Sam laughed softly in the semidarkness. "I wouldn't have characterized it quite so nicely, but I guess I can understand his attitude. I have to say he really pitched in and helped today."

"You said you had something to tell me?"

Sam shook his head. "You kind of stole my thunder. My news isn't as startling as yours."

I reached over and ruffled his hair. "I'm sure it will be quite interesting. Go ahead."

"You're talking to me like a child again."

"Sorry. Tell me what happened today, or I'll beat you senseless."

He snorted. "That's much better." He turned toward me. I could see the outline of his face illuminated by the kitchen light.

"This may not mean a lot to you, but if you'd lived around here as long as I have, you'd find what I'm about to tell you nothing short of amazing. Gabriel Ketterling worked with us all day. I heard him tell Mary he'd hang in there until the work was completed. Even better than that, he seemed to enjoy being with us. He even laughed a couple of times."

I started to tell him that John had mentioned the very same thing, but before the words popped out of my mouth I sucked them back in. Male ego being what it is and all. "Now that *is* big news."

"Don't make fun of me. This is a major step for him. When I left, he and Abel were sitting on your front porch talking. They'd been at it for almost an hour."

"Oh Sam. That *is* wonderful. Really." I'd been teasing him up to now, but knowing that Gabriel and Abel had spent that much time together was encouraging. I thought about Sarah and how much it would mean to her if her father began to reenter the community. "I'm going to pray over this situation," I said quietly. "Wouldn't it be wonderful if. . ."

"Yeah," Sam said before I finished. "It would definitely be wonderful."

"Hey, you spent some time around Mary today. How did that go?"

"Surprisingly well. It's not like we had an emotional moment when we wrapped our arms around each other and forgave everything, but she was civil to me. I'd say it was a step forward."

"She'd better keep her arms to herself." The sentence burst out before I realized what I'd said. I'd spoken in jest, but my words were still badly chosen.

"Why?" Sam said in a low voice. "Do you really care if someone else puts their arms around me?"

"I'm gonna plead the fifth here," I said lightly. Being so near him in the semidarkness, I felt my resolve to keep some distance begin to melt. Time to change the subject. "Hey, we need to talk about our discussion with Levi before the whole fire thing erupted."

Sam leaned back in the seat and sighed. "Oh yeah. With everything else, I kind of forgot."

"Basically we got nowhere. Levi doesn't know anything that can help us."

"So what now?" Sam asked. "I have no idea where to go from here."

"Me either, but someone set that fire, Sam. We find our firebug, and we find our answers."

"Did you check with Ida to see if she noticed anything?"

"Yes, but she slept all afternoon and didn't see anyone at the house."

Sam sighed deeply. "Well then, I have no idea what to do next."

"Me either. I guess we think about it for a while. To be honest, my mind is exhausted."

Sam yawned. "My mind and my body are in agreement. They're both ready for bed." He stood up and held out his hand. I reached out for him, and he pulled me up. Before I knew it, his lips were on mine. I was too tired to resist.

"You know this is only going to make it harder when I leave," I whispered when his lips left mine.

"I don't care." His voice was heavy with emotion. "I only know that right now I want to kiss you more than I care about what happens next week. Can you understand that?"

I didn't trust myself to answer. As if my hands had a mind of their own, I reached up and pulled his face close to me. Although our second kiss was as tender as the first, a feeling of sadness washed through me. I pulled away from him and walked toward the door to the kitchen.

"I—I've got to go to bed. I'm so tired I can hardly stand it."

Sam stepped around me and swung the door open. Light flooded in, and I saw his eyes sparkle with unshed tears. I quickly turned my head. Seeing his pain hurt me deeply inside.

"I'll be going out early in the morning to Ben's," he said in a controlled voice. "I won't see you before I leave. In fact, I may not see you much at all in the next few days."

"I understand. Good night." I'd wanted to say so much more, but instead I fled to my room, confused by the emotions coursing through me. Ever since coming to Harmony, my thoughts and feelings had been jumbled and confused. In Wichita I'd felt that I knew who I was—what I wanted. But here. . . Here everything was different. It was like someone had torn me into little pieces, gathered them up, and thrown them into the air. As they drifted back to earth, all the parts that were Gracie fell into a different picture—one I didn't recognize.

In the hallway outside my room I found Buddy waiting for me. I opened the door, and he ran up on the bed, turned around a couple of times, and curled up in a ball. I changed my clothes, crawled into bed, and pulled him up close to me. Then I stared up at the ceiling for quite a while, feeling strangely unsettled. Besides my jumbled emotions about Sam, something else nagged at me. Something I'd missed. I chewed on it for quite some time without success. Eventually I fell into a troubled sleep.

Chapter Eighteen

The next few days passed quickly. As Sam had predicted, I hardly saw him. When he came home late at night, he was so tired he didn't feel much like talking. I spent the large part of each day giving Sweetie a hand in the orchards. We pruned the trees, which was difficult work, and placed small balls of nitrogen around the bottom of the trunks to fertilize them. By the time we came in for supper, I was exhausted. After we ate, I'd sit in the rocking chair on the front porch and wait for Sam to come home. Usually, I fell asleep before he finally pulled into the driveway.

I'd gone over to my uncle's several times, but each time I'd been told there was nothing I could do there. It didn't take me long to realize that God was doing a special work, and I needed to leave the men alone so He could complete it. In only a few days, Gabriel Ketterling seemed like a different person. Sam and John had bonded as if they were old friends. It wasn't unusual to hear them all laughing together. By Wednesday afternoon I'd completely abandoned my daily visits. Even Mary seemed to realize that something unique was happening. She'd drop off lunch and leave immediately, hardly speaking to anyone.

Thursday afternoon I picked up Hannah and we drove downtown. I brought along a couple of sketch pads that I'd thrown into the car in case I found time to draw while I was in Harmony. I remember thinking my short vacation would be boring and I'd need something to do. Boy, I'd sure missed the mark there. Together Hannah and I sketched the outside of the café, Menlo's Bakery, and Ruth's shop. Hannah wanted to add someone sitting on the empty bench in front of the café, so I roughed in a figure we could detail later, talking to her about how to add dimension to her drawing. I also taught her about using proper perspective. She soaked up my words like they were water and she was a dry sponge.

We had a wonderful time even though we were interrupted so many times it was a miracle we got anything done. Mrs. Menlo brought us warm macadamia nut cookies straight from the oven, along with a cup of coffee for me and a glass of chocolate milk for Hannah. Ruth ran across the street to see what we were doing. She oohed and aahed over our sketches until Esther Crenshaw stuck her head out the front door of her shop and hollered, "If you don't mind, Ruth, I'd rather not live the rest of my life waiting for you to check me out!"

Hannah and I giggled as Ruth jogged back across the street yelling, "Esther, why don't you just keep your silly wig on? I'm not on the earth just to serve you, you know!"

Two of Hannah's friends stopped by to find out what she was up to. Hannah introduced Leah, a vivacious young girl with milk-chocolate brown hair, rosy cheeks, and a glint of mischievousness in her deep doelike eyes. The second girl, Jessica, hung back and stared at me as if she'd never seen anyone like me before. Her dishwater hair hung in thin strands below her dingy prayer covering. One of the ribbons from her cap was missing, and the ill-fitting dress she wore stretched tightly across her chubby body. Leah's face sparkled with life while Jessica's features seemed lost and faded in her sallow skin. Hannah treated both girls with the same enthusiasm, which seemed to help Jessica come out of her shell a little. The two girls stayed only a few minutes. A rather large woman I'd never seen before stepped out of the café across the street and called for them to hurry up if they wanted pie. That was all it took for the girls to say good-bye to Hannah and take off across the street as if the pie would disappear if they didn't eat it right away.

Almost everyone who strolled down the boardwalk stopped to watch us and ask questions. Our venture proved to be a great way to create a successful social occasion, but we didn't get as far with our sketches as I'd hoped. We made a date to meet again on Saturday morning to finish what we'd begun. I hoped some of Harmony's business owners and residents would be at home with their families so we could get some work done.

Friday night when Sam walked in the front door, he informed me that they would probably be finished with the house by Saturday afternoon. I sat at the kitchen table across from him while Sweetie fixed him a late supper.

"I want to do something special to thank everyone," I said. "Do you think we could have some kind of dinner or something?"

Sweetie, who overheard us talking, interrupted Sam's attempt at a response. "How 'bout some of the women and I get together and plan a big picnic in the park Monday evening? There's plenty of room there, and folks could bring their families."

"Oh, that sounds wonderful. Do you think the men would enjoy it?"

Sweetie's coarse laugh broke loose. "I think anytime them hungry men get a chance to chow down, they receive it with gusto."

"I think it's a wonderful idea, Grace," Sam said. He cranked his head around and looked at Sweetie who was busy making him a sandwich. "Hey, be sure to get Levi involved in the party, will you? He helped us out at the house the first day and a half, but then he dropped out. Said he's not feeling well. I'm a little worried about him."

"Sure," she said. "I'll call him first thing in the morning. Make sure he's okay. You know, Levi's not as young as he used to be. Maybe he started feelin' bad tryin' to keep up with all you young men."

Sam shook his head. "Maybe, but Abel's about his age and seems to be doing okay." He shrugged. "Hope we didn't do anything to offend him."

"Oh, pshaw," Sweetie said with a wave of her hand. "Levi and I are two ducks in the same pond. You can't offend us for nothin'."

I raised an eyebrow and smiled at Sam. Sweetie got offended at least four times a day at something or someone.

"I'd sure like to see Gabe come to the picnic and bring Sarah," Sam said, changing the subject. "She could use a friend." He yawned loudly. "I almost forgot to tell you," he said to me when he'd finished. "Gabe's been asking about you. Something about taking some kind of lessons from Sarah? Said he told you no when you first asked, but he's changed his mind."

I clapped my hands together. "Oh, how wonderful! She does the most beautiful wood-block prints. I've heard of the technique, but I'd never seen it done. I'd love it if she'd teach me before I leave. Of course, I'd pay her for her time."

He nodded. "Honestly, Gabe and Sarah could use the money. They don't have much. But I don't think he's got money on his mind as much as he finally wants to reach out to people." He yawned again. "I've had a really bad attitude about him for years. Turns out I really like the guy."

"He's had some tough breaks," Sweetie said. "Tends to make a body careful. That girl's all he's got left. I think he's feared he might lose her, too, and have nothin'."

"Well, he's sure changed."

Sweetie stopped what she was doing and stared hard at her nephew. "Folks don't usually change in a couple of days, Sam. He might be a-comin' out of his shell, but I wouldn't take it as some kind of miracle transformation. He's still got a lotta bitterness inside him. God help any man that tries to touch his daughter."

Sam shrugged. "I don't know about that. I just know he's talking to us and seems to really be enjoying our company."

"All I can say is I hope you're right." She turned back to her meal preparations while I thought about her mention of some man trying to approach Sarah. I had to wonder just how close John and Sarah had become. It was clear they'd been intentionally hiding their relationship. What would happen when Gabriel found out?

"Well, it will be interesting to see if Gabe accepts the invitation for Monday night," Sam said. "It's a purely social invitation. If he and Sarah show up, I'd say we've come a long way this week."

I laughed. "I can hardly believe you're calling him Gabe. Was that your idea or his?"

"Actually, Abel started it. But Gabe seemed to like it. And honestly, it fits him."

"So, do I have any hope you'll call me Gracie someday?"

Sweetie plopped a huge ham sandwich in front of Sam with a side of homemade potato salad. His eyes widened and he sighed with pleasure. "I love the name Grace. God's grace has always been important in my life. Does it bother you?" Without waiting for an answer, he bowed his head, said a quick prayer, and took a big bite of his sandwich.

"I guess not. It's just odd to be called Grace instead of Gracie."

Sam chewed and swallowed. "Why? It's your real name, isn't it?"

I nodded. "Yes, it's my real name." I thought about informing him that there was nothing wrong with the name Gracie, but it was obvious Sam was lost in sandwich heaven and wasn't in a listening mood. Besides, for some reason I liked hearing him call me Grace.

"You seem to be getting along with John, too," I interjected.

Sam chewed silently. I couldn't interpret the look on his face. Finally, he said, "Turns out we have more in common than I thought." He shook his head. "I think we'll end up being pretty good friends."

I started to ask him what he meant about having something in common with John when Sweetie interrupted me.

"I need to drive into Council Grove in the morning." She pointed a finger at Sam. "I'll drop you off at Benny's before I head out. What time do you figger you'll be done?"

He shrugged and swallowed. "Like I said, sometime in the afternoon. But don't worry about me. I'll walk."

"Okay. I'll check on you when I get back. I'm gettin' some groceries for Ida, too. I'll run them to her place and then swing by to see how you all are doin' before I come home. And on the way home, I thought I might stop by Bernie's in Sunrise and pick up some of them chocolate milkshakes you like so much. How many men do you think will be a-workin' tomorrow?"

Sam chuckled. "If word gets out about those milkshakes, we'll have all the help we can use—and more. How many milkshakes can you carry?"

She grinned at him. "I'll have 'em put the shakes in them big carryout boxes. It'll keep 'em from fallin' over on the way home. You figger twenty will be enough?"

"I think that would be perfect. Between Mary and you, I'm liable to actually gain weight working on Grace's house."

There it was again. *Grace's house.* Seemed like everyone was beginning to see Benjamin's house as mine. Even me. I could have corrected Sam's choice of words, but since he'd been working so hard to save the house, it didn't seem important. The effort being made to repair the fire damage meant the world to me. In fact, every time I drove past the house and saw the men laboring in the afternoon heat, tears sprang to my eyes.

"I take it these chocolate milkshakes are something special?"

Sam snorted. "I'll bet you don't have anything like them in Wichita."

"I don't know. Wichita has lots of places with great shakes."

Sam pointed his fork at his aunt. "Pick up one for Grace, will you? She needs to experience a Bernie's milkshake for herself."

Sweetie brought us both a slice of apple pie and ice cream. "I'll do it. You got a treat a-comin', girlie."

I winced at hearing "girlie" again. I kept hoping that particular moniker would eventually fade away, but it appeared it was going to follow me around, much like "Snicklefritz." However, with a mouthful of Sweetie's warm, delicious pie, I had to admit it didn't sting quite as much. As soon as we finished eating, Sam headed to bed.

When Buddy and I woke up Saturday morning, Sam and Sweetie had already gone. I made some toast, took a shower, and headed downtown to meet Hannah. All the way into town, that odd sense that I'd forgotten something persisted. I hadn't mentioned it to Sam, because at this point it was nothing more than a feeling. But I couldn't shake it. When I pulled up in front of the meat market, I found Emily and Hannah waiting for me.

"Good morning," I called out as I got out of the car and grabbed the sketch pads. "Wonderful weather, isn't it?"

They both agreed. I'd just begun to tell them about the picnic when I heard the sound of hoofbeats coming toward us. I turned to see Ida's buggy racing down the street. She came from the direction of the church.

"Whoa, Zebediah," she hollered as she pulled up next to us. Ida pointed at me. "Gracie, I need your help."

I put the sketch pads down on the bench and hurried over to the elderly woman whose face was red with emotion. "What in the world is going on? Are you okay?"

She shook her head. "It is not me. It is Levi. Something is wrong. You have got to find him."

Emily came up behind us. "What are you talking about, Ida? What's wrong with Levi?"

Ida shook her head. "I do not know, but I am afraid for him." She took a deep breath and tried to calm her trembling voice. "I was at the cemetery—putting flowers on Herman's grave. I saw Levi there—which is not unusual because his folks are buried there. But he was wild-eyed and talking out of his head. Something about God's judgment and how he had to find forgiveness. I tried to talk to him, but he just stared at me like I was not there at all."

"Where is he now, Ida?" I asked.

"I don't know. But he said something about washing away his troubles. Could he be talking about Trouble Lake?"

"That lake is huge," Emily said, her eyes wide with fear. "He could be anywhere."

"He asked me if the men were working at Benjamin's today," Ida said. "I told him yes. Then he asked if Sweetie was home." Her eyes filled with tears. "I told him Sweetie was in Council Grove. I should not have done that. I—I just was not thinking. He must be there."

"I'd be glad to check on him," I said hesitantly. "But I don't think he's actually in any danger."

"Levi can't swim," Emily said quietly. "Never learned how. The water around the end of Sam's dock is very deep. If he jumps into the lake from there. . ."

"And there is something else, Gracie," Ida said. "Remember when I told you Sam was the only person at Benjamin's last Saturday?"

I nodded.

"Well, I did not know Levi was driving Sam's other car. It was not the truck I saw at Benjamin's in the early afternoon. It was that other car. The big one. The one Levi drove today."

I turned to Emily. "I'm going to Sam's. Will you find someone to drive over to my house and get him? Maybe Abel should come, too. We might need his help."

"I'm coming with you," Emily said, her face set with determination. She ran up to Ida's buggy. "Ida, please get Mary. Tell her to go to Benjamin's house and get the men over to Sam's as quickly as possible." She ran toward my car while she called out to her daughter. "Hannah, you stay with Ida until we get back. Do you understand?"

"Yes Mama." Hannah may have understood her mother's instructions, but her confused look matched the jumbled thoughts careening around inside me.

I jumped into my car as Emily slid into the passenger seat, pulling her long skirt in after her. Although I was trying to understand Ida's revelation about Levi being at my house on the day the vase was planted there, I was also struck by the sudden forcefulness of Emily's attitude. The timid woman I knew was gone, and someone else had taken her place.

As I pulled out onto Main Street, I looked in my rearview mirror and saw Hannah helping Ida from her buggy. A second glance revealed the young girl patiently guiding the older woman toward the café.

As we sped down the street, I didn't say anything to Emily, but she saw me glance sideways at her.

"Gracie," she said finally, "do you remember me telling you about a man I cared about when I was young? The one who asked me to marry him?"

"Yes. Was Levi that man?"

She nodded. "When I turned him down, after Jacob disappeared, Levi changed. He quit going to church. He was friendly to people, but. . .I don't know. It was like something in him died. He never acted quite the same. Around me, he was especially reserved. And when I married Abel, he almost stopped acknowledging me at all." She sighed. "It wasn't so noticeable that anyone else would see it. But I did."

"You never talked to him about it?"

"No. I couldn't tell him what had happened to me." She stared out the car window, silent for a few moments. When she turned toward me, her eyes were wet. "If Jacob Glick hadn't attacked me, I would have married Levi. I turned him away because I cared for him, not because I didn't. In my mind, I couldn't be the kind of wife he deserved. It wasn't until I met Abel that I had the courage to give love a chance." She smiled sadly. "Abel's the first man I ever trusted completely, but Levi was the first man I ever loved."

Keeping one hand on the steering wheel, I reached over and touched her shoulder with the other. "Emily, if you trust Abel so much, why won't you tell him the truth? You've spent too many years bound by the past. God wants you to be free. Please talk to your husband."

She patted my hand. "Let's take care of Levi first. Then we'll tackle my marriage."

"Fair enough." I put my hand back on the steering wheel and concentrated on driving as fast as I safely could. When we reached the intersection of Main and Faith, I almost turned toward Benjamin's. I really wanted Sam's help. But not knowing what kind of situation we faced with Levi, I drove on to Sam's. I'd been looking in my rearview mirror ever since we'd left downtown Harmony. There was no sign of Mary's truck behind us. I prayed she'd reach the men soon.

As we approached the big red house, I felt relief that Levi's car was parked in the driveway. If we hadn't found him here, it would have been almost impossible to locate him since the lake was so large and surrounded by thick clusters of trees.

Emily and I jumped out of the car and ran around the side of the house toward the tree line. Buddy came running up behind us, barking wildly. We must have been a sight. Me in my jeans and T-shirt, Emily in her prayer cap and long dress, and Buddy frantically bringing up the rear. As we cleared the trees we saw

Levi standing at the end of the dock, staring down into the water. A quiet approach was out of the question, thanks to Buddy. Levi swung around and saw us coming toward him. As we got nearer, he held his hand up.

"Stop right there," he yelled. "Don't come any closer. I don't want your help. Just go away." His eyes were locked on Emily. It was as if I weren't there at all.

"Levi," Emily called back. "What are you doing? Tell me what's wrong."

He glared at her, his face pale and twisted. "What's wrong? I guess that's the big question, isn't it? What's wrong?" He laughed bitterly. "Perhaps you could answer that question better than I." Tears streamed down his round cheeks. "I loved you. I—I still love you, Emily. You're the only woman I ever wanted. In all these years. But you rejected me. And after everything I did for you..."

Emily took a small step closer to him. I had no idea what she thought she could do. If Levi jumped into the water, there was no way we could get him out. He was too big for us.

"I didn't reject you, Levi. I loved you. I—I just couldn't marry anyone then. It wasn't you at all. It was..." Her voice trailed off.

"It was because of Jacob Glick," Levi said angrily. "Because of what he did to you."

Emily's whole body shuddered. "You—you knew? How...?"

"Because Jacob told me. In fact, he boasted of it." Levi spit the words out as if they were bitter. "I was at the church one afternoon, painting one of the classrooms because the bishop had asked for my help. When Jacob came in and found me there, he became angry. He didn't like anyone, even Angstadt, working in that building. He acted like he owned the place. He started taunting me, calling me names. I tried to ignore him, but then he asked if I was the boy who was sweet on Emily Kruger. I—I said yes. That's when he said...it." Levi made his hands into fists and shook them several times in the air. "I—I can't even repeat what he said. It was vicious and disgusting. I ran out of the church, but I couldn't forget his words. I had to know what he meant. That night I followed him down to the lake. I saw Daniel Temple and his girlfriend, Beverly, running away from the clearing behind the Temple's house like the devil was chasing them. I hid in the trees. Jacob was there all right. Rubbing his jaw. Mad and yelling at no one."

"You were there," I said slowly. "I should have realized it. You admitted as much to Sam and me. You mentioned Jacob standing in the open with trees all around him. We never told you exactly where it happened. You knew because you saw him. I knew I'd missed something."

He shook his head. "I didn't even realize I'd said that. I was so panicked after you told me you knew about Jacob."

I took a step closer to Emily. Levi didn't seem to notice. "So you confronted him that night, Levi?"

He looked down at the dock, his body shaking with sobs. "I confronted him all right. He told me what he did to you, Emily. And he was proud of it. Laughed as he said horrible, vile things."

"And that's when you picked up a rock and hit him?" I tried to keep my voice steady. I didn't want to spook him.

He nodded slowly. "It—it was in my hand before I realized it. I just wanted him to quit talking about Emily—to stop saying those things. I—I didn't mean to kill him." He looked up at us, his eyes pleading for understanding.

"I believe you, Levi," Emily said. "No matter what happens, Abel and I will stand with you. You know that, don't you?"

He ignored her and looked at me. "I'm sorry about the vase and the fire. I wasn't trying to hurt you. I just wanted you to leave town. I couldn't risk anyone knowing about Jacob. If I'd known that you already knew the truth, I never would have done those things. Especially the fire. I'd hoped the house would burn down and you'd leave town. Maybe no one would ever dig up the land and find the body." He shook his head. "I set the fire and then drove into town to meet you and Sam. I figured that since most people were still at work, by the time help arrived, the house would be gone." A sob ripped through him. "And then you told me about Ben's letter. I couldn't believe it. I didn't know what to do. Here I'd caused you all this trouble for no reason. Decades of carrying the guilt of murder and trying to keep the past hidden. I—I just can't do it anymore. It's too much to bear."

"But even if the body had been discovered, why would anyone have suspected you?" I asked gently.

He shrugged. "As long as Jacob stayed buried, my sin was buried. I've spent years trying to pretend it never happened. Th–that it was just a bad dream. If Jacob was found, I wouldn't be able to do that anymore. It would be obvious to everyone that he'd been murdered. I would never be able to allow someone else to take the blame. The pressure of what I've done was already too much. That would be beyond comprehension. I'd have to admit to everyone, even myself, that I'm a cold-blooded murderer." He blinked several times and looked at Emily. "I—I wrote a note that explained all of this. It's in the back room of the store. I knew it would be found after—after..."

"Oh Levi," Emily said, her voice catching.

"Did you know it was Benjamin who buried the body?" I asked gently. I knew I had to keep him talking until Sam arrived.

He nodded and refocused his attention to me. "When I realized he was dead, I went down to the lake for a while, trying to figure out what to do. When I finally went back to the clearing, I found Ben digging a grave. I couldn't believe it. At first I wondered if he'd seen me kill Jacob. Then I realized he must have thought his brother did it."

"And you let him continue to believe that all these years?" Emily asked.

"Yes. I know it was wrong, but I was frightened. Scared to go to prison. At first what happened seemed like the answer to everything. Jacob was gone. Everyone believed he'd left town. I thought it was an answer from God. But down through the years it ate at me. And as I watched Ben distance himself from his family, I knew it was my fault." He shook his head. "I was a coward. I just stood by and let it happen. You know, I always told myself that the truth would come out someday. There were just too many people involved. Daniel and Beverly. Ben." He focused his attention to me. "And Sweetie. . . That night, when I found Ben planting Jacob in the ground, I noticed her watching him from another spot in the trees. But she suddenly took off toward the lake. I tried to follow her, to see if she was all right, but she ran too fast. I've always wondered if she saw me. In all these years she's never said a word."

"She didn't see you," I said. "She thought it was Benjamin who chased her."

Levi's eyes grew large. "She never asked him about it?"

"No. But she's been afraid all these years that he thought *she'd* killed Glick."

"So many lies," Emily whispered, tears falling down her cheeks. "So many secrets."

"And so much hurt," I finished for her. "Hurt that didn't have to happen."

"It's all my fault," Levi said, his voice breaking. "If I'd only told the truth." He stepped closer to the edge and stared into the water. "I wonder if it's true—that this lake will wash your troubles away. I—I pray it will wash everyone's troubles away." He took another step. His voice was monotone, and he moved as if he were in a trance. Fear that he would actually jump wiggled inside me. I was trying to figure out a way to rush him—to keep him from jumping in when Emily spoke up.

"Levi Hoffman, you will not take the easy way out this time! Do you hear me?" Her sharp tone caught the distraught man's attention. "You've caused all this pain because you didn't tell the truth. It's time now for you to be a man and take your punishment. If you jump into that lake, the people who need to ask you questions—who need to understand—will be cheated again." Her voice softened a little. "The man I loved would never allow that to happen."

Levi gazed blankly at her. He blinked several times—but then he took another step back toward the edge of the dock.

"Levi, if you really love me, then I want you to come to me." She held out her hands to him.

Levi looked back at the water once more, but then a sob broke out from somewhere deep inside him and he ran unevenly up to us, throwing his arms around Emily.

Thankfully, I heard the slamming of car doors behind us. Sam and Abel had finally arrived. Now, even if Levi jumped into the water, they could save him. I felt my body relax for the first time since Ida had driven into town.

Still holding Levi in her arms, Emily began to lead him back to land. Buddy and I followed her. As we stepped off the dock, Sam and Abel came crashing through the trees, running toward us. Gabriel and Mary were right behind them.

"What's going on?" Sam asked when he got to us.

"I'll explain after we get Levi inside," I said. For some reason, my voice quivered and I lost my balance, almost falling. It was as if my legs were made of rubber. Sam grabbed me and put his arm around my waist.

"It's over, Sam," I said as uncontrolled tears rolled down my cheeks. "It's finally over."

Chapter Nineteen

So what will happen to Levi now?" Ruth asked as she passed around the plate of fried chicken. "I suppose there will be a trial?"

"I doubt it," I said. "Levi admitted to the sheriff in Council Grove what he did all those years ago. I suppose they'll transfer him to a larger city and sentence him."

A sudden shout drew our attention away from the fantastic food brought forth from the good folks of Harmony for the community picnic. My idea for a simple get-together to thank those who'd worked on my uncle's house had turned into a huge event. No one even remembered the original reason for the gathering. Everyone was having a wonderful time sharing a mild spring night with their family, friends, and neighbors.

Another boisterous bellow rang out. The women gathered at the table laughed at the antics of the men who'd put together a baseball game with odd rules and even stranger equipment. Sam had hit a softball past a package of unopened bread that lay on the ground. Abel and Gabe insisted that John had moved the bread when they weren't looking and discounted John's assertion that this signified a home run. However, the argument became moot when Buddy picked up the package in his mouth and began running around their designated playing field. Watching Abel and Gabe run after him while Sam, John, Drew Crandall, and his father yelled enthusiastic comments at the playful dog brought gales of laughter from the rest of us. The men's careful inclusion of Drew, the young man with Down syndrome, into their exploits was touching. He was having as much fun as the rest of them, laughing at Buddy's attempt at disrupting the game. Finally, Sam, who pretended not to be interested in the bread at all, sucked Buddy into his clutches and grabbed the shredded loaf from his mouth. The men were now in a game of keep-away with one another.

"Can't tell the difference between those men and little bitty boys," Sweetie said around a mouthful of potato salad.

"That's for certain." Emily was able to smile tonight after a couple of days of emotional upheaval. Levi's admission that he'd killed Jacob Glick because of his love for her had shaken her deeply. She finally told Abel about the rape. As I'd suspected, he wasn't really surprised. His knowledge of Glick, as limited as it was, and his wife's reaction to the mere mention of the man's name, had caused Abel to suspect the truth years ago. References to Glick had occurred a few times in the past because of Abel's interest in the memoirs and diaries left behind by early Harmony residents. Each time, Emily's reaction had been similar to the one I'd witnessed Saturday at the café. It didn't take a detective to realize something was wrong. Not feeling he should confront Emily before she was ready, Abel had spent a long time praying for his wife. His prayers, along with his undying love and support gave her the strength to finally bring her shameful secret out into the open. When seen in the light of God's love, the darkness vanished, as did the humiliation and guilt. This revelation allowed her to accept God's redemptive power to heal her pain.

She'd finally removed that sad painting off the wall in her

dining room and replaced it with one of Hannah's delightful landscapes. In fact, she and Abel had destroyed the self-portrait together and thrown the remnants on the fire. Now that it was finally vanquished, along with the fear of losing her family, she'd even promised to pick up a paintbrush again. Hannah was understandably delighted, as was Emily's devoted husband.

In an odd twist of fate, although Levi Hoffman may have wanted to protect Emily when they were younger and failed, in admitting his part in Glick's murder, he'd actually helped to set her free. I could only hope he'd find some comfort in that knowledge.

"Well, I can hardly believe what's happened," Ruth said. "Seeing Gabriel and John out there having fun with the other men—why it's nothing short of a miracle."

"Here's another miracle," Emily said with a smile. "Sunday morning we had some very special visitors."

Ida, who sat beside me, reached over and hugged my arm. "That is correct. Gabriel, Sarah, and I came to church together."

"That's wonderful," I said, kissing her on the cheek. "Just a visit or..."

"Not sure," Ida said. "I do not want to push Gabriel. I think it could be a mistake. I just told him I would be going every Sunday I could and would love it if we could ride together. We will have to wait and see what happens."

"Did the investigators fill that hole back up after they dug Glick out of the clearing?" Ruth asked.

I shuddered. "No. Something to do with possibly needing more evidence. They've got crime scene tape all around it. I don't think they'll keep it like that for long. Not with Levi's confession. I'm just staying away. It gives me the creeps."

" 'Twas a might more creepy when Jacob was actually there," Sweetie said. "You should rest better now that that mean old thing is gone."

I sighed and speared a piece of watermelon with my fork. "I guess I do. Honestly, I'm not sure how I feel about any of this. It's just too fresh, I guess."

"Ruth told me you stopped by her shop to get some flowers for Ben's grave," Joyce said. "How did the visit with your uncle go?"

"It was good. I'm glad I went." I smiled at Ruth. "And thank you so much for the lovely flowers. They look so pretty next to his headstone."

I looked around at the people sitting at the large picnic table. "I haven't had the chance to ask anyone before this, but who picked the inscription?"

"Why, Ben did, child," Joyce said. "Who did you think chose it?"

I was pretty sure I knew the answer to my question before she said it, but I had to ask. After I'd found Benjamin's headstone and read the inscription, I could only stand in front of it and weep. Under his name and the dates of his birth and death, these words had been inscribed: 'TIS GRACE THAT BROUGHT ME SAFE THUS FAR, AND GRACE WILL LEAD ME HOME. I couldn't miss the capitalization of the second *grace*. Unless the engraver had made a mistake, my uncle had sent me a final message. He'd trusted me to find a way to lay his pain to rest. Being able to complete the task he'd left for me brought me great peace.

"So did you get. . .what do they call it. . .closure?" Emily asked.

I smiled. "You know, I think I did. I sat down and had a nice long conversation with my uncle. Told him everything that had happened since I came to Harmony. He may not have heard me, but it made me feel better."

"He certainly left a lot behind for you to deal with," Ruth said.

"I know. But now I understand it, and I'm at peace with it."

"I'm sure your father was happy to know you'd put flowers on his brother's final resting place," Emily said.

"Yes—yes he was."

The call I'd made to my dad had really thrown me for a loop. Telling him what Benjamin had tried to do for him was harder than I'd anticipated. I was glad to be free from our awful family secret, but I hadn't fully anticipated how deep the emotional impact would be for my father. When I explained that his estrangement from his brother hadn't been because Benjamin had rejected him but because he'd been trying to protect him, Dad broke down. Then I cleared up another mystery thanks to something Sweetie told me while we were planning the picnic. A few weeks before Benjamin died, she'd asked for the key to my father's old bedroom so she could clean it. Benjamin refused. He'd told Sweetie that he missed his brother so much he couldn't bear to have anything touched or changed. In fact, sometimes he'd pretend Daniel was still living in the house, just on the other side of the closed bedroom door. It shook me deeply to listen to my father cry. Of course, once he got control of his emotions, he went another direction. He chewed me out. Royally.

"Gracie, you should have told me what was going on the first night you got there," he'd said sternly. "I hate that you went through something like this alone. I would have been there for you. You should have known that."

After assuring him it would never happen again, and being pretty confident that I would never run up against a situation quite like this one again if I lived three lifetimes, we'd hung up. After putting the phone down, I'd had a good, long sobfest myself. Not sure exactly why, but I think it had something to do with relieving tension—and hearing my father cry. Not something I wanted to experience again for a long, long time.

"All kinds of changes going on in Harmony," Ida said, pulling me back into the present. "I am getting a telephone!"

"Now that really *is* something," Joyce said with a smile. "What made you decide to do it?"

The old woman shook her head. "After Gracie's fire and Levi's situation, I saw that I could have gotten help for my friends much faster if I had a telephone. I do not intend to let that happen again."

I smiled at her, feeling a great sense of relief. Now if she ever needed help, she'd be able to call someone.

"You know," Sweetie said, "all this goodwill has made me do some thinkin'. I—I was ponderin' the idea of goin' back to church myself." She grinned at Emily. "Don't think it will be your church, though. I don't cotton to dresses, and those caps you wear would just look silly on my old head."

Emily laughed good-naturedly. "Actually, you could wear what you want and still be welcome at Bethel. But you should go where you feel most comfortable."

"I should say you'd be welcome at Bethel!" Abel loudly proclaimed. He and Sam had finished their game and run up to the table. "We can't tell you how much we appreciate what you did for us."

I looked over at Sweetie who wrinkled up her face in a frown. "Now Abel, I told you to be quiet about that."

He shook his head. "Sorry, Sweetie. I think all the blood must have rushed from my head out there with Sam chasing me all over the place. I forgot you didn't want anyone to know."

"Know what?" Ruth asked. "You might as well tell us now, Abel. You know we'll keep needling you until you cough up the truth."

Abel looked over at Sweetie who glared at him. "Sorry, Ruth. It's Sweetie's story to share, and she doesn't seem open to it."

Sam raised one eyebrow. "Well, I know what it is, and I'm not afraid of retribution."

"I told you, boy, I can cut off your food supply if you irritate me," his aunt said forcefully. She waved her hand at the group gathered around the table. "It ain't no big thing, but I'd surely appreciate it if it wouldn't go no further than this group." She shook her finger at Abel. "And that goes for you especially, Abel Mueller. You're a pastor. I shouldn't have to worry about you spreadin' gossip."

Abel bowed at the waist and made a motion as if he were doffing his hat. Actually, his large straw hat was sitting on the bench next to his wife. "My humble apologies for divulging your secret." He straightened up and shook his finger back at her. "But you make it sound like you did something wrong, Sweetie. It's not like you stole Ruth's chestnut vase or something."

Everyone at the table laughed. It was nice to find humor in something that had been so painful only a short time ago. Sweetie guffawed louder than anyone else.

"Well, here's the story," she said when the laughter finally died down. "After I moved into the red house, I was workin' to fix it up. I found an old safe that belonged to that Amil Angstadt character. There was twenty thousand dollars in it. I found out that years ago, a member of Bethel sold some land and donated the proceeds to the church. Seems it never made it to its final destination though." She shrugged. "So I gave the money to Abel—for fixin' up damaged houses and such. You know, like what happened to Gracie here."

Emily reached across the table and took Sweetie's calloused hand. "You're a good woman, Sweetie Goodrich. I'm proud to know you."

Sweetie blinked several times and her eyes got big. "Why. . . why, thank you, Emily. Can't say I heard that too much in my life."

"I remember that money," Ida said. "That property belonged to Mason Guttenberg. After he died, his wife decided to go back to Pennsylvania to live with her parents. Viola wanted to do something in Mason's memory and told folks she was going to sell their land and give part of the proceeds to the church. Funny thing was, we never heard anything else about it. We all wondered what happened to the donation, but then the bishop died, Viola and the kids moved on, and it was forgotten." She smiled at Sweetie. "God used you to put it where it was supposed to go. Praise the Lord!"

Sweetie turned three shades of red. She probably didn't hear herself described as a vessel of the Lord very often.

I could only wonder why Angstadt never gave that money to the church. Was that the secret Glick had held over his head, or was it something else? Did the minister plan to do the right thing someday? The fact that none of the money was ever spent made me hope his intentions were honorable. He'd been a harsh and judgmental man, but was he a criminal? Unfortunately, I would never have the answer to that question in this life.

At that moment, Marcus Jensen and Amos Crandall walked up to the table. "Pastor Mueller," Marcus said with a grin. "I've been sent over here to challenge you to a game of horseshoes. I hear you're pretty good, but I think I'm better. Are you game?"

Abel looked at Emily whose light, lilting laugh made me feel happy inside. "It's fine. You go on. Have fun."

"How 'bout you, Sam?" Amos asked.

"Thanks, Amos, but I have something I need to talk to Sam about," I said. "He'll sit this one out."

Marcus smiled and patted Sam on the back. "Sounds important, Sam," he said in a jovial voice. "I think you'd better tend to it. Catch up to us later if you want to. Abel will probably need the help."

"Pride goeth before destruction, Pastor Jensen," Abel said, winking at us. "I think you're in for a whoopin', as my mother used to say."

The two took off toward the area where the horseshoes had been set up. We could hear their good-natured ribbing as they walked away.

Hannah's friends Leah and Jessica ran up to the table and grabbed her arm. "Let's watch the men play horseshoes, Hannah," they said between giggles.

Hannah looked at Emily who nodded her permission. The three girls ran toward the horseshoe area, laughing and teasing each other.

"Come with me, Mr. Goodrich," I said to Sam. "I think you're in for a whoopin', too."

"Yikes," he said, grabbing Sweetie's hand. "Save me from this vicious woman."

She shook her hand free and laughed at him. "Boy, I think you been in need of straightenin' out for a long, long time. Gracie's got my blessin'!"

"See, there's no help for you here." I grabbed his other hand and pulled him away from the table.

We held hands and strolled over to the fountain. In the dusky glow of evening, lights flickered on and highlighted the fountain and the benches. The sounds of people and children laughing and playing echoed behind us. The aroma of freshly cut grass combined with the sweetness of honeysuckle created an atmosphere so special I wanted to remember the sights, sounds, and aromas forever.

Sam swung my hand back and forth as we walked. I felt a peace inside me that I'd never known before. I wanted to savor it, so I slowed my steps down to a stroll. As if he felt the same thing, Sam matched my unhurried gait with his own.

"Abel's talking about having a funeral for Glick," he said. "He hasn't mentioned it to John yet. He's not sure how John will feel about it."

"Wow. Not sure if that's a good idea. Glick caused a lot of heartache in this community."

"I know, but Abel says funerals are for the living, not the dead. The idea of John burying his father alone doesn't sit too well with either one of us."

I considered this. "You've got a point. Maybe a small, private funeral for John and a few friends." I sighed. "I like John. He shouldn't feel bad about Glick. We don't get to pick our fathers."

As we reached the benches, Mary walked past us. She carried a large box full of pies.

"Boy, that smells good," Sam said. "Need some help?"

She smiled. "Thanks, Sam. But I've got it. These won't last long. You two better get back soon so you don't miss out."

I nodded. "Good point. We'll do our best."

After flashing us another smile, she took off toward the food table.

"Well, that's an improvement," I said.

Sam nodded. "I think we're going to be okay. We had a talk the last day I worked on Ben's house. She finally admitted that she knew we weren't right for each other." He stopped walking and turned to look at me. "You know, after only knowing you a few days, I realized that I'd almost made the biggest mistake of my life. I'd picked someone to marry because I didn't think I had any other choices. I was willing to give up passion for—for convenience, I guess. After Mary and I ended up engaged, I bought her a ring." He laughed. "Funny thing, I could never bring myself to give it to her. With my lightning-fast mind, you'd think I'd have figured out why. But anyway, after you left the other day to pick wildflowers for Ida, I got that ring out of the drawer where I kept it and. . ."

"You threw it into the lake," I finished for him.

His eyebrows arched in surprise. "How did you know that?"

"I saw you. Of course, I didn't know what you'd tossed into the water. I have to admit that I wondered about it."

He grinned. "Did you think I was getting rid of evidence? I couldn't have killed Jacob Glick you know. I wasn't even born. . ."

I put my fingers up to his lips. "Oh hush. I don't know what I thought, but I couldn't have been too suspicious. I actually forgot about it until you just brought it up." I frowned at him. "You could have gotten your money back for the ring, you know."

"For some reason I really needed to pitch it, Grace. I don't know if you can understand that."

I gazed into his eyes. "I understand it completely."

His face flushed slightly, and he guided me to one of the benches. He sat down and pulled me down next to him. "Before you start in on whatever you wanted to say, can I tell you something?"

"Of course."

He took my hand and covered it with both of his. His head hung down as he stared at the ground. "I—I told you that John and I had a lot in common. Do you remember that?"

"Yes."

He hesitated for a moment. "Th–the truth is that I have no idea who my father is. When my mother got pregnant with me, she wasn't married." He breathed in deeply and let it out. "John didn't know who his father was until after his mother died. He was born out of wedlock, too. I may never know my father, but the thought that he might be someone as awful as Jacob Glick makes me feel sick to my stomach."

I squeezed his hands. "Why didn't you tell me this earlier?"

He swung his head up. "I was afraid you'd think less of me. It's embarrassing, Grace."

I shook my head. "Look, I want to be understanding, I really do, but I don't see why in the world you should be embarrassed. It had nothing to do with you."

His face flushed. "It sounds like my mother was loose or something. But she wasn't. She might have made a mistake, but she was a wonderful mother. She did everything she could for me. And she took me to church." He cleared his throat. I could tell this was difficult for him. "And she didn't abort me. She could have."

"I don't believe for one moment that your mother was loose, as you put it. You're the most wonderful man I've ever known. I'm certain your mother had a lot to do with that. We've all made mistakes. It we didn't, we wouldn't need Jesus, would we?"

He shook his head.

"Have you ever thought about trying to find your father?"

"I've toyed with the idea. I get the feeling Sweetie knows something she hasn't told me. But to be honest, this thing with John made me even more reluctant. Obviously, finding your biological family doesn't always turn out like a fairy tale. There's not always a happy ending."

I had no answer to that. His conclusion was probably true.

Sam got up and walked over to the plaque attached to the fountain. "Remember how I told you that Harmony is a special place?" he said evenly. "I believe that even more now. Since—since you came here."

"What do you mean?"

He turned toward me. The seriousness in his expression startled me. "I truly believe you were meant to come here, Grace. There were hurtful secrets buried below the surface of this town. God used you to bring them out."

"Anyone could have. . ."

"No," he said firmly. "Not anyone. Ben couldn't do it. He kept the truth buried for years, letting it cause devastation and pain."

I got up and went over to him. "But it wasn't the truth. It was all a lie. Benjamin protected a lie. If the real truth had come out when Glick died, I'll bet things would have been different for a lot of people. For my family, for Emily, Sweetie. . ."

"And Levi."

I nodded. "Yes, Levi, too. Spending all these years harboring guilt and bitterness is almost worse than being in a physical jail, isn't it?"

"Yes, I believe you're right." He put his hand under my chin and kissed me lightly. "I still believe coming to Harmony was your destiny." He ran his finger down the side of my face. "I want to spend the rest of the week with you. Sweetie said she'd hire some help in the orchard so we can have every possible minute together."

"Thank you, Sam, but that's not necessary."

He frowned. "I don't understand. I know you have to figure out how to get your possessions out of the house, but I can help. Sweetie really wants to buy the land so we can expand the orchards. She'll give you a good price. . ."

"Sam, I'm leaving in the morning. I'm not waiting until the weekend."

He stepped back from me, his face drained of color. "I—I don't understand. I–I'm not ready for you to go."

I sat on the edge of the fountain and looked into the water. "Do you remember when you first showed me this fountain?"

"Of course. It was only a few days ago."

"I told you I prayed for God's will in my life. You warned me that I'd asked for something dangerous. You called it a prayer of consecration. You said it meant that my life might take a turn I hadn't planned on. You asked me if I was ready to accept that."

Sam's beautiful gray eyes locked onto mine. "Yes, I remember."

I could feel the tears that filled my eyes, but I was powerless to stop them. "I wasn't then, but I am now. Since I came to this town my life has been in constant upheaval. I kept thinking how different the world is in Wichita. At first I wanted nothing more than to get home to it."

He took a step toward me. "You said 'at first'?"

I nodded and a sob broke past my lips. "Then all of a sudden, the idea of going back didn't seem so appealing. I finally realized it wasn't the life I wanted anymore."

"I don't understand. What are you saying?"

I reached up and touched his lips with my fingertips while the sound of dancing water played in the background like gentle music. "I'm leaving in the morning so I can go back to Wichita and pack up my things. I've already called my boss. He's willing to let me do freelance work for him. I'm moving to Harmony because..."

Sam's kiss cut off anything else I might have wanted to say. His arms held me close, and I could feel his body tremble. In my entire life, I'd never been kissed the way Sam Goodrich kissed me then and there. When he let me go, it took me a little while to speak.

"There is one thing I need from you, Sam," I finally whispered. "One thing you must promise me."

"Anything," he said in a husky voice. "I would do anything for you. Name it."

I smiled and wiped a tear from his face with my finger. "I can tell you in one word."

He cocked his head to one side. "Tell me."

I couldn't hold back the laughter that bubbled up from inside of me. "Electricity. You've got to help me get electricity."

Laughing and kissing might not seem to go together, but somehow it worked for us.

"You have my word," he said with a grin. "I'll even make sure you have a phone."

"Oh thank you."

From behind us I heard someone call our names. We turned around to see Abel standing a few yards away.

"I'm attempting to save you both a piece of pie," he yelled. "You'd better get over here before it's too late!"

Sam grabbed my hand, and we started walking toward the kind Mennonite man who had become my friend.

"Hey, we're trying to schedule one more game of horseshoes before it gets dark," he said. "What time are you two going home?"

I smiled at Abel and squeezed Sam's hand. "Why, Abel," I said, "we have all the time in the world. You see, Sam and I are both already home."

He stood and watched us as we walked back toward the picnic area. He didn't say anything, but I could hear his hearty laughter floating past us on the gentle spring air.

About the Author

NANCY MEHL is the author of six novels, one of which, *For Whom the Wedding Bell Tolls*, won the 2009 American Christian Fiction Writers' Book of the Year Award in Mystery. Her new Harmony Series takes her a step away from the mystery genre she's used to and into romantic suspense. "This series is a little different for me," she says. "But that element of mystery has followed me to Harmony. I hope mystery readers will find a little something for them in this new venture. It has been so much fun creating the town of Harmony and getting to know the Mennonite people a little better. I hope I've done justice to their wonderful legacy and incredible spirit."

Nancy lives in Kansas with her husband, Norman, their son, Danny, and a Puggle named Watson. She spends her extra time with her volunteer group, Wichita Homebound Outreach.

Nancy's Web site is www.nancymehl.com and you can find her blog at www.nancymehl.blogspot.com. She loves to hear from her readers.

Discussion Questions

1. While working and living in Wichita, Gracie Temple believed her life was everything she'd always wanted. Yet she struggled with a nagging sense of unrest. What caused this feeling?

2. Gracie arrived in Harmony with many preconceived ideas about the people who lived there. Why? Was she wrong, right, or a little of both?

3. Did you like Harmony, Kansas? Would you want to live there? Why or why not?

4. Several people in Harmony had long held secrets. What happens when we bury hurts down deep inside? Do you have anything you've never told anyone? After reading how keeping a secret affected Emily's life, have you changed your mind about staying silent?

5. How do you feel about the way some of the Old Order and Conservative Mennonites live? Do you understand their desire for a "simpler life"? Or do you think it's unrealistic?

6. Do you believe two different churches could really live in harmony in a small town? Why or why not?

7. How did Gracie change from the beginning of the book until the end? Would you have made the same choice she did about whether to stay in Harmony or go back to Wichita?

8. When did you figure out who killed Jacob Glick? Were you surprised?

9.
   What do you believe motivated Amil Angstead? Do you think he was an evil man? Or was he just a man who thought he was right?

10. Do you know anyone like Sweetie or Levi who quit going to church because they'd been hurt? As Christians, what can we do to help people like them?

11. What is the main theme of this book? Finding out that God's will for your life may be different than what you thought it was? Not judging people negatively who may look or live differently than we do? That "secrets buried alive never die"?

Coming soon from

NANCY MEHL

Harmony Series book 2

Simple Deceit

Available Fall 2010